Kandy Shepherd swapped a career as a magazine editor for a life writing romance. She lives on a small farm in the Blue Mountains near Sydney, Australia, with her husband, daughter, and lots of pets. Shepherd believes in love at first sight and real-life romance, which often takes its time. She loves to hear from her readers and can be contacted through her website kandyshepherd.com.

Carrie Nichols grew up in New England but moved south and traded snow for air conditioning. She loves to travel, is addicted to British crime dramas and knows a *Seinfeld* quote appropriate for every occasion.

A 2016 RWA Golden Heart® Award winner and two-time Maggie Award for Excellence winner, she has one tolerant husband, two grown sons and two critical cats. To her dismay, Carrie's characters—like her family—often ignore the wisdom and guidance she offers.

Also by Kandy Shepherd

Hired by the Brooding Billionaire
Greek Tycoon's Mistletoe Proposal
Conveniently Wed to the Greek
Stranded with Her Greek Tycoon
Best Man and the Runaway Bride

Sydney Brides miniseries

Gift-Wrapped in Her Wedding Dress
Crown Prince's Chosen Bride
The Bridesmaid's Baby Bump

Also by Carrie Nichols

The Marine's Secret Daughter

Discover more at millsandboon.co.uk

SECOND CHANCE WITH THE SINGLE DAD

KANDY SHEPHERD

THE SERGEANT'S UNEXPECTED FAMILY

CARRIE NICHOLS

MILLS & BOON

First Published in Great Britain 2019
by Mills & Boon, an imprint of HarperCollinsPublishers,
1 London Bridge Street, London, SE1 9GF

Second Chance with the Single Dad © 2019 Kandy Shepherd
The Sergeant's Unexpected Family © 2019 Carol Opalinski

ISBN: 978-0-263-27213-0

0219

MIX
Paper from
responsible sources
FSC™ C007454

FSC
www.fsc.org

This book is produced from independently certified FSC™ paper to ensure responsible forest management.

For more information visit: www.harpercollins.co.uk/green

Printed and bound in Spain
by CPI, Barcelona

SECOND CHANCE WITH THE SINGLE DAD

KANDY SHEPHERD

To my precious daughter, Lucy.

You're grown up now, but your adorable baby self was the inspiration for every baby I've ever written, including the enchanting little girl in this story.

And, of course, you're my go-to for all matters equine!

CHAPTER ONE

WIL HUDSON WAS a handsome, handsome man. Georgia Lang had recognised his exceptional good looks from day one of their friendship. What red-blooded female wouldn't? But she had never allowed herself to acknowledge even a flutter of attraction to him.

It was way safer to be 'just friends' with a man who attracted women as effortlessly as gorgeous Wil did—and discarded them as readily. Especially when she was just an ordinary girl, attractive enough, but hardly a winner in the head-turning stakes. Nothing like the women Wil dated. *Girl next door* was the way people described her. On self-doubting days, she wondered if that was shorthand for distinctly unexciting. Most of the time she embraced the label as a good fit.

As Wil's *girl next door* pal, his buddy, his good mate from university days, she'd watched as his glamorous girlfriends came and went while their friendship endured. To be sure, it had ebbed and flowed. They'd always seen more of each other when they'd been between relationships; there had been moments when she'd wondered if they could be more than friends. But, fearing rejection, she hadn't dared suggest it; he hadn't either, and they'd each dived back into the dating pool.

But all that had been before Wil's whirlwind marriage. After he'd wed, none of their group of friends had seen much of him. They'd seen him even less after his wife had left him. Georgia hadn't seen him at all. He'd ghosted her—just stopped all contact without explanation. Not a call, not a text, not even a 'like' on social media. She'd seen him interviewed on television, he'd become a reluctant go-to spokesperson for the young generation of millionaires. But he might as well have been a ghost for all the personal contact she'd had with him.

Now, just days into the new year, he stood at the doorstep of the North Sydney apartment she shared with two other schoolteachers. She was so taken aback to find him there she had to clutch at the door frame for support. *Wil.* Her heart started a furious beating. *How she'd missed him.*

Incredulous delight flooded through her at seeing the friend she'd painfully accepted was no longer part of her life. She started to blurt out her pleasure at his unexpected appearance, wish him the happiest of new years. To tell him she was moving house and he was just in time to help her lift some heavy boxes of books and she'd reward him with the cookies she knew were his favourite. But she held herself back. This Wil wasn't her best friend. She hadn't deserved how he'd treated her. This Wil seemed like a stranger.

If it had been any other guy she might have shrieked about what a wreck she looked, in shorts and a past-its-use-by-date vest top, no make-up, hair rioting every which way from the January summer humidity. But she'd never worried about her appearance with Wil; she doubted he'd ever noticed what she'd worn.

But she'd always noticed him. The impact of his

good looks hit her afresh—tall, broad-shouldered, in dark jeans and a white T-shirt that showcased his athletic physique. For a long moment she stared at him as he met her gaze through narrowed eyes. What was he doing here? Why now?

'Georgie,' he said slowly, his voice as deep and resonant as it had always been. His eyes searched her face, acknowledging that it had been a long time between meetings, waiting for her reaction. She met his gaze unflinchingly, drinking in the sight of him.

He was the same, but not quite the same. Wil had always been well groomed in a clean-shaven, country-boy kind of way. Now he was a few days away from a shave and stubble shadowed his jaw. His dark hair, longer than he used to wear it, fell unkempt over his forehead. Fine lines scored the corners of his eyes, the colour of bittersweet chocolate. At twenty-eight, a year older than her, he seemed somehow…weary. Perhaps making so much money so quickly did that for you, she thought cynically. Maybe it had also made him think he'd outgrown his old friends.

'It's been two years,' she said at last, determined not to let a note of accusation edge her voice but failing dismally. Laughter and good-humoured teasing had been the keynotes of their friendship but she couldn't find it in herself to summon them up. It had hurt, the way he had so abruptly discarded their friendship of six years' duration.

Friendship not just diminished—as did happen when friends met 'The One'—but extinguished. As if those years had meant nothing when he had finally fallen in love. As if she had just been a convenient prop, of no further use in his new life. *Good old Georgia—no lon-*

ger required. She couldn't hide that hurt. Couldn't pretend it didn't matter.

And Wil wasn't fooled for a moment. 'I'm sorry it's been so long, Georgie, I really am,' he said.

She attempted to tease but her words fell flat. 'You know whose fault that is.'

'Mine. I know. And I regret it.' He paused.

'Yet you're here now.' She made no move towards him. No kiss on the cheek or hug in welcome—not that their friendship had ever been the kind that involved physical contact beyond the socially polite. There had always been an unspoken 'no touching' barrier between them.

Back in the day, when Wil had smiled there had been a hint of a dimple in his left cheek that, in spite of herself, she'd always found appealing. He wasn't smiling now. Georgia didn't smile either. Once they'd been such close friends they'd joked they could read each other's minds. Now she could see in his eyes that he knew he'd hurt her by the way he'd dumped her. She wasn't inclined to be forgiving. But this was Wil and he had sought her out. She had to give him a hearing.

'I need your help,' he said, his voice gruff.

Georgia could tell the effort it took for him to force out those words. Once she would have immediately jumped in to ask what she could do for him. Good old Georgia would have cancelled prior engagements. Rearranged schedules. Bent over backwards to accommodate him—far more, she realised, than he had ever done for her as his good friend. Now she remained with her feet planted firmly at the threshold. 'I heard you and your wife had divorced.'

Angie, tiny, blonde, with a waif-like air that hadn't hidden her calculating eyes. None of the girls in their friendship group had been taken in by her. Not so the guys. But none had been so smitten as Wil.

'Yes,' he said shortly.

Georgia crossed her arms across her chest. 'I'm no longer available as number one shoulder to cry on when you break up with a woman.' *Not one word from him in two years.* 'I'm afraid my give-a-damn quota has expired,' she said.

Only a tightening of his lips let her know that her words had met their target. He cleared his throat once, then again. 'Angie…she… Angie's dead,' he said.

Georgia clutched a hand to her heart. 'What?' She expelled just the one word, tinged with disbelief. But Wil's bleak expression told her to believe him. 'When? How?'

'Car accident in the Blue Mountains. New Year's Eve. She…she died the next day in hospital. Three days ago.'

'Oh, Wil, that's dreadful. I'm so sorry.' She remembered all the bitchy thoughts she'd had about Wil's fluffy little wife. Regretted every one of them. Also regretted the just-spoken 'not giving a damn' remark. Angie was—had been—twenty-seven, the same age as her. Frighteningly young to die. 'I'm sorry,' she said again, not certain what else she could say. 'Come in. Please. How can I help?'

She stepped aside to let him through the door. Apologised for the half-packed boxes around the place. Led him through to the living room, glad neither of her flatmates was home. Opened her mouth to offer him coffee. Maybe something stronger, even though it was only mid-morning. But Wil spoke first.

'I have a baby. A little girl called Nina.'

'Oh.' Another stab of hurt shafted through her, that

he hadn't cared to tell her something so momentous. 'I didn't know you were a father.'

'Neither did I,' he said.

Georgia was too shell-shocked to find an immediate reply. 'What do you mean?' she eventually choked out. 'How could you not know?'

'Angie didn't tell me. I wasn't aware she was pregnant, let alone that she'd had a baby. We weren't in contact after our short marriage ended. Only through divorce lawyers.'

Yet she was pregnant? Break-up sex perhaps. Georgia couldn't ask. She'd heard the marriage had lasted less than six months. 'Why didn't she tell you?'

Wil swore under his breath. 'I don't know. To punish me. To... Hell. I don't know why. Or if she ever intended to tell me. But she put my name on the birth certificate.'

The Angie that Georgia remembered would have milked a guy for all he had in child support. She'd had dollar signs flashing in her eyes when she'd met successful, wealthy Wil. He'd been an amateur inventor who had made a lot of money through patents after he'd appeared on a television show. 'Then how—?'

'A social worker from Katoomba Hospital in the Blue Mountains contacted me on New Year's Day. Told me my ex-wife had died. After the accident, she regained consciousness briefly and told the social worker she wanted me to take custody of the baby. It...it came from out of the blue.'

Wil a father. Now Georgia realised her old friend didn't just look weary. He looked dazed, as if his world had turned upside down, as if he wasn't sure where to place his feet so he wouldn't topple over. And he had reached out to *her*.

* * *

Wil had missed Georgia's friendship. He hadn't realised quite how much until just now when she'd opened the door to him, not with her customary wide, open smile but tight-lipped and guarded. The full impact of how he had hurt her had hit him like a blow to the gut.

But two years ago, his first loyalty had been to Angie. She had been pretty, sexy and fun—in the beginning. There'd been a vulnerability to her too that had drawn him to her. But she'd got very demanding very quickly. When Angie had begged him not to see his close female friend—not even to say goodbye—he'd had to go along with it. That was what a guy did for his woman. Besides, he'd learned very early that to disagree with Angie wasn't worth it. No matter how large a gap Georgia had left in his life.

When the blinkers had come off, when he'd realised that Angie was too damaged for a normal relationship, he'd cut his losses and ended it very quickly. His gentlemanly instinct had been to let Angie tell people she'd been the one to leave. It had probably been doomed from the start—two people with troubled pasts drawn to each other, he wanting to rescue her, she deciding to blame him for all that was wrong with her life.

But that was in the past. Angie was tragically gone. And he'd found he was a father.

Now his lovely friend of such long standing stood near to him, cheeks flushed, her chestnut hair a riot of waves around her face, her blue eyes warm with both sympathy and a shocked surprise.

'Was the baby injured in the accident?' she asked.

'Thankfully not. Angie's sister was babysitting that night.'

'Thank heaven.' Georgia shook her head as if to clear her thoughts. 'I'm having trouble taking this in. I can't imagine how you must have felt at such news.'

Wil briefly closed his eyes at the intensity of his relief that she hadn't turned him away. Breathed in his friend's sweet scent, immediately familiar, immediately comforting. *Georgia.*

'Nothing could have prepared me for it,' he said.

He still couldn't articulate his shock and disbelief at the call from the hospital. Angie's tragic death had been enough to cope with, without the news of his unexpected paternity. Then he'd had to deal with the anger he'd felt towards his ex for keeping him out of the loop. The doubt that the child was his.

'What did you do?'

'Drove straight to Katoomba. Met with the social worker. Met…met my daughter.'

My daughter. Emotion swamped him as he remembered seeing the impossibly little girl in the social worker's arms. How she had looked up at him with dark solemn eyes—his eyes—then reached over one tiny starfish hand to grip his finger strong and hard. He struggled not to let that emotion show on his face. Not to Georgia. Sensible, steady Georgia to whom he had been so careful never to reveal who he was, what he was, for fear she would turn away from him.

'How…how old is she?' He could see Georgia was struggling with the fact he had a child. He'd only had a few days to get used to the idea himself. But already he thought of himself as a father, determined to give that tiny scrap of humanity everything in life that had been denied him.

'Seven months.'

'That's very young. What are you going to do?'

'Go get her today,' he said without hesitation.

'What do you mean?'

'Angie's sister in Katoomba is kicking up a fuss. Seems to think she has a claim on Nina. She doesn't, of course. Legally she hasn't got a leg to stand on. But the sooner I have Nina with me, the better.'

Georgia's blue eyes widened. 'You mean you intend to bring Nina up by yourself?'

'She's my responsibility. I'm heading up to the Blue Mountains to pick her up and take her home.'

'Whoa.' Georgia put her hand to her forehead. 'I'm reeling here. You're going to be a single dad?'

'I'm her father. She's my flesh and blood. There is no choice.'

'You're sure Nina is yours?'

'Have I done a DNA test? No time for that yet. But she's mine all right. Looking at her is like looking into a miniature mirror. The social worker from the hospital laughed when she saw me. "No doubt about this little one's daddy," she said.'

Georgia nodded thoughtfully, as he had seen her do so many times. 'That's reassuring. And she must be very cute if she looks like you. But have you really thought this through?'

'She's my child and I will do my duty by her.'

He'd been orphaned at five years old. His time in foster care had marked him for life. No way in the world would any child of his go through what he had gone through. But he couldn't tell Georgia that. For all the years of their friendship he'd never told her—or anyone from his 'new life' in Sydney—the truth about his childhood back in Melbourne. He'd made no secret that he'd been adopted. But as far as his university friends were concerned he'd been adopted at five by his wonderful parents. Not at fourteen years of age. Not after having found himself in a heap of trouble for doing what he'd thought was the right thing.

'Good for you,' Georgia said. 'But it won't be easy. I guess you know that.'

'None of it will be easy,' he said. 'Which is why I've come here to ask you for your help. I need a friend—' She started to protest but he spoke over her. 'I know I probably don't deserve your friendship, not after those years of radio silence. But I'm asking you anyway, Georgie. For moral support. Please come with me to Katoomba. Today.'

Her eyes widened and she frowned. '*Me?* Why?'

'You know about kids. You teach elementary school. You have nieces and nephews by the bucketload.' He didn't want to sound desperate. But none of his friends had started families yet. Not that he would expect them to put their own lives aside and rush to his help.

Yet he expected that of Georgia. He pushed the uncomfortable thought aside. She had always been there for him. Until he hadn't been there for her. But Nina needed him. And he needed Georgia.

'That doesn't make me an expert on babies,' she said.

'More of an expert than I am,' he said. 'I'd never even held a baby until the social worker handed Nina to me two days ago.' He'd been petrified he'd drop her, despite the social worker's reassurance.

'I'm one ahead of you there,' Georgia said with a wry twist to her mouth. She'd used to tell him she was the 'afterthought' in her family—eight years younger than her youngest sister, ten years younger than her oldest. They were both married with kids. She'd done a lot of babysitting. If anyone knew how to look after a baby, it was her.

'That's why I thought—' he started.

'Don't you have a girlfriend?'

'No.' The relationship with Angie had burned him too badly to even contemplate dating.

'There must be someone else who could—?'

'There's no one else I would trust.'

She sighed, took a step back from him against the stack of boxes in the middle of her living room. Pushed her fingers through her riot of dark chestnut, wavy hair. 'That's not fair, Wil. After all this time you can't just rock up here and—'

'I've been a bad friend, I know,' he said. Wil didn't expect her to disagree and she didn't.

'I… We… Your friends thought you'd dropped us because when you struck it so rich with your inventions, you wanted to leave us behind.' She looked up at him, her eyes huge with undisguised hurt and bewilderment. He hated that he had hurt her.

'That's not how it happened at all,' he said. *How could she have thought that of him?* Yes, he had made a lot of money but it hadn't changed things, hadn't changed *him*. He clenched his hands into fists by his sides. He never wanted Georgia to think badly of him. 'I felt obligated to do what Angie wanted. She was jealous of you. Thought the others looked down at her.'

By the time he had realised Angie had purposely alienated him from the friends he cared most about, it had been impossible to make amends to them.

'That wasn't true,' Georgia said.

But she didn't quite meet his eye. None of his friends had liked Angie. If only he'd listened to them, instead of being swept along on an ill-founded urge to be some kind of white knight and rescue her from the effects of her troubled past.

'Fact was, Angie didn't like me seeing you. Didn't believe in platonic friendship between a man and a woman. No matter how many times I assured her we were just friends, that we could all be friends. That there was no reason for her to be so jealous.'

'No reason at all to be jealous,' she echoed. 'We rode horses together. Saw indie bands that no one else liked. But there was never any romance.'

'Angie didn't believe me,' he said. Instead she'd screamed awful, ill-founded accusations he had no intention of sharing with Georgia.

'And after your marriage ended? Still no word from you.'

He gritted his teeth. 'I didn't want to admit what a mistake I'd made by marrying her.'

Georgia would never know how many times he'd got as far as the last digit in her phone number before hanging up. How many times he'd driven past this apartment, slowing down only to accelerate away at the thought of confessing what an idiot he'd been to be taken in so thoroughly by Angie. Because to do that would have meant revealing the truth about those hidden years of his life. And not even the comfort and understanding he might have got from his long-standing friend Georgia had been worth that.

'Really,' she muttered. But the icy edge to her voice was melting.

'I'm sorry, Georgie. If I could go back and change things I would.'

She blinked rapidly, something she'd always done when she was thinking deeply about something important. Finally, she spoke. 'I'm not one to hold a grudge. I see things must have been difficult for you. And now—'

'You'll come with me to pick up Nina? That is, if you don't have a boyfriend who has claims on your time.'

'No. There's no one.'

'What about Toby? I thought for sure he'd have a ring on your finger by now.'

'We broke up a year ago,' she said, tight-lipped.

Good. 'I'm sorry,' he said to be polite. He'd been convinced she'd marry Toby. He cursed under his breath. If he'd known Toby was going to exit her life, he mightn't have made that rash decision to marry Angie.

She gestured around her. 'I'm in the middle of moving house. The landlord has put the apartment on the market and I'm going home to my parents' until I find a new place. There are boxes still to pack, cleaning to be done. I—'

'I'll pay for packers, movers and professional cleaners. Please, Georgie.'

She paused, looked up at him with an expression he knew of old, halfway between exasperation and affection, then sighed. 'For past times' sake,' she said. 'No, for the baby's sake. Unless you've changed a lot in the two years since I last saw you, I'm not so sure you'd know which end was up on a seven-month-old baby.' Her smile— that lovely smile that had always uplifted him—danced around the edges of her lips.

Wil didn't realise he'd been holding his breath until he let it out on a *whoosh* of relief.

'Thank you,' he said.

Now that Georgia was back in his life, he wouldn't let her go again too easily. No matter what it took.

CHAPTER TWO

So MANY TIMES during the years of her friendship with Wil, Georgia had escaped the city with him to head for the Blue Mountains, west of Sydney, to ride horses or bush walk. Only never with a rearward-facing baby car seat installed in the back seat of Wil's car. Or four large packets of disposable nappies stacked next to it. 'Just in case they're all needed on the way home,' Wil explained.

Georgia laughed. 'Unless the baby has a particularly explosive digestive system, I very much doubt that.'

He scowled in a way she well remembered. 'I told you, I know nothing about babies.'

She almost said, *You've got a lot to learn.* But Wil seemed only too aware of that. She almost asked if he was nervous about collecting the baby, but the tight set of his jaw and the way his hands gripped the wheel so his knuckles showed white gave her the answer.

'You'll learn quickly,' she said instead, making it her mission to encourage and support him as she'd always done as his friend. And avoid jokes about dirty nappies. He was facing completely new territory without much of a map to guide him. She fought the urge to reach out and place her hand over his to reassure him, but that had never been the way with them. *No touching.*

'I guess I'll have to,' he said.

Her friend had come back so unexpectedly into her life. She was churning with curiosity about what had happened in the two years since she had seen him. So many questions clamoured to be asked. But now wasn't the time to ask them.

Wil was essentially a very private person. It took time for him to confide in his friends. Things must have ended badly for him to have been so estranged from Angie he hadn't even known she was pregnant. Georgia admired the way he had stepped up to his duty as a father. Not every twenty-eight-year-old guy would react the same way to news of a secret baby. But then she'd always thought of Wil as one of the good guys.

She'd met him at orientation day on the first day of her first year at Sydney University. Thrilled by the newness of it all, she'd signed up for various interest clubs and had been searching for the equestrian club when she'd bumped into a tall, dark-haired guy doing the same thing. One glance had told her he was a country boy, his Western jeans, blue and white checked shirt and elastic-sided riding boots a dead giveaway. All that had been missing was an Akubra, the iconic Australian wide-brimmed hat.

'They've closed the equestrian club for lack of interest,' he'd said gloomily.

'But I'm interested,' she'd said.

'So am I,' he'd said.

'That makes two of us.'

Then they'd looked at each other—really looked—and laughed. 'Why don't we start our own club?' he'd said.

'Let's go grab a coffee and talk about how we'd do that,' she'd said.

Excitement had hummed through her. He had been

quite the hottest guy she'd seen on campus. But from
the get-go it had been strictly a hands-off scenario. Wil
had just started dating a girl and she'd still been seeing
her high-school boyfriend. Despite that—perhaps because of that —she and Wil had fallen immediately into
an easy friendship, talking non-stop for more than an
hour. They'd done nothing about reviving the moribund
university equestrian club. But the next weekend they'd
driven up together to the Blue Mountains to horseback
ride in the Megalong Valley.

This time, their hour-and-a-half journey to the mountains took them to a suburban area on the wrong side of
Katoomba. Wil told her that his ex-wife had moved up
there after their final split. The streets were steep and
hilly, lined with small, free-standing houses, the bush
never too far away. Georgia laughed when they had to
sound the horn at a small flock of sheep grazing at the
side of the road. No dimple from Wil. He was obviously
too focused on what was to come to engage in her spec-
ulation about whether the sheep had escaped, or it was
considered okay up here for sheep to wander all over a
suburban street.

He pulled up in front of a shabby but tidy cottage, surrounded by a neat garden. 'This is the sister's place,' he
said. 'She's been looking after Nina since the accident.'
He made no move to get out of the car.

'Nina is such a pretty name,' she said.

'Yeah. I like it,' he said.

Georgia let him sit there, his gaze focused on the bright
blue front door of the house, until the silence got uncomfortable. 'So, *operation baby pick up*,' she prompted.
'What's the next step?'

'The social worker Maree meets us at the house to facilitate the handover. She's in there now.'

'And then you're a daddy,' she said. It scarcely seemed real to her. He would walk out of that house with a baby in his arms. A baby for keeps.

Wil turned to her, the colour drained from his face. 'That's what terrifies me. I want to do the right thing. But what do I know about being a dad? It's not just the nappies or what to feed her. I'll nail that. Suppose I haven't got it in me to be a good parent?'

The anguish in his face told her there was something more going on here. She'd often had the feeling there was more to Wil than he'd ever let on to her. Something, perhaps, to do with his upbringing. She knew he'd been orphaned as a young child. But as a friend she'd never questioned his past. Right now he needed morale-boosting more than anything else.

'The fact that you feel responsible for her is a very good start. That you're actually *here* is a huge point in your favour.'

'Guys usually have time to get used to the idea of being a father.' He drummed his fingers on the edge of the steering wheel. 'I've been thrown in the deep end.'

'That's true. You'll have to learn on the spot. But you're a clever guy. It seems to me that so far you're doing great.'

'She's a baby now, but then she'll be a little girl, then a teenager. I'll be the father of a *teenager*, Georgie. How do I do that?'

'It is a bit hard to imagine, isn't it?' she said. She and Wil had been teenagers when they'd met; it didn't seem that long ago. 'But you'll grow with her and the next thing you know you'll be giving her away at her wedding.'

'Father of the bride? That's a stretch too far,' he said with a hint of that dimple finally appearing.

There was something about his slow smile, the way it lit his dark eyes, that had always made her believe she was special to Wil— *as a friend.* She could only imagine what it might be like to have that smile directed at her in the sensual, exciting way that had had women flocking to him. But she had never allowed herself to imagine it. Too scared that if she ever acted on it he might kindly reject her. She wasn't about to start now.

'Wil, what you're doing will be life-changing. There's no way around that. But take it baby step by baby step,' she said, returning his smile.

'You always know the right thing to say,' he said.

'Not always.' *I'm afraid my give-a-damn quota has expired.* 'But in this case, I say just go in and get your baby. I'll show you how to change a nappy if the need arises. How about that for an act of friendship?'

He grimaced. 'Changing nappies is one aspect of parenthood I'm not looking forward to. Prepared for it but dreading it.'

'Hey, you muck out stables. You'll get used to it.' She certainly hadn't, no matter how much she loved her little nieces and nephews. Maybe nappy-changing would be more bearable if the child was your own. Anyway, Wil could well afford to hire a nanny to help him with the practical aspects of parenting.

'You're right. I'm going in,' he said. He unbuckled his seat belt with a resolute air, as if gearing himself up for action on a battlefield. Four days ago he had had no idea he was a father.

'Do you want me to actually come inside with you?' she asked, trying to sound as if she didn't mind either way. She wasn't sure if he'd just wanted her company on the drive. Of course she was dying of curiosity to see what the baby was like, but mainly she wanted to be there for him—someone on his side.

He turned to her. 'Please. I don't know that I can do this without your support.'

'Of course you could.' She undid her seat belt. 'But there's strength in numbers and I'm very happy to be your wing woman.'

A drier heat than humid Sydney, crisp with the sharp scent of eucalypts from the thousands of acres of national park that surrounded the mountain town. The sound of cicadas serenading summer was almost deafening. She stood with Wil at the top of the driveway to the sister's house and smoothed down the skirt of her grape-coloured linen shift dress. Teamed with a low-heeled court shoe, it was a favourite schoolteacher outfit, smart yet respectable. Just the thing to help her friend claim his child.

'I want to do this,' he said fiercely. 'I'll fight to have this child with me. *She's mine.*'

'I've never seen anyone more fearless on horseback. You can do it. You really can, Wil.'

She didn't want to admit she was nervous. This was so out of her experience, had happened so quickly. One minute she'd been packing boxes, just hours later she was in the mountains with Wil, whom she hadn't seen for two years, to pick up his baby. The baby he hadn't known existed. It seemed surreal to say the least.

He turned to look down into her face, dark eyes sincere and warm with gratitude. *It was so good to be with him again.* 'Thank you,' he said slowly. 'I'll owe you one after this.'

'You don't owe me a thing,' she said. 'I'm happy to help. No exchange of favours required.'

Who knew when she would actually see him again after this? He needed her today, what of tomorrow? Besides, New Wil could be very different from the Old Wil who'd been her friend. Now he was a single dad who'd gone through a nasty divorce and the death of the mother of his child. His life would now be focused totally on a seven-month-old baby. She doubted there would be a lot of time for going to see indie bands, or sharing a meal at a funky city café. There was a real likelihood it might be another two years until she saw him again.

She followed Wil down the pathway. Immediately the sister, Sharyn, opened the door. Georgia saw the resemblance to Angie. The older sister's eyes were red-rimmed, her expression truculent as she glared first at Wil and then at her. The middle-aged social worker hovered nearby.

'I'm so sorry for your loss,' Georgia murmured to Sharyn. 'I knew Angie.' It wasn't simply the polite thing to say, she meant every word. The shocking loss of a young woman, a mother, was genuine cause for sorrow and grief, no matter how she'd felt about her.

'Another loss to come,' Sharyn muttered, still glaring at Wil, who was scrupulously polite in the face of such obvious hostility.

The social worker, Maree, defused the situation and Georgia followed Wil into the house. Small shoes lined up in the entranceway, a stroller leaned against the wall, parked so they had to walk around it, tiny raincoats slung over a rack. A multi-child household. Georgia recognised the signs from her sisters' houses.

The social worker ushered her and Wil into a family

room, clean and tidy save for the toys scattered on the floor. A large playpen, of the old-fashioned wooden kind, was set up in the middle of the room.

'Sharyn tells me little Nina just woke up from her nap, and is playing with her cousins,' the social worker said, indicating the playpen.

Georgia's gaze was drawn to the baby with a shock of dark hair and wearing a pink cotton romper suit. She sat on her bottom on a rug, opposite a little boy of about six who waved a fluffy toy rabbit in front of her. Another younger boy stood outside the playpen hanging on to the railing, calling encouragement. The baby laughed, an infectious gurgling kind of laugh that showed four tiny teeth, two top and two bottom. She waved her little arms around in delight as she made a lunge for the toy. Georgia smiled, a smile that came all the way from her heart.

Wil's daughter. Angie's child too. Little Nina had the best of both of them. Wil's dark hair and eyes; Angie's petite nose and heart-shaped face. Georgia's heart spasmed. Poor little thing to have lost her mother. Poor Angie, to have lived long enough after the accident to know she wouldn't survive to see her baby grow up. But Nina had a good man for a father. She'd won the genetic lottery there.

'She's adorable,' Georgia murmured as she looked up to Wil, standing beside her.

At first, she didn't know if he actually heard her. He was staring, transfixed, at his daughter. Emotions rippled across his face. Trepidation. Awe. A warmth that looked very much like pride. *A Wil she'd never seen before.*

'Yes, she is,' he said softly, his eyes not leaving the baby.

Sharyn approached the playpen, breaking the moment like a rock thrown violently into the gentle ripples of a pool. 'Okay, Kieran, that's enough playtime. Give Nina the bunny and take your brother outside to play.'

The boys obeyed without question. Georgia's schoolteacher eye noted both little boys looked well cared for, in the way of children who were active and well nourished. They were tender and gentle with the baby. The older one gave his tiny cousin a kiss, hopped out of the playpen, took his little brother by the hand, and headed out of a sliding door to a grassed area outside.

Little Nina had turned at the sound of her aunt's voice. Now she put up her arms to be picked up. Sharyn immediately swept her into her arms with a murmured endearment. She stood facing Wil. 'You're still determined to take her?' she said. The baby rested comfortably on her hip.

'She's my daughter, Sharyn,' he said. 'We've gone through all this.' Georgia could see a pulse throbbing at his temple that belied the calmness of his voice.

'You didn't even know you had a daughter,' Sharyn said. 'Angie hated you. Wanted to punish you by keeping Nina from you.'

Maree the social worker placed herself between Sharyn and Wil. 'We've discussed this. Legal aspects aside, your sister's dying wish was very clear. She wanted Nina to be in the custody of her father, Wil. I can understand your sadness at little Nina going but—'

'Rightly or wrongly, all Angie would have been thinking of was Wil's money and Nina having access to it,' said Sharyn. 'I told her that Nina should know her father but Angie wanted revenge on her ex for kicking her out. She wanted her secret kept until one day she could taunt him about Nina and blackmail him for more money in return for seeing his little girl.'

Georgia shuddered at the matter-of-fact tone of Sharyn's voice as she discussed her sister's warped motivation. Wil's expression didn't change but the words must have hurt. 'That changes nothing,' he said.

Sharyn hugged the baby closer to her. 'Nina is happy here with us. I looked after her when her mother was at work. What makes you think you can look after a little girl?' Georgia sensed the pain underneath the anger.

'She's my daughter and belongs with me,' Wil repeated. 'I can look after her very well.'

With Wil's wealth he could give his daughter every advantage. So much more than the aunt could provide. Georgia appreciated that he didn't rub in their difference in social status and income. Besides, she didn't think that was what Wil meant—he meant the special love of a parent, the closest bond a child could have. Father trumped aunt. Wealthy father with doting grandparents, no doubt waiting in the wings, held all the cards.

'You? A guy on your own? A guy who couldn't stay married for even six months?'

Georgia cringed at Wil's sharp intake of breath. 'Yes,' he said, obviously through gritted teeth.

'It's not right.' Sharyn clutched the baby tighter, as if daring Wil to prise her out of her arms. 'If you cared about her, you'd leave her with me. A little girl needs a mother... a woman in her life.'

'She will have a woman in her life,' said Wil. He moved closer to Georgia and put his arm around her. That was the first shock. Then came the second. 'Georgia is my fiancée.'

What?

Georgia stiffened, went to protest. But Wil tightened his grip on her shoulder. She knew what he meant. *Play along.* Back in the day they'd sometimes pretended to be dating to deter an unwanted admirer at a party or out at a bar. Each other's wing person. They'd have a good laugh about it afterwards.

Georgia didn't feel like laughing now. 'Uh, yes.' She forced a smile. *This wasn't a game.*

'Congratulations on your engagement,' said the social worker, looking very pleased.

'Th-thank you,' said Georgia, not able to meet her eye, furious with Wil for putting her on the spot.

'She's an elementary schoolteacher and knows all about little kids,' Wil added. He squeezed Georgia's shoulder again in an unmistakable prompt.

'Uh…yes, I do,' she said. 'And babies. I have five nieces and nephews and have looked after them all. Ask me anything you want about babies.'

Sharyn looked her up and down as if she were something loathsome. 'Angie told me all about *Georgia*. The *best friend* she thought her husband fancied. Looks like she was right not to trust you, if you're now engaged.'

Georgia gasped at the accusation. Went to deny it. Bit her tongue. *This wasn't real.* She was, in truth, just his friend. She had nothing to feel guilty about.

'Not true, Sharyn,' Wil said. 'Georgia was indeed just a friend then.'

Irrationally—because that was all true—his dismissal of her as a woman his wife had had no cause to fear hurt. Georgia schooled herself not to betray just how much it hurt. She'd never tried to be more than *just a friend*, she reminded herself.

Georgia was aware of the woman's narrowed glance at her empty ring finger and she fisted her left hand in response and put it behind her back. Of course people would expect an engagement ring. Guess Wil hadn't thought of that with his spur-of-the-moment comment. Unless he'd planned to say she was his fiancée all along?

She put that thought aside to consider later. By not denying his from-out-of-nowhere claim—how could she have?—she had committed to playing along. Especially as Wil's former sister-in-law seemed still determined to fight.

Wil pulled her closer. She tried to relax against him, difficult when she was so intensely aware of his strength and warmth, the utter masculinity of him. *He still smelled the same.* She'd always managed to deny how attractive she found him. Pretending to be his wife-to-be took her denial to a whole new level.

Sharyn continued. 'But that doesn't qualify you to be a mum. Especially to a little girl who has lost her own. She looks cheerful enough now but she knows her mummy is gone, that something is very wrong in her world.' She choked up but scowled at Georgia's look of sympathy.

Georgia glanced up at Wil, trying to seem like a concerned fiancée seeking reassurance, then back to Sharyn. 'I'll do my best. I should imagine Nina would be a very easy child to…to love. Just because Nina is going to live with her dad and…uh…me, doesn't mean she has to say goodbye for ever to her aunty and cousins. I'm sure Wil will want you to be part of her life.'

Georgia sensed Wil still beside her. Had she overstepped the mark, gone where a pretend fiancée shouldn't go?

'Really?' said Sharyn, relief softening her combative expression. 'We'll get to see her?'

Georgia was so disconcerted at the situation she found herself in, she struggled to sound normal. 'Of course.

Family is important.' She looked back up at him. 'Isn't it, Wil?'

'Yes, it is,' he said with a vehemence that surprised her.

'So I don't have to tell the boys they'll never see their baby cousin again?' Sharyn said.

'No. Uh…in fact they could be pageboys at our wedding.' Georgia had to suppress a grin at the look on Wil's face. Served him right for dropping her into this. 'They'd make cute little ring-bearers, wouldn't they, Wil?' she said, perhaps a little too sweetly.

'Uh, yes,' he muttered.

Sharyn's face lightened. 'Pageboys? I'm not sure they'd stay still long enough for that,' she said. 'But you're serious about keeping in touch?'

Georgia gritted her teeth. How could she possibly be expected to answer such a question? She pasted on a fake fiancée smile as she gave Wil a glance she hoped he would recognise as *over to you.*

'I'll make sure Nina keeps in touch with her cousins,' he said.

His former sister-in-law nodded and reluctantly handed her little niece over to her father. 'Make sure you do,' she said.

Wil took Nina from her, a little awkwardly but with growing confidence. Georgia caught her breath as she watched him.

There was something about a tall, broad-shouldered, manly guy holding a little baby in strong, protective arms that was heart-stoppingly appealing. Even more appealing when the guy in question was her friend Wil, and the little daughter he had only just discovered. He so big and powerful; Nina so small and vulnerable. The way he held her, the intensity of his gaze were as if he was silently assuring Nina he would protect her from every possible bad arrow the world might have in wait for her. But the way the tiny girl looked back up at him with the same dark eyes made Georgia's heart turn over. There was a connection there. Now she really believed it—Wil was a father.

A wave of yearning swept over her. Not for Wil—of course not for Wil. He was just a *friend*. Or for his daughter. Her days were filled with looking after other women's children. She wanted her own baby one day. At twenty-seven going on twenty-eight, her biological clock had started to tick insistently. But as her track record with marriageable-type males was abysmal, that particular dream might not be coming true any time soon.

She'd knocked back three proposals, the first while she'd still been at uni. Commitment was what she'd craved but the guys just hadn't been quite right. The most recent had been Toby. She'd let the relationship go on for too long, wasting her time and his. But she'd thought that pathway was expected of her—marriage to the steady kind of guy everyone had liked. Children to follow. Even to the fact that Toby had been a fellow schoolteacher—just think how convenient all those school holidays would have been when it came to vacation childcare. But that hadn't been enough for her to want a ring on her finger. Even after Wil had married and dashed any deeply suppressed hope she'd had of their friendship developing into something deeper.

Wil turned to her and smiled. The dimple was in full force. 'Do you want to hold her?' he said, as if offering a gift of inestimable value.

Hold baby Nina? As a potential stepmother? Of course

she wanted to hold the dear little thing. But she wasn't sure what Wil expected of her. To gush that she couldn't wait to be little Nina's mummy? That would be going too far in this crazy charade he had thrust her into. She wouldn't—couldn't —lie. Instead, she would try to behave as she normally would when offered a cuddle of an adorable baby.

She held out her arms with a smile, was rewarded with the deliciousness of a soft, sweet-smelling baby in her arms. 'Hello, Nina,' she murmured. 'I'm Georgia.' The baby replied with her cute, four-toothed smile and a string of babble that just might have meant *pleased to meet you*. Nina was, without a doubt, enchanting.

But how dare Wil put her in a position when she had to pretend to be a doting mum-to-be? Engaged to be married to him? It stretched the boundaries of a newly ignited friendship a step too far. She didn't want to fall back into the *good old Georgia* trap—always obliging, always helpful, making excuses for the inexcusable—not for her family, not for her friends and especially not for Wil, who had ignored her for two whole years.

CHAPTER THREE

WIL RISKED A sideways glance at Georgia where she sat next to him in the car as he drove back towards Sydney. Her eyes were closed, but he knew she wasn't asleep.

In two years, she hadn't changed a lot. Her hair, glinting reddish highlights in the afternoon sunlight, was cut a little shorter into a more sophisticated style. Her cheekbones seemed more pronounced and made her look more grown up, more womanly, though the scatter of freckles across the bridge of her nose was still delightfully girlish. She must have had her ears pierced as she was wearing stud earrings he'd never noticed before—she'd never worn earrings for fear of them getting caught in her horse-riding helmet. But she was still riding horses if her toned arms—bare in her sleeveless dress—were any indication.

He was struck again, as he had been many times since they'd reconnected, by how lovely she was. Not in an obvious *look at me* way, but in a quieter way that needed a second glance to be truly appreciated. He'd appreciated her beauty from the get-go, even more so as he'd got to know her. But it wasn't just a tumble of dark hair, deep blue eyes and an oval-shaped face that made her so attractive, it was her warm, generous heart, ready laughter and her smile. Georgia smiled not just with her lips but with her eyes, her whole face lighting up and warming those who were lucky enough to be on the receiving end.

There had been years in Wil's life where smiles bestowed on him had been rare. When he'd first met Georgia, back during his first days of university, her smile had been like a gift. She'd been as disappointed as he had about the lack of an equestrian club, but her good humour about it had soon had him planning how he could continue to see her. Fortunately, riding horses had been an immediate shared interest. He'd had to be convinced by the quirky indie music she favoured but he'd gone along with it as an excuse to see her. Then he'd got to genuinely like it. And to like her. A lot.

He hadn't straight away relegated her to the 'just friends' zone. Far from it. He would have asked her out like a shot that first day at uni if each of them hadn't already been dating other people. As neither of them were the types to cheat, it hadn't happened. Turned out the opportunities where they'd both been single and available at the same time had been rare. But there had been undeniable moments when neither of them had followed up on the chance to step up their friendship to something else. Then he'd got to thinking she was way too valuable as a friend to risk losing her friendship. Yet. Maybe one day he'd take that chance. It had seemed to him that Georgia had 'commitment' stamped all over her. He hadn't been ready for 'for ever'. Girlfriends had come and gone. Georgia had stayed. Until the big mistake that had been his marriage.

Now Georgia was annoyed with him. The tight set of her mouth, the uneven breathing told him she was seething while she pretended to sleep. He knew why.

He should have consulted her before introducing her as his fiancée. But it had been a spur-of-the-moment decision. A gut response to the criticism that he wasn't capable of looking after a baby. Fear that, despite the baby being legally in his custody, somehow the sister and the social worker would block him from taking his daughter home with him.

Georgia had been shocked when he'd made the outrageous claim, though she'd hidden it well. The rigid way she'd held her shoulders had told him she was less than pleased. Yet she'd stepped up to the plate. She'd made the perfect pretend fiancée. Things wouldn't have gone as smoothly without her intervention. He could never thank her enough.

From the back seat, where baby Nina was strapped into her brand-new baby car seat, came a sudden loud murmur. Georgia's eyes shot open. 'Is Nina okay?' She twisted around to check on her. 'She's still snoozing. Must have been dreaming.'

'I wonder what a seven-month-old baby dreams about?' he said.

'Who knows?' she said. 'Food? Comfort? A former life, perhaps, if you believe in that.'

'Whatever that dream might have been, she sounded happy,' he said with relief.

'She seems a happy baby. Healthy and well cared for too. Angie must have been a good mum.' Georgia's tone was guarded.

Wil knew what his friend had thought of his ex-wife. With good reason, as it had turned out. Angie had made manipulation into an art form. But he'd been so intent on seeing in her an echo of someone from his past, a chance to right a long-ago wrong, he'd been blind to the reality of Angie. He'd cut his losses as soon as he could, paid her what she'd wanted. Hadn't seen her again after she'd moved to Katoomba. Married and separated within six months—not a great track record. Not something he was proud of. Not a mistake he intended to repeat any time soon.

'According to Sharyn, Angie was a good mother,' he said. 'Sharyn told me that when Angie discovered she was pregnant, she reformed her party-girl lifestyle and looked after her health.'

Georgia sighed. 'What a tragedy. Lucky for Nina she's got you.'

'I want to give her everything,' he said fiercely. *Everything I never had.*

Georgia fell silent as they started the descent from the Upper Mountains. The Great Western Highway twisted through charming small townships that Sydneysiders liked to visit for the autumn colour, the winter chill, to enjoy the distinct seasons that didn't really apply to sub-tropical Sydney. Much of the road was through bushland with eucalypt forest growing right to the edge. In the summer heat, he was aware of the sharp tang of the gum leaves, the faint chime of the bellbirds.

When he stopped at a traffic light, Georgia turned to him. She was flushed high on her cheekbones. The words that had obviously been brewing spilled out. 'Why? Why the fake fiancée thing? Why put me on the spot like that?'

Wil wished he could tell her the real reasons. Unload some of the burden of his past. Confess how he distrusted social workers. His dread of leaving a child—any child—in the care of an aunt. That his fears had festered since he was a five-year-old, orphaned and left in the reluctant custody of his father's sister, who had kept him out of a grudging sense of duty and absolutely no love. He'd run away. More than once. The last time had delivered him into the welfare system. Many social workers had followed, some better than others, all overworked and not inclined to spend more time than necessary with a boy labelled as trouble. But the masks he'd been forced to wear for all those years for self-protection were too firmly in place to risk letting Georgia see behind them.

'You heard Sharyn's scorn at the idea of me looking after a baby. *A man.* As if I wasn't capable.' His former sister-in-law's words had triggered his own deep-seated fears about the sudden fatherhood that had been thrust upon him. He'd fought back with his best defence— Georgia.

'She didn't think too much of me looking after a baby, either,' said Georgia with a strangled laugh. 'In spite of you trumpeting my extensive childcare experience.'

'Sharyn was out of order. I'm sorry you were exposed to her attack,' he said, grateful that the light changed to green and he didn't have to directly face her.

'She was grieving. I didn't take offence. In a way she was right. Looking after other people's children must be very different from caring for your own, with day-in, day-out responsibility.'

As he was about to find out. 'Point taken. But I didn't want to argue with her. Or the social worker, who'd whip a child into care sooner than not if they had any doubt about the parent's capacity.'

Georgia tilted her head questioningly. 'What makes you say that? I thought she was supportive of you. It's a social worker's priority to keep children with their parents.'

Wil sensed Georgia's frown, the unasked questions

about his childhood. All he'd ever told her was that he'd been adopted, lived with his adoptive parents and their birth son on a historic rural property raising cattle and growing wheat in south-western Victoria. He'd gone to boarding school in Melbourne and then university in Sydney. A seemingly idyllic, privileged life. The years between five and thirteen, in and out of foster homes and children's institutions, were the blanks in his history he had no intention of filling in. Not for Georgia, not for anyone if he could avoid it.

'But did you note Maree's relief when she heard I had a fiancée?' he said.

He knew Georgia rolled her eyes even without having to see her. 'Which of course you don't. The social worker might have believed your fabrication. Sharyn sussed out something was fishy because I wasn't wearing an engagement ring. I hope this deception doesn't come back to bite you. Or me, for that matter.'

'How could it? The "deception" won't go further than today. It was a temporary ruse. When I see Sharyn again, I'll just tell her it didn't work out for us.'

'As easy as that,' Georgia said too lightly.

He cursed himself for his thoughtlessness. She'd been such a good sport about all this. 'I didn't mean our friendship. I meant—'

'I know what you meant,' she said drily.

She had been so calm, so unflustered, rising to the challenge of playing a fake fiancée beyond even his expectations. As far as friends went, Georgia was the gold standard.

'Thank you,' he said. 'You're being very gracious about it.'

'I'm not, actually. I'm cranky as hell. Not with Sharyn.

With *you*. She was fighting for a child she loves, her last link with her sister. You took advantage of me, threw me into the situation totally unprepared. We've only just re-established contact with each other. You went too far, Wil. It was a crazy thing to do.'

'It wasn't premeditated, I assure you. But I can't regret my strategy, not for a moment. You were brilliant. I'm so grateful to you for going along with me.' Thank heaven he'd found the guts to call on her that morning.

Georgia frowned. 'I still don't get why you did it. Surely introducing me as a good female friend would have been enough?'

'A fiancée sounds more stable. These government people are looking for stability and continuity.'

'Why should you worry? It wasn't an adoption. You're the father. Her closest blood relative. Your name is on the birth certificate. Nina's mother's dying wish was that you have custody. Sharyn doesn't have any rights.'

Wil simply didn't trust the system, not when he'd been a victim of it in the past. Perhaps it had changed since he'd been a ward of the state, perhaps not. But his memories of his experience of the welfare system would always be raw. 'I wasn't going to allow anything—or anyone—to get in the way of me claiming my daughter. Bringing you into the picture was a good way to get Sharyn off my back.'

'Actually, I didn't think Sharyn was that bad either. She obviously cares for Nina in her own way.'

Of course Georgia would try to be fair. Her determination to see the good in people was something he'd always liked about her. He didn't refer to her comment about the pageboys. When she'd made the teasing remark, a sudden image had flashed through his mind of

Georgia walking up a church aisle, radiantly beautiful in a white wedding dress, with Sharyn's two little boys walking earnestly ahead of her balancing wedding rings on satin cushions. Where the hell had that come from? It wasn't something he wanted to revisit, that was for sure.

'Were you serious about maintaining a relationship with Nina's aunt and cousins?' she said. 'Or was that another expedient lie to help you get what you wanted?' Georgia had always been quick to the point.

'Not a lie. Those little boys seemed like good kids.' As, perhaps, he had been before his young life had shattered into pieces around him.

'It would be good for your little girl to grow up knowing her cousins. I loved my boy cousins, though at times they seemed like a different breed.'

'That's why I agreed to it. I don't care much for Sharyn. But it's all about Nina. What's good for her. That's all that concerns me now. Whatever she needs I will make sure she gets. If it's extended family, I'll go along with it for her sake.'

Wil recognised that from now on his own needs would come a very poor second to the tiny person asleep in the back of the car. His life would never be the same. He needed Georgia. He had to make sure she stuck around. As his friend. As Nina's friend. He couldn't lose her again.

What next? As they finished their descent from the mountains and joined the motorway that would take them back into Sydney, Georgia wondered—not for the first time—if Wil had fully thought this single-fatherhood thing through.

'Do you really not know how to change a nappy?' she asked.

'What single guy my age would know about nappies? But I've read the instructions on the packet. It doesn't look too difficult. The woman in the pharmacy where I bought them gave me a demonstration.'

Georgia tried to smother her laugh but without success.

'So you think it's funny too?' he said, that scowl back in force. 'The pharmacy lady seemed to think it was highly amusing.'

With his dark brows and eyes, Wil had always managed an impressive scowl. Georgia put up her hands, as if to ward him off. 'I'm not saying anything,' she said, mirth still bubbling through her words.

'No. But you're still laughing,' he said. 'I also watched some online videos. Nappy-changing tutorials. How to bathe a baby. That kind of thing. And I signed up to follow some mommy bloggers. They seem to know everything. It's all there if you know where to look.'

'What's all there, Wil?' she asked. She found the idea of handsome, clever Wil earnestly watching childcare videos more than a tad endearing.

'How to be a parent,' he said very seriously. 'The practical stuff, anyway.'

'Okay,' she said cautiously.

'And Sharyn gave me a comprehensive list of Nina's likes and dislikes. Even packed that toy rabbit she loves into her bag.'

'Sounds like you're all sorted, then,' Georgia said, biting her tongue. And reminding herself again that he could afford an around-the-clock nanny. She wasn't going to jump in doing her *good old Georgia* thing again, always first with the offer of help.

She was over being taken for granted by anyone. Her

people-pleasing had always been part of her. Perhaps because of being born the 'accidental' third child, whose unexpected arrival had interrupted her mother's career and disrupted the family dynamics, she'd been so amenable to try and earn her place.

Until recently she'd kept it up, house-sitting, cat-sitting, babysitting for her family—even when inconvenient, even when she'd resented their assumption that she would always be on call. She'd overdone it with Toby, being too compliant, perhaps to make up for her instinct that she didn't love him enough. She'd been super sweet to his overbearing parents. Had spent weekends, where she'd rather have been horse riding, cheering him on in the rugby games she'd found tedious beyond belief because he'd liked her to be there.

Looking back on her friendship with Wil, trying to puzzle why he'd ghosted her, she'd realised the caring and sharing element had been unbalanced there too. To a certain extent, she'd been there for him to pick up and put down when he'd pleased. When she'd ended it with Toby, she'd decided to put herself first for a change. Follow her own interests. And it was working out great. Now Wil was back in the picture and she'd have to stick to her resolve—no more being a doormat for anyone.

'Where are you actually living these days? Still in Pyrmont?' she asked. She shuddered at the thought of a baby learning to walk in his harbour-side penthouse with balconies on two sides and hard, shiny surfaces everywhere.

'I kept the apartment as an investment and bought a property in Ingleside after my marriage broke up.'

'Wow. I'm envious.' Ingleside was a suburb on Sydney's northern beaches, close to both bushland and sea.

Once home to market gardeners, now known for large plots of land with big houses and priced way out of the regular wage-earner's reach. But not, it seemed, her wealthy friend Wil's. 'Is there room for horses?'

'You betcha. I have two stabled there for me to ride. An Arab gelding and a thoroughbred mare.'

'Country boy in the city,' she said. 'Lucky you.' She wanted to ask could she come down and see them, beg for a ride on one of the horses, but she wasn't sure what shape her friendship with New Wil, single dad Wil, might take.

'It's a big house, a big garden,' he said. 'I didn't know about Nina when I bought it, but it will be a great place for her to grow up.'

'She's a lucky girl to have you as her dad. And not just because, no doubt, she'll have her own pony.'

'Starting with a miniature as soon as she's big enough to mount one,' he said.

'But that's a while off. What preparations have you made for her now? Babies seem to need a lot of stuff.' She wasn't as confident as he seemed to be on the value of online tutorials. Yet she didn't want to undermine his confidence in his parenting skills.

'All sorted,' he said. 'The day after I got back from my first trip to Katoomba I visited one of those big baby stores. A very helpful girl helped me get everything I needed and it was delivered the next day.'

There would, no doubt, be many very helpful girls extending a hand to this handsome, wealthy single dad and his cute baby. He'd be bowled over with offers of help once the news got out. His care for his daughter only made him more attractive.

Despite her annoyance at him about the fake-fiancée

fiasco, she was glad she'd been there for him today. It was a privilege to have been present to witness the moment he'd first taken charge of his daughter—an emotional, significant occasion. She wished… *No.* She didn't want to become more involved. She was as vulnerable as anyone else to the appeal of this gorgeous man with his adorable little girl. *Just friends*, she reminded herself for, quite possibly, the millionth time since she'd met him.

'Have you been able to get a good nanny at this short notice?' she asked.

'There won't be any nanny. I told you, I'm going to look after my baby myself. I need to bond with her. Not leave her with strangers.'

'Okay,' she said. She admired him for his conviction. Didn't want to make any comment that might be construed as sexist. 'What about your work? How will you manage both working and being a stay-at-home dad?' Her sisters seemed to be endlessly juggling.

'These days I run a design and engineering solutions consultancy. My staff are mainly freelance. I intend to shift my centre of operations to a home office. I've had to think on the spot. Fortunately, January is our quiet time.'

'You seem to have it sorted,' she said.

'It will be more a work in progress. I just want to do my best for my daughter.'

'Keep in touch, won't you?' She didn't want to go back to friend limbo with Wil. Not after this dramatic reconciliation. 'I'll be wondering how you and Nina will be managing.'

'I'm sure we'll be fine,' he said, with typical Wil confidence.

'The entire Internet is on standby to give assistance,' she said lightly.

Not to mention all the other resources available to a millionaire. Those resources would not include her. *Good old Georgia*, always on hand, had gone on strike. She'd told her sisters to count her out for free babysitting all summer. She had a life of her own and at age twenty-seven she darn well wanted to develop it.

'When I drop you back at your apartment, give me all the details I need to organise the movers for you,' he said.

'That won't be necessary, I—'

'No arguments,' he said. 'It's the least I can do for your help today.'

'Okay, I won't argue,' she said. In truth, his offer was more than welcome. She'd be packing all night otherwise.

'How long do you plan to stay at your parents' place?'

'Long enough to sort out where I really want to live. I want to go to Greece in the July school vacation. Then I'm thinking of maybe getting a transfer to a rural school. I don't know that I'll ever be able to afford to buy my own place in Sydney.'

'You're really planning to leave Sydney?' Wil sounded shocked.

'Maybe. One day. It's an option. That's a good thing about teaching. There are jobs in the country. The other good thing is the holidays, of course.'

'Have you got the rest of this summer vacation off?'

'All of January.'

'Are you going away?' He still seemed disconcerted at the revelation she might be leaving Sydney. Did he think she'd put her life on hold these past two years? That now he'd got back in touch she'd be always on tap?

She shook her head. 'I have to work. Well, I don't know that I can really call it something as onerous as work when it's a dream come true for me.'

'Something to do with your art?' *He remembered.*

'I got a publishing contract. A children's picture book. I wrote and illustrated it.' Excitement and disbelief bubbled through her voice; she still could hardly believe it was true. But it hadn't happened until she'd made her own interests her priority.

'Congratulations,' he said, sounding genuinely pleased for her. 'I always knew you were talented. Well done.'

'My first book comes out in March. My next deadline is February. That will keep me very busy over the holidays.'

'My friend the author,' he said slowly. 'I like the sound of that.'

'Not as much as I like it,' she said, laughing.

'You'll be busy. But if you could find time to visit me and Nina, I'd like that.'

'Me too, Wil,' she said.

Her heart gave a skip of pleasure at the thought. Wil back in her life. She didn't want to get too involved. His ghosting of her still stung, and she wasn't convinced he wouldn't do it again. Then there was the way he'd dropped her into the pretend engagement without any consultation. But they had a lot of catching up to do. She ached to know more about what he'd been doing. Of course the presence of a third little person would change the dynamics. But she could see no reason why she and Wil couldn't ditch the fake-fiancée thing for good and pick up their friendship again. On her terms.

CHAPTER FOUR

WHAT THE HECK was she doing back in what had been her childhood bedroom at age twenty-seven—turning twenty-eight next month? Georgia finished stuffing her carefully curated selection of clothes into the three skinny drawers her parents had allocated for her use; the rest of her stuff was in storage. When she'd left home, they'd turned her old room into a study for her mother. All traces of her occupancy were long gone, but there was a disturbing sense of déjà vu about it. Under the coat of tasteful dove-grey paint that covered the acid yellow she had favoured for her bedroom, she swore she could still detect the shadows of her horse posters taped to the wall.

It was ironic, because the room had actually started off as a study. It had become a bedroom for Georgia when she'd been born eight years after the youngest of her two older sisters. Their 'happy accident', her parents had called her, but she'd always felt they'd tacked on the 'happy' in an effort to make her feel better about it. She'd been their disappointment too. After two daughters, they'd hoped their 'afterthought'—she'd also had to live with that label—would be a longed-for son. They'd been saving her great-grandfather's name of George for his birth. But they'd got Georgia instead.

She sometimes wondered if that was why she'd turned out such a tomboy, happier in jeans and riding boots than the girly dresses her sisters loved. Perhaps trying to live up to the name they'd really wanted.

It wasn't that she hadn't been loved. Her parents were wonderful, her mother a lawyer, her father a university professor. She had good relationships with her sisters too, even if they did have a tendency to think they knew what was best for her. Sometimes she'd felt she'd had four parents expecting her to fall into line, needing to please. To their credit, her family had taken her new stance on not being as available to help out as she'd always been with good grace, if not without some good-natured teasing.

Georgia placed the last folded T-shirt in the over-stuffed drawer, along with her mother's staples and sticky tape, sliding it carefully shut.

It had come as a shock when the landlord had given her notice on the North Sydney apartment, but in a way it had been a kick-in-the-butt blessing. Her life had been on hold for the last year since the split with Toby. Same flatmates. Same job. There were places she longed to see, stories she ached to tell, new experiences to embrace. Now was her chance to pole-vault out of the rut her life had become as she headed towards thirty. She had stopped being such a people-pleaser but she had to take control of the direction her future would take. And that included not rushing into any long-term leases on apartments.

When Wil's ID flashed up on her mobile phone she looked at it for a long moment before picking up. Two years since she'd been used to seeing calls from Wil. She still wasn't sure what she thought about his sudden reappearance. How to handle her mixed feelings about a rekindling of their friendship. 'I was just about to call to thank you for the professional movers you arranged for yesterday,' she said. 'They got me all packed up and moved without any fuss.'

'Glad that worked out,' he said. 'It was the least I could do for disrupting your day.'

'I appreciated it,' she said. She was still a little cranky with him over the fake-fiancée thing. The more she'd thought about it, the more she'd realised how out of order he'd been to spring that on her. 'How's Nina? And you, of course. Transition to fatherhood going well?'

'It's okay,' he said. But it wasn't. Even without seeing him, she could tell he was on edge. The old connection between them was still there.

'Is it really okay?'

There was a deep intake of breath. 'I could do with some help.'

Why was she not surprised? Help from good old Georgia required, no doubt. 'Is that Nina I hear wailing in the background?' she asked.

'I can't get her to settle.' She could sense a quiet note of desperation in Wil's voice, usually so confident and self-assured. 'She's been howling like that for more than an hour.'

'Have you fed her?'

'Yes.'

'Same food Sharyn was giving her?'

'I followed instructions precisely.'

'Changed her?'

'Yes. I'm getting the hang of it. That sticky tab system could do with some improvement, though.' Georgia smiled to herself at that. Nothing like a challenge to Wil's fix-it soul.

'Cuddled her?'

'Who knew I could rustle up the words to "Rock-a-bye Baby"?'

The thought of Wil rocking his sweet little daughter in his strong, muscular arms and singing to her sent a spasm to her heart. This was definitely a New Wil. But should she be so surprised? He'd always been scrupulous in his care of the horses he rode, kind and affectionate towards them. Not all riders were. He'd always been kind to her too. Until he'd so brutally terminated their friendship.

'But nothing is working?' she asked.

'The struggle is real. She was fine yesterday. I don't know what's the matter with her today.'

Georgia didn't have the heart to suggest baby Nina could be missing her mother, her aunt and everything familiar in her young life.

She dredged her memory for any other strategies her sisters used to calm a crying baby. 'Have you tried popping Nina in her car seat and driving around the block? That can work.'

'I hadn't thought of that but I'm prepared to try anything.' He paused. 'Georgie, could you—?'

'Come down to your house?' So much for being on strike. But this was a baby in distress. And possibly a dad in distress. It would be heartless to stand on principle. 'Now?' The wailing in the background got louder and angrier.

'Please.'

'Shall I pick up something for lunch on the way?' She'd been just about to make a sandwich.

'No. There's plenty of food. Just get here.'

'I'm at my parents' place in Lindfield. Give me thirty minutes.'

'Be quick. I really need you.'

Until the next Angie came along?

Georgia put a tight rein on her urge to say she'd do anything she could to help. Seeing him again had brought the pain he had caused her rushing back. His sudden severing of their friendship had hurt as much as any relationship break-up. More. She wouldn't risk that kind of pain again too easily. She had to be careful to keep her distance from Wil's domestic dilemmas. This would be just the one time she rushed to his help.

Forty minutes later—even with satellite she'd got a bit lost—Georgia drove along a narrow road lined with bushland to reach Wil's house in Ingleside. She pulled up at the address he'd texted her. Then sat there, gaping.

This was Wil's house? High sandstone walls formed a boundary on either side of wide wrought-iron gates. Through the gates, she could see a long gravel driveway that ran up to the house, an imposing colonial-style building with sandstone foundations and wide verandas on three sides. The house was framed by palm trees and surrounded by lush gardens, the centrepiece of which was a three-tiered fountain that splashed and sparkled in the midday sun.

For just the teensiest moment, she felt intimidated, as if her small white hatchback, a gift from her parents on her twenty-first birthday, didn't belong among such opulence. Her parents were reasonably well off. She herself was comfortable on a schoolteacher's salary, with a decent advance on royalties for her book. But this place represented wealth right out of her league. Wil was only a year older than she was—man, had their paths diverged. Maybe she should have dressed for this occasion, instead of wearing shorts and sandals. She told herself not to be so silly—he was still Wil—and buzzed the security device set in the sandstone pillar. The gates swung open.

Wil strode down the driveway to meet her. 'You're here,' he said, his relief obvious as he opened her car door for her. He looked impossibly handsome in khaki shorts and a black T-shirt. He also looked exhausted, his stubble halfway to a beard, dark circles around his eyes.

'I got here as fast as I could. How's Nina?'

'Hallelujah, the car trick worked,' he said, pumping his fists above his head in victory. 'She's asleep at last.'

Georgia swung her legs out of the car. 'You mean I've come all the way down here for nothing?' As she looked up at him, she pretended a pout of annoyance.

He shook his head. 'Not a wasted journey at all. Trust me, I need you.' For a moment she thought he might hug her.

She wanted him to hug her. She hugged her friends of both sexes all the time. Kissed them on the cheek. But not Wil. Never Wil. The 'no touching' rule, which neither of them had ever formally agreed to but had been there from the beginning, appeared to be still firmly in place. 'When it comes to Nina, you're a miracle worker,' he said.

'I'm not sure about that,' she said, bemused. 'I only suggested what my sisters do when they get desperate.'

'I don't have sisters to learn from. The staggering depth of my ignorance when it comes to babies is becoming all too apparent.'

'No luck with the online videos?' she said with a sly sideways look. Maybe teasing wasn't appropriate but she couldn't resist.

'A fail, I'm afraid,' he said with a hands-down gesture. His wry grin brought that irresistible dimple to life in his left cheek. 'It seems only miracle worker Georgie has the goods.'

'I hope I'll live up to expectations,' she said, determined not to feel too flattered. Liking to be needed was one thing, to be at the beck and call of someone quite another. It was a trap she'd fallen into one time too often. Including, at times in the past, with Wil.

'Come on in,' he said. 'But you have to walk on your tiptoes and talk in whispers.'

She laughed. 'You're learning fast,' she said. 'Do not wake slumbering baby at any cost.'

'Laugh out loud now,' he said dramatically. 'Once you enter these doors, make a noise at your peril.'

He put a finger to his lips as he led her through double carved wooden doors and into a spacious, marble-tiled entrance hall. Walking with an exaggerated tiptoe, he indicated for her to follow. She smothered another laugh, not with complete success, which earned her raised dark eyebrows and a mock glare. His reprimand only made her want to laugh more. Old Wil, playful Wil, was still there.

He indicated for her to follow him. As she did so, walking on tiptoe, she couldn't help but notice that his back view was as hot as ever: broad shoulders tapering to a perfect butt, long legs strong and tanned with just the right amount of dark hair. She took a deep breath and chanted to herself the familiar mantra: *just friends*—then repeated it again to make sure her libido got the message.

As she dutifully followed him, she forgot even the fabulousness of Wil's butt as she took in the fabulousness of his house. An interior designer had obviously been given a no-expense-spared budget. Every room deserved a place on the cover of a high-end interiors magazine. In the expansive, high-ceilinged living area, luxurious furniture was placed around an outsize fireplace set around with river stones. The house would be toasty warm in winter, but now air conditioning cooled the January heat to a blissful temperature. The kitchen was over-the-top, chef-equipped, but warm and inviting at the same time. The adjoining informal family room was just as elegantly decorated and furnished as the more formal areas.

Yet among the designer perfection, Georgia noticed heart-warming evidence of a baby in residence—a fold-up stroller in the entrance hall; in the family room a high chair; a tray of feeding bottles on the marble kitchen countertop. And toys. The family room had soft toys and educational toys and baby books wherever she looked. For all the size and elegance of the interiors this was a family home. Wil's home with Nina. And, man, had he shopped for his baby! There was enough stuff here for triplets. Georgia smothered a giggle, successfully this time.

She followed Wil through folding glass doors to emerge onto an expansive deck that looked out across greenery and gardens, through to bushland and then the sea gleaming blue in the distance. There were no immediate neighbours in sight. A multimillion-dollar view.

The deck was sheltered under wide eaves and positioned to take advantage of sea breezes. Like the interiors, it was styled to magazine perfection, with vintage-style cane furniture, brightly coloured cushions, and a profusion of broad-leaved potted plants. On a level down to the right was an infinity-edge pool that seemed to stretch to the horizon, inviting her to plunge into its cool, aquamarine depths. Ahead of them sloped gardens with banks of hydrangeas blooming in multiple shades of lavender and blue. She breathed in the air, scented with the richness of frangipani, the sharpness of eucalypt, a hint of salt. And the indefinable tang of wealth.

She turned to Wil. 'Can we talk now?' she whispered.

'If we keep it low,' he said.

'I really want to shout *wow* at the top of my voice,' she said. 'Wil, this isn't a house, it's an estate.'

'More than five acres,' he said with a wave that encompassed the surrounding land and an unmistakable note of pride in his voice.

'Five acres so close to both the city and the beach.' She couldn't even imagine the multiples of millions it must be worth. That was when she noticed the tennis court. 'Not just an estate. Tennis court. Swimming pool. It's a resort.'

'But totally private, exclusively for the use of my family and friends,' he said. 'For you, the best is yet to come. Beyond the hedge are the stable complex and the arena.'

'And your horses?'

'In residence and waiting to be introduced to you.'

Excitement bubbled through her. 'I can't wait,' she whispered.

'We probably don't have to whisper out here,' he whispered back with a hint of dimple. 'Nina is sleeping in her room.'

He indicated the chairs set around a round table. 'Take a seat while I get us some drinks.' From an outdoor fridge disguised as a bench, he pulled out beers and mineral waters and placed them on the table along with some chilled glasses. 'I'm offering you a beer, but as you're driving I guess you'll want fizzy water as usual.' It appeared he still drank his beer straight from the long-neck bottle.

She accepted the cool drink, and Wil settled himself in the chair opposite her. He pulled out an intercom receiver from his pocket and placed it on the table in front of him.

'All the high-tech stuff to hand,' Georgia said. 'Just what I'd expect from an inventor.'

'There's a nanny cam in her room too,' he said.

'Of course there is.'

'Listen,' he said, putting his hand up. 'You can hear her breathing. I find it reassuring to know she's safe and secure under my watch.'

Georgia took in the rapt expression on his face, transcending the dark shadows and weary lines. 'You're a fully fledged dad already, aren't you?' she said softly.

'I was a dad the moment Nina looked at me with those dark eyes, eyes I recognised from my mirror. The same eyes I think I remember my mama having. It was as if—' Abruptly, he stopped, as though realising he'd spoken about something he'd never shared with her before, and regretted it.

'It was as if what, Wil?'

His gaze didn't meet hers. Rather, he looked down at the monitor. 'Not important.'

'I think it is. As if you were with family again?'

Immediately, he went on the defence. As he had always done if she had dared to venture into any kind of discussion about his life before he was adopted. 'I have family. The best parents a man could have. The best brother. You don't have to be connected by blood to be family.'

'Yet your connection with Nina was immediate, intense.'

'And totally unexpected,' he said, finally looking up at her. 'It was as if we already knew each other. Took me completely by surprise.'

'I saw the resemblance immediately. She's like a mini Wil. You told me once you were only five when your birth parents died.' *Approach with caution.* She'd never pressed Wil on the details of his childhood. But now he was a father of a little girl who looked so like him her desire to know more overrode her usual restraint.

He clammed up. 'That's right.'

'Was it an accident?'

He paused, and she wondered if she would get an answer. 'They both drowned,' he said eventually.

'Oh, no, Wil.' Again she wanted to reach out to him, again she knew she couldn't.

'By all accounts, Mama wasn't a good swimmer. She got into trouble in the surf. My dad died trying to rescue her. Unsuccessfully, as it turned out.'

Georgia took a sharp intake of breath. 'What a tragedy.'

'I was there, on the beach. They found me wandering along the sand, crying out for my mama and daddy. Of course I don't remember much, just fragments. But it was all over the newspapers at the time. *"Little Boy Lost."* I read the accounts of the incident much later.'

Georgia clutched her hand to her heart. 'Oh, Wil. I... I have no words.' She was crying inside at the thought of young Wil, kindergarten age, wandering the beach in distress, looking for his parents. She envisaged him in a pair of wet swim shorts, legs streaked with sand and holding a little plastic bucket and spade, tears streaking down chubby childish cheeks and sobs putting hiccups in his voice as he called for his mummy.

'I try not to think about it,' he said gruffly. 'Being with Nina is making me relive stuff I would rather have left forgotten.'

Georgia was grateful that the connection with his baby daughter had been so profound it had opened up channels in Wil so he was, at last, willing to share his past with her. 'You were so young.' Her heart ached for that little boy, recognised his vulnerability in the adult Wil.

He nodded. His eyes had a distant look, as if he was talking about people he didn't know at all. Which, she supposed, he didn't. She thought back to when she had been five years old but couldn't dredge up many memories. Her parents and her sisters had always been there from her birth until right now and memories mingled with memories.

'Was there any other family? Grandparents?'

'My father's parents were dead. Mama's parents were from a traditional, strictly religious family and had disowned her. Much to their displeasure, my parents had never got married. They wanted nothing to do with me. There was only an aunt, my father's sister in Melbourne. I went to live with her. It didn't work out.' His words were terse, his expression grim.

He so obviously didn't want to talk further about it but Georgia couldn't help herself. While the portal was open she felt compelled to probe. 'So then you got adopted by a lovely family.'

'After a while,' he said, not meeting her eyes.

'So in a way, it turned out okay in the end. As okay as it could considering the...the tragedy.'

'You could say that.'

Georgia waited for him to say more but was met by a heavy silence that stretched out for too long to be comfortable. She took a sip of her drink. 'Thank you for sharing that with me. I always got the impression you didn't want to talk about what had happened to you as a child.'

She'd never before got up the courage to pry behind the sky-high barrier he had put up against emotional in-

timacy. Not just to her. To all their friendship group. To
his girlfriends—a number of whom had sobbed on her
shoulder after the inevitable break-up, a process she had
found excruciating as she'd imagined how she'd be feeling if it were her. That impossible-to-breach barrier had
always made her glad she had kept any attraction to him
so firmly in check. Until Angie, he'd evaded committed relationships. She'd begun to wonder if he was capable of them.

'I didn't. I don't. I don't often give my birth parents a
thought. But Nina seemed immediately familiar. I looked
at her and I recognised her. It was the weirdest thing.
Brought back flickering thoughts of a smiling, loving
face. Of laughter. Of a kind voice with an accent. My
mama's family was eastern European—she was back-
packing around Australia when she met my father and
never went back home.'

'Did you ever try to find her family?'

Wil's face hardened. 'That would have seemed dis-
loyal to my new family. Besides, if they were the kind
of people who would abandon their daughter and their
grandchild, I never want to meet them.'

'You're determined not to ever abandon your daughter.'

'Never. She lost her mum even earlier than I did mine.
But she has me, and she won't grow up wondering where
she came from.'

'Which is why you agreed to her keeping in touch with
Sharyn. So she knows her mother's side of the family.'

He scowled. 'Don't mention that woman. She's already
called me three times to check how Nina is settling in.'

'That's well meaning of her.'

'Or interfering, depending how you interpret it.'

'You're still committed to an ongoing relationship with her and her boys, for Nina's sake?'

'Of course, but not until I've established myself as her father. Bringing Nina up myself without interference is something I have to do. It would be easy enough for me to hire nannies around the clock and leave them to it. But I want her brought up by her parent—not an aunt, not a nanny.'

Georgia took another sip of her drink. Thought carefully about what she might say. Schoolteachers had a reputation for being bossy. She didn't want to be perceived that way. 'It's really worthy of you to think you can do it all by yourself, Wil. But I don't know that it's that easy.'

He sighed, a great heaving of broad, manly shoulders. 'I'm beginning to see that. I'm getting the hang of the changing, the feeding, getting her dressed, though I'm going to ask you to help me with her bath when she wakes up. But there's one thing I hadn't counted on, Georgie.' He looked directly into her face and she was stunned by his perplexed expression, the sadness in his eyes.

'What's that, Wil?' she said carefully.

'I don't think my daughter likes me.'

CHAPTER FIVE

GEORGIA STARED AT WIL, stunned by his woebegone expression, shocked by his words. 'What on earth would make you say Nina doesn't like you?'

His mouth turned down in a half-scowl, not the full brooding Wil scowl but enough to indicate his disappointment and dismay. 'She might only be seven months old, but she's got quite the personality, my little Nina. She's made it very clear she's just putting up with me and she'd rather be somewhere else.' There was an edge of hurt to his voice he couldn't disguise—certainly not from Georgia.

'I'm sure that's not the case. Didn't you say you thought she recognised you, the way you recognised her? I don't know that I can make a judgement about the opinions of a baby her age. But I'm wondering…well, it might be…' She struggled to find a tactful way to say it. 'She's probably missing her mum and her aunty.'

The scowl deepened. 'I thought you might say that—and of course it crossed my mind. Maybe a dad really isn't enough. Not that I will ever give up trying to be the best dad I can possibly be. But she needs more than I can give her. Like the care of a woman in her life.'

'Perhaps. That's what she's used to. I'm no expert on

babies, Wil, in spite of your faith in me. I believe a dad can fulfil her needs, but this particular little one is used to being parented by a woman. It might take her a while to adjust to the fact her sole carer is her father. And… I'm not sure how to put this but, in her own baby way, she must be grieving the loss of her mum.'

'Yeah, I get that. I just want to do what's best for her. If the best isn't me, then—'

Lights flashed on the monitor as it started to sound— grizzling baby whimpers that increased in crescendo. 'She's awake,' Georgia whispered.

'Here she goes again. She's only just got to sleep. What am I doing wrong, Georgie?' He seemed grey and drawn and she wondered how much sleep he'd got in the time since she'd last seen him.

'Nothing you're doing is "wrong",' she said. 'My older sisters say caring for a baby is a steeper learning curve than anything they did at university or in their high-powered jobs. Their husbands agree. They had their kids with them from the day they were born—you're starting well behind the starting gate. Should we go to her?'

'Give her a moment to see if she settles down,' he said. But as he finished speaking Nina started to wail, an urgent cry for attention, increasing in crescendo, impossible to ignore.

Georgia looked at Wil. 'Let's go,' he said at the same time she did.

Georgia followed Wil across the living room, down a corridor and through an open door into Nina's room. The spacious room had obviously started life as a guest room, elegantly decorated and so luxurious a guest would never want to leave. The cot, change table and pretty pink alphabet floor rug made it instantly a nursery.

Nina was sitting up in her high-sided white cot. She wore a pink onesie printed with white bunnies over her nappy. Her face was red and tear-streaked, her dark hair damp and sticking up on end.

'Nina, sweetheart, it's okay, Daddy's here,' said Wil.

Even through her concern for Nina, Georgia marvelled at the depth of affection in his voice. Without a doubt, Wil had bonded with his daughter.

'She looks a picture of misery, poor little pet,' Georgia said.

'I know,' said Wil, wearily.

'Shall we try a different voice?' Georgia headed for the crib. 'That's a very big noise for such a little girl,' she cooed. Nina looked at her, blinked, stopped wailing, hiccupped, then settled into a lower volume grizzling.

Georgia turned to Wil. 'May I pick her up?'

'Please. Anything to keep the volume down.' He ran his hands through his hair so it stuck up on end. Which made him look as frazzled as his little daughter.

Georgia approached the cot. 'Remember me, Nina? I'm Georgia.'

Nina immediately quietened. When Georgia leaned down to pick her up, Nina went willingly into her arms. Nina wound her arms around Georgia's neck and looked into her face. Yes, her eyes were like Wil's eyes. She was definitely her father's daughter. But there was a difference. Nina was her own little person. They were Nina's eyes. And the expression in them made her believe Wil could be right about the strength of her personality.

'I think she likes you,' Wil said.

'I'm a different pair of arms, a distraction.'

'A female distraction.'

'There's that.' Georgia disengaged Nina's arms so she

could look at her more closely. Gently, she smoothed back the damp wisps of dark hair from the baby's forehead. 'I wonder if she's teething?'

'I wondered that too,' he said. 'I typed in "why is my baby crying?" into a search engine and teething came up as a possible cause.'

Georgia ducked her head, kissed Nina's sweet little neck, so Wil wouldn't notice her smile. 'Did it?' she said. She enjoyed the way he took his new duties so seriously.

'But when I looked up "teething" she didn't seem to have those symptoms. A rash and frothing at the mouth. Hell, if she'd been frothing at the mouth I would have rushed her to hospital.'

'Me too,' she said, turning to look at him. 'Did it really say "frothing at the mouth", Wil? Surely not. That sounds more like rabies. Or poison.'

'Excessive drooling and foaming is what it said and that sounded alarming. Anyway, she didn't have a rash or swollen gums. So I don't think she's teething.'

'Your guess is as good as mine. Seriously. Just because I'm a woman doesn't mean I'm a baby expert. Just because you're a man, doesn't mean you can't be.'

Nina reached out and patted Georgia on the face with her tiny hand. Georgia immediately gave the baby her full attention and was rewarded with a gummy smile. 'Oh, you're such a sweet little thing,' she said. 'Your daughter is adorable, Wil.'

'Yes, she is,' said Wil with a catch to his voice that surprised her.

Georgia's head bent close to Nina's, his daughter's tiny hand on her cheek, her solemn dark eyes searching Georgia's face was a sight so entrancing Wil couldn't tear his gaze away. He wanted so desperately to believe he could be everything to the daughter he hadn't known he had. But perhaps that wasn't possible. He was prepared to spend any amount necessary to get her what she needed. Turn his life upside down so he could spend time with her. But he couldn't give her what she'd had with her mother and her aunt. What she was getting right now with Georgia. A woman's touch.

Georgia was a natural with Nina. His little girl was now all smiles and gurgles. Nina wouldn't be his daughter if she didn't respond to the illumination of Georgia's smile the way he always had—by basking in it. Watching his friend and his daughter together, he felt an unexpected shaft of emotion stab his heart. A sudden yearning for what might have been if, one past day, he had given into that long-simmering attraction to Georgia. If he'd found the courage to try, even knowing the risk she might have turned him down. Perhaps she might now be the mother of his child. An unexpected joy prodded him at that thought, impossible as it was.

He had damaged their friendship, and any hopes he'd had of one day it becoming something deeper, by his hasty and ill-advised marriage. He fought against the bitterness he felt towards Angie, not only for depriving him of the first months of Nina's life, but also for engineering his estrangement from Georgia by her jealousy. But whatever Angie's shortcomings, she had bequeathed him this wonderful little girl.

And Georgia, lovely Georgia, had accepted his explanation for why he had cut her from his life. To a point, she had forgiven him. But he knew the foundations for their new friendship were laid on shaky ground. She was reserved, holding back the wholeheartedness of her friendship that had always meant so much to him. Now Georgia didn't trust him. Whatever it took, he would win that trust back.

'Wil, are you a tongue-roller?' Georgia asked, still engaging totally with Nina.

'No,' he said, startled at the question.

'I am. I wonder about Nina.'

'It's an inherited tendency, isn't it?' he said. 'And not something I'd given a second's thought.'

Georgia poked her tongue out at Nina, then rolled it into a tube. Nina reacted with chortles of laughter. In return she poked out her tiny, pink, very flat tongue. It was Georgia's turn to laugh.

'No rolling. She either takes after you or is too young to be able to do it. I haven't a clue how old she'd need to be.' Nina poked her tongue out again, then dissolved into her delightful baby laughter again. 'Clever girl,' said Georgia, planting a kiss on his daughter's cheek.

Nina was delightful. So was Georgia. Relaxed, confident and utterly lovely. No wonder Nina was enchanted with her. No wonder she was loving being kissed by her. *He had never kissed Georgia.* Georgia glanced over to him. 'I think she's learned a new party trick,' she said. *Why had he never kissed Georgia?*

Her eyes met his in a moment of sheer mutual delight in his child. He smiled, not wanting to break the moment. She smiled back and he saw something he'd never seen before, something more than a shared complicity in the cuteness of his daughter. Something that made him want to keep on looking into her blue eyes until he could figure it out.

Then Nina seized upon Georgia's moment of inattention to tug at a lock of Georgia's hair. Georgia's laughter turned to squeals. 'Ouch! That's quite a grip you've got on you, young lady. Ouch!' Which only made Nina laugh more.

Wil laughed too. The tension that had been building since he had first found himself in this large, empty house with his baby daughter, and pretty much clueless except for an overwhelming desire to do everything right for her, started to ease.

Georgia. She was the answer. Georgia would know what to do. She had an instinct for children. It had led her to her career teaching them. To her hobby of drawing and now writing for them. And here she was with Nina, immediately bringing laughter into the rooms of the big empty house where he had lived alone.

Alone and, until now, glad of it. Angie hadn't been able to keep up her fun, loving act much past the honeymoon. He'd tried to understand how childhood abuse had shaped her and had made allowances for her behaviour. But life in the Pyrmont apartment had become hellish. She had insisted on knowing what he was doing every second of the day. There'd been tantrums and excesses of behaviour that had shocked him, then scared him. He'd longed for privacy, time for himself and a door he could lock behind him. He'd found it here. And vowed to stay single. How could he ever again trust his judgement when it came to a woman?

But he trusted Georgia. Believed in her innate goodness and honesty. Loved the energy she brought with her. *He had to keep her in his life.* And not just for Nina's sake.

Georgia gently disentangled her hair from his daughter's tiny fingers. 'I think she's inherited your strength,' she said with a wry smile.

'Good,' he said. 'I want her to be strong in every way.'

During his years in the welfare system, he'd seen what could happen to vulnerable girls. He'd make sure his Nina would be able to hold her own whatever situation she found herself in. Like Georgia.

Georgia shifted Nina around so she rested comfortably on her hip in that instinctive way women did with babies. 'She's off to a good start, I reckon.'

'Nina is obviously at home with you,' he said. 'You're right. She responds to a woman's touch.'

'It's what she's used to, Wil. She'll get used to you. But she might need more than two days to adjust.'

'I know you're right,' he said. 'I guess I don't like to admit she didn't fall for me as quickly as I fell for her.'

'I'm sure she will—just give her time. She's very relaxed and happy with you now.'

'Let's hope it stays that way, though I suspect it's because of you.' There was something so warm about Georgia that had drawn him to her from the get-go. His daughter seemed to feel it too.

'I'm a novelty. She seems a bright little thing. I suspect she might get bored easily. Why don't we take her outside? A change of person worked wonders. A change of scenery might too.'

'That's a thought,' he said. *We.* Georgia working alongside him to care for Nina seemed an eminently sensible option. Certainly for him and for Nina. But what would be in it for Georgia?

'Has she got a sunhat?' Georgia asked.

'It's hanging in the closet. I bought everything I thought she might need.'

Georgia walked over to the closet, Nina still comfortable on her hip, and pulled open the door. Her laughter pealed out. 'Heavens, Wil, did you buy the baby store out? They mustn't have had any stock of cute outfits left after you visited.'

He shrugged. 'As I told you, the assistant was very helpful to a clueless father. Please note, while admiring my purchases, that each of Nina's garments is there in three sizes, one to fit now and two for when she grows bigger. That way I won't have to endure shopping for baby stuff for quite some time.

'Endure? Did you say *endure*?'

'You know I don't like shopping. What guy does?'

Did she, in fact, remember his loathing of shopping? During those two out-of-contact years, had she thought about him much at all?

Georgia had rarely been without an adoring boyfriend in tow, with another one waiting in the wings. It had seemed to him that as soon as the poor sucker had fallen for her, she'd finish with him. Which was another reason he'd been happy to keep her in the friend zone. Even in those rare times they'd both been single he'd never broached the possibility of more. He hadn't been ready for the commitment a relationship with her would demand. But apparently neither had she, in spite of what she'd often said about wanting the long-term and serious, the big white wedding. To his knowledge, she'd turned down two proposals. More now, perhaps.

He doubted she'd missed him. However, he had missed her and having her back in his life was more wonderful than even he could have imagined in those years he'd exiled himself from her warmth and positivity.

'But, Wil, shopping for a gorgeous baby like Nina would be a pleasure. I didn't like dolls when I was a kid, much preferred stuffed animal toys.' She dropped another kiss on his daughter's cheek. 'But a real-life baby girl is a different matter altogether. And, boy, have you got a choice of little outfits for her.'

He laughed. 'She's not a doll, Georgie.'

'But I'll have so much fun dressing her up,' she said. She pulled a tiny garment out of the closet. 'What about this adorable little shirt with the embroidered collar, Nina?' she said. 'It's hot out there and we need to protect you. You've inherited your daddy's olive skin but our Aussie sun in January can really burn.' Nina waved her arms about, reaching for the shirt, babbling as if she were trying to say something.

'Next time I shop for her, I'll invite you along,' Wil said.

'I'd love that. And Nina would come too, of course. I suspect she's going to have strong opinions of what she likes and dislikes.'

'Is that your professional, schoolteacher opinion?'

She paused with that thoughtful expression he knew so well of old. 'In a way, I guess so. Even on this brief acquaintance I can sense a strong personality.' She looked up at him. 'Like her dad. You've always been strong-minded.'

'I've had to be,' he said, not wanting to be further drawn. 'But right now this little girl just turns me to mush.'

'Me too,' she said. 'She really is a sweetie. Now, where's that hat?' She pulled out the pale pink baby-size fedora, popped it on Nina's head. 'This is the most adorable little hat I've ever seen. Did you choose it?'

'As a matter of fact I did,' he said, pleased at her reaction. 'I thought it was cool. Because I bought so much stuff at the baby store, the assistant threw it in for free.'

Nina took the fedora off her head and before Georgia

could stop her had thrown it to the carpeted floor. His daughter's bottom lip jutted out in a way he was beginning to recognise. Georgia looked down at the hat, back to Nina and then up to Wil. Her expression was so dismayed he had to laugh.

How he'd missed her. He wanted to sweep her into his arms, Nina and all, and tell her that. But they'd always had a 'no touching' relationship, instigated, he realised, by him. There was a reason he'd never kissed her. Because he'd feared that hugging her, kissing her even in the most informal way, would unleash feelings he had thought he would not be able to handle.

'Well, I guess that tells us what your daughter thinks of our taste in hats,' Georgia said. She took out a tiny, wide-brimmed hat in white cotton.

'The shop assistant said that hat was more practical,' said Wil. 'What would I know?' The world of baby fashion was a mystery to him. He just wanted the best for his daughter and he could afford to give her the best.

'It ties under the chin so we might have more hope of keeping it on, mightn't we, little missy?' Nina went to grab it from her, but Georgia held it out of her reach. 'No hat, no walking down to see the horsies—uh, sorry, I mean horses.' She looked apologetically to Wil. 'That was a mistake for a schoolteacher to make. No baby talk if she's to develop proper language skills. Starting with the correct name for animals. We should make it a rule.'

'Of course,' he said. He hadn't really thought about things like that. When it came to parenting, he had so much to learn. But with Georgia's input, it suddenly seemed a whole lot more achievable.

'Come on, Nina,' she said. 'Your dad and I are going

to change you, dress you and introduce you to some special new friends.'

'Who do you think is going to be more excited at meeting these "friends"?' Wil said, making quote marks with his fingers. 'Nina or Georgia? I think I know who is dying to get down there and see the horses.'

'Of course I am,' she said, her mouth curving into a smile, her eyes dancing. 'You know me so well, don't you?' Their gazes held for a quick, glancing moment, an exchange of questions without answers.

Wil wasn't sure what to say in reply. Did he really know her any more?

'When it comes to horses, I think I know you well,' he said. 'Otherwise, I have some catching up to do. Starting from now.'

'You were right—again,' Wil said to Georgia not long afterwards. 'Nina is responding so well to a change of scene.'

'So am I,' said Georgia. 'I can't wait to meet Sultan and Calypso.'

As soon as he strapped Nina into the buggy—who would have thought just days ago he would own a buggy?—and headed down the pathway to the stables she was alert and excited with no hint of a grizzle.

The two horses were grazing in the paddock under the shade of the eucalypt trees. At the sight of him, and with the possibility of treats, they came trotting over. He didn't disappoint them about the treats. He and Georgia fed them a carrot each, which they munched with gusto. Nina seemed to find the process fascinating, her little head turning from horse to horse, her arms flailing in excitement.

His horses seemed to know that Nina was an infant and stood placidly while he held his daughter close enough so she could pat their cheeks with her tiny hands. When she let out squeals of excitement, they didn't spook. The horses were on one side of the wooden fence, he, Nina and Georgia on the other. Horses could be flighty creatures and he didn't want to take any risks around his daughter and his friend.

He was getting used to the fiercely protective instincts his daughter aroused in him, which had sprung up the moment he'd looked into those dark eyes. As for Georgia, he had always been in the habit of watching out for her, whether they'd been around unpredictable horses or fending off unwanted admirers in a Sydney club. There had always been admirers. Right now, in denim shorts that showed off her long, toned legs and shapely behind and a T-shirt that made no secret of her curves, she was the tantalising blend of wholesome and sexy that men found appealing. He was no exception.

'So, what do you think of Sultan and Calypso?' he asked.

'They're beautiful. Well bred, well natured and well trained. And I think I sense a real rapport between them and Nina. You should encourage that. A love of animals is a good thing for a child. I think she loved them.'

'Is that a sneaky way of saying you'd like to see the horses again?'

'Perhaps.' Georgia gave him a mischievous sideways grin. 'But isn't this all about Nina?'

Was it? Suddenly it seemed to be as much about Georgia. About ways he could see more of her. Rebuild their friendship. Restore her trust in him. Georgia and Nina together seemed so right. He'd had too many years of refusing to let himself imagine how Georgia and Wil together as a couple might be, to allow that thought any real air time. Especially not now when his life had been turned upside down by the arrival of Nina.

Nina was back in her buggy and was happy for him to wheel her along as he showed Georgia the stable complex, which included four individual stables, a feed shed, tack room and a wash bay. Nina was very taken with the big ginger cat who lived in the stables. So was Georgia.

'I wonder if Nina has seen a cat before?' said Georgia. 'We don't really know what her experiences were in Katoomba.'

'She doesn't seem worried about the horses or the cat. The previous owners left him behind, so he came with the house,' he said. 'He's not the friendliest of felines, so we need to be careful.'

The cat had refused any overtures from Wil. The second Georgia called, 'Kitty, kitty,' the animal ran to her and wound around her legs in an ecstasy of purring. When Georgia picked him up to cuddle and then show Nina, the cat stood still and docile while his daughter patted him.

What was it about Georgia that had this aloof creature instantly besotted? Georgia was truly an exceptional person in every way. Had he been guilty of taking their friendship for granted all those years? Of thinking he could put anything deeper than friendship on ice until it suited him? That had all gone awry when she had met Toby and then he Angie. He'd made some very bad decisions.

'What a gorgeous big boy,' Georgia said, putting the cat down. 'He'll help keep the mice down in the feed shed.'

'He doesn't live on mice alone. My housekeeper feeds him every day.'

Georgia turned to him. 'You have a housekeeper? I wondered if you had help in a place this size.'

'She doesn't live in, rather comes in every weekday. I like my privacy. There's a gardener too. And a stable hand, a student who works here and lives in the apartment that's at the end of the stable complex.'

'This place is awesome. Nina is so lucky she can grow up here. You were so lucky, Wil, growing up on a farm where you could have your own horse.'

'I was very lucky,' he agreed.

If only she knew how different his life had been until he'd been adopted by the Hudson family. How damaged he'd been and how his new father had encouraged his interaction with horses as a form of therapy. But he still couldn't bring himself to reveal the truth about himself to Georgia. He'd shared some of it with Angie because she had told him she'd had a similar background, and she'd used it against him.

'It was my dream to have my own horse,' Georgia said wistfully.

'You can come and ride mine instead. They need more exercise than I can give them.'

'I might take you up on that,' she said. 'Be careful what you offer. You might wake up one day to find I'm living down in the stables, sharing a straw bed with the cat.'

'In that case, I would have words with the cat about him illegally subletting his stable.' She laughed. Nina started to chuckle too, not that she could have any idea of what was funny. It was just that Georgia's laughter was contagious. So he joined in the laughter too.

It was *so* good having her back. Even if he did have to battle the sudden image of Georgia in his bed that flashed into his mind. The cat could have his straw bed to itself. The thought of making love to Georgia was one he'd fought to keep at bay so many times over the years. If it were not for the complication of having Nina now in his life he might be thinking it was time to stop fighting those thoughts.

Georgia, thank heaven, was oblivious to his lascivious thoughts of her in his bed. She was instructing Nina on how to say goodbye to the kitty. He almost corrected her to say 'cat' not 'kitty' as per their new rule but decided against it.

'Next time Nina won't settle, bring her down here with all the distractions,' Georgia said. 'I guarantee she'll stop wailing.'

As he had to stop getting distracted by Georgia's legs in those abbreviated shorts. Or the swell of her breasts under the snug-fitting T-shirt.

He cleared his throat. 'Yeah. Good idea.'

He didn't want her to go.

As he pushed the buggy back up to the house, Georgia by his side, Wil's brain was whirring in hyper-drive, trying to think of ways he could entice Georgia to spend more time with him and Nina.

He was an inventor. An engineer. A creator of design solutions. He saw a problem, then found the solution. The problem in this case was obvious. Nina needed Georgia. He needed Georgia. By the time they reached the house he'd come up with an ideal solution.

CHAPTER SIX

WIL WAITED UNTIL a tuckered-out Nina had been fed, bathed and put to bed for her nap before he broached his idea to Georgia. They were sitting around the round marble-topped table in the family room, eating a late lunch of sushi and Japanese salad delivered from a favourite restaurant in the nearby beachside suburb of Narrabeen. The room looked out over the pool and was one of his favourite places in the house. To have Georgia sitting opposite him, relaxed and enjoying her lunch, made it even better. *She belonged here.*

'I seem to be grovelling with gratitude every time I speak to you,' he said. 'But I really want to thank you for your help with Nina today.'

She took a sip from her mineral water. 'Grovel away, I like it.' She smiled her lovely Georgia smile. 'Seriously, Nina is delightful and you're very welcome. It wasn't a hardship.'

'My daughter likes you,' he said.

'I hope so. I like her too,' she said.

Wil took a deep breath. 'It goes without saying that I like you.'

He was finding it difficult to believe that she was actually here in his home. Seeing her interact with his horses had brought back so many memories of the good times they'd shared over the years. He'd never met anyone else with whom he'd felt so at ease, supported and encouraged. When he'd bought the horses, he'd found himself wishing she'd been with him to give her opinion. Had he chosen Calypso with the thought in the back of his mind that one day Georgia might enjoy riding her? *How he'd missed her.*

She flushed high on her cheekbones; her eyelashes fluttered in the way that happened when she was disconcerted. 'I could say the same. About you, I mean. We go back a long way.'

'We do. And I'll grovel some more to say how glad I am that you didn't slam the door in my face when I turned up out of the blue on your doorstep two days ago.'

'I won't deny that I wanted to. But curiosity overrode caution. Then when you told me about Nina, I just had to listen to you.'

'I'm so glad you did. What a hit you proved to be with her. I suspected she would be comfortable with a woman caring for her. You proved that today.'

'That could be so.' Georgia paused. 'Perhaps you could reconsider your stance on a nanny, Wil?' Her expression was delightfully serious as she leaned across the table towards him. 'Why not get some help? There's no shame in it. No one but me would even know you're backtracking on your "parent only" stance. I had a nanny when I was young. I loved her.'

'You're right. I don't like to backtrack. I was determined to do everything myself. But I'm beginning to come to the same conclusion.'

Her eyes lit up. 'That's great, Wil. I'm so glad to hear that. Getting help won't detract from your role as her father. And I'm sure you'll be more relaxed and be able to enjoy getting to know your daughter.'

'Yes to all that,' he said.

'You'll have to get the right person, of course. Most importantly, make sure Nina is comfortable with her.'

'I know just the person for the job.'

Her eyes widened. 'Really? That's good. Who?'

'You,' he said.

Georgia put down her fork with a clatter on her plate. 'Me? Be your nanny?'

'It makes perfect sense. You're on holidays. You said you needed extra cash for your vacation in July. I think I speak for Nina, too, that you would be the ideal person. Just until you go back to school. I should have everything sorted by then.'

Georgia stared at him without speaking for so long, he thought he'd shocked her speechless. The colour drained from her face, leaving her freckles stark against the creamy paleness of her skin, then flushed back warm and angry.

Wil had a sinking feeling that perhaps his idea for keeping Georgia close by might not have been one of his best ones.

Her eyes narrowed, sapphire ice in their coldness. 'You mean pay me?'

'That's the plan.'

'You become my employer?'

'I wouldn't put it like that.' This wasn't going quite as planned.

'You'd be paying me to work for you. That would make you my boss. What on earth made you think that was a good idea?'

He frowned. 'It makes sense. You got on so well with

Nina. I really like having you here. From what you said you could do with the extra money. I'll offer a very generous salary. It will only be for three weeks. To help Nina get used to me. And vice versa. You could perhaps do weekends during term time if you wanted to if it worked out. I haven't really thought that far ahead. Right now, Nina needs you. I need you.'

She slowly shook her head as if in stunned bewilderment at his words. 'Wil, have you got more money than sense? We've only just reconnected as friends. I've spent two days helping you with Nina purely out of friendship. And you want to turn all that on its head by making my help into a financial transaction. Where I would have to answer to you, defer to you, hold back on speaking my mind. Working for friends is a terrible idea. I actually consider your offer of employment to be an insult.'

'It certainly wasn't meant that way,' he said slowly.

Georgia pushed her plate away from her and got up from the table. 'I think it's time I left you to it.' She glared at him. 'Look up nanny agencies and find your nanny that way.'

She was seething. He knew her well enough to know that. Unwittingly, he had hurt her feelings. If she walked out now he would never see her again. And he couldn't bear that. How had things gone so wrong, so quickly?

He pushed away from the table so quickly his chair fell backwards with a clatter onto the marble-tiled floor. He made no effort to retrieve it. 'No. Don't go.' He closed the distance between them with a few brisk strides, reached out and took her arm. His action brought her close, closer than he had been to her for a long, long time. So close he was aware of her scent, familiar and heady; the warmth of her skin.

She stilled under his touch. Shocked, he thought, at the fact he had actually touched her. Surprised, perhaps, at the strength of his grip on her arm. Immediately, he let her go. His grip left the impression of his fingers on her arm, pale on her lightly tanned skin. He took a step back from her so the distance between them was not as intimate or confronting. She glared back up at him but behind her combative stance, the icy accusation in her eyes, he could see her hurt.

'I didn't mean to insult you, Georgie. My offer was meant more as a compliment. Ever since you got here I've been trying to figure out how to get you to spend more time with me. I mean Nina. I mean me and Nina. Without taking advantage of your kindness and generous spirit, I mean.'

Dammit. Why didn't the words come out the way he wanted them to? He was usually so sure of himself when it came to negotiating a business deal. His shoulders sagged. That was the trouble. This wasn't about business. It was personal. And he'd gone about it in quite the wrong way.

'I don't work for friends, Wil. Golden rule. Of course, I'm dealing under the assumption that we are friends again. For the time being, anyway.'

'Of course we are,' he said. *More than friends.* There had always been a deeper bond than ordinary, everyday friendship with Georgia. For him, anyway. Perhaps because of the way it had started. Perhaps because it had never been entirely platonic with him. Perhaps there had always been an echo of *one day* about it for him.

That one day could very well be now. They were both single and unattached. Each facing a crossroads in their life. Now it looked as if he had messed it up—again. He had to make good on his mistake and keep her on his side.

Georgia fumed. She could scarcely look at Wil, she was so cranky. How could she ever have thought there was any chance of re-establishing friendship—or anything deeper—with New Wil when he had obviously moved so far away from Old Wil?

She and Wil had started as equals, both students. The scales could have tipped another way when he'd gone on that television show and become a celebrity because of his cleverness and extraordinary good looks. He'd got very wealthy, very quickly. His inventions had kicked it off, then he'd made a killing in crypto currencies. He'd upscaled his car and bought the luxury apartment in Pyrmont. Started to move in different circles. But still they'd stayed pals. He'd never made her think she was lesser because she was a schoolteacher on a salary that would never make her rich.

Then Angie had come along and everything had disintegrated. Actually, Toby had come before Angie and for a while there it had looked as if she would marry before Wil. Two years apart while Wil, it seemed, got even richer. And acquired some more arrogance along the way. *While she'd missed him every day.* She'd thought that for all his wealth he was still the same person who had been her best friend. But now he obviously saw her in a different, lesser light. As his inferior.

He looked bemused, his dark brows drawn together. Did he not realise what was so wrong with his offer? She'd sometimes wondered about his emotional intelligence. Now she was convinced he didn't read cues the same as other people. What made him a brilliant engi-

neer might not make him great in everyday people trans-
actions. Or so his ex-girlfriends had told her as they had
bewailed the way it had ended with him.

'I'm not for sale, Wil. What made you think I was?'

'I didn't think that for one moment,' he said. 'I saw it
as a clever solution to a problem. A win-win situation. I
couldn't entrust Nina to a stranger.'

Georgia felt slightly mollified by the sincerity of his
expression. 'You know I can be trusted with Nina.' When
his baby looked so like Wil, she was predisposed to be
fond of her. Already she had fallen under Nina's spell.

Wil sighed. 'I hate to admit failure of any kind. But
you can see that I'm barely treading water with her. I
need help. You really are the only one I could trust with
this little person who has become so important to me,
so quickly.'

No way in the world would Georgia agree to be Nina's
nanny. Yet she felt torn when she thought about the story
of his birth parents Wil had finally shared with her. She
shuddered at the thought of the accident that had deprived
him of his family, sent a lost and lonely little guy into the
harsh embrace of state care.

Yet he seemed to have grown up undamaged. She was
touched by the way he had so immediately recognised
that family in his little girl. How he had stood up to his
responsibility, not grudgingly but with love. A lesser
man might have walked away from a child bequeathed
to him under such circumstances. There was much to
admire in New Wil.

But that still didn't make her want to work for him.
Under any circumstances.

'Surely there must be someone else you could trust
with Nina?' she said. 'What about your parents?'

'Mum is thrilled at the news she's a grandparent. Dad too. But they're not here. They're at a wellness spa in Phuket.'

'Thailand. Nice.'

Wil's parents were wealthy farmers who ran the large, historic farm holding Five and a Half Mile Creek, near the border of New South Wales and Victoria. Over the years, Wil had said he would like to take her there but it had never happened.

'Yes and no. Mum hasn't been well.'

'Oh. I'm sorry to hear that.' Georgia had met his parents a few times over the years when they had visited their son in Sydney. She could see the struggle on Wil's face whether or not he should share the details with her. 'Is she okay now?'

'She's getting over chemotherapy. Breast cancer. She had a mastectomy last year.'

'I'm so sorry, Wil. Your mum is lovely. I liked her a lot when I met her.'

'The prognosis is good, thank heaven. She's in remission. But she needed a complete break. Relaxing. Eating well. Meditation. Mum being Mum, as soon as she started to feel better, she wanted to throw himself back into work. Dad had to take her away.'

'What about the farm?'

'My brother, Ned, is looking after things. He's in partnership with Dad now. He'll be taking over when Dad decides to hang up his boots and retire.'

'Okay, so obviously your mum can't help you with Nina. I'm glad to hear she's getting the rest she needs.'

'Which brings us back to you.'

She put up her hand to stop him. 'No, Wil. That doesn't bring us back to me.'

'Hear me out. Please.'

She glanced at her watch. Didn't really register what it said. 'I should be going.'

'Just five more minutes,' he said.

'Okay,' she said. 'And not a minute more.' She walked over to the family-room sofa where she had left her handbag. Sat down. Wil followed her to sit on the other sofa, placed opposite hers, a coffee table between them.

He leaned forward, elbows resting on his knees, gaze not leaving her face. 'You're living at your parents' home, right? How long do you think it will last before you get in an argument with your dad?'

He knew her so well. Still. 'Maybe I've already had a difference of opinion,' she grudgingly acknowledged. 'I love Dad dearly but the second I'm back under the same roof we clash.'

'There must have been a reason you didn't move on to another shared household with your flatmates?'

'You mean apart from flatmate number one's ghastly boyfriends and flatmate number two's apparent allergy to housework?'

Wil indicated their luxurious surroundings with a sweep of his hand. 'So living here could possibly have some appeal. Your own bedroom and private bathroom, use of a swimming pool and tennis court. With the added attraction of horses and somewhere to ride them. Oh, and proximity to the beach as an added bonus. Plus a housekeeper, and commercial cleaners to do the heavy stuff. Isn't that an attractive proposition?'

'Very attractive.' This was, in every way, her dream house. Though he hadn't added, as an enticement, attractive man for company. 'That is, if I was in any way interested in working through the vacation. I mean, working on anything apart from the illustrations I have to have finished by the end of the month. My parents think of it as my "little hobby". But it's not a hobby. I'm being paid. I have a deadline to meet. It's a job.' She knew she was doing a rotten job of keeping the rising frustration out of her voice.

'You're fighting to be taken seriously. I get it.'

Of course he did. He always had got her frustration at being a creative person in a family of business-minded achievers. They'd talked her out of art school. She'd seen the common sense in getting her teaching degree and the subsequent steady income. But she'd never stopped sketching, painting and dreaming of making her art her life.

'I know you do,' she said. 'Now is my chance to do what I've always wanted to do. Maybe make it a full-time career.'

'I've still got every card you ever made for me,' he said. 'The birthday cards. The good luck cards. The congratulations cards. All Georgia Lang originals. All brilliant.'

'Really? You saved them?'

'They'll be worth something one day, I'm sure.'

If there ever was a moment she wanted to kiss Wil, this was it. And not a friendly peck on the cheek, either. Memories of all the good times they'd shared together came flooding back. Of how miserable she'd been without his presence in her life.

Wil leaned back into his sofa. She was struck again at how tired he looked. Although the dark shadows under his eyes, the shadow on his chin and the tousled hair only added to his appeal. He was hot. The hottest of the hot.

'I understand how important your art is to you,' he

said, the tiredness apparent even in his voice. 'Of course you wouldn't want to be distracted by Nina. It was a mistake to ask you. I can muddle along on my own. Maybe Mum can stay with me when she gets back from her trip. And I hope you'll still visit me and Nina here when you can lift your head from your sketchbook.' He got up. 'I should let you go.'

She got up too, so hastily she nearly tripped over the coffee table. 'Wil. Wait.'

The bleak expression in his eyes made her heart contract. He thought he'd lost her. That she'd walk out of here and that would be it.

'I have an idea. Why don't you rewind to when we were eating our lunch and talking about what fun we'd had showing Nina the horses,' she said.

He narrowed his eyes. 'Rewind?'

'Start all over again. You don't ask me to work for you as your nanny. You take a different tack.'

He frowned. 'I'm not sure what you're getting at.'

'Listen and learn.' She started to pace up and down the room as she warmed to her subject, much as she sometimes did in her classroom. 'You say to me that, while Nina is adjusting to you as her primary carer, it might be nice to have some female help with her. Not a nanny, because you wouldn't trust a stranger with your precious daughter. You mention how Nina seems to like me. I say I like her.'

He nodded thoughtfully. 'Subtly different to what I actually did say.'

'Correct. This is a rewind, remember. You certainly don't insult me by making me an offer of employment.' Wil went to protest but she put her hand up to stop him. 'Instead you point out that I, Georgia, am on school vacation, have illustrations to finish, and am sure to go stir crazy living with my parents. You suggest that I move into this enormous house for the rest of the holidays as a housemate, on the understanding that I spend time with Nina. Out of friendship, it's understood, not for money. For the duration, I pay rent and—'

It was Wil's turn to put up his hand to stop her. 'No rent. Now you insult me by suggesting such a commercial transaction. You're quite right, no money should exchange hands and sully the purity of our friendship.'

Taken aback, she stopped her pacing and looked at him. 'I couldn't have said it better. You've caught on completely.'

'I'm a fast learner.' He smiled a little smugly, which made her smile too. 'So then I say, you help me care for Nina in lieu of rent.'

'Quite right, too,' she said. 'I've never been a freeloader.'

'You've spelled out what I should say, Georgie. So what do you say in response?'

She looked up at him, at his handsome face, his dark eyes searching her face. This was Wil, her friend. Asking for her help in such a way she couldn't say no. She smiled but it was a bit wobbly at the edges. 'I say, "Why, Wil, what a fabulous idea. I would love to be your housemate and share this amazing house with you and Nina. Thank you for your kind offer."'

He drew those dark brows together; the dimple revealed itself in his left cheek. 'So that's a "yes"?'

'It most certainly is. When can I move in?'

A huge grin of relief spread across his face. 'Tomorrow.'

'It's a deal,' she said, her own grin less exuberant but as heartfelt. 'Shall we shake on it?'

She put out her hand in a businesslike manner for him to take. Then thought better of it. 'Heck, Wil. I don't want to shake hands. I want to hug you. But we never hug, do we?'

'No, we don't,' he said slowly.

'Why is that? When did we decide not to hug or even kiss each other on the cheek in greeting? Was it you? Was it me?'

'I suspect it was me, Georgie.' He looked down at her, his eyes half-lidded and sensual. The look she'd seen him give other women, but never her. He was looking at her not as his horse-riding buddy but as a woman. And letting her know he liked what he saw. Perhaps had always liked what he saw.

She felt breathless at the look in his eyes, had trouble choking out the words. 'Why was that, Wil?'

His voice was low and husky, intensely masculine. 'Because I couldn't trust myself not to want to kiss you for real. To kiss you and want so much more than kisses. I didn't trust myself to be able to hold back from something that might put off course the friendship I valued so much. I wasn't ready back then for where that might take us. Not with you, you were a keeper. And I wasn't ready for you. Not then.'

Her heart started to hammer so hard, she swore he must hear it. 'And I complied for the same reason,' she choked out. 'It was safer than starting something at the wrong time that might ignite, then burn out of control to leave us with nothing but the ashes of what we'd had. You always brutally dumped your girlfriends as soon as it got serious. Then I had them sobbing all over me. They thought I, as your friend, would know the secret

of hanging on to you. But I didn't. By sticking to friendship, I got to keep you in my life.'

'You did the same to your boyfriends. As soon as the
poor infatuated guy started to talk about happy-ever-
afters, you ran. And you never stayed friends with them
afterwards. They were consigned to oblivion. I didn't
want to be tossed into oblivion if I kissed you and you
liked it but then decided you didn't like it—or me—any
more.'

'I didn't want to be dumped and have to say goodbye
to our horse riding and the other things we shared that
were so important to me.' Her voice threatened to seize
up. 'I…I couldn't have borne to have lost you. We were
better as friends than as…as lovers.'

'And now?' he said. His head lowered to hers as he
took a step closer. So close she could feel the heat of
his body, feel intoxicated by his scent both familiar and
unfamiliar at the same time. Quite unconsciously, she
swayed towards him, aching for his touch, frightened of
it at the same time.

Panic grabbed her and she stepped back. 'Then you
dumped me anyway. Even our friendship didn't protect
me from that. And it hurt, Wil. It really, really hurt.'

'I'm sorry,' he said hoarsely. 'If I could make it up to
you, I would.'

'I'm not sure we can go back to what we had. Or even
if I want to. Or to risk moving on to something else. It's
different now. We're different people. And there's Nina to
complicate things. We're going to be sharing a house. And
I'm still not sure I—'

Wil laughed. A low, husky laugh that ran shivers of
awareness through her. *Wil as a lover.* She had never al-

lowed herself to think about him in that way. *Now it was all she could think about.*

'So we keep the status quo?' he said. 'No touching, no kissing, no acknowledging at last that we both want more?'

'Um, yes.' She didn't want to think of him like that. It was too risky. He could hurt her too much.

'You're sure about that?' He picked up her hand as if to shake it. But his touch was not businesslike at all. He lazily circled the sensitive palm of her hand with long, strong fingers, unimaginably pleasurable. She shuddered. If holding her hand could make her feel like that, what would it be like to make love with him? *And then to lose him if it didn't work out.*

Her voice came out in a choked half-sob. 'I'm not sure about that at all,' she said. 'I... I'm scared, Wil.' Give in to impulse and she could end up with the horror of all heartbreaks.

'We could start with a hug,' he said. 'A friendly hug.'

She thought of all the hugs she'd avoided with him over the years. Things were different now. How could a hug do any harm?

He drew her close, wrapping his arms around her tenderly as if she were something precious and valuable. She hugged him back and, for a brief moment, laid her head against his shoulder. His breath was warm and ragged against her cheek. Pressed against the hard wall of his chest, she was aware of the rapid beating of his heart.

'Just a friendly hug,' she echoed. 'Why didn't we do that years ago instead of making such a big deal of it?'

He cleared his throat. 'A harmless hug,' he said as he dropped his arms and she stepped back from him.

'Didn't feel a thing,' she lied, hoping the overbright

tone of her voice didn't give her away, knowing that Wil could still read her as well as he ever had, and hoping he wouldn't use that knowledge to hurt her.

But as she drew away from the hug, the vulnerability in his eyes was visible for a fraction of a second before he masked it with a smile and that disarming dimple. She became aware she also had the power to hurt him. And that was equally terrifying.

CHAPTER SEVEN

THE NEXT DAY Georgia was running late on her way to Wil's house, her first day as his housemate. It was already mid-morning, later than she'd intended to move in and get unpacked. As it was Saturday, her parents were at home and had demanded to know why she was moving out of the family home when she'd only just moved back in.

When she'd told her mother about Wil and Nina, the attitude had changed. Dear Wil was a widower now? Technically he was a divorcee but they obviously thought widower sounded more romantic. Of course Georgia must move down to Ingleside and help him and his little girl. They'd always liked him so much. Thought it such a shame she and Wil had never dated. Wil had always been a 'catch'. Now that he was so wealthy in his own right, even more so. It was no use protesting that she and Wil were just friends and had never been anything more. Her mother had laughed, as if that were the most amusing thing Georgia had ever said. 'You two were perfect for each other—only neither of you could ever see it,' she'd said.

Maybe we did see it, Georgia thought afterwards as she drove down to the northern beaches. *Saw it and ran from it, too scared of changing the status quo. We missed our chance.*

Could there be a second chance for them?

She hadn't been able to stop thinking about how she'd felt in Wil's arms the day before. *'A harmless hug.'* It could never be 'just a hug' with Wil. Not now that the awareness that had simmered underneath their platonic friendship had been acknowledged. Nothing and everything had changed since they'd made the unspoken 'no touching' pact. Fact was, she was no more ready for a relationship with Wil now than she had been when she was nineteen. And he certainly wouldn't be promising commitment any more than he had then.

Maybe there'd been a chance with Old Wil if they'd got their timings right. However New Wil came as a package deal. No longer was it just about him. Now every decision Wil made would have to be made with Nina in mind. Particularly when it came to women. As it should be. He would have to be extremely careful who he let into his life. Nina's safety, Nina's welfare had to be paramount. Already, she herself felt that about his enchanting little daughter.

Then there were her secret deep-down fears when it came to her and Wil. *If* anything were likely to happen between them. Nina was an eminently lovable little person. But to be thrown into motherhood headfirst would be a scary thought. Georgia had never dated a man with a child. She wasn't sure how she felt about being a stepmother. Would she be able to love Nina as deeply as she would love a child she bore herself? What if other children came along?

Even in just a few days she was starting to care for Nina. To step further than friendship with Wil would now be doubly dangerous. Double the risk to her heart. If she'd been too wary to risk a relationship before for fear of losing him altogether, how much riskier would it be now? If things went wrong, she'd lose not just Wil but Nina too. And Nina would suffer from the loss of another mother figure from her life.

For her and Wil, there could only be a friends-with-benefits arrangement. And she certainly didn't want that—certain heartbreak lay at the end of that path. Double heartbreak where Nina was concerned.

Far better to have Wil and Nina as part of her life, but not the focus of her life.

Friends. That was what they did well. That was the way it should stay. *Without benefits.*

Driving in Sydney on Saturday meant negotiating streets blocked with the vehicles of hordes of parents transporting kids to school sport venues all across the city and suburbs. By the time Georgia drove through the gates to Wil's house—home for the next three weeks—she was feeling decidedly frazzled. A dip in that glorious pool as soon as she got there might be just what she needed.

Wil had given her the passcode for the gates and the security keys for the door. As she pushed open the front door her phone buzzed. She paused to check it. A few missed calls. All from Wil. No point in picking up now. She'd be seeing him in just a minute.

As Georgia headed into the hallway she prepared an explanation for why she was later than expected. An explanation that did not include outrageous levels of matchmaking from her mother. Then she paused when she heard voices. Wil hadn't said he was expecting visitors.

To have other people there wasn't a bad thing. In fact

she was relieved. Conversation might cover any awkward moments between her and Wil on the occasion of her actually moving into his house. Especially after that hug the day before. And her sleepless night pondering and discarding possible scenarios that involved her and Wil in something rather more intimate than a hug.

But the last people she expected to see when she walked into the family room were Wil's parents, sitting around the table where she and Wil had had lunch the day before. A teapot and cups were set there and plates of cake and cookies. Nina was in her high chair, gnawing on a baby rusk.

'Georgie.' Immediately he noticed her, and Wil got up from his chair. Her heart did the familiar flip. In long shorts and a dark T-shirt, he was heart-stoppingly handsome. She remembered how good it had felt to be held close to his chest in that fleeting 'just a hug'. How would she be able to keep her hands off him? 'We've been waiting for you,' he said. 'Did you get my calls?' His expression told her she should have listened to his messages.

'Sorry, no,' she said, puzzled and unable to read the silent message he was trying to send her via the raising of his eyebrows and the nod in the direction of his mother. 'I had my phone muted to placate my father, who has a thing about mobile phone addiction, and forgot to unmute it.'

Wil's mum and dad sat on either side of the high chair, smiling adoringly at Nina, who was waving the half-chewed rusk around like a conductor. They looked up at Georgia, their smiles embracing her too. Georgia smiled back with genuine pleasure. She'd last seen them three years back when they'd treated Wil and a group of his friends to dinner at an exclusive harbour-side restaurant.

Now she had to hide her shock at the change in Wil's mother. She'd been slim before but now she was bone-thin. Her hair that had once been tinted blond was now a dull grey. Even her hazel eyes seemed faded. Where once she had been vibrant, now she seemed fragile. No wonder her family had wanted her to recuperate and be looked after at a luxury resort after the ordeals of chemotherapy and surgery. Wil's dad was tall and stocky with thinning ginger hair and the sun-reddened skin and faded blue eyes of a man with Scottish ancestry who'd spent his life farming outdoors in the harsh Australian climate. He'd aged too, more than the years warranted.

'Mrs Hudson, Mr Hudson,' Georgia said. 'So nice to see you.'

'Please. It's Jackie and Dave,' said Wil's mum as his parents got up from the table. 'Now that we're family.'

Family? How did becoming Wil's new housemate translate to *family*? A loose interpretation, Georgia supposed. Someone to care for Nina, help Wil adjust to fatherhood? But it was a big jump from friendship to family. 'Jackie and Dave,' she murmured obediently.

Jackie gave her a hug, warm and genuine. 'I was so thrilled at your news. To hear I have a granddaughter one day and then just days later to discover you and Wil are engaged to be married. I couldn't be happier. It's almost too much excitement to deal with.'

Engaged?

'Er,' Georgia choked out, frantically looking to Wil for an explanation.

She stepped politely back from Jackie's embrace, fisted her hands by her sides, forced a smile. Could Wil see the steam coming from her ears? Surely he hadn't pulled that stunt on her again? If so, she was going to turn around and drive straight back to Lindfield.

Wil came to stand beside her, brushed his hand against hers, caught her eye. He read her annoyance. She read the response in his eyes and the slight shrug of his shoulders: *not my fault.* 'Mum and Dad were in Phuket when I called to tell them about Nina. I thought they were still there.'

'There's only so much lying about the pool, drinking vegetable juices and nibbling on exotic fruits a person can take,' said Jackie. 'We certainly weren't hanging around once we discovered we had a grandbaby to meet. We got the first flight out we could so we could meet Nina, a.s.a.p. What a little treasure she is.'

'Jackie thought it would be nice to surprise Wil,' said Dave.

'You certainly did that, Dad,' Wil said, his eyes still connected to Georgia in silent conversation. 'I had no idea until you and Mum turned up on the doorstep.'

Jackie continued, 'Of course, once we got to Sydney, we had to call Angie's sister to offer our condolences. Such tragedy amidst our joy.'

'Of course,' Georgia murmured through gritted teeth, still looking to Wil with a silent plea. *Get me out of this.*

'Sharyn told us the good news about you two being engaged,' Jackie said. 'Why we had to hear it from her and not Wil, I don't know.' She looked pointedly at her son in reprimand.

'We, uh, wanted to tell you face to face,' said Wil.

'I suppose so,' Jackie said, not sounding in the slightest bit mollified. 'But with important news like that we would have liked to hear it straight from you and Georgia.'

'It's only been a recent development,' Wil said. 'Just days, in fact.'

Georgia refused to jump in and help him out.

'No matter, we're absolutely delighted,' said Jackie. 'We always liked you, Georgia. Had hopes… Well, had hopes this might have happened years ago. Instead—I don't wish to speak ill of the dead—there was Angie, who wasn't right for our Wil at all. I'm glad you two finally saw sense.'

'Uh, thank you,' said Georgia. The effort of pasting on a fake smile actually hurt.

'We're over the moon, actually. You deserve happiness, son. We think you're perfect for him, Georgia, and you'll be getting a marvellous husband in Wil.'

Husband! Georgia gritted her teeth. This was getting completely out of hand.

'Thank you, Jackie. That's very kind of you. But could you excuse me for a moment? I need Wil's help to bring my bags in from the car.' She'd left her stuff—just the three drawers' worth—in the car, until Wil showed her which room would be hers for the duration of her stay.

'Let me help, too, son,' said Dave taking a step towards Wil.

'No need, Dad,' said Wil. 'You keep Nina entertained. She's very taken with her grandma and granddad.'

Georgia didn't say a word to Wil until they were outside in the driveway, beside where her car was parked, the solid double doors closed behind them. Then she whipped around to glare at him.

'What the heck, Wil? Why didn't you tell them we're not really engaged? Why am I caught up in this fake-fiancée farce again?'

'I was as shocked as you were. Who knew they would ever contact Sharyn? I started to explain but Mum was bubbling along about how happy she was, and I couldn't get a word in edgeways. Then she said that the news about our engagement, on top of the joy about Nina, gave her something to live for. I just didn't have the heart to disillusion her. Mum has been so unwell, Georgie. We thought we might lose her last year.'

'That's really sad, and I can see how worried you must have been, but *this*. No good can come of deception on this scale. I say we march right back in there and tell them it's a complete misunderstanding before it goes any further.'

He groaned. 'Can you play along just for a few days? Phuket was a stop for them, on the way to Italy, where they're booked into a villa in Tuscany with her sister. They're only here until Wednesday. She's so happy at the thought of us together.'

Georgia closed her eyes in exasperation. When she opened them it was to see Wil with hands gripped together as if in prayer and one knee bent in mock supplication. She couldn't help but laugh. 'No, Wil. Beg all you like. I won't be a part of this. It's madness. Blame it on Sharyn if you want. Say she got it wrong.'

He didn't laugh. Rather, he straightened up with a sigh. 'I'll tell them the truth when we go back inside.'

'Good,' she said. 'I'll get my bags from the car.'

'Wait.' Wil put his hand on her arm to stop her. The third time he'd touched her. The third time she'd realised how much she liked his touch. How she had to block her desire for more of his touch.

He cleared his throat. 'Before we go back in, there's something I need to fill you in on. It's actually another reason my parents are so delighted about our "engagement". Apart from the fact they've always liked you, that is.'

Georgia frowned at the seriousness of his tone. 'Fire away,' she said with a sense of foreboding, that something was about to change. As she waited she was aware of the splash of the fountain, the raucous squawk of rainbow lorikeets feasting on the orange flowers of a grevillea bush, the incessant background thrum of cicadas. The sun was warm on her shoulders in her sleeveless sundress and she pushed her hair, damp with humidity, away from her neck.

Finally, Wil spoke. 'It's something I've never told you before but they will expect you would know. The reason Mum is so over the top about all this.' He looked down at the ground, where he kicked the gravel with the toe of his canvas shoe. 'She so wants me to have a normal life and…and to be loved.'

'What do you mean? You have a great life. A millionaire's privileged life. One that many would envy.' She couldn't speak with any authority about how well he'd been loved.

'It wasn't always that way.' He looked back to face her. 'I've let you think I was adopted when I was five years old after my birth parents died, after I ran away from my aunt so many times she relinquished custody of me. I've let all the friends I made after I moved to Sydney believe that.'

She frowned. 'But it wasn't true?'

'An angry five-year-old runaway boy isn't high on an adoptive parent's wish list. I was in and out of foster homes and children's homes for years. Some okay. Some very much not okay.'

She couldn't help her shocked gasp. 'Wil. How awful. Why didn't you ever tell me?'

'I wanted to put it behind me,' he said tersely.

'So when did Jackie and David adopt you?'

'The year I turned fourteen. When I was thirteen, I was incarcerated in a children's home in Melbourne. I say incarcerated because it was like a prison to me. That year, Jackie and Dave decided to take a child from the institution for Christmas to give a deprived city kid like me a holiday in the country.'

'Do people do that?'

'Kind people like them do. They were taking a risk with me. I had a reputation for being a troublemaker. The manager tried to talk them out of choosing me. But they told me later they saw something in me that no one else seemed to see and they insisted. Me or no one.' He looked hot and uncomfortable, and she realised how difficult this was for him.

'How wonderful,' she said slowly. Why had Wil never shared this?

'I thought it was wonderful, all right. I had every intention of running away as soon as I could, hitching a ride on a truck and never going back to that place I hated.'

'But you didn't.'

'I loved it there. Five and a Half Mile Creek was like heaven. Jackie and Dave knew just how to handle me. Dave told me later it wasn't much different from taming an unbroken horse using the kind, natural horsemanship methods he preferred. And I got on really well with Ned, their only child, who is six months older than me.'

Georgia had never met Ned, but Wil had always spoken of him with affection and regard. 'That was fortunate,' she said. 'It could easily have gone the other way.'

'He didn't resent me, the intruder with an attitude. Ned has the same quiet strength and confidence as his father. He told me he got lonely over the long summer vacation and welcomed the company of another teenager. At the end of the holidays, he begged them not to send me back. My parents are the type of people who should have had a brood of kids but they couldn't. Cut a long story short, by the time I turned fourteen they'd adopted me and I became part of their family. During term time, I was sent to boarding school in Melbourne with Ned. That was a challenge. But Ned looked out for me. I was a year behind him as I needed to catch up on my broken schooling.' He paused. 'I really hit the jackpot when they took me home with them.'

Georgia was so taken aback by Wil's story she was finding it hard to keep steady. It explained so many things. The feeling she'd always had that he was holding back. His difficulty in sustaining relationships. That emotional distance. Her heart ached for the troubled boy he must have been. 'Why tell me this now?'

'My parents will assume you know. I didn't want any awkwardness.'

'You mean apart from any awkwardness around pretending to be engaged?'

'Yeah. That. Mum will be disappointed but she'll get over it. She thought my past had made it difficult for me to…to, well, love. When she thought she might die, she feared leaving me behind to make another bad choice like Angie. Or be on my own. That's why she was so overjoyed about us. But you're quite right, it's best she finds out now it was a misunderstanding. She might be more disappointed if we leave it until further down the track.' He took a step towards the car. 'Come on. Let's get your bags. They'll be wondering where we are.'

Georgia stayed where she was. 'You sure know how to tug on the emotional heartstrings. After hearing that, how on earth can I possibly disillusion your lovely mum if the thought of you being happily engaged is sustaining her in a struggle with cancer?'

He shrugged. 'I don't mean to do that, Georgie. Just stating facts. I don't regret using the engagement tactic with Sharyn.' She'd puzzled over that at the time; now she knew where he got his fear of the welfare system. 'However, I do regret my parents finding out the way they did. I never dreamed they'd contact her.'

'Guess that's the type of kind, well-mannered people they are.'

'You're right about that,' he said.

'How long did you say they're staying?'

'Just until Wednesday. Then they take off for Italy to resume their holiday.'

She sighed. 'I suppose we could fake it until then. While they're in Italy, you can tell them it didn't work out.'

'Which wouldn't surprise them at all, with my history,' he said with a downward twist to his mouth.

Georgia ached to find out just what had gone wrong with Angie, but now wasn't the time to ask. 'They'll still have Nina, remember.'

'Yeah. And maybe we should leave it at that. You're right about the deception. I don't like lying.'

'I'll lie too if you think it's that important to your mum.'

'Really?' He looked down into her face and she could see more than weariness in his eyes. He had had it so much tougher than she had ever imagined. He'd masked it so well during the years they had been friends. And she had the feeling that she still didn't know the whole story. 'You'd do that for me?' he said.

She nodded, finding it difficult to keep up a cool façade when inside she was crying at what Wil had gone through, at what he hadn't said about his time in the welfare system. During her training she'd taught in some disadvantaged areas around the state. She'd heard the horror stories. She'd seen some of the sad outcomes in her classrooms. Heaven knew what fate Jackie and Dave had saved Wil from. 'I couldn't bear it if some action of mine compromised your mother's recovery.'

'I'll really owe you after this, Georgie.'

'Yeah. You will. I'll need time to think about how you can repay me.' Her attempt at light-hearted humour fell flat.

'Thank you,' he said simply. He briefly put his hand on her shoulder. *Touch number four.* Then took a step towards the car. 'Okay. So let me get your things from the car so I can take them to our room.'

Georgia stared at him. 'Stop right there. What do you mean *our* room?'

CHAPTER EIGHT

WIL THOUGHT HE had stunned Georgia into a total state of shock she stared at him for so long, her blue eyes wide with disbelief. He wished he'd had time to talk this through properly with her.

She put up her hand. He noticed it was trembling. From anger? Fear? He doubted it was from excitement at the prospect of sharing a bedroom with him. Not now.

'Correct me if I'm wrong,' she said, 'but wasn't it our agreement that I have my own bedroom and bathroom? With just me sleeping in it?'

'That was our agreement,' he said. 'Our housemate agreement. Of course, things would be different for an engaged couple agreement. My parents would think it odd if my fiancée didn't sleep in my room with me.'

'Your fake fiancée, you mean,' she hissed. 'Whom you have never even kissed, let alone…let alone done things engaged people might do in…in bed.' She cursed under her breath, which shocked him more than anything else she might have done. Georgia rarely swore.

'You wouldn't have to share my bed.' The sudden vision of a naked Georgia in his bed smiling, teasing, inviting him to join her on his cool sheets, made him catch his breath. And force his body not to react. 'If you don't want to, that is.'

Her eyes flared. He wondered if she might have had the same thought of how it might be in his bed with him. There was a sensual heat flaming within her righteous anger. He couldn't help but observe that the cotton sundress she wore, all splashes of orange and yellow, wrapped around her waist. It would be easy to untie it and have it slide down her body. What underwear did Georgia wear? Plain and practical, he surmised. Not that it would stay on for long if— *Stop!*

'Of course I don't want to,' she said. 'You can sleep on the floor.'

'That won't be necessary,' he said. 'There's a sofa I can bunk down on. Alternatively, once the lights were out, I could head on down to the stables and take your place with the cat.'

'What?' Her reaction was half stifled laugh, half disbelief.

'I know. The cat will be disappointed I'm not you. It hates me. He'll stalk off and I'll have the straw to myself. Bit scratchy, probably.'

'This is serious, Wil.' She reprimanded him with her best schoolteacher manner. He wondered if any of the lads in her class had crushes on her. He certainly would have.

'Sorry,' he said, not in the slightest bit sorry at raising a laugh from her.

'You're assuming I will agree to this revised arrangement. I'd rather have a room on my own. After all, we're only meant to be engaged. Not married. Your parents might actually approve that we're in separate rooms.'

'Unlikely,' he said. 'They're very broad-minded. But

the room-of-your-own thing isn't going to happen anyway. Not while my parents are here. There are six bedrooms but they're not all set up as actual bedrooms with beds in them. There's mine, of course; the room that's now Nina's nursery; and the one I'd earmarked for you. Mum and Dad have taken that one as they always use it. In fact, Mum decorated it for her taste.'

'What do you mean by that?'

'She's an interior designer. Mum is responsible for all the interiors in this house. Many years ago she was employed to go up from Melbourne to redecorate at Five and a Half Mile Creek after Dad inherited. She fell in love with the client and never left.'

'Jackie is very talented. I love everything she's done. And that's a very romantic story. But I still don't want to share a room with you. No matter how beautifully decorated. Why don't we get some bedroom furniture delivered from a furniture store in time for tonight? Problem solved.'

'Do you seriously think that's going to happen between now and bedtime?'

'Throw money at the shop and it might.'

Did she hate the idea of sharing a room with him so much? 'We've shared a room before, Georgie.'

She scuffed the gravel with the toe of her espadrille. The shoe laced around her ankles with wide, white ribbons. She was all wrapped up like a beautiful gift. 'It was different then…' She cleared her throat and looked up at him. Her cheeks were flushed. Just as they'd flushed in his fantasy of her naked in his bed.

'I know,' was all the response he could come up with. Sharing a room with Georgia without wanting her in his bed for real would be a challenge. The stable was looking more and more like a viable option.

'The last room I remember sharing with you was the back of a horse trailer parked at a rural showground,' she said. 'We were both wearing riding breeches and boots and had our sleeping bags laid out on the top of the horses' straw.'

'I still remember. We had leased those good horses we competed on. How could I ever forget the aroma of our sleeping quarters?'

She wrinkled up her nose. 'The smell of horse lingered. No matter how carefully we'd swept the floor.'

'But we wanted our horses nearby and we figured the trailer would be more comfortable than a tent.'

He'd never forgotten waking before Georgia had. She'd been lying on her back with her arms flung behind her head, the sleeping bag tucked right up to her chin. It had been so cold in the trailer she'd been wearing her riding gloves and he'd been able to see her breath in tiny puffs of white vapour. During the night, her wavy hair had come loose and a shaft of early morning sun had illuminated her face and picked up auburn glints that had shone in the gloom of the trailer. Her expression had been peaceful, her lips slightly parted. She had trusted him and felt totally safe. *That was how she had to feel with him now.*

Back then, he'd had to fight the urge to trace her features with his fingers, learning the shape of her pretty ears, her nose she despaired of because it wasn't quite straight, her mouth with the slightly irregular cupid's bow. Then to kiss her, the way he'd fantasised about so many times. There'd been a long piece of straw caught up in the wisps of hair around her temple. Gently, being careful not to wake her, he'd reached over to lift it out.

But he hadn't been careful enough. Her eyes had opened and slowly focused on him. For a long moment her gaze had connected with his. Then she'd smiled, a slow, lazy, sweet smile. 'Thank you,' she'd murmured. Then she'd closed her eyes again and within seconds had resumed her rhythmic breathing. Whether or not she actually went back to sleep, Wil had never known. Or that she'd even remembered waking to see him so close. Nor did he ever know whether the 'thank you' had been for him taking the straw from her hair, or for not kissing her and complicating their easy friendship.

He'd kept that piece of straw in the pocket of his riding jacket for a long time afterwards, only losing it because he'd once forgotten to remove it before he'd sent the jacket to the dry cleaner.

There'd been a few of those type of 'maybe' moments throughout the years of their friendship. The mutual, unspoken acknowledgment that there could be something more between them. The 'one day' promise he had perhaps been guilty of hanging on to. Until the day, with eyes sparkling, she'd told him she thought she'd met 'The One' she might marry. Friendly, fun Toby, who had doted on her and let it be known in a not unsubtle male way that any other guy had better back right off. Even a so-called platonic 'friend'. Not long after that, Wil had met Angie.

'You'd better hope your sofa is more comfortable than the floor of that horse trailer,' Georgia said now.

She turned and started to stomp back towards the house. Wil caught her arm and pulled her back to face him. He grinned. 'I suggest you ditch that scowl if you're going to make our engagement seem believable.'

'Hmmph,' she muttered.

'In fact you might want to look friendly, affectionate and even, dare I say it, loving.'

'*Loving*, Wil? That particular emotion might be rather difficult to conjure up, considering the situation you've shoved me into.'

'Maybe a touch of passion might be in order.'

'Passion?' That would not be difficult for him to feign. The sudden flare in her eyes told him it might not be impossible for her either.

'The only passion I'm feeling towards you at the moment, Wil Hudson, is of the angry kind. Anger for putting me in this position. When I was trying to do you and your mum a good deed. Sharing a room was not part of the deal.'

'But pretending we're crazy about each other enough to want to get married is.'

Her eyes narrowed. 'Time for a new rule that has nothing to do with the language we use with Nina. I'm talking about PDA only while in the direct presence of your parents.'

'You mean Public Displays of Affection?' he said.

'Correct.' He liked the way she said *correct* like the schoolteacher she was. She'd always been a little bossy, and he'd always liked it. 'And there's to be none of the other type of PDA.'

'Other type?'

'Private Displays of Affection. I mean, there can't be any. We really do have to return to the status quo when we're alone.'

'The old "no touching" way? Forget the friendly hugs?'

'Yes.' Her voice broke. 'I won't be able to deal with it otherwise. Last night we both admitted we had used the old way as protection. I... I still need that protection. The hug... Well, it seemed more than friendly to me. We have to be platonic in private when we're pretending to be engaged. If those first kind of PDAs spill over and become the second kind, we won't know where we stand and it could get very awkward and...and hurtful.'

'You're scared,' he said slowly.

'I told you that last night,' she said a little stiffly. 'I really value you as a friend. We've only just found each other again and I don't want to mess it up. This fake-fiancée thing complicates everything.'

'Yeah. It does.' Adjusting to his new life with Nina was change enough on a momentous scale. After his disastrous marriage, he certainly couldn't see himself rushing into another permanent relationship, especially considering what that might mean to Nina. And a no-strings fling with Georgia where he kissed her goodbye when it ended was unthinkable. The friend zone was still the best place for them. The safe zone.

'I'm glad we're thinking the same way,' she said.

He looked back to Georgia. 'While this is theoretically a private moment. Perhaps we should think about the public moments. About how we handle it when—'

She screwed up her face and, for an alarming moment, he thought she might cry. 'This is crazy, Wil. Pretend engagement. Fake fiancée. Mapping out fake shows of affection. We're not those people out of some...some rom-com. We're straight-talking horse people.' Her voice broke on a half sob and she buried her face in her hands. 'I want to walk inside and tell your parents that Sharyn mistook fiancée for friend. Then I think how frail your mum looks, how the thought of you finding love gives her something to live for and—'

'Georgie, look at me.'

She dropped her hands from her face and looked up at him. Her eyes were glistening with unshed tears, an intense shade of blue like the summer sky at noon. He reached down and smoothed a wispy lock of her hair that was falling into her eyes. 'This is stressing you. It is a crazy idea and I'm a crazy man for having dropped you in it.'

She sniffed. 'Now I understand why you did it in the first place. And how very special your mother is to you, so you want to keep it going. It's just I—'

'I would never force you into something you didn't want to do. Ever.'

'I know. And it's because of that I really do want to help you. I also want to be your housemate and help you with Nina. If I tell the truth now, I'll have to go back to my parents' place. Otherwise, it would be incredibly awkward staying here under the scrutiny of your disappointed parents.'

'Now's your chance to back out. Seriously. I'll still be your friend even if you break off our "engagement".'

That brought a watery smile from her. 'I'm in. I'm your fiancée until Wednesday.'

He stepped closer. Took both her hands in his. She looked down to their joined hands and back up to him, alarmed. 'It's only pretend, remember,' he said. 'But we need to be convincing. As you reminded me, I've never kissed you. Engaged people should probably have some knowledge of what it's like to kiss each other.'

Georgia looked up at him, her eyes wide and wary, but still with a trace of smile lingering at the corners of her lips. She usually didn't wear much make-up, but today she'd put something on her eyes that emphasised their blue and the thickness of her dark lashes. Her mouth was slicked with cherry-red gloss and it looked eminently kissable. He'd always found that slight unevenness of her top lip very appealing—now he wanted to know how it felt under his lips, how she tasted, how she felt in his arms.

'Okay, so we kiss,' she said.

'Right,' he said, taken aback by her practical approach. 'Shall I be the first?'

'What do you mea—?'

Before he could finish his question, Georgia had tugged on their linked hands to pull him close and pressed her mouth against his, soft and warm and, to his surprise, hesitant. For all her show of bravado, she was nervous.

Wil wasn't the slightest bit nervous. More like exultant that he had her so close. *Kissing Georgia at last.* He took command of the kiss, being careful to keep his lips on hers tender and undemanding. A shiver of surrender ran through her as she relaxed into the kiss. He tightened his grip on her hands. She parted her lips to welcome his tongue with a little murmur of what he couldn't be sure was pleasure or trepidation. He vowed, with a fierce surge of protectiveness, he would make sure she felt only pleasure from his touch.

Her curves were soft and yielding against his chest. He slid his hands around to grasp her waist and pull her even closer. The wrap skirt of her dress had swung open to the top of her taut, toned thighs and her legs were bare against his. When her tongue met his, tentative at first and then meeting his in a sensual tangle, he was stunned by the sudden and intense shock waves of pleasure that rippled through his body—and his heart.

* * *

Her first kiss with Wil. It was so much more than Georgia could ever have imagined. She was almost overwhelmed by excitement. *This isn't real*, she tried to remind herself, but she couldn't think logically when she was so overwhelmed by sensation. This was Wil, familiar, yet, oh, so unfamiliar. His mouth, tasting of coffee and his favourite chocolate cookie. His scent, citrus shower gel with a heady touch of fresh, manly sweat. His hard, perfect male body in such intimate contact with hers.

What had started as a harmless practice kiss had flamed into something else altogether and escalated to a passionate exchange that surprised the heck out of her. Her heart hammered, her body pulsed with want. They'd always had a connection, mental, spiritual, now it was physical. The difference between friend and potential lover. Her heart gave a huge jolt. She broke away from the kiss to catch her breath, to find her balance. If she didn't pull away from him, she'd be dragging him behind the house and pushing him up against the wall.

She came up for air, panting, holding on to her heart. Wil was the same, his eyes dazed and unfocused. He seemed as knocked out as she was by what they had unleashed.

'What happened there?' she gasped.

Wil was drawing in great gulps of air in an effort to steady his voice. 'Eight years of wanting to kiss you? What's your guess?'

'Same,' she managed to choke out. The thought struck her. 'Or was it an act? On your part, I mean. You know, to look authentic.'

'I sure as hell wasn't acting. What about you?'

She shook her head. 'No. It…it was real.'

Georgia looked up at him and, as had happened so many times before, their eyes connected and they laughed. She felt exhilarated, high almost. Her buddy Wil. The best kisser she'd ever kissed.

He planted a firm, hard kiss on her mouth. 'Who knew?' he said, then proceeded to answer his own question. 'That's why I held off from ever kissing you. I suspected it might be like that for us. Did you not wonder why I never did, in those rare times when we were both single?'

'I could as easily ask you the same thing. A woman doesn't just hang about waiting to be kissed, you know. Not this girl, anyway.'

At that he laughed and pulled her back for another kiss. A kiss that caught her mouth when they were both still laughing, that made it seem an extension of their friendship. Which was so much more powerful than any impulse fuelled purely by desire.

She pressed her body close to his with a moan of impatience. Slid her hands up and under his loose shirt to feel the warm, bare skin of his back. She forgot where she was, why she was there. If she and Wil had been in the middle of George Street in Central Sydney with the world buzzing around her, she wouldn't have cared. *Him*. Wil. And the revelation of how much she wanted him.

But the sound of the door opening made her still. Wil too. She murmured a curse against his mouth, so low only she and Wil could hear it. Pulled away from the kiss. Looked up into his face. Saw the same dazed look of being pulled back into reality too quickly so her feet were scarcely holding her to the ground, still in the dizzying world where it was just her and Wil and their bodies in tune with each other.

They both turned as one towards the front door to

the house. Jackie. His mother stood there, holding on to the door frame, as if what she had seen had come as a shock. But she was grinning, a huge grin that lit up her face and made her look ten years younger.

'Sorry to interrupt,' she said, laughter lacing her voice. 'Nina's getting a little grizzly with just old folks for company.' She turned to head back inside, the grin dialled down now to a happy smile. 'But she can wait a little longer for her dad,' she said as she disappeared inside.

Now it was Wil's turn to curse, much more strongly than Georgia ever would.

She fought to get her breath back. 'It's okay,' she said. 'We did leave Nina for longer than we probably should have. They're still strangers to her. If you think about it, that worked out better than we could ever have planned. I suspect your mum is in there telling your dad how happy she is to have witnessed what she witnessed. That all is well with their son and his girl. And that's what this is about, isn't it?'

'It did the trick,' he said. 'But, play-acting aside, I enjoyed it.' His eyes drilled down into hers, dark with desire and something else she couldn't read, asking questions she was incapable of answering.

'Me too,' she said, unable to resist reaching up to give him a quick kiss on his mouth. He snatched her hand and kissed the palm. Even that felt thrilling. Shivers of excitement coursed through her. 'But I'm not sure what we should do about it,' she said.

He grinned. 'Now you consign me to oblivion.'

'What? Oh, yes, I remember. But you've got it wrong. Didn't you say I would consign you to oblivion if I didn't like you kissing me?' She narrowed her eyes, pouted her lips. 'Who said I didn't like it?'

With a triumphant whoop, he drew her back into his arms and kissed her again.

Georgia knew she should be breaking away and talking about keeping the two different types of PDA apart. That otherwise they'd be heading to heartbreak. But all she could think about was that she'd be sharing a bedroom with Wil that night and what the heck was she going to do about it?

CHAPTER NINE

GEORGIA LET WIL take her hand as they headed back into the house. *Holding hands with Wil.* Who knew it would feel so good, his much larger hand enfolding hers, warm and relaxed? It felt so natural and uncontrived, she couldn't imagine ever walking along beside him without holding his hand. But it wasn't real. It was an act, one in which she was willingly colluding.

Already she had started to talk herself out of what had seemed so very real outside—those passionate kisses. Obviously, they were both healthy young people who liked each other and no longer denied they found each other attractive. Of course their first kiss would ignite all sorts of feelings. But her reaction—and she supposed his—was purely physical. A friends-with-benefits scenario could work, if it remained strictly physical. *But that wasn't going to happen.*

Her feelings towards her long-time friend went beyond the physical. But there was too much in the way, blocking them from proceeding to anything deeper. Give in to a physical fling with Wil and she would lose him for ever. That first kiss aside—that exciting, wonderful, arousing kiss—the way she had handled her attraction to him for so long must still stay in play. Keep him as a hands-off friend or risk him becoming a lost former lover she would mourn? The choice was obvious.

The table in the family room, where morning tea had been set, had been cleared and she could hear Dave rattling around in the kitchen. Jackie was sitting on the sofa with Nina asleep against her chest, her little head with its cap of dark hair so like Wil's resting on her grandmother's shoulder. It made a beautiful picture and warmed Georgia's heart. She itched to sketch them. Although there was no actual blood connection, Jackie and Dave had instantly welcomed Nina as their own. 'Just a little wind bothering her, I think,' Jackie whispered. 'The old patting-the-back trick still works a treat—a good burp and she was fine.'

Wil sat down on the sofa and Georgia sat close to him a little hesitantly. How did he want her to play this from here? He put his arm around her to bring her closer, so close their knees were nudging. She tugged her skirt around her so at least skin wasn't touching skin in a situation that was already way too distracting. Then he took her hand in his again.

Georgia noticed Jackie glance at her hand linked with Wil's and was treated to a smile of warm approval. Her 'all is right with my world' look of contentment made Georgia glad she had agreed to carry on the charade of the engagement. This was a good woman; Georgia was doing a good thing in helping make her happy.

'Wil, I notice Georgia isn't wearing an engagement ring,' Jackie said. 'Have you decided not to get one or...?'

Wil, so obviously taken by surprise, didn't answer for a moment that seemed to stretch on and on. Georgia was just about to jump in with a hastily thought-out explanation when he finally spoke. 'We haven't had a chance to get one yet, Mum. I told you, our engagement is only a very recent thing.'

'That's right,' said Georgia, thinking on the spot. 'Wil…he wanted me to choose my own ring. Not him doing the old-fashioned thing of him buying it without any input from me.'

As poor Toby had done, with the lovely diamond ring he'd bought to surprise her when he'd proposed. She would never forget his heartbreak when she'd said 'no'. She'd realised she didn't love him enough to marry him. But along with her anguish at hurting him had been exultation. The realisation that she didn't have to compromise her own happiness just to make someone else happy had been like a bucket of ice water thrown over her, awakening her from her people-pleasing, 'good old Georgia' ways.

'Right, yes,' said Wil. 'After all, Georgie is the one who'll be wearing it. She can have any ring she wants.'

Georgia cringed inside at his words, though she kept a sweet fake-fiancée smile glued to her face. The thought of Wil buying a ring for another woman made her feel more than a touch uncomfortable. After that kiss, the thought of him even holding hands with anyone else hit her with a painful spasm of jealousy. The last time she'd seen her, Angie had waved an enormous diamond around on her ring finger. At the time, Georgia had thought it was an effort to incite envy, a tribute to Wil's bank account rather than to any kind of loving commitment.

Georgia forced the memories away. She had never given a thought to what kind of engagement ring she might want if the day ever came when she found someone she actually wanted to marry. She had turned down three proposals of marriage from three very nice men she'd been deeply fond of but not enough to commit to a lifetime of togetherness. There had always been something missing, but she didn't know what it was. Intensity perhaps. She wanted to be head over heels in love with the man she married. Nothing less. In some deep, hidden corner of her heart she was beginning to wonder if she would *ever* love anyone like that. *Maybe she didn't have it in her to be a wife.*

'What kind of ring do you like, Georgia?' Jackie asked.

Georgia thought quickly. 'I think a coloured stone.'

'Then a coloured stone is what you shall have,' said Wil, a little too heartily, Georgia thought. But his mother didn't seem to notice the strain in his voice.

'The reason I ask,' said Jackie, 'is that I have my mother's engagement ring. It's dated in style but quite magnificent with a huge emerald and surrounded by diamonds. You could have it remodelled if you think that might suit, or just use some of the stones.'

'Mum, I—' Wil started to protest.

'I know you can well afford to buy Georgia any ring she wants, but it was just a thought. A way to welcome Georgia to the family with a link to the family past.' She looked to Georgia. 'Your choice, of course.'

'Mum, that's what I was going to say. About the family past. Shouldn't Grandma's ring go to Ned? Not… not to me.'

Wil tightened his grip on Georgia's hand without, she thought, realising he did it. Her heart ached at the naked vulnerability on his handsome face. He must at times have felt second-best to their birth son but would never show it. However, both she and his mother had seen it now, breaking through his happy, just-engaged mask.

'Why would that be?' Jackie said. 'I've always said, as I didn't have a daughter, whoever of my sons first got married could have first choice of Grandma's jewellery. Ned is way behind—he isn't even dating anyone. Besides, there are other rings for when his turn comes.'

Wil let go of her hand, put both his hands on his knees as he leaned towards his mother. 'But, Mum—' Georgia could see now what Wil had meant when he'd said he found it difficult to get a word in when his mother was on a roll. He was too respectful to simply barge in and interrupt.

'If you're going to say something about Ned being my birth son and you my adopted son, you can forget about it. You know I consider you equally both my sons, end of story.'

Georgia wanted to hug her. She and Dave had given Wil such unconditional love he had overcome the disadvantages of his youth to be the confident, successful man he was. They obviously had a lot of love to give— extending it immediately to Nina and, she realised, to her. It made her feel doubly bad about deceiving them.

'Mum, thank you,' Wil said, and Georgia could hear the love in his voice too. Thank heaven they had come along when they had in his life.

'So what are your thoughts about the ring?' Jackie said. 'Georgia?'

The vintage emerald ring sounded like just the kind of thing she would love. But she was never likely to lay eyes on it. No emerald rings for platonic pals. By the time Wil's parents got back from Italy, Georgia the fiancée would have shrunk back to being just the friend. She wouldn't dare meet with Jackie and Dave again. They were so protective of Wil, they would assume she had hurt their son. Toby's parents had actually hated her for 'leading their son on'. Right up to the moment Toby had said, 'Will you marry me?' she had planned to say yes. Toby had ended up hating her too.

'Er…it sounds amazing,' she said. 'I guess I… We… need to see it first. Thank you for your very generous offer.'

'My parents were very happily married,' said Jackie. 'So the ring comes with good karma.' Georgia couldn't help but wonder what kind of bad karma this deception would bring with it.

'That's good to hear,' Georgia murmured, not daring to meet Wil's eye.

Wil patted her on her knee as a fiancé might and she had to stop herself from flinching. Not because she didn't like it, but because she did. From never feeling Wil's touch, she now had lost count of the occasions she had revelled in his touch. *That kiss!*

'It's a very generous offer and Georgia and I thank you,' he said.

Georgia couldn't—wouldn't—point out the elephant in the room that no one was acknowledging. Wil actually had already been the first son to get married. But the parents had so obviously not approved of his choice. She, Georgia, was the favoured one. But she was the fake. She wanted to be far away when Wil told them they had broken their engagement.

'I'll make sure you get a chance to see the ring as soon as possible,' Jackie said. 'Now, while we're all here together, there's something else I want to ask you.'

Georgia exchanged a quick glance with Wil. What next to test them? He looked relaxed but there was tension in the way he held his shoulders, the set of his jaw.

She still couldn't believe she was sitting here pretending to be engaged to him while fighting as hard as she could to quell the insistent little voice telling her how nice it was to be considered a couple. Her and Wil. Not to be actually engaged. Of course not. That could never work with Wil. But sitting here so close to him. *Belonging* felt very good.

'What's that, Mum?' Wil asked.

'Have you and Georgia thought about Nina's christening?'

Wil was hit from left field with that one, but only Georgia seemed to notice. 'No,' he said. 'You know I'm not particularly religious, but I guess a christening or a naming ceremony might be a good thing.'

Georgia had no opinion on Nina's religious upbringing. As a fake fiancée, she didn't think she should proffer any ideas.

His mother, however, had strong opinions. 'According to her mother's sister, Nina has not been christened into any faith, or even had a naming ceremony. If you don't have any feelings either way, your dad and I would like to see her christened in our denomination as she is the newest member of our family.'

'Sure,' said Wil.

'What do you think, Georgia, as Nina's future stepmother?' asked Jackie.

If her 'engagement' was real, she'd know who she could talk to about her fears of being a good stepmother. Here was Jackie, proving again and again her mother's love for Wil—the child of strangers—whom she had not even met until Wil was thirteen. 'I hadn't really thought,' she said.

Jackie smiled in understanding. 'The word *stepmother*

has such bad connotations, doesn't it? Is there ever a non-wicked stepmother in stories? But as his adoptive mother, I genuinely love Wil as my own, and you will come to love Nina too. And she you   the love goes both ways.'

'Of course,' said Georgia, suddenly aware that she could be giving the game away if she didn't show some enthusiasm for her future—though fictional—parenting duties. 'Nina is adorable, such a cute baby.'

'You have a head start with her,' Jackie said.

'What's that?' asked Georgia, genuinely interested.

'You already love Wil, and he loves you. You two have got a strong love that goes back a long way. Because you love Wil, you'll learn to love and cherish his daughter. She looks so like him, doesn't she?'

Georgia flushed. She felt like such a hypocrite. Wil took her hand again and squeezed it in a good semblance of lovingly. But she noticed he looked straight ahead instead of at her. He felt it too.

'Yes, I can see that,' she said faintly. She hadn't expected this and she was squirming with guilt and discomfort. How lovely Jackie was, to include her in the family from the start. How duplicitous she and Wil were. But it was what Wil thought was best. And she was—had always been—on his side.

'Back to the christening, what are your thoughts, Georgie?' said Wil.

'My mother always says, apart from the spiritual aspect, being christened is important to get into some of the top private schools in Sydney.'

Wil stared at her. 'That's extremely cynical,' he said. 'I don't know that I like it.'

Wil might not have come from wealth, but he had been adopted into it. Then amassed his own fortune. Georgia shrugged. 'Fact of life in posh Sydney circles. You attended a prestigious private boarding school in Melbourne. Perhaps you'll want the same kind of school for Nina.' Darn. She'd said *you* not *we*. She darted a look at Jackie. Thankfully, she didn't seem to have noticed the slip-up.

'She's right, Wil,' said Jackie.

'I hadn't given a thought to Nina's schooling,' Wil said. 'Getting her from one feed and nappy change to the next is all I've been focusing on. Regarding schools, I...we...will decide what's best for Nina when the time comes.'

'Of course,' said Georgia. By that stage she wouldn't have anything to do with the decision. Except to give an informed schoolteacher opinion to her friend Wil, who she wouldn't see much of as he was so caught up being a single dad. Or not. *No.* She wouldn't let herself think of Wil with a new wife helping him with Nina.

'Mum, if it's important to you to welcome Nina into the family with a ceremony, I'm okay with it.'

'Me too,' said Georgia, as it seemed to be expected of her.

Jackie beamed. She shifted Nina, who had been sleeping soundly through the entire exchange, to her other shoulder. 'We're leaving for Italy on Wednesday. Would it be possible to get the christening organised for the Tuesday?'

'Tuesday?' said Wil, shocked. 'Today is Saturday. How could we—?'

'We've never organised a christening. Can you get it done in that time?' said Georgia.

'Wouldn't it be better to wait for you to come back from Italy to have the ceremony?' said Wil.

'Nina is already seven months old,' said Jackie. 'We don't want to leave it much longer. Besides... I... Well, there's no beating around the bush. I'm feeling well now. But who knows what the future holds for me?'

'Mum,' said Wil, anguished. 'Don't say that. Please.'

'It's a fact of life, son.'

Georgia put her hand comfortingly on his arm, now she was 'allowed' to do that. 'We'll see what we can do, Jackie.'

'If we can organise a christening for Tuesday, we will,' said Wil.

'If you don't mind me putting my oar in, I know the priest at a church in Manly—he used to be in our parish,' said Jackie. 'That's not too far from here. I'll see what he could do about fitting us in for a quick christening. It might be okay on a weekday, if we take whatever time they give us. Not to mention a generous donation on offer.'

'Sure,' said Wil. 'Georgie is on school holidays and my time is my own.'

Georgie actually has illustrations to finish, Georgia thought, but how could she protest? She had the uncomfortable feeling she was being steamrollered, even if it was for the best of reasons.

'What about your family, Georgia?' said Jackie. 'It will be short notice for them. Do you think they will be able to attend the christening?'

Georgia stared at her, unable to speak. Her throat closed over. 'My family?' she managed to choke out. 'Oh, I...er...don't think so.'

'They may want to see their step-granddaughter christened,' Jackie said.

Step-granddaughter? Of course, they would be Nina's step-grandparents. If this were for real.

Wil came to the rescue. 'We hadn't actually thought that far ahead.'

Georgia had no intention of telling her family anything about the fake engagement. She'd hoped she could keep it confined to Ingleside. This was in serious danger of spiralling out of control.

If her mother thought she was engaged to Wil, she'd cancel a court case to be there and meet his family. Her sisters would be agog. They always teased her that she'd let Wil—who they were convinced was her Mr Right—get away. Once they knew, half of Sydney would know.

'We only want a very small ceremony, Mum,' said Wil. 'Ideally, just you, Dad, me and Georgie. That's what I want.' Georgia could see him improvising as he went along. 'For one thing, it would be in bad taste to have anything other than to keep it very small and very private when you consider it's so soon after Angie's death. I know we were divorced, but just out of respect. That's my final word.'

'I agree with Wil, of course,' said Georgia. In this case she most certainly did.

Jackie nodded. 'I can see your reasoning behind that decision. Small and private it shall be.'

Georgia looked to Wil and smiled, hoping she was masking her intense relief. He smiled back. Crisis averted.

But Jackie hadn't finished. 'But I'll need to get in touch with your parents anyway, Georgia,' she said. 'After all, we'll all want to pull together to organise the wedding. Have you two set a date?'

CHAPTER TEN

LATER THAT EVENING Wil was alone with Georgia in his bedroom. Not so much a bedroom but a luxurious hotel-like suite with the finest of furnishings in muted neutrals. His mother had pulled out all the stops on the master bedroom when they'd redecorated the house. Wil shut the door firmly behind him and Georgia to ensure their privacy. Nina's room was the next down the corridor; the bedroom his parents were sharing at the other end.

'What a day,' exclaimed Georgia, laughing, whirling around to face him. 'Your mum! She's a darling, but she never stops.'

'Never stops trying to organise my life, you mean,' he said, his tone mildly exasperated yet not masking his love for his mother. 'And now yours.'

'The look on your face when she asked us had we set a wedding date—I nearly cracked up,' said Georgia.

'Coming on top of the urgency of the christening, I'd really had enough, much as I love her,' he said.

'I couldn't look at you or I would have laughed out loud when you laid down the law. When you told her in such a controlled voice that we'll get married in our own good time—and that it wouldn't be until after she comes back from Italy.'

'I really had to grit my teeth when she suggested we might consider a destination wedding in Tuscany and that, if we liked, she could set the wheels in motion while she was over there.'

'I had to stop myself getting excited about that one. I mean, if it were real, if we really were getting married. Tuscany.'

'I didn't want to get cranky with her, but I'd had enough. I'm not as good at creating fibs on the spot as I thought I would be.'

'That's actually a good thing, Wil,' she said. 'I'm not a natural-born liar either. It's exhausting.'

'Mum kept us both on the spot,' he said. 'But you played your part so well, Georgie. I'm having another grovelling with gratitude moment.'

Wil threw himself down on one of the upholstered armchairs that were arranged around the marble fireplace. In winter, it kept the room toasty warm. Now a ceiling fan flicked overhead to supplement the air conditioning on a steamy summer night. He indicated for Georgia to take the other, tried not to notice the way her wrap skirt slid away from her legs when she sat down. She glanced up, noticed the direction of his eyes, tugged the fabric more modestly around her.

It was the first time they had been alone since the kiss outside on the driveway. There had been lunch with his parents at the house around the pool, then dinner, Nina included, at a waterside restaurant in Manly. Not surprisingly, the Manly trip had also included a drive-by of the proposed church for the christening.

'The highlight for me was when your dad came out of the kitchen with a dishcloth dangling from his hand and told your mum we would decide a date for our wedding when we were good and ready and not before,' said Georgia as she settled into the chair with a delightful wiggle of her bottom. Wil was noticing so many habits and quirks about her that he'd never noticed before. Though he'd admired her back view clad in tight riding breeches on many occasions over the years of their friendship.

Georgia continued. 'Then your dad said you'd only just found out you're a father and to give the boy some space.'

'Dad's a man of few words, but he keeps his finger on the pulse,' he said.

Georgia drew her dark brows together. 'Do you think he suspects something isn't right? Between us, I mean?'

'No. He lets his sons get on with their lives. He's always there if I need him, I can count on that. Otherwise, he doesn't interfere.'

'Except when he entered you for the reality inventors show without telling you.'

'For which I will always be grateful. At that age, I would never have found the guts to enter it myself. The exposure gave me such a kick-start. I wouldn't be where I am without the contacts it brought.'

'And now you've got all this,' she said with a wave around the room. 'This bedroom is like a six-star hotel.'

But has only come to life with you in it, Wil thought. Her megawatt smile, the brightness of her eyes, the vivid splash of colour from her dress were like a series of lights being switched on to illuminate the stark loneliness of the space.

He got up to fetch a bottle of white wine and two wine glasses and placed them on the low glass coffee table in front of them. Nina's baby monitor was on the mantelpiece. She had been put to bed by her doting grandmother but it would be Wil who would get up to her during the night, if needed.

When his mother had interior designed this room, she had thought of everything. An enormous king-sized bed dressed with fashionable linen and rather too many cushions for his taste, a comfortable sofa, these chairs, a walk-in dressing room, even a small fridge hidden behind custom cabinetry. She'd had the existing bathroom ripped out and replaced with elegant new fittings and marble tiles with underfloor heating. It was a bedroom that a boy in residential care sharing a room with other boys, sleeping in a narrow bed with an envelope-thin mattress and a metal locker for his few possessions, could never have imagined would be his.

Georgia sipped at her wine, looking at him over the rim. 'I know we're having a laugh at your mother's expense, but it's lovely the way she's so excited about it all. If we really were organising a wedding, she'd be a great help.'

'I have to admit, I thought only as far as an engagement. Mum threw me when she asked about a wedding date.'

Georgia leaned forward in her chair. 'And yet, you've been married before.'

He put down his glass, unable to take even a sip of his wine for fear he might gag on it. 'I don't count that as a marriage. More a…a short-term spell in prison.'

Georgia couldn't disguise her gasp. 'Was it that bad?'

'Yep,' he said.

'Are you ready to tell me about it?'

'As you've become so involved in my life, I guess you should know,' he said.

'Only if you want to share,' she said, thoughtful as ever.

How different his life might have been if she hadn't met Toby and he hadn't met Angie and they'd decided to try out where that deeply buried attraction between them might have led to. Too late now. All this talk of engagement rings and weddings made him shudder. He had no plans to re-enter that trap called marriage any time soon. Perhaps never. Besides, looking after Nina took up all his energies. Though having Georgia here to help would make a huge difference. He wouldn't let himself think about how it would be, when she'd leave to go back to school.

'Angie caught me on the rebound,' he said.

Georgia screwed up her face in concentration. 'Who were you dating then? Oh, yes, that nice red-headed physiotherapist.'

'Yeah,' he said.

That wasn't the rebound he was referring to. But he had no intention of telling Georgia that she had been the one he'd lost and, in his loss, he had been vulnerable to a woman like Angie.

At the time, Georgia had seemed so keen on Toby. Wil hadn't actually needed the 'back off from my girlfriend' confrontation with Toby one night when their group had all been out at a pub. Wil had already realised he'd left his move too late, that there'd been no chance then of suggesting he and Georgia step out of the friendship zone and try dating. Not when she was more serious than he'd ever seen her about another guy—and Toby about her. As Georgia had said, their stars had never aligned.

'Where did you actually meet Angie?'

'In a takeaway coffee shop. She'd just been served and she accidentally spilled some coffee on me. I brushed it off, but she insisted on buying me another coffee, even suggested she pay for my dry cleaning.'

'Meet cute,' said Georgia.

He frowned. 'What do you mean?'

'It's a movie term to describe a cute, uncontrived meeting.'

'There was nothing uncontrived about it, I discovered later,' he said grimly. 'That meeting was totally contrived. Angie had been watching me as a hunter watches its prey. She'd seen me on TV, you see. Knew my worth down to the last dollar.'

'I don't mean to defend Angie, Wil. But there might have been more to it than that. You are extraordinarily handsome, you know.'

Dear Georgia, always wanting to be fair. But there had been nothing fair about the way Angie had behaved. 'That's nice of you to say so,' he said.

'So what happened next?'

'She was very attractive, she pursued me, and I allowed myself to be caught.'

'You were quite the player in those days.'

'Perhaps,' he said.

'So how did you end up marrying her so quickly?'

'More wine?' he asked. Georgia held out her glass for a refill. Wil topped up his glass. 'To answer that, I have to go back again to those times of my life I'd rather not remember.'

'Are you sure, Wil?' Her eyes were warm with sympathy. He knew she'd been shaken by hearing about his childhood. But he hadn't told her everything.

'Yes. You should know. Now that you're so caught up with me and Nina.'

He left the wineglass on the table, after all. He needed to be sober for this. Not to mention clear-headed enough to face the challenge ahead of having Georgia in his bedroom all night.

'Angie reminded me of a girl named Tegan I met in foster care—my last foster home when I had just turned thirteen. Tegan was the same age as me, dainty, blonde and very pretty.'

Georgia smiled knowingly. 'You had a crush on her.'

'I guess I did. I liked her a lot.'

'Hormones kicking in,' she said.

'Unfortunately the foster father had his eye on her too.'

'Oh, Wil, no.' Her smile disappeared like ice thrown onto a fire.

'As a foster kid, I learned the hard way to shut up and make myself compliant. I was very young for my first placements. Apparently I cried and screamed at being shunted into a house with strangers. Regressed to bedwetting. Tried to run away. Got the label of troublemaker from an early age.'

'Five years old,' Georgia whispered. She raised her hand as if reaching out to comfort him but lowered it. The 'no touching in private' rule was back in place.

'I soon learned that the amiable kids do best in foster care. Yes, sir, no, sir, do as you're told. Don't get attached to any of the nice foster parents, when you know you won't be staying. When I was younger, I saw stuff I didn't understand. I thought it was bad but I didn't know why. You learn to turn the other way if you see something scary, otherwise you'll be in trouble.'

Georgia snatched her hand to her mouth. 'Were you abused?'

'No, I wasn't. Other boys were, but thankfully not me.'

'Thank heaven.' She breathed out a huge sigh of relief. 'What happened with Tegan?'

'When I realised this guy was grooming Tegan for abuse, I couldn't turn a blind eye. I warned her never to be alone with him, no matter what threats or promises he might make to her. That didn't keep her safe. When Tegan told me what he'd tried to do, I went for the guy. I was nearly as tall then as I am now. And used to defending myself at school. He was taken by surprise and I was angry. I managed to do some serious damage—broke his nose, knocked out a few teeth. That's when I got put into the care home. Got myself some respect from the other boys for beating up a foster parent.'

'But not much from the authorities, I'll bet.'

'None. I never went back into foster care—no one wanted me, not surprisingly. The foster father didn't press charges. He didn't want to be looked at too closely. So I was spared Children's Court and a spell in a juvenile justice centre.'

'And Tegan?'

'Thankfully, one of the social workers believed me when I told her Tegan was in danger. The guy denied everything, of course. But she was taken out of that house and supposedly sent to somewhere safer. I never saw her again. But I never forgot her.'

'So Angie reminded you of her?'

'Not just in looks. She and Sharyn came from an abusive family situation. Angie had spent time in care too.'

Georgie nodded thoughtfully. 'If you couldn't rescue Tegan, you could rescue Angie.'

He knew his mouth had turned down in a bitter line. It always did when he thought about that disastrous time in his life. 'Not that she really needed rescuing. Her survival technique was manipulation, learned from a very young age. Pretty little Angie could twist the truth like no one I've ever encountered before or since. Though of course she was all charm at first. Until she'd got me on her hook.'

Georgia frowned. 'That begs the question, Wil, why did you marry her?'

'The oldest trick in the book. She told me she was pregnant.'

Georgia sat bolt upright in her chair. 'What?' He could see her going through a mental timeline, realising he didn't mean pregnant with Nina.

'By then I'd started to see beneath the veneer of her pretty ways. Was ready to end it. Angie must have realised that. I'd told her something of my background by then. She knew I would never risk having a child of mine going through what I went through. She gambled that I would marry the mother of my child—no matter what. That's why the hasty marriage at the register office. That's why she didn't want my parents involved in the wedding.'

'You're too honourable to have made any other choice.'

'Too gullible as it turned out,' he said, unable to keep the bitterness from his voice.

'What happened about the baby?'

'Conveniently lost just two weeks after the wedding. I was sympathetic. Sad for her, and sad for me too. I blamed her erratic behaviour that followed on hormone disruption from the miscarriage. Then she told me in one of her screaming fits that she'd never been pregnant at all. The positive pregnancy test kit she'd shown me had come from another woman.'

'Surely not,' Georgia said, visibly shocked. 'How could someone do that?'

Such deception would be beyond someone as thoroughly decent as Georgia. That was the reason he had never told her the truth of his sordid past—fear she would scorn that violent foster kid whose own family hadn't wanted him. That kid masquerading as a wealthy landowner's son. He'd believed he'd be punching above his weight if he'd tried to get serious with Georgia.

'I left. But she begged me to come back. She knew what strings to pull. I didn't want to admit defeat. Felt I had to give the marriage a fair go. I'd made a commitment. I tried and tried to make it work. But it became more and more toxic.'

'So what happened to make you finally end it?'

Wil angled himself to look directly into her face. 'I'm going to tell you this just the once, Georgie. I don't want to revisit it ever again. I'm only telling you now because I know I can trust you.'

'Of course you can. That goes without saying.'

Wil threw his head back, stared at the ceiling as he spoke. He didn't want to see pity or condemnation in Georgia's eyes. 'She started to push me further and further. I couldn't do a thing right. She undermined me at every opportunity. Alienated me from my friends. Even tried to do the same with my family.'

Georgia audibly caught her breath. 'Wil, are you telling me she became abusive?'

'A big man and a tiny little woman? Who would believe it? What male wants to admit to being an abused husband?'

'That happens, though, doesn't it? The abused becomes the abuser. Angie was abused and repeated the cycle. The poor woman—in spite of everything you've told me, I feel some pity for her.'

'So did I. At times I could see flashes of the person she could have been. But Angie wouldn't acknowledge she needed help. I actually began to fear I might end up with a knife in my back. I had to admit defeat and walk away for good.'

'How did she take it?'

'Badly, as you can imagine. I paid her off very handsomely when we divorced. But she wouldn't accept my decision. I told her I never wanted to see her again.'

'But it turned out she was pregnant for real.'

'And saw a way to further manipulate and punish me. Stubborn, scheming and plotting revenge.'

Georgia shook her head. 'Keeping your child from you when she knew how much that would hurt you.'

'Until she was ready to strike, according to her sister, Sharyn.'

'What a horror story. Yet for all that, she cared for Nina and looked after herself.'

'Although I only have Sharyn's word on that. Angie abused both alcohol and chemicals—that was part of her problem. Apparently she kept clean through the pregnancy and after the birth. Nina is certainly in excellent health, which points to that being true. I like to believe, for Nina's sake, that perhaps she was Angie's salvation. Who knows? I'll certainly never tell Nina the truth about her mother. Only the good things.'

'I'm reeling, Wil, that you had to go through all this by yourself.'

'Not by myself. There were my parents and Ned and the solace of Five and a Half Mile Creek. I stayed down there as often as I could. Worked remotely. Talked to Mum and Dad. Rode my horse. When I was in Sydney I worked on this house. Another reason you and our other friends didn't see me.'

'I honestly don't know what to say, Wil. You've gone through hell.'

'Now you can see why I was prepared to fight and even lie to keep Nina. And why I'm so damn grateful to my parents, I lied some more.'

'I just wish I'd been able to help you.'

'You're helping me now, Georgie. That's what counts.' He got up from the chair. Paced up and down in front of the fireplace until he came to a halt in front of her chair. 'Now you know the worst of me, where I came from, what I really am. Do you still want to help?'

CHAPTER ELEVEN

GEORGIA JUMPED UP from her chair to face Wil. 'The worst? What do you mean the worst? More like the best,' she said fiercely. 'Over the last few days you've told me an incredible story of a boy who had a terrible start in life and won through by his strength of character and intelligence to be the amazing man I'm proud to call my friend.' She had to blink away tears, but didn't want him to notice.

He tilted his head. 'You mean that?'

'Of course I mean that. How could you think I wouldn't? I didn't think it could get any more tragic than the five-year-old lost on the beach while his parents drowned. But the thirteen-year-old white knight saving his vulnerable friend from a terrible fate and then being punished for it comes very close. I want to run out of this room and bang on your parents' door and kiss their feet for rescuing you from that dreadful situation. Though in reality, I think you rescued yourself.'

He swallowed hard before he replied, she could see by his Adam's apple. 'That means a lot, Georgie. You and your family are so…north-shore respectable, I suppose is the word for it. I was concerned you would think less of me because of my past.'

'Why? That you were somehow not worthy because of the dreadful childhood you suffered through no fault of your own? Because adults let you down? I hate your aunt, by the way. I hope you never see her.'

'No chance of that, even if I'd wanted to. She moved house and left no forwarding address.' He couldn't hide the pain of rejection from his voice, after all that time.

'I hope she came to a horrible end,' she said with narrowed eyes and a melodramatic tone.

He laughed and it warmed her heart to hear it. 'Loyal Georgie,' he said.

'To think what you've made of yourself since that start. I'm so proud of you, Wil.'

'Thank you,' he said simply.

She ached for him—it literally felt as though she had a pain in her chest—for all he'd gone through as a kid. 'How strong you must be to have won through all that. And then to have to cope with that terrible marriage.'

'I guess,' he said gruffly.

She looked up at him. 'I don't give a flying fig about the "no touching" rule right now, Wil. I have to hug you.' She put her arms around him. He felt so good, warm and hard and so utterly male. He tightened his arms around her and held her close. For what seemed like a long time but probably wasn't even minutes, she stood in the circle of his arms, willing all his past pain away. Finally she murmured against his shoulder, 'If your friends had known what you were going through in your marriage, you know we would have rallied around you. Tried to intervene.'

'It wouldn't have done any good. I got myself into the mess and I had to get myself out of it. Besides, you would have been the worst person to have offered help.'

She pulled away, still within the circle of his arms. 'Why was that, Wil?'

'I told you. Angie didn't believe we were platonic friends. I don't know how many times she accused me of, as she said, having "the hots" for you.'

'Funny, Toby said the same thing.'

'You know he warned me off you?'

'I didn't know, but I'm not surprised,' she said. 'He was possessive.'

'He cared for you.'

'He did.'

'What went wrong? Did he cheat on you?'

'No!' Georgia laid her cheek back against his shoulder. It was easier, somehow, to talk about this intensely personal stuff without looking into his face. 'I broke his heart.'

'You told me Toby was "The One", that you were going to marry him.' There was a harsh edge to Wil's voice that she didn't understand.

'I thought I wanted to marry him. He was so nice, good-looking, we had a lot in common, got on well, he made me laugh. We talked about moving in together, but something held me back.'

'The fact that you're the marrying kind?'

'Probably. I'm a romantic, as you know. I wanted the big wedding with all the frills, one day. The head-over-heels-in-love thing.'

'Toby was that,' he said. 'Head over heels, I mean.'

'I know, and I did love him. But in hindsight, I didn't love him enough. Everything pointed to us getting married and I went along with it, thinking it was what I wanted. I knew from all the hints and allusions from our families and friends that he was gearing up to propose.'

'Just as you'd hoped,' Wil said.

'Yes. Though I had a dream one night that the two of us were waiting on North Sydney station to catch a train. When the train came, he got on the train we were meant to be on but I turned around and got on a different train on the other side of the platform. He looked back from his train to see where I was, as I was meant to be with him. But I was on the other one, behind closed doors, looking out of the window at him as my train drew away in the opposite direction. I woke up shaking and in tears.'

'That dream was telling you something.'

'But I didn't listen to it. Then when Toby did propose, on his knees in the most romantic way I could have wished for, I opened my mouth to say "yes" but "no" came out instead.'

'Ouch. For Toby, I mean.'

'He thought I was joking at first, but I wasn't. I just knew I couldn't marry him. That I loved him but not enough to want to spend my life with him.'

'Let me guess,' said Wil. 'Toby wasn't happy about your decision.'

She looked up at him again. 'You could say that. Needless to say, he ended up hating me. His family hated me. Some of my friends took his side and didn't have nice things to say about me either. And no more golf games between the potential fathers-in-law.'

'Better that happened before you married him than after.'

'So my family said. My mother works in the family law court. She said I did absolutely the right thing. She sees the results of the wrong decisions in court all the time.'

Wil looked down at her. 'Poor Georgie,' he said. He

traced a line from her cheekbone to the corner of her mouth.

She stilled. Their gazes connected for a long time. Then he kissed her. He pulled her close and she kissed him back. The kiss escalated quickly from a tender affirmation to a passionate hungry exchange. Wil hadn't shaved since the morning and Georgia found the scrape of his beard unbearably exciting against her skin, his scent familiar and exhilarating. When Wil slid his hands down the sides of her breasts, her nipples hardened and she ached for him to touch her, stroke her and go so much further than kissing. When his hands slid down to cup her bottom, and she began to push her body insistently against him, she pulled away.

'Not a good idea,' she said, panting and trying to get her breath back. Not to be kissing like this, alone with him in his bedroom with that big bed beckoning.

He turned his head from side to side in disbelieving amazement. 'All those years, holding back on kissing you. Now *this*. Who knew how mind-blowing it would be? You know what this means?' He pushed a curl gone frizzy with humidity away from her forehead.

'What does it mean?

'We'd be sensational together in bed.'

'Wil!'

'It's true. You feel it too, don't you?'

Her heartbeat had started to slow down from the kiss. Now it started hammering again and a shudder of anticipation went through her. 'We'd better stop that line of conversation right there.'

'Practical Georgie,' he said, huskily.

'Cautious Georgie who knows this can't lead anywhere but heartbreak,' she said. 'Friends with benefits can't work. Not for people like me, anyway. Sex has to be part of an ongoing relationship, one I think can go somewhere, even if it ends up not to be that way.'

He groaned. 'You're right, as usual.'

'What we have as friends is not worth risking.'

'Not even for mind-blowing sex?'

Georgia flushed at the very thought of it. Moved a step closer to stand under the breeze generated by the ceiling fan. If just kissing Wil could make her feel like this, what would making love with him be like? 'I'm fanning myself at the thought. But you know it wouldn't work.'

That big, empty bed with all those cushions loomed in the room. If she took him by the hand and led him over, would he follow? She clenched her hand into a fist to stop herself from even contemplating it.

'I know,' he said slowly, with what seemed like genuine regret. 'You're right. We should keep that "no touching" rule in place unless required for purposes of enhancing the illusion that we're engaged.'

She hesitated before she replied. 'A few times today, especially when it came to Tuscany, I found myself wondering what it might be like to be actually engaged to you and then—'

His face tightened. 'I'm sorry, Georgie, I can't see myself getting married again. And I know you too well to believe you would settle for anything less than whole-hearted commitment.'

'You misunderstood,' she said. She schooled her face to ignore that unreasonable stab of hurt at the thought he could marry a woman like Angie but would never have considered her. *Just friends*, she reminded herself yet again. 'I was going to say that I don't let myself think any further along those lines. Perhaps if we'd acted on…

on whatever it is that makes our kisses so mind-blowing several years ago, we might have had a chance. But not now.' She paused, trying to summon up the right words.

She turned away from him. Picked up the baby monitor from the mantelpiece and put it hastily back down as it emitted a blast of static. 'Back then, there wasn't Nina. It's not just about us any more. You don't want to marry again. You've made that clear. I do want to get married and have a family some day. That means if we did have a fling for a while, or a "friendship with benefits" thing, it would be a dead end for me.'

'I'm not sure where you're going.'

'Where would that leave Nina when I left? Crying for me like she cried for her mum? I don't want to be responsible for adding further trauma to that precious little girl's life.'

'Yeah. I get that.'

'Do you? Because I'd be crying too, having to leave her. I might be glad to see the last of you because it didn't work out. Not so Nina. It's too easy to get attached to children. Like the kids I teach and have to say goodbye to at the end of the school year. If I allowed myself to get attached to them, I'd be an emotional wreck.'

'But—'

'You'll have to keep that in mind when you start seeing other women. Think about how any relationships you have could affect Nina.' It killed her to think of him with another woman. But she'd had to get used to that over the years. What was different now?

'I have no plans to see other women,' he said bluntly.

'You will sooner or later,' she said, forcing her words to be even and emotionless. 'And I look forward to playing some ongoing role in Nina's life, maybe like a surrogate aunty.'

Wil paused for a long moment. Georgia thought he had never looked more handsome, his hair all ruffled from her hands running through it, his eyes dark and thoughtful, the sexy shadow of his beard. 'Our stars never aligned, did they?' he said eventually.

'And it looks like they never will,' she said, unable to keep a note of sadness and regret from her voice.

She leaned down to pick up her glass of wine, took a sip, but then put it back down. 'Not a good idea at this time of night. I've had enough.'

She made a show of yawning, putting her hand over her mouth. In truth, she wasn't tired at all. Not after that kiss. Her body was throbbing with want for him. *We'd be sensational together in bed.*

She could happily make love to Wil all night and not sleep a wink. But she valued their friendship too much to throw it away for a physical thrill that could go nowhere.

He placed his hands on her shoulders so she had to look up at him. 'Georgie, I'm not going to sleep in here tonight. Before, it would have been okay for me to sleep here. Like we did in the horse trailer. But not any more. All day I've been wondering what it might be like to unfasten your dress and watch it slide off your body.'

She gasped. 'Oh.'

'I've been wondering what underwear you have on.'

She cleared her throat. 'Black lace,' she choked out.

He groaned, dropped his hands from her shoulders, stepped back. 'You weren't meant to answer that question, Georgie. Now I'll be in torment all night.'

She screwed up her face. 'Sorry. But I like wearing nice underwear. French lace by preference.'

He groaned again. 'I had you down for simple and white. Which has its own charms, of course.'

Maybe she'd had one glass of wine too many. But she was a little tired of being underestimated by Wil. He thought she wore white granny panties and a sturdy white bra? She was a schoolteacher, not a nun.

'But not quite the same as black lace?' she said, very sweetly.

'That does it.' He kissed her hard and swiftly on her mouth. 'I cannot be in this room with you, imagining you in that underwear.'

'But I don't sleep in my underwear.'

'What do you—?' He put his hand up. 'Don't answer that question.' He searched her face with a quizzical look. 'Georgie, I didn't imagine you could be such a tease.'

She wound her arms around his neck. 'There's a lot you don't know about me, Wil Hudson.' *Never underestimate a girl next door*, she thought.

She kissed him briefly, flicking her tongue between his lips, then stepped back from temptation. 'I don't want to boot you out of your bedroom. That doesn't seem right. The sofa is yours.'

'There's a sofa in Nina's nursery. I slept there the first night. I'm going to head in there now. My parents wouldn't be surprised to find me there in the morning. I'll probably have to get up with her during the night anyway and wouldn't want to disturb you.'

'That's our cover story,' she said. 'I'll back you all the way.' She reached up and kissed him chastely on the cheek. 'Goodnight, Wil.'

CHAPTER TWELVE

WHEN GEORGIA WOKE up on Wednesday morning, it was to the vastness of Wil's empty bedroom. The room was still and quiet, save for the chorus of kookaburras outside. Yet Wil's presence seemed to linger, in the shape of his body moulded in the chair where he most often sat, in the scent of the soap in his bathroom, in the starkly simple black-and-white artworks by a coveted Sydney artist he'd chosen for the walls. For the past four nights he had kept up the pretence of sleeping in his room with his 'fiancée', while in reality sleeping on the sofa in Nina's nursery.

She had offered to take his place but he'd refused. 'I got you into this situation, Georgie, the least I can offer you is a comfortable bed,' he'd said.

There'd been no more kissing, touching or flirting when they'd been alone together. At her request. Back to no touching. *Just friends.* It was simply too difficult to deal with the sensations and emotions physical contact aroused. And they'd kept the public displays of affection muted in front of Jackie and Dave. Even if they'd been engaged for real, she and Wil had agreed, they wouldn't be getting passionate in front of his parents anyway.

It was still very early but Jackie and Dave had left

with Wil while it was still dark. They were booked on a crack-of-dawn flight to Italy from Sydney's Kingsford Smith airport. A sleepy Nina had been bundled into her car seat to go with her father and grandparents on the trip out to the airport. Her grandparents had wanted to enjoy the company of their newly discovered baby grand-daughter for as long as possible.

Georgia had been invited to go with them in Wil's car, but she'd demurred. Instead she'd waved them off and then crawled back into bed. She'd thought it important that the family spend some time alone together without the fake fiancée present. Now, more than ever, she re-alised how very important his parents were to Wil. She'd never got around to kissing their feet, but the sentiment was still there. If Wil ever did marry again, Jackie and Dave would make marvellous parents-in-law. *But not for her.*

Ned was important to Wil too. She'd finally met Wil's older brother on Tuesday at Nina's christening. Ned and his cousin Erin, also a farmer, had flown up from Albury to be godfather and godmother. Ned was like his father with the same colouring and broad shoulders but with more of his mother's energy. Afterwards, at the chris-tening lunch at a beachside restaurant in Manly, Geor-gia had enjoyed talking horses with him and Erin and heard more about Five and a Half Mile Creek. She'd felt a curious sense of loss as she'd realised she would most likely never get the chance to visit the historic property. Now she knew why Wil had kept her from visiting: she might have discovered the secrets of his childhood he had so successfully kept hidden from his Sydney friends.

The christening had gone off like a charm—friendly, intimate and with Nina on her best baby behaviour. The only thing Georgia had felt uncomfortable about was Jackie's insistence that she hold Nina through most of the ceremony. There had been constant well-meant comments on how quickly Nina had taken to her stepmother-to-be. She knew Nina was too young to understand, but she'd felt as if she were deceiving her too.

On the Monday, Jackie had insisted on taking her on a 'girlie' shopping trip to the posh shops in Mosman to buy her a new dress and hat for the christening. Never had Georgia felt more guilty about the fake engagement than when she'd had to gracefully accept the beautiful, flowing tea dress in a gorgeous muted floral in shades of orange, pink and cream and an elegant wide-brimmed cream straw hat. She'd never be able to wear the outfit again, of course. It was finery bought for a future daughter-in-law, not a fraudulent fiancée.

She got out of bed, slipped on her wrap and padded down the corridor, the marble floor cool beneath her bare feet. The door to the room that would now be hers was open, and she popped her head around it. The room was stylishly decorated in up-to-date shades of duck-egg blue and white. The bed had been stripped and the en suite bathroom cleared of towels. Wil had told her the housekeeper would get the room ready for her to move into tonight. She was glad. It was too unsettling to continue to sleep in Wil's bed.

Instead of drowsing off, she'd spent way too much time wondering what it would be like if Wil were between the linen sheets with her. *Wishing* he were there with her. Putting her hand on the pillow and fantasising his dark head lay there beside hers. Who could blame her for such imaginings, after those passionate kisses? And his seductive talk of mind-blowing sex? She had no doubt making love with Wil would indeed be mind-blowing and memorable. And she had to stop wishing she could challenge him to prove it.

Now, in the kitchen, even the splash of the water pouring from the tap into a glass sounded loud in the silent stillness of the house. It seemed so empty without the visitors. Quiet without Nina. Most of all, it was lonely without Wil. She missed him, even though he'd be back home within a few hours. She put away the three coffee cups she had found washed and drained on the sink. Then stood looking at the window over the pool and to the view of the sea, at a loss of what to do.

It was her first day as a former fake fiancée. She was now back to officially being Wil's housemate and friend. She didn't know when he intended to tell his family that their 'engagement' was off. That was up to him. He'd got them into this mess and he could extricate them from it as gracefully as was possible.

The day was forecast to be a scorcher. She thought about a swim. The family—her included—had spent quite some time around the pool during their visit. No, she knew what she wanted to do in the relative cool of the morning. Ride Sultan.

She went back to Wil's room and moved her stuff into 'her' room, which took all of a few minutes, got into her riding gear and headed on down to the stables.

The stable hand Wil employed was there to help her saddle up. So was the ginger cat, who wound himself around her legs and demanded attention. Georgia normally wouldn't choose to ride by herself. But she knew she wouldn't be alone on the bushland trails that adjoined Wil's property. She wouldn't be the only horse lover with the idea of getting out early before the heat of the day set in.

Sultan whickered to her as she approached him in his stable. Whether he was pleased to see her or the carrot she had for him, she didn't know or care. He was a magnificent boy and she told him so as he munched messily on his treat. She'd ridden him on Sunday, putting him through his paces on the sand arena under Wil's watchful eye. Despite his haughty, aristocratic good looks, Sultan had a sweet nature and was impeccably well trained. She'd felt immediately at home on his back. 'He's perfect for you,' Wil had said. 'Ride him whenever you want.'

Once in the saddle, Georgia urged the horse forward with a nudge of her heels. She couldn't imagine a better place to live than here. Lucky, lucky Wil. And lucky her to be sharing it with him for the next two weeks.

From where he stood outside the stables, with Nina in her stroller, Wil watched as Georgia cantered Sultan up the final stretch of the trail and slowed him to a walk as they approached the gate to his property. She reached down to pat Sultan on the neck and Wil knew she was thanking the horse for the ride. Ever since he had first known her, she had always thanked her mount. She loved and respected horses as much as he did. Even if she hadn't left a note in the family room telling him where she'd gone, he'd known she would have gravitated to the stables.

He had always admired how Georgia looked on horseback. She looked particularly good on his big gelding, horse and rider well matched in terms of skill and temperament. As she neared the stable, she dismounted in one graceful, fluid movement and led Sultan by his bridle towards the bay. She handed him to his very competent stable hand, who would wash Sultan down, feed him, rug him in a summer sheet and turn him out to pasture.

As he had done so many times over the years, Wil admired how hot Georgia looked in form-fitting cream breeches, shiny high black boots and a plain white polo-style shirt. It was a sexier look than the skimpiest of provocative dresses. Although Georgia had certainly looked beautiful in the dress she'd worn to the christening—elegant and very feminine. She'd been more of a tomboy when he had first known her and he'd rarely seen her out of jeans and riding gear. He liked both her looks. And had spent a disproportionate amount of time wondering what she actually did wear to bed.

Now she took off her protective helmet and shook her hair free. It fell around her shoulders, glossy in the morning sun. Her face was flushed with a fine sheen of healthy perspiration, her eyes shining with the exhilaration that came after an energetic and enjoyable ride. She looked up and caught his eye. He was treated to the full radiance of her smile.

'Wil,' she said, making the sound of his name like a caress. 'You're back. And Nina too.' She put down her helmet and walked towards him. He went to hug her and then remembered he shouldn't. That the 'no touching' rule was back in place. 'Not a good idea,' she said. 'Besides, I'm sticky—it's getting really hot.'

She squatted down to Nina's level in her buggy. 'Good morning, Miss Nina. Did you have a fun trip to the airport? Did Daddy show you some planes taking off?'

Nina chortled and made baby noises that sounded happy, waving her little arms around. His daughter seemed excited to see Georgia. But that equally might have been excitement at seeing the horse or the ginger cat that had appeared at the sound of Georgia's voice.

'She was fascinated by everything at the airport,' he said. 'Looking around her, taking everything in, not in the slightest bit intimidated by the noise and the activity.'

'You might enjoy travelling, Nina, like your nana and granddad,' Georgia said to Nina. He liked the way she spoke to her, not using baby talk and over-the-top endearments. 'Don't worry, you'll see them again before too long. In the meantime, Daddy and I will do our best to keep you entertained.'

She straightened up to face him. 'Sultan was magnificent,' she said. 'We had a really good trail ride. Your stable hand gave me some advice on which way to go. I met one of your neighbours on the trail and asked him could we ride on the beaches anywhere around here. He said not any more, which is a shame.'

He? Wil felt a surge of jealousy at the thought of Georgia chatting with some good-looking guy on horseback. She was *his*. Jealousy was something new to him when it came to Georgia, born after he'd held her in his arms and kissed her. He dismissed the thought as irrational. She was *his* as in *his friend*. And that didn't preclude her from meeting another guy, dating another guy, even marrying another guy when she found her head-over-heels person who would give her the love and commitment she craved. When that time came he would have to grit his teeth and— He scowled as though a cloud had scudded overhead and blocked the sunlight from the glorious day.

'You okay, Wil?' Georgia said, head tilted.

'Absolutely fine,' he said. 'Thinking about breakfast. I'm hungry. Have you eaten?'

'No,' she said. 'What about Nina?'

'She enjoyed a hearty meal of puréed oatmeal and peach.'

'Nice breakfast. I could do breakfast for us both if you'd like,' she said. 'Maybe a grown-up version of Nina's—muesli and yogurt with fruit? Eggs?'

'I'll gladly accept that offer. You know I'm not much of a cook.' He ate out or ordered in all but the most basic of meals.

He had assumed they would have meals together while they were living under the same roof. Maybe platonic housemates didn't do that. He'd never shared his living space with a housemate to know what behaviour was expected. After being in residential care and then boarding school, he liked his privacy and would pay to maintain it. Georgia, however, could invade his privacy all she liked.

He made his voice sound casual, nonchalant. 'The neighbour you spoke to. Who was he?'

'I didn't get his name. An older man. Very pleasant. On a handsome chestnut stock horse. He told me this whole area had been rezoned and was up for massive redevelopment.' The older guy didn't sound like someone he needed to worry about. Georgia had been more interested in his horse.

'That's true,' he said. 'But I won't be breaking my land up into housing plots. I like it just the way it is.' This property had already experienced a huge increase in value, which was gratifying. Building wealth was important to him, not just for the comforts, but for the security it brought with it. Even though he never had to work again if he didn't want to.

'That's a relief to hear,' she said. 'Your place is heaven, Wil. You must never want to leave it.'

'When I move some of the work operations home, I

won't have to,' he said. 'However, I'll still have to travel and hold client meetings in the city office. That's when I'll have to seriously consider employing a nanny.'

'In the meantime you and Nina have me to help,' she said. 'You know, when I was out riding, I was wishing you were with me on Calypso. I realised we were only able to ride together on Sunday because your parents had Nina. We'll have to ride on our own as one of us will have to be looking after Nina.'

'I realised that too,' he said. 'This has really been a crash course in parenting for me, and I'm not anywhere through it yet. Having you here is such a help.'

'As I said, I'm no baby expert. But we can muddle through together like real parents have to learn to, I guess.' *Parents.* Nina only had one parent. Georgia was— what had she called herself?—a *surrogate aunt.*

'When she's older, Nina can ride out with us.' Georgia paused. 'That is, if I'm still coming to visit.'

Her words left so much unspoken. Such as by then she might have a family of her own, and no time or inclination to ride with her old friend. Or a husband like Toby who wouldn't appreciate their friendship.

And him? No action on his part would stop her from visiting him here. He point blank wouldn't get involved with a woman who couldn't deal with his friendship with Georgia. No other woman could be as important to him as Georgia. The realisation hit him with the force of a rearing stallion kicking him in the chest. He didn't want another woman. He wanted Georgia. He cared for her. *There could be no other woman for him.*

'I hope you'll always be coming to visit,' he managed to choke out.

'I hope so too.' She smiled but it was a dimmer version of the high-wattage Georgia smile. Did that sadness in her eyes mean she was envisaging a future that didn't include him in it, even as a friend? *He couldn't bear that.*

Wil cleared his throat. His thoughts were twisting around in a vortex. 'What are your plans for today?' he said casually, as a housemate might.

'After breakfast I really have to catch up on some work. It's been wonderful having your parents here and all the excitement of the christening. But I want to enjoy finishing the illustrations, not rushing them so they become a chore.'

'What's your first book about?' he asked, genuinely interested.

'It's a picture book for very young children, early readers. About a little pink tree frog living in the Queensland rainforest where all the other tree frogs are green.'

'That sounds fun,' he said. 'Cute. I like frogs.'

'It's got a message about ecology, but mainly about friendship and inclusion. And yes, it is fun. I wrote it in rhyming verse. The language is quite rhythmical and I hope kids might clap along to it.'

'I'm sure it's brilliant. You created it. That's guarantee enough. Of course, I'll buy a copy for Nina and ask you to sign it.'

She beamed, the full wattage Georgia smile. 'It will be my pleasure to give you one of my advance copies for Nina.'

'You know you said you were proud of me? Let me return the compliment. I'm really proud of you, Georgie. I don't know much about publishing but I know it's a real achievement to have a book published that you've both written and illustrated.'

'Thank you,' she said, looking pleased.

The cat had come to sit by the buggy, much to Nina's delight. It kept a safe distance from Nina's grabby little hands.

'What's the story you're working on now?' Wil asked Georgia.

'A companion book about a lizard. Don't laugh. It's a very cute lizard.'

'Why would I laugh?' he said. 'I'm agog with admiration at your talent. Do you see your books as a possible future career?'

'It's my dream. I have so many more ideas bursting to see the light. Which is why I'd like to sit down with you over breakfast and plan just how we're going to manage our time between our respective work and caring for Nina while I'm staying here. I have to earn my rent and horse-riding as per our agreement. But I also have to have some uninterrupted time for work.'

'You mean draw up a roster? Day to day, hour to hour?'

'That's not a bad idea,' she said. 'But can we make it flexible enough, not just to account for a baby's unpredictable behaviour, but also so we can enjoy this good weather in your spectacular home? The house that isn't just a house but, as you said, our own private resort.'

'I want to do whatever makes you happy,' he said. 'And Nina.' He meant that to the core of his soul—and he wasn't referring to the roster.

'And you too, Wil,' she said.

He knew exactly what would make him happy about having Georgia in his house. The schedule would include provision for very adult and pleasurable recreational activities for him and Georgia to enjoy. All when his sweet daughter was asleep.

Now was perhaps not the time to discuss those activities in detail with her. A change in the nature of their relationship. It was not the type of conversation that could easily be scheduled. Push her for more than she was ready to give and he could lose her from his life altogether.

CHAPTER THIRTEEN

MID-MORNING, ONE WEEK LATER, Georgia sat cross-legged on the floor in Wil's family room, close to Nina, who was on her padded pink play mat surrounded by toys. The baby's already extensive collection had been added to by her doting and generous grandparents. She was playing gleefully with a soft toy hammer that sounded snatches of music when she gripped it to bang on her rainbow-coloured plush building blocks. Nina's play time with the hammer was limited as the sound eventually drove adults crazy. Right now it was making Georgia laugh. And when Georgia laughed, Nina responded with her utterly adorable baby chuckle.

While Nina was playing, Georgia was sketching her favourite new subject—Nina. She'd filled page after page, capturing moments with Nina with her cap of dark hair, ever-changing expressions, sweet little feet and hands. Nina awake, Nina asleep, Nina laughing. Even in the two weeks since she'd first met her, Wil's daughter had changed and grown. Georgia found it fascinating to observe. Felt proud of Nina's every little milestone achieved. She knew all the milestones to expect, as Wil was an expert from his internet parenting research. He could quote them verbatim.

Georgia put down her pencil and had one of the conversations she so enjoyed with Nina, with her speaking in full sentences and Nina replying with babble that sounded like speech but didn't yet make sense.

Accepting Wil's invitation had been such a good move. Georgia couldn't remember when she had felt happier. She had the run of Wil's fabulous house and grounds. She was well ahead on her book illustrations and inspired daily by the beautiful surroundings of Wil's property and the adjacent bushland.

Then there was Wil.

And the bittersweet edge to her happiness.

She'd known Wil for eight years—minus the two when he'd been off-limits to her—and thought she'd known him well. She'd liked him a lot. Respected him. Laughed with him. Thought he was a good person—one of the best. All the while fighting her attraction to him. Then when they'd reconnected, he'd shared with her the secrets in his past that had shaped him, and she'd understood him on a deeper level.

But *this*. Living with him day to day. This was getting to know him on a whole new level. Discovering his strengths, his habits and quirks. All endearing in their own way—because they were particular to Wil. She loved being so close to him, sharing with him the everyday life of a newly fledged single dad getting to know and care for his daughter.

She appreciated how considerate he was to both her and Nina. Admired how he treated his staff with respect. Discovered that they were both morning people. Found he always picked the 'twist' when they watched crime shows on television but didn't ruin it for her, just gloated afterwards that he'd been right. Noticed how he poured her favourite drink without her ever having to ask him. Wondered why he picked out every piece of red pepper from his salad or pasta sauce. Recognised he got 'hangry' if he went too long without food. Noticed he walked along the beach with her and Nina, but never went in the surf. Speculated on why he never, ever rinsed out his coffee cup so stains didn't set on the expensive Italian porcelain. Smiled that he didn't care if he wore odd socks.

She'd got to know him so much better.

And to care for him way too much.

At the sound of the sliding door to the back deck, she looked up. And dropped her sketchbook. The pages splayed open, pencil strokes and shading possibly smudged. But she didn't even look down at the book, let alone do anything to protect her precious work. Her entire attention was focused on Wil. Her heart started to hammer.

Wil was clad in nothing but his black swim shorts, his body slick with water, his hair damp to his head. He had a black-and-white-striped towel slung around his shoulders but it did nothing to disguise the power of his muscular arms and chest, the defined hardness of his six-pack, his long strong legs. *Turn around so I can admire your gorgeous butt*, she silently willed him. But was glad when he didn't. She already felt light-headed with desire. Too giddy to be able to get up from the floor. Get turned on at the sight of Wil's back view and she very well might faint from lack of oxygen.

As a man he was perfect, she thought. Not just his body. His heart, his soul, his mind. Well, nobody was perfect—not even Wil. She settled on perfectly imperfect.

'Good swim?' she asked, managing to make her voice sound halfway normal.

'Awesome,' he said.

'You were churning through the water.' She'd been keeping an eye on him through the glass doors as he did laps. He didn't like to swim alone.

'I'll head for the shower,' he said.

I'll join you there. She said it in her head. Of course she didn't dare say the provocative words out loud. No matter how much she might want to. As he headed towards the bedroom wing, she tried to force her heart-rate back to normal with a series of deep, calming breaths.

She couldn't endure this for much longer. Living with him. Wanting him. *Falling in love with him.*

She couldn't deny it to herself any longer. Her feelings went way beyond friendship. But it was futile to allow them to flourish. Nothing had changed. There was no hope that it would. She was happy here, but it was a half-life. Studiously playing at being *just friends* when the more time she spent with him, the more she knew she wanted so much more. Stay in this house for too much longer and she might one day do something foolish like follow him to the shower, slip off her shorts and cotton broderie anglaise top and join him there, let him strip her of her pink lace underwear, then wind her arms around his neck, press her naked body against his, together under the stream of water and—

The direction of her thoughts made her flush all the way down her neck. Besides, she couldn't join Wil in the shower for so many reasons. Not the least of which, she was looking after Nina. *Nina.* That was another issue.

She glanced over at where Nina was lying on her tummy on her mat, reaching out for her hammer. 'What's my darling little girl doing? That hammer is—' She stopped herself, aghast.

What had she said? Slip of the tongue. Nina wasn't *her* little girl. She buried her face in her hands when she realised something else she'd been denying—she was falling in love with Nina too. Risking her heart getting broken, not once, but twice. *How had she allowed this to happen?* All those years of resisting her attraction to Wil and now this.

With hands that weren't quite steady, she put her sketchbook back into order and tucked it under a cushion on the settee. She didn't want Wil to see her sketches of Nina just yet. They were too rough and unfinished.

By the time Wil returned to the room, thankfully her flush had faded and her heart rate was approaching normal. Only for it to accelerate at the sight of him in loose, white cotton drawstring trousers and a white vest that emphasised his muscles, played up his tanned skin and dark hair. His hair was still damp from the shower he had taken, unfortunately, alone.

She got up from the floor to greet him. Unaware of her blatant ogling, he headed for the kitchen, brought her back a tall glass of fizzy mineral water packed with ice and lime wedges. 'Just what I needed,' she said, taking it from him. She sat down on the sofa, making doubly sure the sketchbook was concealed.

'I know,' he said, his smile unleashing that devastating dimple. 'You look a little flushed. Do I need to adjust the air conditioning?'

'Er…no. I've been playing with Nina.' She made a show of pushing her hair back from her face to avoid meeting his gaze, for fear he might read the out-of-bounds thoughts she'd been having about him.

He took his favourite place on the other sofa, put his frosted iced tea on the coffee table, looked dotingly over at his mini-me daughter. 'Time to take the musical hammer away, perhaps?'

'She's tossed it out of reach. Let's hope she's tired of it.'

'No chance of an adult conversation over the sound of that thing.'

Georgia resettled herself on the sofa. 'Wil, about that. Conversation, I mean. I need to talk to you. School goes back in ten days. That means I'll be moving back to my parents' place. I think you need to start looking for a nanny. I'll be able to help you interview so we…you get the right one.'

Georgia had rarely seen Wil stuck for words. Now he seemed flabbergasted. 'This is from left field.'

'We always knew I'd only be here for the holidays,' she said gently.

'I…I can't bear to think of you leaving here. I don't want that. Nina doesn't want that.'

Georgia didn't want that. But it would be too painful to stay, continuing the act that she only cared for him as a friend, whereas she was on the edge of falling in love with him. How would she endure it if—when—he started to date again? What would she do if he brought a woman home to his bedroom? To overstay her time here could end in disaster—and the complete loss of her friendship with Wil.

'The time has gone so quickly,' he said. 'Don't be in a rush to go. Do you like it here?'

'I love it. In fact, I can't imagine a better place to live anywhere.'

'So why can't you stay?'

'What do you mean?'

'The living arrangements are working well, aren't they?'

'Yes,' she said. *Except for all the sleepless nights when I lie awake wishing I were in your bedroom with you.*

'Then why not stay on as my housemate? Indefinitely, I mean.'

Georgia hadn't been hoping for anything more romantic. Of course she hadn't. Wil had made it very clear he couldn't promise commitment. She had made it clear that both for her and Nina's sakes, she couldn't settle for anything less. She was cranky at herself for feeling so deflated. Hadn't she herself pointed out that their stars would never align?

'It wouldn't work, Wil. I teach at North Sydney. It's quite a long trek from here in peak-hour traffic. Besides, theoretically I'm a housemate. But in reality this is your house, your rules. Really, I'm just a guest. I need my independence, my own place—even if it's a room in my childhood home—my own life.' *My own man.* Her heart gave a painful lurch at that thought. She didn't want another man. She wanted Wil.

If she and Wil had never hugged, had never kissed, had never flirted about the possibilities of mind-blowing sex, she might have agreed to extend their housemate situation into the school term after she went back to work. But they had and the dynamic of their friendship had changed irrevocably.

'We could make it work,' he said.

'How? The reason I'm here is to help you with Nina. I'll be at school all day. How could that work?'

'I could hire a nanny for when I had to work, and you could help with Nina after you get home. You'd have the school holidays, too.'

'What if I want to go out after work? Or go away on the holidays? I'm already planning to go to Greece in the midwinter break. I need my own life, remember? I have to move on.'

'We must be able to reach a compromise.' He paused. 'Nina would really miss you. Sultan and Calypso would miss you. That orange cat would miss you.'

'And you, Wil?' She tried to make her voice light-hearted but it betrayed her by breaking. 'Would you miss me?'

He scowled his darkest Wil scowl. 'Do you have to ask that? Of course I'd miss you. Georgie, I want—'

Whatever he was going to say, she didn't hear it for the sudden chimes of music emanating from Nina's hammer. Georgia immediately glanced over to her charge; Wil did the same. Then he looked back to her. 'Nina got the hammer by herself,' he said.

Georgia jumped up from the sofa and clapped her hands. 'She crawled to get it by herself. On her belly and not very elegantly. But she crawled for the first time! Now she's off again. Look at her go. Oh, clever girl. She's going to be an athlete when she grows up. Where's the camera?'

'My phone is on the countertop.' Wil got up to get it. 'Another milestone to check off the list.'

'And many more to come. I'm so proud of her.'

Wil looked down at her. 'You care about Nina, don't you?'

There was little point in hiding the truth. 'Yes. I do. More than I could ever have imagined I would, even though I tried not to get attached.'

She thought back to what Jackie had said. That she would grow to love Nina because she was part of Wil.

There was that. But it was more. Nina was a little person in her own right, with her own personality, quite independently of Wil. Georgia had come to care for her because she was Nina, not just because she was Wil's daughter. She wanted to be around to see her develop into a toddler right up to the teenager Wil joked about and beyond. To celebrate the milestones with Nina as someone important to her. Not just someone on her periphery. The idea of being her stepmother didn't seem as scary as it had.

Jackie's words came back to her. *'Because you love Wil, you'll learn to love and cherish his daughter.'* Had Jackie seen what she couldn't see for herself? She wasn't *falling* in love with Wil, something she could stop. She was already head over heels in love with her best friend. Totally and irrevocably.

Wil took photos and video of his daughter from every angle, urged on by a delighted Georgia. While pleased about his Nina's new mobility, he was more excited by what he'd seen in Georgia's eyes when she was watching Nina. Something that could change the course of their misaligned stars. Because he didn't really want a nanny for Nina. He wanted a mother.

And for himself?

He wanted Georgia.

Since she had moved in, this big, expensive house had become a home. A home full of the spirit, energy and generous heart of this beautiful person. All these years, she had been there right under his nose masquerading as his friend. When all along she had been his ideal woman. Deep down, he thought he'd always had an inkling that Georgia was 'The One'. Yet he'd resisted it, knowing he wasn't ready, promising himself *one day*.

That one day had crept up on him. This time, he was not going to easily let her go. Problem identified. Solution in progress. Plan of action to be determined. Pronto.

'Let me get a shot of you with Nina,' he said. 'I think she might have had enough of crawling.'

Her hands went to her head. 'My hair. It's a mess. The humidity.' Her hair had indeed gone off in all wavy directions. But he liked it. Ached to run his fingers through it, gently tug on it to tilt her head back for his kiss. This last week of the 'no touch' rule had been hell. If he had his way, that was about to change.

'Your hair looks great. It always looks great. *You* always look great.' She looked particularly good today in denim shorts and a peach-coloured blouse in that cotton lace stuff with tiny holes in it. There was a smear on the shoulder that looked like puréed carrot transferred by tiny fingers, but he didn't have the heart to tell Georgia. After all, the colour sort of coordinated.

She flushed and looked pleased. Did he pay her enough compliments? Did she even realise that the friend-zone barriers were crumbling?

Georgia bent down to pick Nina up. Wil shot off a series of candid photos as she dropped a kiss on his daughter's downy little head without seeming to realise she was doing so, it had become so automatic when she was with Nina, before folding her into her arms. A huge surge of emotion swept over him at just how right his two favourite people looked together. No one seeing them together would disbelieve that Nina could belong to Georgia as much as to him. That they could be a real family. *His* family.

He'd never been one to curse and rail against the misery and injustice of his childhood. Resilience and sheer determination not to allow himself to be broken had seen him through. Then he'd hit the adoption jackpot with parents like Jackie and Dave, so how could he regret the rest? But those years in care, when survival was all he'd had on his mind, had stifled his ability to dream. Now, he found himself believing that finally the richness of the life that stretched ahead of him could make up for the aridity of the past. When Georgia suggested a selfie of the three of them, he had to swallow hard before he could manage a cheerful reply. But it wasn't difficult to smile for the camera when he had his arm holding both Georgia and Nina close. He dared to dream that both of them were his.

All the excitement inevitably ended in tears from an exhausted and over-stimulated Nina. Georgia was rostered on baby duty and while Wil got Nina's bottle ready, Georgia was the one who gave it to her then took her to the nursery to settle her for her second nap of the day. Wil left her to it. He needed some time alone to strategise.

By the time Georgia came back—wearing a snug-fitting, clean white top that made no secret of the shape of her breasts—he was ready.

'She's out like a light,' she said.

'There's some stuff from the gourmet deli in the fridge for lunch, if you'd like to join me.' He tried to act like a housemate and not assume they would always eat together. Even though they'd shared every meal since Georgia had got here. He didn't want to be guilty of taking her company for granted. Far from it.

'Sounds good,' she said. 'But first, we really need to continue our discussion.'

'We do,' he said. 'I have a plan.' He looked down into her face. Knew he had to choose his words carefully. She might need convincing. He didn't want to scare her off. Not when he wanted this so very much.

She raised her eyebrows. 'Really? So quickly? I'm all ears.'

'I think we should get married,' he said.

CHAPTER FOURTEEN

GEORGIA STARED UP at Wil. She felt the colour drain from her face and her mouth went dry. Her heart tripped into an erratic beating of anticipation. 'Wil, did you just propose to me?'

'It makes sense, doesn't it?' he said. 'That we get married, I mean. Checks all the boxes, in fact.'

'Boxes?' she said. She suspected that didn't include the type of tiny velvet box in which nestled a glittering engagement ring. Her heart commenced a slow, disappointed sinking from the heights of elation to which it had soared.

'We get on so well,' he said. 'You're my best friend. You like living here, I like having you here. You're the perfect mother for Nina. My family all think we're engaged already so we'd be continuing as expected.'

Her heart sank even further. She put up her hand. Noticed it trembled. 'Wait. You're proposing a fake marriage following on from our fake engagement?'

'Hell, no. I'm talking a real marriage. In every way. I think we both know we'd be okay in that, uh, department.'

Who was this person? So sober and stilted and totally lacking in spontaneity. *Where was Wil?* 'You mean, to be specific, in the mind-blowing sex department?'

'Exactly,' he said, without a hint of his devastating dimple.

Georgia waited for him to take her in his arms, to kiss her senseless and let her know exactly what she had to look forward to in her marriage bed. If that was indeed what he meant.

'Anything else to add? Another box?' *Had someone put him up to this?*

'It goes without saying that as, uh, my wife you'd be totally financially secure. You can be sure of that.'

'You're talking a pre-nuptial agreement?'

'Only if you want one. I trust you.'

Trust. What about *love*?

Her disappointment was so intense it threatened to choke her. 'You sound like you're setting out a business proposal. Not a proposal of marriage.'

'Does it sound like that? I didn't want you to think this was a hastily constructed response to you wanting to move out. That it wasn't a genuine offer.'

'It's all very convenient, isn't it?' she said, trying to keep the edge of bitter disappointment from her voice, not sure she succeeded. 'Long-time schoolteacher friend slots in as mother for your child. The child you only recently acquired. It's like insta-family. Just add wife. Even more convenient as your parents approve. My parents would too, by the way. Everyone would be congratulating you on your excellent decision to secure me.' *Good old Georgia to the rescue—a lifetime of rescue.*

'I wouldn't put it like that,' he said with something like alarm in his eyes.

'How would you put it?' she said.

'That it would be a very good idea for you to marry me. For all concerned.'

Tell me you love me, Wil. Tell me you love me and I'll say yes.

But he didn't.

She took a deep, steadying breath that didn't do much to take the wobble out of her voice. 'In that case, I must respectfully decline your proposal.'

He stared at her for a long moment. She wasn't sure how to read the expression on his face. Disbelief. Disappointment. Surely not anguish.

'You're saying no,' he said.

'Yes. I mean *no*. I'm saying I don't think marriage to me is the solution to your problems.'

If only it could have been different.

She knew by saying no, she was waving goodbye to not only sharing her life with the man she loved, but also any hope of an ongoing friendship with him. How could they come back from this? All the ease that had marked their friendship would be gone for ever. She knew only too well how a man behaved towards a woman who had turned down his proposal.

Wil furrowed his brow. 'I can't change your mind? Georgie, I think we'd have a great life if we got married. We'd be happy. Think of the fun we could have. You. Me. Nina. The horses.'

Just tell me you love me.

Crickets.

Georgia sighed. You couldn't force a person to love you. If she pursued the issue, of course he would parrot the words she wanted to hear, to get what he wanted. A convenient wife and a mother for Nina. But she wanted the real thing. One hundred per cent. Not second best. Not second thoughts. That was all she'd ever wanted.

Georgia, who should have been George, was never going to settle for less.

'Wil, I'm sorry I can't give you the answer you want. It would have solved a lot of problems.' She gave a short, mirthless laugh. 'Not the least of which would be somewhere for me to live.'

'But you have a home here.'

'That's kind of you, but you know I can't stay. Not even until the start of term. I'm sorry to leave you in the lurch with Nina. But I actually think it's best for me to leave now.'

He caught her arm with his hand. She stilled. 'Don't go like this,' he said.

Don't propose like this, she thought. *Take me in your arms, tell me you love me and I'll stay.*

When she didn't reply, he dropped his hand from her arm.

'I'm not going to pack my bags and make the big dramatic exit,' she said, looking at a slight discolouration in the marble tile of the floor, ironically in the shape of a heart. If she met his gaze, she knew she would cry. 'But I don't think I should stay here tonight. It would be too awkward. I'm going to check in to a hotel. The big one by the beach in Manly if I can get a room. Give us some space. Then come back for my stuff tomorrow. And to say goodbye to Nina.' The thought of losing Nina from her life made her want to double over with pain.

Her parents' house was not an option. She couldn't endure the questions and demands for explanations. And the good friends she could have called on for a spot on their sofas were all away for the holidays.

'Nobody is asking you to go, Georgie.' There was such an edge of sadness to his voice that for a moment she wondered should she reconsider. Give up her dream of reciprocal head-over-heels love to accept what Wil was offering. But she would never be happy with compromising her heart.

'It's my choice. No hard feelings, Wil.'

She couldn't, wouldn't, kiss him goodbye. That would be just too painful. Not when she yearned for so much more from him. 'I'll let myself out,' she said as she turned and headed to her room to pack an overnight bag.

Wil followed Georgia to the front door, despite her refusal of his offer to carry her backpack to the car. She didn't say anything as she walked out; he raised his hand in farewell. He stood behind the solidly closed doors, heard her car take off down the driveway, the skid on the gravel when she stopped for the gates, the clang of the gates closing behind her.

Feeling as if he were pushing his way through fog, he made his way to the family room. The empty room where such a short time ago, in what already seemed another world, her laughter had pealed around the walls.

He heard a scratching sound, turned to see the ginger cat with its paw plaintively up against the outside of the glass sliding door. Looking for Georgia. The cat had never come up to the house before. But it knew, in that instinctive way of animals, that she had gone. 'Sorry, mate, she's abandoned us all,' Wil said.

Then slammed his hand on the back of the sofa so hard the pain jarred all the way up his arm. He cursed long and hard and viciously, his anger aimed at himself.

He had completely stuffed up the proposal that was meant to secure Georgia as his wife. It was as if his brain had planned to say one thing, his mouth had decided on a different pathway. He had wanted to tell Georgia how much she meant to him, how happy he would be if she would share her life with him. Instead he had blurted out a business proposal. All the solution on offer without any of the joy. Without any of the *love*.

No wonder his beloved friend had looked at him as if he were a stranger. No wonder he had lost her.

Did his inability to express what he really felt, how much he loved her, track back to his blighted childhood where to show love was to risk showing weakness that could be exploited? Had he got so good at wearing the mask of indifference he couldn't rip it off? That was no excuse. He was an adult now. He knew better.

Wil slammed the back of the sofa again. In doing so, he dislodged something hidden under one of the cushions. Georgia's sketchbook. She always snapped it shut when he came near. He'd teased her about what she could possibly have to hide about her lizard.

The book had fallen open when it had been dislodged. Not a drawing of a lizard but an exquisite sketch of Nina's face in repose. So skilfully rendered, it brought his daughter to life on the paper. Beautiful. Innocent. Precious. He stared at the front of the book and flicked through every page. All drawings of Nina. Some of the images weren't finished, as if Georgia had been interrupted or Nina had demanded her attention. He stopped on a sketch of him looking down into Nina's face and her looking up at him. Just like the moment when he had recognised his mama in his baby's eyes and Nina had seemed to recognise him. It made the hairs on the back of his neck stand up. This had been drawn with compassion and love. For Nina. For *him*.

He'd made such a terrible mistake. Let something of

inestimable value slip through his fingers. *The woman he loved.* And who might love him. When he'd suggested marriage, he'd hoped she would learn to love him. This picture gave him hope.

He had to go find her. Bare his heart to her. Get right back into grovelling mode and grovel for his life. Carefully, he put Georgia's sketchbook back under the cushion. Then stopped as he heard the front door open and close, and Georgia's footsteps—already so familiar—tap their way down the hallway towards him.

Georgia had barely got to the end of Wil's street when she had realised she had to turn back. *Wil was her friend.* She couldn't leave him like that, with pain and bewilderment in his eyes. Not after all the awful things that had happened to him in his life. The people who had let him down. In that tall, powerfully built, successful wealthy man was still the soul of the five-year-old boy on the beach, the thirteen-year-old white knight who'd saved the damsel in distress and been thrown into a dungeon for his pains.

All that time he'd been checking off the boxes, she'd been silently urging him to tell her he loved her. But she hadn't said a word about love. She'd been knocked for six by his sudden suggestion of marriage—she really couldn't call it a proposal—but couldn't she have come out and said, *What about love, Wil?* Instead of *thinking* it and expecting him to read her mind?

She was going to march down that hallway and tell him how she felt about him, and how she wished he felt about her. If she didn't like what she heard in response, at least she would have tried and could walk away without regrets.

Then he was there, in front of her. 'You came back,' he said hoarsely. 'I was about to set off to find you.'

He held out his arms and she didn't hesitate to go into them. *Wil.* As she snuggled in against his chest, her head against his shoulder and his arms tight around her, she felt as if she was coming home. She stood there for what seemed like an age, eyes closed in sheer relief, breathing in the intoxicating, familiar scent of him, rejoicing that she was there, *loving him.*

Finally, when she could feel the tension between them ease, the relief that they had found each other, she pulled back. Resting against the circle of his arms, she looked up at his face. He smiled and she smiled back.

'Remember how we sorted out our last problem? About me moving here, I mean?' she said. 'Perhaps we could try that again.'

'You mean, you tell me I need to tell you how much I love you?' he said.

'Sounds like a plan,' she said with a slow smile and a heart soaring to elation from the unfathomable depths to which it had plunged.

'Then I say, "Georgia, I love you. I've always loved you, since the moment I saw you standing there in the university quadrangle, stamping your foot because there wasn't an equestrian club."'

She reached up and kissed him on the mouth. 'Really? That far back? Was I truly stamping my foot?'

'With your dainty riding boot.'

'I'm not sure I believe you. About the boot, I mean. But I'll take the way-back-then love.'

He laughed and she delighted in the sound of it. Wil deserved so much laughter in his life.

'Now let me continue,' she said. 'Then I tell you, that

all I want is to be head over heels in love with the man I marry.'

'And then I ask you, "Georgia, are you head over heels in love with me?"' Wil's tone was light-hearted, in keeping with their game, but his eyes told her that her answer was important.

'And I say…' Her voice started to break and she had to swallow the lump in her throat before she could continue. 'I say, yes. I am totally head over heels in love with you, Wil Hudson. And I'm glad. You see, I was beginning to worry that I couldn't love, that I was incapable of loving a man. Now I realise it's because of you. *It was always you.* I couldn't love another man because there wasn't room in my heart. It was already full of love for you. I just didn't recognise it.'

This time he kissed her, a passionate possession of her mouth. The kiss was long and sweet and full of promise. Finally they came up for breath. Wil was first to speak. 'Now you pose the question to me: is my love for you the head-over-heels kind? The kind where I pick you up and whirl you round and declare myself?'

'Well, are you? Will you? Do the whirl thing, I mean?'

Wil didn't reply, but rather put his hands around her waist, picked her up and whirled her around the room until she was breathless and laughing. 'I'm head over heels, crazy in love with you, Georgia Lang. Will you marry me?'

She didn't hesitate. 'Yes, Wil, yes. I will marry you.' She wasn't sure whether she was giddy from the whirling, or delirious with joy. Then she got a little more giddy from the passion of Wil's kiss as he held her tight.

'Now for the ring,' he said. 'A proper head-over-heels-type proposal of marriage is always accompanied by a ring.'

'You wouldn't have had time to buy a ring and I wouldn't expect—'

He pulled out a little black velvet box from the side pocket of his trousers. Then flipped open the lid to reveal an exquisite vintage emerald and diamond ring.

Georgia gasped. 'Your grandmother's ring. But how—?'

'Ned brought it up with him from Five and a Half Mile Creek. Gave it to me at the christening.'

'You didn't say anything.'

'I was waiting for the right moment. Do you like it? If not, I can get you another ring more to your taste. Or we can have the stones remodelled into something more contemporary.'

'I love it just the way it is. It's utterly perfect. And I love what it represents too. The love of your family for you.'

Wil took her left hand. 'I wonder will it fit?' He slid it onto her third finger. 'Yes. Perfectly. Meant to be. Good karma, remember.'

Georgia splayed her hand and held it away from her to admire her engagement ring, the way it caught the light and glittered. She sighed from sheer joy. 'I never want to take it off.'

'What do you think of an Easter wedding at Five and a Half Mile Creek?'

She looked up to his beloved face. 'Perfect. Thank you, Wil. Thank you for everything. Thank you for Nina. I love her too, as if I had borne her. And I promise to always be a good mother to her.'

'I know you will,' he said. 'And to any sisters or brothers we might give her.'

She kissed him for that. A kiss of affirmation that rapidly escalated into something more insistent that sent desire throbbing through her. 'Wil, about that mind-blowing sex?'

'Yes,' he said, nuzzling her neck so she murmured in pleasure.

'Your room or mine?'

'Definitely mine,' he said. 'Shall your head-over-heels husband-to-be pick you up and carry you to the bed?'

'Why not start as we mean to continue?' she said, as he lifted her up and into his arms. 'With love and passion and a whole lot of fun.'

'I'm looking forward to marrying my best friend,' he said.

'Me too,' she said. 'Friend, lover, husband.'

'Put *adoring* in front of those and you have me to a tee,' he said with a dimple-revealing grin.

She smiled. 'We're going to have such a wonderful life together.'

'Count on it,' he said.

* * * * *

THE SERGEANT'S UNEXPECTED FAMILY

CARRIE NICHOLS

This story is dedicated to my late big brother, Norman, who was an avid amateur astronomer and teller of amusing stories.

Acknowledgments

I want to thank Dr. Warwick Dell of First Sight Hixson for returning my call and patiently answering my questions on CRVO. Any errors or misconceptions are entirely my own.

Chapter One

"If you're going to nag me, you're gonna have to marry me." Former army sergeant Brody Wilson heaved an exasperated sigh and propped his hands on the polished wooden counter of Loon Lake General Store.

From the other side, seventysomething Octavia "Tavie" Whatley pointed a crooked, arthritic finger. "As God is my witness, you stood right there—right there on that very spot, Brody Wilson—and swore to me you'd given up those cancer sticks."

"I did." Brody blew his breath out between his lips. "I am… I will." Brody shook his head. The residents of Loon Lake might be eccentric, but they were decent, caring people, and he enjoyed living in this quaint corner of Vermont. But sometimes…

Looked as if today was turning into one of those sometimes. If he lived in a city, he'd be nameless and no one would know or care if he smoked himself to death. But damn, the woman was right, because if he lit up now, he'd be throwing thirty-two smoke-free months down the tubes. May was a tough month for him, but cigarettes wouldn't change the past, only complicate his future. Yeah, smoking was a stupid move if there ever was one; nevertheless, he glared at Tavie as if she were the one in the wrong.

"*Humph.* And don't think you can flash those pearly whites down at the Pic-N-Save to get those smitten girls to sell you any. I know their mamas." Tavie sniffed and touched her halo of teased hair as if she were in sole control of the thing that ruled a soldier's life in peacetime—the unit's training schedule.

"Aha." Tavie snapped her fingers, reached under the counter and slapped a small box on the ancient wood. "Here, try these."

Brody eyed the box with suspicion. "What are those for?"

"If'n you have to have *something* dangling outta that pretty mouth of yours," she said as she pushed the rectangular box closer, "at least give these a try. They'll hang out of your mouth just fine and won't pollute your lungs."

He picked up the mint-scented box and turned it over several times. "Toothpicks?"

She nodded once. "On the house."

"Gee, thanks." The sad part was he couldn't fault Tavie for treating him as if he didn't have enough sense to come in out of the rain. Thirty-five years old and still trying to decide what he'd do with the rest of his life. What did that say? In his glory days, he'd achieved more than most—including those smug Rangers—when he'd passed the army's rigorous physical and mental training to become a covert operator for Delta Force. That phase of his life had come to a halt two years ago, but that didn't give him an express ticket to pity town. Not when a trust fund and an army disability check eased financial concerns while he considered his options.

Tavie wore a smug smile. "Thank me in thirty years, when you're still healthy."

"You planning on being behind this counter that long?" The cellophane crinkled as Brody unwrapped a toothpick.

"And why wouldn't I?" She crossed her arms over her bosom.

He smirked and stuck the toothpick in his mouth. "Figured you and Ogle would be enjoying life in sunny Florida by then."

After leaving the army, he'd craved isolation, somewhere to lick his wounds. He'd expected to find it in rural Vermont, but it would seem the residents of Loon Lake had, at times, other ideas.

"*Pfft*, I know what you—" The ringing of Brody's cell phone interrupted her.

Saved by the bell, he dug into his pocket and pulled out the phone. "Huh."

"Who is it? I can't see." Tavie leaned over the counter and scowled at him when he held the phone out of range. "Hey, I don't get out much."

"It's the hospital, and you do just fine from behind that counter."

"Want me to call Jan to see what they want? She might—"

"Why don't I just answer…" Brody swiped his thumb across the screen. "Wilson."

"Brody? It's Jan over at Loon Lake Regional Hospital. There's a woman by the name of Mary Carter in our ER with her seven-month-old son, Elliott, and they're ready to be released."

Brody jerked his head back. What the…? He frantically searched his memory, but the names meant nothing to him. "And this concerns me…how?"

"Well…she insists you're the baby's next of kin—"

"Whoa, hold on." He turned his back on Tavie, who was craning her neck over the counter, and, if he didn't know better, he'd swear her ears had grown bigger. "Tell me how I'm supposed to be related?"

"Don't panic." Jan chuckled drily. "She listed you as the infant's uncle."

Uncle? Him? Did he even know anyone with an infant? Let alone someone who'd go as far as listing him as next of kin. "But I…"

"Paramedics say she was quite adamant about you being the baby's uncle when they brought her in."

Still trying to place the names, he took a deep breath to help counter the effects of a sudden adrenaline rush. "What happened?"

"They were involved in a chain-reaction car accident out on the state four lane."

As he listened, an image of sparkling dark eyes and long, wavy hair the color of a Guinness rose to the forefront in his memory. Mary. Yes, that was the name of the attractive woman, his brother's girlfriend, he'd met at their father's funeral. If he was her baby's uncle, how did his half brother fit into all of this? Where was Roger and why wasn't the hospital contacting him? He and Roger had been estranged for years but the thought of—

"Brody? You still there?"

His thoughts scattered at the sound of Jan's voice in his ear. "Sorry. What sort of injuries did they sustain?"

"Yeah…no. Even Tavie can't get me to break HIPAA laws," the nurse chided. "I *can* say they've been treated and are ready to be discharged. The doctor suggested

CARRIE NICHOLS

she not go home alone. He wanted a responsible party picking her up."

Brody slouched against the counter and released the breath he'd been holding. The fact Mary and her son were being released after such a short time had to be good news, even if he didn't know what any of this had to do with him. He was acutely aware of Tavie listening to his end of the conversation, so he tried to make light of this, even if it felt the opposite. "Responsible? Ha, then I guess that lets me off the hook."

"Nice try, but sorry, tag, you're it…unless of course you want me to bundle an injured woman and her poor infant into a cab and send them off to God knows where."

How did the women of Loon Lake see past the bad-ass special forces persona he'd been cultivating so people would leave him alone? He learned explaining why he'd left the army led to undeserved sympathy. The guys whose lives he'd endangered on that mission were the ones who mattered.

He sighed. Jan could've saved her manipulative breath because he was already halfway out the door. "Tell them I'll be there as soon as I can."

Mary Carter shoved her arms into the sleeves of a red plaid flannel shirt someone had scrounged up. The crisp white blouse she'd cut the price tag off this morning was now covered in blood, so a nurse had brought her a shirt from a lost and found box. Except the nurse had failed to mention Paul Bunyan had lost the shirt. Mary struggled to get her hands free of the endless sleeves so she could button the hideous thing.

"It's a bit big, but better than the one you were wearing, or going home in a disposable gown." The nurse bustled around the treatment area. "Head wounds are such notorious bleeders. On the plus side, they glued yours, so no stitches to remove."

The sleeve flopped around as Mary reached up to touch the skin glue patch above her eyebrow. Memories flashed in her mind like slides in a PowerPoint presentation. A car in front of her spinning out of control…she'd braked…swerved…had no place to go. The screeching of brakes. The crunching of metal. A crying baby. *Elliott!* She choked on the bile rising in her throat. How could she not have asked for him before this? What was wrong with her? "Please. Where's my baby?"

"I assure you, he's fine, dear." The trim fortysomething nurse, whose name tag identified her as Jan, gave Mary's hand a sympathetic squeeze. "He's charming the nurses at the triage desk."

Mary's shoulders slumped. "I don't understand why I didn't already ask you that."

"But you have, dear. Several times in fact." She squeezed Mary's hand again before letting go. "It's the concussion. Even a minor one can cause some confusion. That's why you need someone to check on you. Plus some good, old-fashioned rest."

"Concussion" explained the jackhammers in her head. "If he's not hurt, where is he? When can I see him?"

"Soon. We wanted to get you situated before we brought him in. No need to stress yourself. Elliott was snug and safe. Good job with the car seat, Mom." The nurse grinned. "Everyone here is quite taken with him. Such a doll."

It was easy for someone else to say don't stress, but at seven months, Elliott was her whole world, and she ached to hold him. "Can you bring him to me? Please."

"We'll have him brought to you in a jiff." The nurse checked her watch. "Now, let's get you ready to leave before Brody gets here."

"Brody?" Mary gasped. "You mean… Brody Wilson? He's coming here?"

"Why, yes, dear, I let him know you're being discharged," the nurse said.

"But I…" Good Lord, what had she started? She'd met Roger's half brother, Brody Wilson, once before. What would he think of her barging into his life with her son? This was not how it was supposed to go. Without any family of her own, she'd come to Loon Lake to get to know Brody, let him get to know Elliott, but not like this. Since Roger had refused to acknowledge Elliott as his son, chances were he hadn't told Brody about his nephew.

"You were very insistent when they brought you in that he be notified about Elliott."

After the accident…the police, the paramedics…the ambulance ride. She'd been petrified about Elliott's future if her injuries proved fatal, so she'd grabbed the hand of anyone close to her and insisted they tell Brody Wilson he had a nephew. She remembered wondering if fate would be so cruel as to rip her out of this world before she could introduce Brody to Elliott, before they could form a bond that would reassure her that her son would never be alone should anything happen to her.

She pivoted and swung her legs off the narrow gurney, but, still feeling a bit shaky, she remained seated, not wanting to do anything that might delay being reunited with her son.

"I'm sorry but your jeans are covered in blood." The nurse held them up, and Mary wrinkled her nose at the blood-spattered denim. The nurse laughed. "Yeah, if Brody was picking me up I'd want to look my best, too. He may be a decade and a half younger, but— Oh, dear, listen to me babbling on."

"You know Brody?"

Jan nodded. "I met Brody when he agreed to pasture my dad's old Holstein on his farm. After Dad's stroke, we sold off the herd but no one wanted Gertie. Dad had a soft spot for her and I'd heard Brody might let her stay on his farm. But enough about cows, let me see if I can find some scrub pants for you to wear."

"I'd rather you find Elliott for me." Was there something they weren't telling her?

"I will. I promise." The nurse patted her leg and gave her an appraising glance as if judging her size, then left, the curtain fluttering in her wake.

Mary straightened her shoulders and tried not to think about being in a strange place in borrowed, ill-fitting clothing. She was no longer at the mercy of others, no longer that forlorn little girl. If Brody wanted to find fault with her that was on him because all she cared about was holding her son.

But she did have to admit that Brody coming to the hospital for a virtual stranger was proof he was different from Roger. After she and Roger's breakup, acquaintances of the family had told her Brody was the most respectable one—too bad that information had come too late for her to see through Roger's charming lies.

She may have met Brody only once, but she'd witnessed his kindness firsthand. During the calling hours before his father's funeral, he'd feigned interest as a confused elderly woman clutched his arm and told him a story—for the fifth time.

Unemployment had given Mary the time to search Brody out, something she'd planned to do after she was diagnosed with a blood clot that could've killed her. Elliott had been in danger of being orphaned, as she had been. She'd had no relatives willing to take her into their home. A motherless child caseworkers had to pick up and transport to another set of frowning foster parents who couldn't see past her shyness or unfortunate overbite.

Elliott was an adorable baby and she'd been a with-drawn pre-teen. Still, she wanted Elliott to have relationships with his blood relatives and Roger had made it plain he didn't want to be a father. She backed down from requesting child support when Roger threatened to seek full custody. Call her a coward, but she could support them and wasn't taking a chance on losing Elliott. Instead, she'd conceived of a plan to seek out Elliott's uncle, possibly even finding a legal guardian in Brody Wilson, should something happen to her.

The untimely death of a colleague had convinced her not to put off finding Brody and losing her job had sealed the deal.

Sighing, she held up the jeans, sticky with blood and who knew what else, and folded them. Those were her best ones, so she would try to salvage them. A childhood spent in the foster-care system had taught her to appreciate and take care of her possessions. Maybe the nurse would come back with pants that fit better than this shirt.

Someone with a purposeful stride approached and Mary sat up straighter, pushing her shoulders back. She didn't want to give the doctor any reason to change his mind about releasing her. She ached to hold Elliott close and reassure him—and herself—everything would be okay.

Brody paused for a second outside the curtained area. Mary was calling her baby his nephew, so did that mean she was his sister-in-law? If so, where was Roger? At their father's funeral, Roger had introduced Mary, who had seemed reserved, but shyness wasn't a crime. After the brief service he'd hoped to have a word with her, but she'd disappeared, and he hadn't hung around either. What would he have said if he'd found her? Warn her against getting involved with his half brother and that nest of vipers Brody called relatives? That sort of discussion would've been in poor taste. But wasn't that an apt description for his family?

Inhaling, he pushed aside the curtain. "Mary?"

She glanced up, and her mouth dropped open.

What the...? For someone who'd insisted on contacting him, she didn't look happy to see him. "I...uh..." He waved his hand in the direction he'd come. "They said... the nurse...she said it was okay to come back here."

"Yes. I'm dressed and decent. In a broad sense of the word, anyway." She ended on a breathless laugh and tugged on the hem of a huge shirt that threatened to swallow her whole.

"I got here as soon as I could." He put her initial reaction down to embarrassment and approached the gurney where she sat, her bare, slender legs dangling off the side, her hands resting between her knees. Even in ill-fitting clothing, she made his breath hitch in his chest and had him thinking thoughts that were anything but brotherly.

She blushed, drawing his attention to a gash above her eye. Even the injury didn't detract from her beauty.

"You probably don't remember me. I didn't realize they were going to call you to pick me up. When they brought us in, I was frightened and..." She trailed off, shrugged, then winced as if the movement or the thought was painful. "I don't know anyone else here, and I panicked for my son."

"I'm glad they did. Where's...?" He glanced around but saw no evidence of a baby, and his stomach somersaulted. Jan had told him they were releasing both, hadn't she?

His apprehension must've shown, because she reached out and brushed his arm with her fingertips. It was a simple gesture of reassurance, but her touch spread warmth across his chest.

"They've assured me Elliott is fine. Not even a bruise. But I haven't been able to get anyone to bring him to me. I just keep remembering him crying—" She sniffled, squeezing her eyes shut.

Oh, God, not that. Anything but a woman turning on the waterworks. You'd think, having witnessed his mother's histrionics during his childhood, he'd be immune. He clenched his jaw at the unwanted memory of his mother's many tearful rants designed to get everyone around her to cave in to her demands. For all the good it had done, since nothing seemed to please her.

He set his memories aside because Mary's tears were genuine, not manufactured for effect.

"Want me to go and see if I can get someone to bring him to you?" He was ready to march out there and demand— heck, he'd beg if he had to—and not stop until they brought Mary her son.

She drew in a shaky breath. "The nurse said—"

"If my patient gets any more popular, I may start handing out numbers like the deli on Saturday mornings." Nurse Jan stepped into the treatment area, a pair of blue scrub pants folded over her arm and a uniformed deputy at her heels. "Of course, if all her visitors are this good-looking, who am I to complain?"

"Glad to see you're okay, ma'am." The deputy side-stepped Jan, nodded to Mary then turned to Brody and stuck out his hand. "Wilson."

"Cooper." Brody shook hands with his friend's husband. He'd met Meg McBride, now Meg Cooper, when she'd come to the farm, asking if he had any extra eggs she could buy. When he learned she wanted them for the weekly community luncheon at the church, he'd donated them. And continued to. How many eggs could he eat, anyway?

Deputy Riley Cooper didn't act surprised to see him. Even for Loon Lake, the information about Mary and Elliott had spread quickly, unless… "Are you here to investigate the accident?"

"No, that's for the state troopers. My big mistake was stopping at Loon Lake General Store when I got off duty. Tavie *voluntold* me to go and see if I could salvage the personal belongings out of Ms. Carter's car at the tow yard. Tavie figured my uniform would get me in. It did." Riley's mouth twisted upward on one side at the admission. "You were at the store when the hospital called?"

Brody nodded, rolling his eyes. "And Tavie was having a double-duck fit because I left before giving her a full report."

The nurse patted Brody's shoulder. "*Ha.* Tavie was on the phone demanding details before you even turned your key in the ignition."

Brody had been watching Mary, and his heart gave a quick thump at her sudden grin.

"Sir? Were you able to get anything from my car?" Mary sobered and directed her question to Riley.

"Yes, ma'am, I found a diaper bag and your purse, but I couldn't unlatch the trunk. Must've been damaged by the impact. They frowned on me taking a crowbar to it until the investigation is completed." Riley rested his hand on his duty belt.

Mary frowned. "Investigation?"

"Don't worry, ma'am, just a formality." Riley smiled. "The accident was a chain reaction. According to accident investigators and witnesses, you stopped in time but the guy behind you didn't and pushed you into the car in front of you. Luckily no one sustained serious injury. A sudden change in wind direction blew smoke across the road from a smoldering wildfire and reduced visibility."

"I see. Thank you, Officer," she said and gave Riley a wobbly smile.

Brody unwrapped a toothpick and stuck it in his mouth, wishing that enchanting smile was directed at him. How crazy—as in, asking-for-trouble-crazy—was that?

Riley nodded. "Tavie insisted I bring a brand-new car seat. You're not supposed to use the old one after it's been in an accident."

"But how did anyone know I even needed one?" Mary asked.

Brody gave Jan a sideways glance.

"Hey, she's my mother-in-law. Ducking her calls is not an option, but I didn't break any privacy laws when I mentioned you might need one," Jan said and spread her arms to herd the men to the opening in the curtain. "All right, you two wait in the hall and let the poor woman finish dressing. Unlike the deli, our goods aren't on display for all and sundry."

"C'mon, Wilson, I have the car seat and some of Ms. Carter's things in the trunk of my patrol car. Help me get 'em." Riley turned back to Mary before Jan could close the curtain. "Ma'am, my wife says if you need anything—anything at all—to let her know."

"That's very kind of her. Thank you," Mary replied.

"I'll get your things," Brody said over his shoulder and fell into step beside Riley.

"She your sister-in-law?" Riley asked as they marched through the ER toward the ambulance bay.

"Who knows." Brody shrugged but acid was burning

a hole in his gut. Roger still hadn't returned his call. He was trying to give his brother the benefit of the doubt but it was getting hard.

He knew women found Roger handsome and charming. And Roger had enough money to flash around if the first two didn't work. He frowned. The woman back there didn't look like a gold digger. *Or are you letting those dark eyes and sweet mouth blind you to facts?* And why should he care? Roger could look after himself. But it wasn't Roger that bothered him—it was Mary. He hated the thought that Roger might have taken advantage of her. That was an absurd notion, since he barely knew the woman. But he did want to know what had happened between the two and why his brother wasn't with her. Or why Mary apparently hadn't tried to contact Roger.

Riley cleared his throat. "It was just the two of them in the car. The trooper I talked to said it was a chain reaction. Not her fault. She was in the wrong place at the wrong time. If that means anything to you."

"Thanks," Brody said, but fault didn't matter, nor did her character, since it looked like everyone expected him to pick up the pieces. Even though he hadn't even met his nephew yet, Brody felt responsible for him, protective of him. And Mary, too. "I don't know her, despite the connection she's claiming through her son. I haven't spoken with Roger since our father's funeral. Not that I've ever been privy to his love life, thank God."

"Do you—" Riley paused to open the exit door and glanced around "—want me to run a check on her?"

"Nah." Brody's chest tightened as the image of Mary's dark, distress-filled eyes popped into his head. If they hadn't brought her son to her by the time he got back, they'd have him to deal with. Something about this woman pulled at him, touched something he kept buried deep.

* * *

After the nurse left with a promise to bring Elliott, Mary unfolded the scrubs, stuffed her legs into them and eased off the gurney to pull them up, careful not to jostle her pounding head too much. At least these pants fit better than the shirt, but she still hated Brody seeing her like this. She would've sworn the thoughtless comments from foster parents no longer had the power to wound, but in times of stress those voices from the past threatened her self-confidence.

Even with her occasional blurry vision from the concussion, she'd noticed how Brody's slim-fitting Western-stitched chambray shirt complemented his wide shoulders, and the rolled-up sleeves had revealed the corded muscles on his tanned forearms. His faded jeans had showcased his long legs. All that, and the scuffed boots, made Brody Wilson appear more cowboy than farmer. Having lived in Connecticut, she had no idea what Vermont farmers looked like. Maybe they were all just as mouthwatering as Brody.

It was crazy, but she'd thought about him from time to time since that brief meeting at the funeral. At times she'd wondered if her imagination had conjured up those deep blue eyes fringed with sinfully long eyelashes or the sculpted cheekbones. Nope. If anything, her memory hadn't done him justice and her guilt deepened. She'd had no business noticing Brody while she'd been dating his brother, even if the cracks had already begun to show in their fledgling relationship.

She touched a hand to her brow. *Plan your work and work your plan, Mary.*

She'd tracked him down so Elliott could connect with family. So much for her plan of getting to know Brody, making sure of his character, letting him get used to the idea of being an uncle to Elliott. She didn't want or need romance of any kind in her life, no matter how tempting the depths of those blue eyes. Roger had fooled her with his charming façade, and she wasn't about to jump into another relationship. She blamed herself for not realizing Roger was one of those men who enjoyed the pursuit but not so much being a couple. And definitely not being a father. More fool her if she turned around and got involved with Roger's brother, of all people. She had a son to consider in all her decisions from this point forward.

Pushing unproductive thoughts aside, she secured the drawstring at her waist. Too bad the deputy couldn't get to her suitcase with her clothes. But at least with her purse and credit cards she could buy new clothes and pay for a motel room and anything she or Elliott needed. She'd received a severance package that included insurance for a short time and her natural tendency toward frugality ensured she had a decent bank balance to fall back on until she secured another job. She'd researched opportunities in the area and hoped to find something not too far away from Loon Lake and Elliott's uncle.

Rather than try to get back on the gurney, she perched on a hard plastic chair to put her socks and sneakers on. Maybe the faster she got dressed, the sooner they'd bring Elliott. But when she bent over to pull a sock on, her headed pounded and the room swayed. She straightened, fighting the dizziness.

"Hey, hey, should you be up?" Brody dropped several bags and an empty car seat on the gurney. "Where's Jan?"

"Who?"

"The nurse." He glanced around the enclosed area as if he expected to find the missing nurse lurking in the corner.

"She went to get Elliott. They tell me he's okay, but I need to see for myself." She wanted her son, needed to feel his reassuring warmth and sturdy little body. Except for when she'd been working, she'd rarely been separated from Elliott. Even at work, he'd been in the nursery her employer had on the premises, so she often spent breaks or lunches with him. "Why won't they bring him to me?"

Brody studied her for a moment, opened his mouth but shut it again. He bent and snagged the sock from her fingers. "Here, let me help you."

He crouched in front of her and lifted her foot to rest on his thigh.

She drew in a sharp breath at the contact with his hard thigh muscles. Brody didn't have the physique of a body-builder, but he was leanly fit, the kind of strength that came from physical labor, not hours in a gym.

"You okay?" He peered up at her. "You look kinda peaked again."

"Yes... I'm...yes." He was so close, the dark blue outer ring around his irises fascinated her.

He gave her one last look, then arranged the sock over her toes and slipped it on, repeating the process with the other.

The warmth from his thigh seeped into her foot. Her eyes stung and her throat clogged with emotion. When was the last time someone had treated her with such caring and kindness? Roger had given the appearance of solicitousness, but with the help of hindsight, she realized that's all it had been—a façade. But this was real and what had started as an embarrassing situation had turned into something that felt intimate.

"Mary?" He looked up. "Where are your shoes?"

Pay attention to his words, not his lips. She scowled at the gold toes on her socks, but it was like trying to make sense of a spreadsheet written in Sanskrit. Why couldn't she— Oh, yeah, she'd been attempting to put her socks and shoes on when Brody came in.

"Never mind. I see them over there." He stood and retrieved her sneakers from the other side of the gurney.

Mary reached for the shoes. Despite looking like a pauper, she wasn't someone who needed rescuing. She'd been taking care of herself for most of her twenty-six years. "I can do that."

He ignored her outstretched hand. "I got it."

He crouched again and put her sneakers on and tied the laces.

"Thank you." So much for all her plans to demonstrate how she had everything under control, how she wasn't looking for charity, how she was a strong, twenty-first-century woman. Brody needed to see her as Elliott's mother, not as someone he needed to take care of, or worse, pity. Never again would she allow anyone to cluck over her and murmur, "You poor thing," as those caseworkers had done. She and Brody were close enough in age to be considered contemporaries, equals.

"Someone's been waiting to see you." A nurse around Mary's age came in carrying Elliott, who was babbling to a teddy bear clutched in his hands. He glanced up, and as soon as he spotted his mother, he burst into tears and reached for Mary.

Brody rose to his full height of several inches over six feet and stepped aside, but Mary wasn't aware of his presence as she reached out to enfold Elliott in her arms. Ignoring her protesting muscles, she clasped onto his warmth, the stuffed animal crushed between their bodies, and rained kisses into his dark hair. Sobbing in earnest now, Elliott clung to her, his chubby fingers clenched around the soft flannel of her shirt. She rubbed his back in soothing strokes. "Shh, it's okay, sweetie, Mommy's here. Mommy's got you."

He lifted his head, tears clinging to his lashes, and sucked in air in short sobbing bursts. She could still hear the crunching noise as cars collided, feel the impact, and he was so young he wouldn't understand what had happened. "Mommy's here, sweetie."

Mary's brow furrowed as she spoke to the nurse over Elliott's head. "Are you sure he's okay?"

"Physically he's fine. He's had quite a fright. I 'spect he'll be emotional and clingy for a few days. He's not at the stranger-anxiety stage yet, so he did well with us until now." The nurse rubbed a hand over Elliott's riot of dark curls. "He's just happy to have his mama."

Brody watched the tearful reunion, his brows drawn together in a frightening glower. Her stomach clenched. Had she been wrong about him? Maybe he wasn't the person she'd imagined him to be. She'd been wrong about Roger, so it shouldn't be a surprise if she'd be wrong about Brody, too. Maybe this was a wasted trip.

"Brody?" An elderly woman with a purple volunteer button pinned to her chest appeared outside the opening to the curtain. "There's a phone call at the desk for you."

"For me?" He jerked his head back and turned to the newcomer. "Tell them I'll be right there."

The woman left, and he glanced back to Mary. "Wait right here. I'll go see what this is about."

"As if you wouldn't want to wait for him." The nurse sighed, then leaned toward Elliott. "Are you going to let me fasten you into your seat, sweetie?"

Elliott clung tighter, babbling something that ended with a hiccup.

"We'll let him settle for a few more minutes," the cheerful brunette said.

Mary hugged him close, needing the contact as much as he did. She tugged the toy clear of where it was wedged between their bodies and held it up. "Who's this? Have you got yourself a new friend?"

"One of the police officers on the scene must've given it to him." The nurse removed the sheet from the gurney and rolled it into a ball. "The women's group at the church collected donations last year to buy enough stuffed bears so each of our deputies would have several in their cruisers for emergencies involving children."

Mary's throat clogged as she recalled the glimpse she'd had of a state trooper cradling her son while paramedics put her on a stretcher. "I'll be sure to thank them."

The nurse tossed the discarded hospital gown onto the sheet. "People around here stick together and help one another. It's a wonderful community. I wouldn't want to live anywhere else."

Mary envied the other woman's ties to a community. Would she and Elliott be accepted, grow roots here, if she found employment and decided to make Loon Lake her permanent home? "Do you have Uber around here? Or should I call a cab?"

"No Uber that I know of." The nurse picked up the pile of laundry. "But don't worry, I'm sure Brody will take you wherever you want. Did you have someplace in mind?"

"The nearest motel, I guess." What else could she do? Driving back to Connecticut or anywhere was out of the question until she could rent a car.

"Oh." The nurse paused, adjusting the bundle in her arms. "I'm not sure the doctor will agree to that."

Mary had been digging one-handed in her purse for her phone, but the nurse's words halted her search. "Why can't I go to a motel?"

"It might take a day or two for the effects of the concussion to go away, and it's best that you not be alone during that time."

"But, I—"

"That's no problem. Mary and Elliott will be coming home with me," Brody said from the opening in the curtain.

Chapter Two

"Wait...what? No," Mary protested. "We'll find a motel room."

Brody was still waiting for Roger to return his call. What the heck was Roger's deal? His brother should be here, dealing with those beguiling dark eyes, hair that begged to be caressed and those long, slender legs that— Hold on! He needed to stop this...this... "Nonsense... I...uh, I mean, I have plenty of room."

"Our Brody rattles around alone in that big house. Do him good to have some company," Jan said cheerfully. She held the curtain open as the younger nurse left with the wad of laundry.

Brody rolled his eyes at Jan, but she was too busy entering information into the laptop attached to the wall to notice. He wasn't anyone's Brody, and he was content to rattle around alone, thank you very much. He preferred keeping his life uncomplicated. His gaze shifted to Mary. Yeah, he talked tough, and yet here he was bringing complicated with a capital *C* home with him. Damn that irresponsible Roger. Where was he, anyway?

The baby—his nephew—had recovered from his earlier outburst and was blowing spit bubbles, one chubby hand patting Mary's chin. Brody tried to swallow the sudden lump in his throat as he watched the pair. He took a step closer.

"Really, I—*mmmfff*—" Mary stopped and pried Elliott's exploring fingers from her mouth. "That won't be necessary. Elliott and I will be fine in a motel."

Great, now he sounded like an unwelcoming jerk. He stepped back.

His reaction—that frisson of awareness racing up his spine when he looked at her—wasn't Mary's fault. "All the local motels will be full. There's an annual triathlon that attracts people from all over the country."

Mary tucked a dark curl behind her ear. "But I—"

"The doc doesn't want you to stay alone in a motel room," Jan interrupted as she turned away from the computer. "Don't worry, Brody might try to act like that big green ogre all alone on that farm of his, but he's an ole softy who lets store clerks substitute toothpicks for cigarettes."

"How did…? Tavie." Cripes, he was never going to live that down. "Is it any wonder I stay on the farm?"

"*Pffft*, you'd die of boredom without all of us minding your business and you know it." Jan patted his shoulder. "Don't forget she needs wake-up checks to make sure she's all right and remembering well."

"Elliott tends to take care of the periodic wake-ups," Mary said.

"But he can't ask you questions." Jan whipped the curtain back with a jangling of metal hooks as they rattled against the rod. "Let me fetch the paperwork and you can spring Mary from this place."

After Jan left, Mary cleared her throat as if to renew her protests, and he lifted his hand. "I don't know what happened between you and Roger, but if this little guy is my nephew, then I'd like a chance to get to know him, so staying at the farm makes sense."

And that was the truth. He was an adult and could deal with any physical attraction he might feel toward Mary. She was too good for his brother, but—

"If?" Mary choked out, her eyes flashing with anger.

"Huh?" Why had she turned on him?

"You said *if* like you're questioning my word. I can assure you that—"

"Hold on." He raised his hands in a gesture of appeasement. "It was a figure of speech…not an indictment of your character."

Oh, man, what had Roger done to put such suspicion in her eyes, and why was good ole Brody always the one stuck smoothing hurt feelings caused by his family? Mary didn't look convinced, and he laid a hand over his chest. "I swear…just a poor choice of words."

She studied him, her dark eyes piercing him before she nodded. "I believe you. My plan was to go forward at a slow pace but the accident changed all that."

"Forward with what?" Brody shuffled his feet. What did she have planned?

"I brought Elliott to Loon Lake so he could meet his uncle, and I thought maybe after that you two could get acquainted."

Okay that made sense and she wasn't flat out refusing to come to the farm. A feeling resembling relief swept over him. But that was crazy, considering he didn't want to be involved in any mess with Roger. "Thanks. I *would* like to get to know him."

She coaxed Elliott to turn his head by cupping her fingers around his chin. "Can you say hello to Uncle Brody?"

Brody squatted so he was eye level with the baby, who turned to study him with big dark eyes. "Hey there, big guy, want to come to my house? Do you like animals?"

Mary brushed a kiss across Elliott's temple. "He was fascinated by the cows we saw on the way here. He squealed every time we passed some."

"Is that right? You like cows?" Gazing into the baby's large, expressive eyes, some of the invisible barrier Brody had established around himself shifted.

Elliott laid his head on Mary's shoulder and stuck his thumb in his mouth, his gaze intent. *Hey there, little man, you've got your mama's pretty eyes.* Brody rose and stepped back as if he could return to that protective circle. "Have you called Roger to let him know you two are okay?"

Mary's smile faded, her expression closed up and she gave a slight shake of her head. "That won't be necessary. Roger isn't a part of our lives."

"I see." And the sad truth was he did. Born from an illicit affair, Roger had a giant chip on his shoulder, and Brody couldn't totally fault him. No, blame lay squarely on their father for getting the maid pregnant. But Roger had learned early to play the victim card, and Brody, like many others, fell for it until…until he didn't.

Of course, Roger might be done with Mary, but that didn't mean Mary was done with him. So Brody had no business noticing or admiring her radiant eyes and shiny curls. Besides, he didn't need or want a woman—

any woman—in his life right now. Even one as appealing as Mary.

"Is everything okay with you?" Mary asked. When he gave her a questioning look, she continued, "Your phone call at the nurses' station."

"Oh, that." More of Tavie's meddling, but the woman's heart was in the right place, so he couldn't be angry. Trouble was, once Mary and Elliott left, the entire town would notice and be full of questions. He'd swear the women's group at the local church could give any matchmaking websites a run for their money. Yeah, not looking forward to any of that.

He'd casually dated a few women since leaving the army and settling in Loon Lake but was careful not to get too serious. Although he hadn't thrown himself into the town's activities, he didn't want those awkward meetings if the relationship ended badly. And in a town this size, you couldn't enter the Pic-N-Save without running into someone you knew, so even casual hookups could become embarrassing.

Mary had just arrived, so why was he already thinking about her departure? He pulled a toothpick from the front pocket of his shirt, wishing like heck it was a cigarette.

"Do you have to explain to someone why you're here?" Mary drew her lower lip between her teeth.

Only the whole damn town. "It was Tavie Whatley. She pretty much runs the town from her perch behind the cash register at Loon Lake General Store. She's the one who got Deputy Riley Cooper to go and get your personal items from your car. She called to say Meg dropped off some clothes for you."

Mary looked confused. "Meg?"

"Sorry. Meg is Deputy Cooper's wife, and she's about

your size—or was…she's pregnant." He rolled the tooth-pick around in his mouth.

"That was very nice of her." Mary blushed. "But I can provide for myself and my son."

"I'm sure you can, but these people love to help out, and saying no to Tavie is, well…you'll understand once you meet her. She said she's sending her husband, Ogle, to drop the clothes off at the farm."

Mary drew her tongue over her top teeth. "My son and I are not charity cases."

"No one will think that. As I said, people in Loon Lake look out for one another. Whether you want the help or not, it's just the way it is." No matter how he'd tried pushing the people away, they continued to try to engage him in town life. So much for spending time alone while coming to terms with having caused his unit's last mission to go sideways. "If you're going to be here awhile, you may as well get used to it."

Like you have? his inner voice mocked.

"I understand, but—"

A nurse tech came in, pushing a wheelchair. "The paperwork is done, and the doctor is discharging Mary and Elliott."

She engaged the brake on the wheelchair and gave Mary some papers attached to a clipboard to sign, along with a list of instructions. "If you get any of those symptoms on that list or just don't feel right, don't hesitate to come back in."

Mary scooted forward and struggled to stand while keeping a grip on Elliott.

"Here." Brody's innate chivalrous code slapped him upside the head and he held out his hands toward Elliott. "Will he come to me?"

"I guess we'll find out." Mary gave the baby a noisy kiss on his cheek. "Want to go see Uncle Brody?"

She handed over Elliott, who studied Brody while waving the teddy bear around and rattling off a string of babbled sounds ending with a spit bubble and a toothless grin.

Brody hadn't had much experience with babies; the only child he'd had much interaction with was Meg's daughter, Fiona, who was six years old. A feeling he couldn't identify tightened his chest as those dark, trusting eyes studied him, threatening to scale that barrier he kept around himself. Holding the warm, chunky body close made him want to deck Roger. Why wasn't he here accepting responsibility? Was Brody's past willingness to bail his brother out of trouble to blame for Roger's laissez-faire attitude?

Brody sighed. Roger wasn't his responsibility but being three years older, Brody had felt protective of his younger sibling when their father used Roger's existence as proof of his affair to retaliate against his wife. And here Roger was, saddling Elliott with the same feeling. Brody would be having it out with Roger at some point, for sure.

The nurse assisted Mary into the wheelchair and unlocked the brake. After Mary settled in the seat, she reached for her son. He reluctantly handed off the baby.

Mary's sweet smile made Brody's breath catch in his throat. Yep, she was gonna be a complication. And he'd had enough complex family dynamics growing up. Mary was here because he was her baby's uncle. She wanted a family connection, nothing more, and that was perfect, because he wasn't looking for any romantic entanglements—no matter how stunning her smile.

He picked up the infant carrier, diaper bag and Mary's

purse and followed the wheelchair. At the exit he said, "I'll get my truck and pull it up."

Tossing all the items in the back seat of his battered extended-cab pickup, he drove to where Mary waited with the nurse. His heart skipped a beat at the sight. Was this what it felt like when a new dad picked up his little family? Not that he ever wanted anything like that. His father was gone but years of being put in the middle of his parents' toxic and tangled relationship had left scars. Photos captured all the family smiles and missed all the simmering tensions and passive aggression. But holding Elliott in his arms had satisfied something he hadn't even known he'd wanted.

He shook his head at his stupid thoughts. Thinking like that was dangerous. *Repeat after me, Wilson: this is temporary.*

At the hospital entrance, he put the truck in Park, jumped out and opened the rear door. He battled to get the infant seat strapped into place. The buckle clicked, but he backed away, saying, "You should double-check. I haven't had much practice with these things."

Brody stood behind Mary while she secured Elliott in his seat and did his best not to stare at the way the fabric of the scrubs stretched across her backside. She gave her son a noisy kiss on his forehead, then scooted backward and bumped smack into Brody. "Oh, I'm sorry."

He held on to her hips to steady her, lingering longer than necessary before releasing her. Damn, what happened to no entanglements? Not to mention the poor woman had been in a car accident and had hurt her head. He cleared his throat. "My fault."

"If you don't mind, I'll sit in the back with Elliott." She drew her tongue across her bottom lip.

"I wouldn't mind, except that the other seat belt doesn't

latch. You're my first back-seat passengers in a long time, so I haven't gotten around to fixing it." He should feel guilty for preventing Mary from sitting next to her son, but the fact she'd be sitting ncxt to him outweighed that.

"I guess he'll be okay. He looks like he might end up sleeping anyway. Car rides tend to do that to him." She offered him a smile but continued to worry her plump lower lip.

As if rewarding him for his procrastination with the seat belt repair, Mary's enticing sweet scent filled his head as he drove through Loon Lake toward the county road that would bring them to his place. He glanced in the rearview mirror at Elliott. Cute kid, but what the heck was he getting into, bringing them to the farm?

He pushed those thoughts aside and concentrated on driving. Loon Lake was a quintessential New England town, complete with a wooden covered bridge and pre–Revolutionary War architecture. The state tourist board photographed the quaint Main Street to feature in pamphlets designed to lure tourists. The population increased during summer cottage rental season, but the town had one small motel, keeping the transient population low. While tourists flocked to other parts of the state, Loon Lake remained secluded—by design or happenstance, he hadn't figured out which.

"I had no idea places like this existed outside books or television," Mary remarked, her tone wistful.

Brick-front businesses and rectangular, gable-roofed early-nineteenth-century homes gathered around the town green, which boasted a restored gazebo that doubled as a bandstand for concerts in the summer. An iconic Greek Revival white church with black shutters and steeple bell tower anchored the green at one end.

"It's real. Filled with real people." He didn't tell her he'd chosen this place more for the people than the picture-postcard appearance. Sure, they liked to get up all in his business, like Tavie and her toothpicks, but their actions lacked malice, and when neighbors hit a patch of bad luck, instead of searching for ways to take advantage, they gathered around and helped. And he liked the farmers and their straight-up, no-games approach to life. Not to mention most residents left you alone if you signaled that was your true preference. No, his mistake had been going *into* town, to the general store instead of the more anonymous gas station on the outskirts. If he needed someone to blame for this morning, all he had to do was look in the mirror.

"It would be nice to raise Elliott in a place like this," she said, glancing around.

"Is that why you came?" Was she planning to stay?

"I came because I wanted Elliott to know he had family. Where I settle will depend on finding a job to support us." She half turned and glanced into the back seat.

Her long hair brushed his arm and shoulder as she checked on Elliott. Brody couldn't place the scent, but it reminded him of the sweet, cleansing smell of cooling rain after one of those occasional Vermont summer heat waves, how everything smelled new and fresh afterward. He inhaled deep into his lungs, his fingers tightening on the steering wheel. What was he thinking, bringing them to his farm, into his personal space? *Repeat after me: this is short-term.*

She must've been satisfied Elliott was comfortable, because she shifted around, her gaze meeting his. A man could get lost in her dark eyes. He'd have to guard against letting that happen. He didn't do permanent, and Mary Carter had hearth and home written all over her. Did she think she'd found that with Roger? Evidently seeing how their father treated women hadn't made his brother want to do better.

Dragging his focus back to the road, he turned off the state highway onto the county road that climbed the hill leading to his farm. The narrow road wound past rolling pastures broken up by fences or dense stands of sugar maples tapped for their sap in February and March.

Her head swiveled between the view ahead and the passing scenery. "How far out of town do you live?"

"About five miles. Once we get over this next rise, you'll be able to see the place," he added with a sense of pride. After the army he'd struggled to find a purpose until he began working on the historic farmhouse. Once he started, he decided the house deserved restoration, not renovation. Now he spent hours tracking down the right piece of hardware or learning to recreate what he needed. He'd gone from breaking down and reassembling his carbine to retrofitting plumbing.

"You live alone on this farm?" She scrutinized the passing scenery.

"Yep. It affords me all the privacy I need, plus the land to bury all those dismembered bodies." Oh, man, he was the devil himself teasing her, but he enjoyed that quick grin he'd glimpsed in the ER and the way it lit up her face. He raised an eyebrow. "That's where your mind was going, wasn't it?"

"Yeeaahh," she admitted, her mouth curving into a smile, her face red. "Sorry. Too many late nights watching *Investigation Discovery* when Elliott was a newborn."

When was the last time he'd considered a woman's blush sexy? He shifted in his seat. "S'okay. Besides, Tavie knows you're here, and if Tavie knows it, the whole town knows it, including Deputy Cooper. We'll be the talk of the town before sundown."

She turned to him, a mischievous grin playing around those full lips. "I've also seen shows where the whole town is in on the cover-up."

He chuckled, enjoying her playful side. "Have you given any thought to watching cooking or decorating shows instead of true crime?"

"I think you're onto something there." She laughed, but it was replaced with a sharp intake of breath and a pointing finger. "Is that your place?"

He didn't need to follow the direction of her finger to know what she was seeing, and his lungs expanded as he took in several deep, satisfied breaths. His pride and joy, the white two-story farmhouse, with its newly replaced red metal roof gleaming in the sun, sat on a large tract of relatively flat land. A covered porch ran across the front and wrapped around one side, and, although he couldn't see it from here, the porch ceiling was painted sky blue. The big red barn had white-painted split rail fencing extending from the back. The smaller chicken coop with wire enclosure was hidden by the barn, as was a smaller bunkhouse that now stood empty. "Yup, three years of hard work."

"It's beautiful." She brushed a curl off her cheek, squeezing her eyes shut for a moment.

"How're you holding up?" He resisted the urge to reach out and take her hand in his. What the heck was wrong with him?

"Guess I'll have a headache for a while." She dropped her hand to her lap. "Did you restore all of it?"

"The house and part of the barn. The rest is still a work in progress." For the past three years, he'd thrown himself into the restoration, keeping anchored in the present, not getting mired in the past or facing the future. A twist of fate had proved how little control he had over his life or his choices. Mary and Elliott's arrival was a reminder he wasn't immune to fallout from choices made by his family.

"I don't see any cultivated fields. What do you grow?" She gestured to the surrounding grassy areas.

"Grow? I don't grow anything." Well, he baled hay every summer and sold what he didn't use himself, but he didn't consider that a crop. Not like grain or potatoes.

She turned to face him. "Then what kind of farm do you have?"

"The usual kind." He lifted a hand off the steering wheel to run a finger under his collar. The term "gentleman farmer" came to mind, but he shied away from saying it out loud.

"I'm a city girl through and through, grew up in Bridgeport and moved to Hartford for college. Help me out here. What's the usual kind?" She tilted her head and studied him.

"The kind with a cow and a few chickens."

She raised a bruised brow. "Okay, I may be a city girl, but even I know farms need lots of…something. Like herds of dairy cows. Isn't that one of the things Vermont is famous for?"

"No herd." He'd come here looking for isolation, not a career as a dairy farmer.

"Okay. How many chickens do you have?"

"A half dozen." He was an adult. He could have as many or as few chickens as he chose. Besides, his chickens laid so well Meg Cooper came every other week to get the extras for the soup kitchen. Her farming questions took him by surprise. The restoration contractors who'd sought him out at the farm hadn't been interested in his animals, just in his advice or to see how he'd recreated unavailable pieces.

"Not enough to produce mass quantities of eggs." She rubbed a finger across her lips. "Hmm, what else do you have?"

He cleared his throat. "A horse and two alpacas."

"Alpacas? You mean, like those late-night commercials I used to see about alpaca farming?" She laughed, glancing back at Elliott once more.

"Yeah, except you don't see those anymore, and with good reason. People who didn't know what they were getting into sank a lot of money into alpacas, and when the bubble burst, some walked away." And who was he to throw stones? He'd walked away from his family and then his army career when they wanted him to sit behind a desk, not that he blamed his superiors for that decision. His compromised eyesight had endangered the others in his unit. Even if what happened wasn't his fault, he carried the guilt for injuries sustained by his fellow soldiers.

"You mean someone abandoned their animals? Is that how you ended up with them?"

He dragged his attention back to alpacas. "They sold all but one."

He didn't go into detail about how sick that animal had been. And he wouldn't have been able to live with himself if that one had died while he did nothing. Oh, yeah, he was a sucker for an animal in distress. He glanced over at Mary. Looked like that extended to damsels, too.

"One? You said you had two."

He shrugged. "They're social animals and never do well alone. I had to locate a companion."

"That's so sweet," she said.

He shook his head but her comment shifted something in his chest, satisfied some unknown need. "It's just a fact."

The truck's tires rumbled over the metal cattle grid

as he turned onto the half mile dirt driveway that led to his home.

"Ooh, is that one of the alpacas in that fenced-in area?" she asked, leaning forward to look past him.

He stopped the truck and glanced to his left. "Yeah, that's Lost."

She chuckled. "Is the other one Found?"

He shifted in the seat, warmth rising in the back of his neck. "It was just a silly—"

"It's perfect." She reached over and gave his arm a gentle squeeze, all traces of laughter or teasing gone.

She captured his attention and he swallowed, hard. Undone by the tenderness in her eyes, he glanced at her fingers on his arm. They were free from adornment, but they were feminine, slender and elegant. He resisted the urge to touch, but he'd bet those hands could turn a man to putty. Clearing his throat, he eased his foot off the brake.

"What's your horse's name?"

"Patton."

"I like—Oh, looks like you have company." Mary dropped her hand.

He dragged his wayward thoughts away from her and his reaction and gazed at his house. Sure enough, two teenagers unloaded items from the bed of a truck parked in front of the house, while a barrel-chested older man, dressed in denim overalls and a Vietnam vet ball cap, supervised. Ogle Whatley.

Brody slowed his truck and pulled up beside Ogle's restored cherry-red 1949 Mercury M47 truck. His chest tightened as memories of Sean, one of the guys in his unit, assailed him. The first day they'd met, Sean had bragged about restoring one belonging to his grandfather. Sean was one of the guys whose life had changed that day due to traumatic brain injury. Brody pushed the memory aside. Now wasn't the time for old wounds.

"I thought you said she was sending over some clothes."

Mary's voice broke into his morose thoughts, and he turned off the engine. What the...? He gave a low whistle and got out. His porch looked as if a Kmart had exploded.

Going around the front of his truck, Brody opened the passenger door and took Mary's hand to steady her as she stepped down. *Maybe she would be worth the complications.* Now where had that thought come from? She pulled her hand away, and he stepped back. Complicated never had a good outcome.

Ogle sauntered over and nodded. "Afternoon, folks."

"This is Ogle Whatley. He runs the garage in town. Ogle, this is Mary Carter."

"A pleasure to meet you, Mr. Whatley." Mary shook hands and smiled.

Brody grinned at Ogle's flustered reaction to Mary's smile. *Yeah, I feel ya, Ogle.*

"It's just Ogle." The older man hooked his thumbs under the bib of his denim overalls. "As promised, I'll take a look at your car and see if it's salvageable."

"Thank you." Mary nodded, then canted her head. "Wait...you promised?"

"Yeah." Ogle hitched his chin in Brody's direction. "Brody here asked me to check into it."

"I figured you'd want someone to take a look at the damage to your car." Brody slipped his hands into his pockets. Mary's expression was apprehensive, and once again he had the urge to reach out. "Ogle's the best mechanic in town."

Ogle laughed, his belly jiggling like a department-store Santa. "Mebbe because I'm the only one. But don't you worry, the young feller I hired knows all about them new cars and all their fandangled computerized parts."

"No problem. My car isn't brand-new or...fandangled," she replied, a smile lighting up her face.

Kevin Thompson, a tall, gangly kid with spiked black hair and an eyebrow piercing, hefted a box marked Portable Crib. "Hey, Sergeant Wilson, you want Danny and me to take this on into the house and get it set up?"

"May as well. The door's not locked," Brody told him and nodded to Danny Simmons, who was waiting on the porch. Both boys hadn't had the best starts in life but Riley and Meg Cooper had been mentoring them about making better choices.

Kevin shifted the box and grinned. "Yeah, we know, but Mr. Ogle said to wait till you got here anyway."

"Start bringing the boxes in and I'll be in to decide where to put everything," Brody told Kevin before turning his attention to the older man once more. "Ogle, where did all this come from?"

His thumbs still hooked over the bib of his overalls, Ogle flapped his arms, elbows turned outward. "The baby things were left over from all the items we collected when that young family, the Dodges, got burned out of their place. 'Member that fire last winter?" Ogle didn't wait for a reply. "Anyway, folks who'd donated said to go ahead and keep things for the next family that needed help."

Brody glanced at the chaos on his porch. "But that's an awful lot of stuff."

"Yeah, ain't it amazing how much stuff a tiny person requires?"

Eyes wide, Mary stared at the stack of baby merchandise. "I can't possibly accept all this."

Ogle shook his head. "You'll have to take that up with

Tavie. I don't argue, just follow orders. Kinda like the years I spent in the corps. She says you're gonna need all this, and if there's one thing I've learned in the past fifty years, it's that Tavie is usually right."

Brody tugged his ear. "I don't…"

Ogle clapped him on the shoulder. "Oh, son, a baby changes everything."

Mary surveyed the makeshift nursery on the second floor of Brody's two-hundred-year-old farmhouse. With Brody's help and Ogle's supervision, the boys had set up a portable crib, a rocking chair and even a changing table in what had been an empty room. What was with this town? It was as if she'd returned home or something. With all the furniture, the room looked as though she and Elliott intended to take up permanent residence. She winced. Brody had tried to hide his reaction, but seeing all the baby paraphernalia the boys were unloading had thrown him. He clearly hadn't realized picking her and Elliott up at the hospital and offering them a temporary place to stay was going to cause such an upheaval in his life. She hadn't meant to barge into his personal space. At least Brody had attempted to hide his consternation. Roger hadn't tried to hide anything. Told her flat out he had no time or inclination to make room for a baby in his life.

Mary sighed and rubbed Elliott's back while he slept in the crib, unaware of all the commotion he'd caused. She went into the Jack-and-Jill bathroom that connected this room to the one she would be using.

She bent to splash water on her face, and a wave of dizziness hit her. She gripped the edge of the counter, straightening with care.

"What were you thinking, just showing up like this?" she asked her reflection in the mirror.

Poor Brody had looked as if he'd been struck by a tornado. And who could blame him? She patted her face dry with a towel from the rack, taking extra care around her glue patch. Ogle was right when he said a baby changed everything. She'd had nine months to prepare, and she often felt overwhelmed and unqualified. She and Elliott had been thrust on Brody with no warning whatsoever. Despite her fatigue, she hung the towel back up and went downstairs to look for Brody.

He was standing in the kitchen, drinking a glass of water and staring out the window above the sink, his broad back to her.

She paused in the doorway and admired his wide shoulders and the thick black hair that curled over the top of his collar in the back. Would it feel as silky as it looked? She cleared her throat. "I apologize for disrupting everything like this."

He refilled the glass from the faucet before turning. "Don't worry about it."

He hadn't reacted to her presence. Had he seen her reflection in the window? If so, he'd caught her staring at him. Warmth rose in her face. Even with Roger she hadn't felt like a middle schooler in the throes of a crush. Looking back she could see her mistakes. Charm and good looks had been the sum total of Roger Wilson, but that realization had come too late.

Brody turned toward the bags piled on the wooden farmhouse table, and a muscle in his cheek twitched. More unwelcome chaos?

She needed to make things right. Brody and Elliott could get to know one another just fine without living together. "I'm sure Elliott and I can find a place of our own within the next few days."

"There's no rush. I have plenty of room here." He sipped the water.

"But we're imposing on your privacy and…and…" She shook her head, wishing she'd kept her mouth shut when the paramedics had arrived at the accident scene.

"It's okay—it's not as if I had plans to walk around naked…for the next few days, anyway."

His statement set off flutters in her stomach. The picture of Brody Wilson naked did things to her that she had no business exploring. He was off limits as the brother of her ex. Her face hot, she coughed. "Well, I don't have any plans for that, either."

"Then we're good." He set the empty glass in the sink and leaned against the counter.

They stood in the silent kitchen, Brody staring at his feet and Mary's stomach churning at the plastic bags strewn on the table. How often had she collected her few possessions in a black plastic trash bag to take with her to the next foster home? To this day, she hated the smell of those black bags, and she'd sworn she'd never do that again. And yet here she was. Not quite the same situation, but close enough to sour her stomach.

The refrigerator's motor kicked on, and he straightened, stepping away from the counter. "I've got to check on the animals. Why don't you get settled? Take a nap. After I finish with the chores, I'll see if there's something in the freezer for supper. If you get hungry, feel free to help yourself to whatever you can scrounge up."

Mary crossed the kitchen to the window over the sink as soon as the back door shut. Brody sauntered across the yard to the bright red barn and rolled open one side of the giant double doors. He stood in the entrance and stared back at the house. Had he needed to see to his animals, or had he been in a hurry to get away? She couldn't blame him if it was the latter. She and Elliott had descended on him and disrupted practically his whole house. That nurse at the ER had made it sound as if Brody enjoyed being out here alone on his farm, so it stood to reason he wouldn't welcome the intrusion. She stared at the open barn door after Brody had disappeared inside.

Sighing, she turned away from the sink and opened the bags until she located clothes the deputy's wife had sent. At least she could take a nap, then change into something decent while Brody checked on his animals.

He cared a great deal for those animals, going so far as to locate a second alpaca to keep the first one company. He'd tried to laugh off their names as a joke, but she didn't think they were a joke or even random. Although their names may have been subconsciously chosen, they were a clue to Brody. And telling herself she wanted to get to know him better for Elliott's sake alone was an outright lie.

Brody rolled his shoulders, trying to ease the tension that had settled there as he trudged toward the house. Maybe he should've found a motel for Mary and Elliott. He was under no obligation to look after his brother's… his brother's what?

And that was the heart of the problem. What was Mary to Roger? And what was he to her? Had they had a fight and she left, hoping his brother would chase after her the way his father did his mother? If that were true, then he'd be smack-dab in the middle of all that family drama—a place he swore he'd never be again.

And if this wasn't family drama, he didn't know what was. This wasn't just any woman or any baby staying with him. This was fallout from Roger's callous actions. Sure, he'd picked up after Roger in the past, but this wasn't the same as paying to replace the neighbor's busted mailbox or getting Roger's car from the impound when his parking tickets had mounted up.

Brody wasn't any more responsible for Roger's actions than he'd been for their father's, and yet here he was, disrupting his life to pick up the pieces. He'd done so in the past to shield his mother or appease his father, but they were both gone and he'd washed his hands of Roger years ago. So why did he have an alluring stranger and her baby in his house?

Stretching his neck, he made a conscious effort to relax his tensed muscles. The situation was temporary. Concussions didn't last forever, and if her car couldn't be repaired, he and Ogle would help her find a replacement. A few days and Mary would move out and he'd get to know his nephew without the distraction of her sleeping across the hall. He could withstand anything for a few days—his time in the army had taught him that. The gossip chain was already started, so he might as well do right by his nephew.

Entering the house, he toed off his dirty Roper boots in the mudroom. A welcoming aroma and Mary's voice drifted from the kitchen, and he stood on socked feet in the doorway. Mary sat at the antique oak table with her back to him, spooning something into Elliott's mouth as he sat in the high chair. The baby seemed as intent on pushing the food back out with his tongue as he was with eating it.

"C'mon, sweetie, you like rice cereal. You gotta eat if you want to grow up big and strong."

Brody's breath caught in his chest at the scene. *Don't get used to her presence in the house. Remember, this is temporary.*

Clearing his throat, he stepped into the kitchen. Mary

glanced over her shoulder. Her welcome smile tightened his belly and he tried to remember the last time he'd had a woman in his kitchen. The few he'd gotten involved with for any length of time had either complained about the mess when he was in the middle of restoring this room or disliked being so far from town. Would Mary feel the same? *You can soldier through a couple of days.*

"I was giving Elliott some supper," she said before turning back to her task.

The scent of garlic and tomatoes filled the kitchen, reminding him he'd skipped lunch. "That's not *his* supper I smell, is it?"

She laughed. "No. I found a lasagna casserole in the refrigerator and put it in the oven. I hope that's okay... I mean, you said you were going to have to look for something."

"Lasagna? You found lasagna in my refrigerator?"

"I'm sorry, was I not—"

He held up his hands. "No, it's okay. I have no idea how—oh, wait, I'll bet Tavie sent it with Ogle. I saw him come into the kitchen with something, but I was busy helping Danny and Kevin get the baby things into the house and set up."

"I thought you might be hungry after working all afternoon. The foil covering the casserole dish was dated with reheating instructions on it and I wanted to help, since it looks like we've been dropped on you for a few days."

He washed his hands in the sink. When was the last time he'd shared supper with anyone? Huh, maybe Jan was right and he was an ogre. Watching Mary, he would be hard-pressed to remember why he wanted isolation. "How are you feeling?"

"Better. I took a nap while Elliott slept. That and some ibuprofen helped take the edge off the headache."

He threw the towel onto the counter. "I'm glad."

She glanced over at him, the spoon poised in midair. "If we get in your way, just tell me. I know we must be a distraction, but I don't want to be a burden, too."

"You're not." *A complication? Yes. A distraction? Yes. A burden? No.* "Don't worry, having to wear clothes walking around the house isn't as disruptive as I'd feared."

"That's a relief," she said and that grin—the one that made his heart thump against his chest—skipped across her face.

"I'm glad I could set your mind at ease." Danger signs flashed in his head, but he ignored them.

"Let me check on the lasagna." She set the cereal bowl on the table and rose.

Elliott must've thought she had stopped feeding him, because his face scrunched up and he started to fuss. His fingers splayed, he reached for the cereal bowl.

"Oh, sweetie." Mary turned back toward the baby, but Brody waved her off.

"I got it." He took Mary's place in the seat, picked up the spoon and began feeding his nephew, who decided he was done spitting the cereal back out and ate with gusto while intently tracking his mom.

Elliott wasn't the only one keeping an eye on her. Brody watched as she puttered around the kitchen. He couldn't help but admire how great she looked in the figure-hugging jeans and snug hot pink T-shirt. Dragging his attention back to his task, he scraped the bowl and spooned the last bit into Elliott's mouth. Such a cute kid, with Mary's dark hair and eyes.

"Thank you." She wiped Elliott's face and hands with a washcloth. She even managed to get him clean, despite the squirming protests. "The lasagna should be done by the time I get him bathed and into his pajamas. I can give him a bottle while we eat, if that's okay. You must be hungry after farming all afternoon."

Damn, but he didn't want to be charmed by her. He needed to remember some families didn't have cheerful, welcoming kitchens at the end of the day. His certainly hadn't. *Don't let that smile make you stupid.* "Don't worry about it. As you said, this isn't like a regular farm."

"I hope you know I was teasing about the animals or lack of." She folded the wet cloth and wiped the plastic high-chair tray. "As a matter of fact, I would have given anything to stay someplace like this during the summer for a week or two when I was a kid."

"On a farm?" Was she still teasing?

She licked her lips. "You laugh, but when you've spent your life in a city, a farm with live animals can sound exotic."

His gaze went to her mouth, and he had to concentrate on following their conversation. "I hate to disappoint you, but my cow and chickens aren't very exotic."

"You have alpacas." Her eyes sparkled with humor. Blushing, she turned away and went to the sink.

He suppressed an urge to pull her onto his lap and kiss her. Or hold her and celebrate their playful moment. "True, but their names don't make my alpacas exotic. Just proves I'm a bit of a nerd."

Turning around, she made a tsking sound. "Oh, believe me, you're not like any nerd I've ever known, and I have a degree in accounting."

"What about farmers? Know any?"

"You're my first. Although I've had a dream of—" She shook her head. "Never mind."

He needed to know what had put that faraway look on her face. "Tell me."

She glanced around as if checking to see who might be listening. "I've had a dream of opening a summer camp on a farm for city kids who have no idea places like this exist or kids whose home life is rough...you know, kids like Kevin and Danny." She pulled in her lower lip. "Although I suspect Kevin and Danny would argue that they're too old for camp."

"How do you know so much about Kevin and Danny?" He suspected she was the type of person who drew people to her. *Whereas you do your best to push them away.*

"Ogle told me about Kevin's father's drinking and neglect and Danny dropping out of school. He explained how Deputy Cooper and his wife were mentoring the two boys. I'd like to be a part of something like that."

"There's plenty of ways you can help. Programs are already in place." He wasn't into volunteering, but there were several opportunities in town. "The church on the green—the one we passed on our way through town— they run a soup kitchen. Meg Cooper helps with that."

"Thank you." She swallowed. "I'll be sure to ask her about it when I thank her for the clothes."

"Opening and running a summer camp..." He wanted to kick himself for the closed expression on her lovely face. "There must be a ton of paperwork, regulations and bureaucracy involved in that sort of undertaking."

"I'm sure it would take a lot of work to get it started. But what's wrong with that?"

She put a great deal of effort into wringing out the wet cloth. Was she imagining his neck between her hands? He laughed to himself. It would serve him right.

"It would be a bureaucratic nightmare." He regretted the callous remark as soon as it left his mouth. His upbringing might have been privileged in material wealth but when it came to emotional support, his experience was similar to Kevin and Danny. Which was why he'd done what he could for the teens. He tugged on his ear and reached for a toothpick, but his pocket was empty.

"True." She folded the washcloth, her movements slow and precise. "But just because something is difficult doesn't mean it's not worth pursuing."

Aw, man, was he some sort of special jerk or what? He'd pursued getting into the Deltas, even though the army put up rigorous roadblocks at every turn. How many people would consider spending weeks tracking down restoration hardware pieces instead of popping into the nearest home improvement store a waste of time?

If she wanted to face all those hurdles to realize her dream, who was he to argue?

She adjusted the high chair's tray and lifted a droopy-eyed Elliott, who popped his thumb in his mouth and snuggled against her shoulder.

Regret gnawed at his gut, and he struggled to explain. "Bureaucracy is…"

"A special kind of hell?"

He released a ragged breath. "You sound as if you've had experience."

"Something like that, yeah." She hugged Elliott. "I'm going to get him ready for bed. Be back in a minute to get supper on the table."

He put a hand on her arm before she left the room. "I'll have it ready when you're done."

Brody snatched the pot holders off the counter and knocked the washcloth Mary had used onto the floor. He bent to pick it up and his muscles protested. Dang, but what little work he'd accomplished today couldn't account for the fatigue. Mary's hurt expression sprang into his mind's eye. Swearing under his breath, he straightened and threw the wet cloth into the sink.

Guilt was a heavy burden, and he was getting tired of lugging it around. And guilt was futile, since he couldn't go back and change the events of that day, how his helplessness had put others in danger.

He reached into his pocket before remembering it was empty. He damned Tavie and her concern for his health and went in search of a toothpick.

Chapter Three

It was two in the morning, and Mary was in the kitchen preparing a bottle with Elliott perched on her hip and swaying to a tune she hummed under her breath.

"Is everything okay?" Brody hovered in the doorway.

She turned, and her breath caught in her throat. Dressed in sleep pants and a faded T-shirt, a yawning, rumpled Brody was even more tempting than the man who'd sat across from her at supper that evening. Way too tempting. He ran a hand through his disheveled hair, mussing it further as he strolled into the dimly lit kitchen. Her stomach fluttered. His feet were bare. Who knew that could feel so…so…intimate?

"Sorry if we woke you. I tried to be as quiet as possible." At Elliott's first cries, she'd rushed to get him and come downstairs to fix him a bottle.

"That's fine." He yawned again. "Elliott okay?"

"Yeah, just wet and hungry. He's started sleeping through the night, but…" She shifted him from one shoulder to the other as she got his bottle ready. "Between the accident and being in a strange place, it's playing havoc with his schedule, I think."

"May I?" He approached and reached for Elliott. "You've got your hands full."

"Thank you." *Nice, but don't get used to sharing and having an adult to talk to in the middle of the night,* she cautioned herself as Brody took Elliott. As soon as she had a car, she'd be out looking for employment and a place to live. As exciting as that prospect was, she'd miss Brody's farm and the welcoming farmhouse. *One day and you're becoming attached?* But knowing this home had been here housing families for such a long time made her yearn for a history she'd never have, although she was determined to give one to Elliott. She glanced at Brody cradling her son against his shoulder. This farm could be a part of Elliott's life, a place he'd remember from visits to his uncle—if that's what Brody wanted.

"How did you end up on a farm in Vermont?" As far as she knew, he and Roger had grown up in Hartford.

"My father's family had a farm and I enjoyed spending time there as a kid. While I was in Afghanistan I thought about that place a lot but by the time I got out of the army, the farm had been sold." He shrugged. "It's now a subdivision full of tract homes."

He may have brushed it off, but she could see his disappointment. "You're doing a great job of preserving this one."

"Maybe big guy here will want to farm it someday," he said and laughed.

She laughed, too, but Brody's words made the back of her eyes burn. Blinking, she finished readying the bottle and was prepared to take Elliott back, but Brody reached for the bottle.

"You want to feed him?"

He pulled out a chair and sat at the table. "If you don't mind."

"Of course not," she said, but Brody's offer stirred up mixed feelings. This was what she'd wanted, the whole reason she'd come to Loon Lake, so Brody could bond with his nephew. And she was glad he was jumping in and even speaking in terms of Elliott and the future. She was…and yet, placing Elliott in someone else's care was like handing over her heart.

After giving Brody the bottle, she poured herself a glass of water at the sink, not because of thirst, but because she had to move to help release some of the building tension. Seeing Brody holding, feeding and talking with Elliott turned her insides to mush, made her think things she had no business thinking. This moment wasn't a happy family moment, but two strangers thrust together because of circumstances.

Brace your backbone and forget your wishbone.

A child services worker had given her that piece of advice when she'd been in foster care and it still held true today. Maybe she should have followed that advice and proceeded with greater caution with Roger. But then she wouldn't have Elliott, and she couldn't imagine her life without her son. She slammed the door on what-ifs and sipped her water. What did Brody think? He hadn't said much about his brother.

She ran her finger along the rim of the glass. "It didn't last long."

"Hmm?" Brody looked up.

"Roger and I." Mary took her glass and sat at the table across from Brody and Elliott. "He…he wasn't the man I thought him to be, but I guess maybe I wasn't what he was looking for, either."

"Oh?" He adjusted the bottle when it began to slip from Elliott's hands.

"I think for him it was all about the pursuit, not making something lasting." She rolled the glass between her palms. "In my defense, Roger knows how to turn on the charm."

"He does, but don't sell yourself short. I'm sure you're what most men are looking for."

Most? What about you? Could I be what you're *looking for?* "Thanks, but I have this little guy here to consider in every decision from now on. Whom I'm with also affects him. Lots of guys don't want the responsibility of another man's child, but Elliott and I do fine." She drew circles with her index finger on the table. "It's just that I have no family, and I want my son to know his."

"Tell me that at least Roger stepped up financially." When she didn't reply, he blew out his breath and swore. "Wait till I get my hands on that—"

"That's not necessary."

"Why not? He needs to step up." Although he was whispering, Brody's anger was loud and clear.

Elliott had fallen asleep, the bottle slipping out of his mouth, so she reached over. "Here, let me take him."

Brody placed him back with Mary, and she put him on her shoulder and rubbed his back. "I can support both of us. I'm a CPA. I'm sure I can find work. I have a solid employment history. A company buyout was the reason I lost my job. They'll give me good references."

At least a concerned caseworker from her time in the foster care system had convinced her to take full advantage of educational opportunities and she'd gone to college on grants and scholarships, keeping student loans to a minimum. It hadn't been easy, but she'd done well financially. And would continue to.

Brody frowned. "That's not the point."

"If you must know, when I approached him regarding child support, he threatened me with a custody battle." Frightened by his threats, she recalled feeling helpless despite swearing to not get into a situation like that as an adult. Roger having the means to hire high-powered attorneys didn't mean he deserved his son.

"And you let him get away with it?"

"What could I do? I won't take the chance of losing Elliott under any circumstances. If he wanted to be involved in Elliott's life, I would do everything in my power to see that happen, but he doesn't and that's the end of it." Her voice rose an octave, and Elliott stirred.

"It shouldn't be." Brody tugged on his ear, a habit she'd noticed he displayed when irritated.

"Don't worry. We're not here to disrupt your life. I wanted to give you an opportunity to get to know your nephew. My arrival might seem strange, but I think family is important, and when I met you at your father's funeral, I realized you were…different than Roger." She patted Elliott's back, wanting to be sure she didn't put him back to bed with a tummy full of gas. He was good about getting it up, but she liked to be sure at night.

"That's not what this is about."

"Isn't it?" She shouldn't have said that. Brody had been nothing but kind and caring, and he didn't deserve her anger over Roger's behavior directed at him.

"Look, I—"

"No, I—"

Elliott's loud belch interrupted them. Brody laughed first and Mary soon joined him, their disagreement forgotten. She rose and started to leave.

"Mary?"

She turned back, but didn't speak.

"I would like that. To get to know Elliott."

* * *

Brody roused to the smell of coffee brewing. After a restless night spent tossing and turning, caffeine was welcome. He regretted arguing with Mary over his worthless brother. Whether to press Roger for child support was Mary's decision, not his. He needed to respect her judgment, but that didn't change his feelings. Could he have done more for Roger? Was he complicit in Roger's actions? The circumstances of his brother's birth had nothing to do with him, but being the son from the right side of the bed had caused Brody a certain amount of irrational guilt.

After pulling on jeans and a T-shirt, he stopped long enough to brush his teeth and run a comb through his hair before seeking out the promising aromas coming from the kitchen.

Mary was at the stove cooking scrambled eggs, and Elliott was in an infant bouncy seat, chewing on his fist. As it had last night, his breath caught in his throat at the appealing domestic scene. His functional kitchen had come to life, filled with warmth. Was this what lured people in? Made them fall for the idea of family?

Brody laid his hand on Elliott's belly. "Hey there, little dude. Does that hand taste good?"

"I think he's teething." Mary turned away from the stove. "You're just in time. The eggs are ready. I'm afraid it's nothing fancy. Eggs and toast. And there's coffee."

"Mmm, I could smell it." He poured some and stirred in cream and sugar. "I don't expect you to cook for me while you're here."

She shrugged and divided the eggs onto plates. "I enjoy cooking, so it's no bother. Besides, it's more fun preparing meals for someone other than myself."

As if by tacit agreement, they avoided the topic of

Roger over breakfast. After Elliott dozed off, they discussed movies they liked and books they'd both read. Although Mary admitted she preferred romances and he wouldn't touch one, they both enjoyed some of the same thrillers and nonfiction. He basked in Mary's wry smile when she admitted to loving mindless action movies.

When Mary stood to clear the dishes away, Brody jumped up. "Sit. You cooked. I'll clean up."

She shook her head and continued to load the dishwasher. "I want to repay your kindness, and putting dishes in the dishwasher isn't labor-intensive."

"I know, but—"

The sound of a diesel engine in the driveway interrupted their discussion.

She looked up. "Were you expecting anyone?"

"No." He didn't tell her the people who came out here had business. He justified his omission because he didn't want her to feel uncomfortable about staying here, but deep down, he didn't want her to realize how pathetic that made him sound.

Mary scowled. "Please don't tell me people are bringing more things."

"We'd better go see." He picked up Elliott's seat and they went onto the front porch to find a dually truck with a green sixteen-foot livestock trailer hitched to the back.

Brody set Elliott's bouncy seat on the porch floor and shrugged in answer to Mary's unspoken inquiry about their guest. He'd seen the truck in town, but other than that, had no idea why its owner was here. He stepped off the porch and strolled over.

A stranger got out of the mud-spattered truck and adjusted his blue-striped train engineer's cap. Nodding to Mary, he stuck out his hand to Brody. "I know you're

Brody Wilson, but I don't think we've officially met. Bill Pratt from Hilltop Farm."

"Pleasure to meet you, Bill." Brody shook the farmer's hand. Hilltop was a dairy farm, so chances were good Bill hadn't come about boarding horses or restoration hardware. While a friendly and caring bunch, farmers didn't have a lot of spare time for idle socializing. Oh, man, was that a calf in the trailer?

"Bill, this is…" Brody turned as Mary climbed down the steps and stood by his side as if she belonged there. But she didn't and he needed— Why was she looking at him like that? He cleared his thoughts and his throat. "This is Mary Carter. She and her son, Elliott, are visiting Loon Lake."

"Welcome, Mary. Hope you're enjoying your stay."

"A pleasure to meet you, Bill." Mary shook hands. "Thanks, I am. It seems like such a friendly place."

The dairy farmer nodded. "Hope that means you'll be staying awhile."

Mary's answer was a noncommittal "We'll see."

Brody shifted his stance but didn't move away from Mary; he stared down at the top of her head as her fresh scent teased him. Visiting implied she'd be leaving, and the thought of her departure bothered him but he refused to examine the causes. The farmer cleared his throat and dragged Brody's attention back to his other visitor. Hilltop Farm was clear on the other side of the county. Bill hadn't come to chat.

"What brings you out here this morning?" Brody asked, as if he didn't already know.

The farmer adjusted his cap again. "Got a problem I heard you might be able to help with."

"Problem?" Yep, that *was* a calf, and this wasn't good news. Brody's attention shifted back to Mary when she reached up to remove a strand of hair from her bottom lip. His fingers itched to brush it off. Yeah, enough problems of his own making, without others bringing him more.

"Be easier if I just show you." The man went to the back of his trailer and released the gate with a clatter. "Her mama rejected her. I tried to get one of the others to adopt, but no luck. I bottle-fed for a bit, but I ain't got the time or manpower for it. I can't keep up with that level of care, but my granddaughter has taken a shine to this one and..."

Good old Bill wasn't just asking for help, he was upping the stakes with a little show-and-tell. Great—if the town saw him as a soft touch, then his reputation had been cemented by rushing to the ER and offering Mary and Elliott a place to stay. Probably why the farmer thought he could dump a calf in his lap. "What makes you think I can take care of it?"

"My granddaughter is friends with Riley and Meg Cooper's little redhead, Fiona, and she put the notion in my head that you could help. Fiona said her mom brought her out here to see some of the animals you've taken in. My granddaughter wouldn't let up until I promised I'd bring the damn thing to you."

"Uh-huh." Brody shifted again. Mary's bottomless dark eyes studied him as if she was trying to see inside him, as if this was some sort of test of his character. Why should he even care what she thought? He shouldn't have brought her here. A motel, that's where she belonged, not here watching him with those expressive eyes. But she and the baby had looked so vulnerable in that ER, the thought of abandoning them seemed wrong. Oh, man, he was a soft touch.

The farmer pulled off his hat, revealing thinning gray hair. He scratched his scalp. "Never thought I'd see the day when a six-year-old told me how to run my farm. I tried to fight it, but, as my granddaddy used to say, a bull-dog can whip a skunk, but in the end, it just ain't worth it. So here I am."

Brody chuckled at the farmer's wisdom. "You do realize I'm not a vet."

Bill dipped his head. "I don't need a vet, just someone to take her off my hands without breaking my little Elena's heart."

The calf began bawling, and Brody tunneled his fingers through his hair, bowing to the inevitable. "Bring it out."

The farmer led the skittish calf out of the trailer. "Wish I could pay you for your trouble, but things are a bit tight and…"

"Don't worry about it," Brody assured him. Helping Farmer Bill had nothing to do with Mary or the way her big dark eyes were watching him. Nothing at all. Who was he kidding? He could hardly pay attention to the damn conversation with her so near. "I can't guarantee results, but I'll do my best. If she survives, she'll be company for Gertie, the Holstein I took in."

"Gertie? You mean Hank Finley's cow? The one who didn't get pregnant last few go-rounds, but he kept her anyway?" When Brody nodded, Bill belly laughed. "Always was a softhearted ole geezer. Too bad about the stroke but his daughter's taken good care of him. Just like you're taking good care of Gertie."

Brody rolled his eyes and the farmer chuckled as he went to his truck, reached in and pulled out a small carton.

Mary walked to the brown calf and scratched behind its ears, murmuring, "You sweet girl. I'm sure you've come to the right place."

The dairy farmer studied Mary a moment, then

winked at Brody as he handed him the box. "Milk replacer. And thanks."

Brody nodded. "Yeah, glad to help."

"I can pick up more milk replacement and bring it out here."

Brody waved a hand. "I can take care of it."

The metal drop gate clattered as the farmer pulled it back up and secured it. The calf balked at the commotion, and Brody shifted the box under his arm and stooped to pick up the end of the rope tied around the calf's neck. Mary soothed the animal with gentle stroking motions.

Brody sighed. "Mary, I should—"

"Nice meeting you, Mary. I hope to see you at the Independence Day picnic," Bill shot back over his shoulder as he hauled himself into his truck, a huge grin splitting his weather-beaten face. "I appreciate this, Wilson."

Mary caught Brody's attention. "Maybe his granddaughter could come and visit the calf?"

Brody shifted his weight to his heels as he mumbled, "We'll see."

The dairy farmer stuck a hand out his window and waved before driving off, the now-empty trailer rattling and bouncing behind his truck.

Mary waved at the farmer and continued petting the calf and talking to it. Brody sucked on his teeth. He hated what he was about to say, but he had to warn her. "Don't get too attached."

Her head jerked up, and she frowned. "But you said you'd—"

"And I'm going to do my best, but she's not out of the woods yet."

Mary's fingers dug into the calf's thick hair near its ears. "What do you mean? Why not?"

"Bottle-fed calves don't always have a happy outcome."

Dang, she needed to quit looking at him with those expressive eyes. He wasn't some damn calf whisperer. Experience had taught him Mother Nature could be cruel. "They can succumb to something called scour. I'll keep a close watch."

She swallowed. "But it's not always fatal?"

Her hopeful expression twisted his gut. *Be brutally honest; don't give her false hope.* "Not always, no."

She smiled and patted the calf's head. "I'm sure you'll do your best. Otherwise that farmer wouldn't have brought her to you."

"He was happy to hand off his problem, that's all," he told her, and yet a strange tingling curled through his belly when she looked at him.

"I don't believe that for a minute." She flashed a smile. "He was doing it to keep his granddaughter happy, and he wanted to do the right thing by both her and the calf."

Brody grunted. "Believe what you will."

He rubbed the back of his neck. Why were people always expecting him to make things right? Just once he'd like to see what it was like to be selfish, like the rest of his family. You'd think his time in the army would've taught him to recognize his limitations. And yet here he was, tasked with keeping a calf alive when he knew the odds. He'd been tasked with bottle feeding calves as a kid on his grandparents' farm but that didn't make him a calf whisperer.

"What are you going to name her?"

He gave Mary a quizzical glance. "Who?"

"The calf…she needs a name."

"What part of 'don't get attached' did you miss?" He regretted his harsh tone. But dang, she looked at him as if he *was* a calf whisperer.

Instead of the hurt he'd expected, her expression turned mulish.

"She *has* to have a name."

"Be my guest." He sighed, thinking of Bill's analogy involving skunks. At least he'd warned her. He'd remind her of that if… No, he wouldn't. He'd do his best to console her, but there wouldn't be any I-told-you-so. Yep, his Special Forces badass days were over.

"Thanks." She grinned and bounced on her toes. Her impish grin made her appear younger than the midtwenties he'd first guessed. "I'll let you know what I decide."

"Yeah, I'll be waiting." God, he sounded like such a cynic. "I'm going to get her settled."

She went over and picked up a still sleeping Elliott and his infant seat. "Is it safe for him to be in the barn?"

If he told her no, she'd go back into the house, out of sight, and he would be able to ignore her appealing smile and her optimism over the calf. He'd be able to ignore *her*. He closed his eyes. Opening them again, he shrugged. "Sure. There's a small office. He'll be fine."

He guided the skittish calf toward the barn and slid the doors open. Grinning, Mary followed them.

Inside, she paused to let her eyesight get accustomed, then gawked at the cavernous interior, her expression full of awe. He glanced around, but all he saw were repairs and upgrades he'd yet to finish. He'd accomplished a lot in three years, considering he'd done most of it alone. The physical labor had acted as a kind of therapy, clearing his head after the things he'd seen and done in the army. He'd been a professional soldier, something that branded his soul. Despite being cut short, his time in the military had been intense and those experiences plunged that brand deep inside. And close contact combat had added a callus that would be with him forever.

The barn still needed a lot of attention, but Mary looked around as if it was the most wonderful thing she'd ever seen, and while pride filled his chest cavity, his gut twisted at the same time. She was stirring things inside him he wasn't sure he wanted disturbed.

"You can put Elliott's seat on the desk in the office." He pointed toward a walled-off corner. "The door isn't locked."

He led the calf toward an empty stall.

"I'm counting on you to cooperate and survive," he muttered in the calf's ear and glanced back toward the open office door. "You wouldn't want to break her heart, would you?"

Mary put Elliott's seat on Brody's desk. His office was neat and tidy, as was his house. At least it had been before she and Elliott had swept in and disrupted everything.

She left the door ajar as she came out of the office so she'd hear Elliott when he woke up. Back in the other part of the barn, she found Brody preparing bottles for the calf. She wrinkled her nose at a pungent, musty, sour smell and glanced around. "Yuck. What's that?"

"The milk replacement."

"Oh." Why had she thought it would be like table milk? Elliott's formula wasn't.

Brody quirked an eyebrow at her. "Still want to help?"

"You can't scare me." She raised her chin. Did he think she was a city slicker who would balk at a smell? "I've changed diapers that smelled worse than that."

He handed her one of the bottles. "Let's see if she'll take it with you standing in front. Bill said he'd been bottle-feeding already, so I assume she will."

"What happens if she won't?"

"We'll have to try straddling her, but like I said, I doubt if that will be necessary."

Despite her enthusiasm, she'd planned on a careful approach, but the calf had other ideas. Eyes wide, the animal tilted her head back, opened her mouth, and out came a tongue longer and wider—and sloppier—than Mary had imagined.

She held tight as the calf latched on to the bottle and tugged, splattering milk replacer and drool everywhere. "Wow, hope I don't have to burp her, too."

Brody's answering chuckle launched a series of flutters in her stomach. She glanced away, hoping to distract herself from the awareness starting to simmer between them, and she eyed a shelf with more bottles. "How come you already had some bottles if you don't have but the one cow?"

He rubbed his chin and frowned. "Remember when I said the outcome wasn't always happy?"

"Oh." Her chest tightened, and she did her best to put that thought aside. She of all people knew life's harsher realities, but whenever she fell into the trap of feeling sorry for herself or unable to find joy in the simple things in life, she remembered one exceptional foster mother. Aunt Betty, as she'd wanted to be called, had instilled in Mary an optimism she clung to when things got bad. Even now, she heard Betty's voice telling her to be thankful for having something worth mourning when it was gone. Mary had had hopes of staying with Betty until she aged out but Betty got sick and her grown children had convinced her caring for foster kids was too much. But as ill as she was, Betty had put up a fuss when the social worker had pulled out a black trash bag for Mary's belongings. Betty had insisted on giving Mary one of her own suitcases, and before Mary left, Betty had gripped her hand and pleaded with her to remain optimistic. Mary had done her best to keep that promise.

"Mary?"

"Sorry. What do we have to do other than feed her?"

"Most important is to keep her warm and dry. Keeping her in here for a while will help with that."

She looked around at the empty barn. "Didn't you say you had another cow?"

"Yeah, she's in the pasture, but we'll keep this one sequestered until the vet can come and make sure she doesn't have anything that might infect Gertie."

"Is that a possibility?"

"Not a big one, but I'd rather not take that chance." He patted the calf's back and went to the hay bales stacked in one corner. With a grunt he lifted one, his biceps straining the fabric of his T-shirt. He carried the hay to the stall, let it drop to his feet in a shower of dust and wiped his face on his sleeve. No wonder he was so hard and lean. He used a knife from his pocket to slice the twine holding the bale together, then a pitchfork to spread the hay in the stall.

"Is she going to eat that?" She pointed to the hay.

"No, but it keeps the stall drier and makes cleanup easier."

Mary rubbed the calf's neck. She'd never been this close to a cow before, and she enjoyed the opportunity to interact. "I don't understand how her mother could reject her."

Brody grunted as he threw down another hay bale. "Sometimes it's just Mother Nature going a little haywire, or maybe the mama suspects something is wrong so she rejects the calf. Take it from me, not all mothers love unconditionally."

"But…" Mary shook her head. It wasn't as if she hadn't experienced it herself. Her mother hadn't rejected her, but she'd made no provisions for her daughter in case of her death, so Mary had ended up in foster care. Even the line for "father" on her birth certificate had been left blank.

She vowed to do better by Elliott. That's why she was here, setting aside her pride by letting Brody know Roger had rejected not only her but Elliott, as well.

Brody glanced over at her. "But what?"

"Nothing." How could she explain her feelings if Brody didn't believe in unconditional love? What if coming here had been nothing but a waste of time?

She rubbed her arms. Planning her work and working her plan wasn't…well…working. She swallowed her disappointment and smiled as she had done countless times, when all she wanted to do was cry and shout. Life wasn't fair. Yeah, she got it, so why did she keep thinking that it was?

Chapter Four

"Does this happen often?" Mary asked as she got the hang of feeding the calf. The whole process was sloppy but satisfying.

He glanced up from spreading hay. "People bringing unwanted animals?"

She blew her bangs off her forehead. The man was nothing if not frustrating. "I was going to say people turning to you for help."

"Is that what you call this?" He scowled.

"Yes, I think that farmer demonstrated a lot of trust in you." And she was doing it, too—coming to Vermont to track him down so he could meet Elliott.

He grunted and went back to his task.

As the cow suckled on the bottle, Mary recalled the biological kids in her first foster home talking about summer vacations spent on their grandparents' farm. That memory had stayed with her because—despite never having set foot on a farm—she'd come up with an elaborate essay for a school assignment several years later, rather than admit she'd spent the summer hiding out at the local library, day after day, in order to get away from one of the boys in the home who'd picked on her. To this day her gut burned when she thought about writing that paper, not because she'd resorted to stealing someone else's summer to write about, but because she'd resented her absent mother with every poached word of that stupid how-I-spent-my-summer-vacation essay.

Even now it distressed her how she could relive that shame but had trouble recalling memories of her mother. What her mother had looked like, smelled like or the sound of her voice…all lost. What did that say about her? Well, she wasn't going to let that happen to Elliott. She'd get to know these people at Loon Lake, and if something happened to her, they'd be able to help Elliott retain his memories. And maybe someday she'd even build a summer camp for kids in similar situations she'd been in as a child. Give them something special, a memory uniquely theirs, something no one could ever take away. They could carry that with them even if they were bounced from place to place.

Brody set the pitchfork aside and patted the calf's broad back. "I'm going to give her some shots."

"Shots? Why?" Mary's stomach knotted. The calf was so young—was that safe?

"Some antibiotics and vitamins. Preventative measures." He pulled out a first-aid kit.

"See?" Relieved, she balanced on her toes. "I knew you'd know what to do."

He readied the hypodermics. "Knowing what to do isn't the problem. It's whether it all works."

"Even if the worst happens, we'll know you did your best." Did he think she'd hold him responsible?

He had a furrow between his eyebrows as he studied her. "Will we?"

"Yes, of course." She hoped her smile would reassure him.

"You have an awful lot of confidence in me." He tugged on his ear. "Why?"

Why was he arguing with her? Did he think she was lying? "It's a choice I'm making."

"Choice? What kind of choice?"

"I choose to believe in you." She could think the worst, spend her time worrying, but as Aunt Betty used to preach, time spent worrying was time wasted, time you couldn't get back. *Now, child, wouldn't you rather spend the time God gives you being happy? Wouldn't you rather be remembered for spreading joy around?* Aunt Betty had made Mary happy, and she hated to disrespect that memory by not following the other woman's example with Elliott.

"I'll tell you what I told that farmer—I'm not a veterinarian. Her rump's a large target, but hold her steady just in case."

She wrapped her arms around the calf's neck while he injected the needle. "See? Getting a shot isn't so bad. I'm not talking about your abilities, I'm talking about your dedication to doing your best and taking in animals. I suppose most wouldn't do that."

"You talking to me or the calf?"

"Both. I believe this calf wants to survive and you want to do your best to see that happen."

"You barely know me," he scoffed, shaking his head.

"I know enough." When he frowned, she explained, "I remember how patient you were at the funeral with a woman who had no short-term memory—she told you the same story five times."

"No wonder Roger saw you coming from a mile away," he muttered. Stalking over to a plastic tub, he tossed the used needles into it.

She stepped away from the calf, ground her teeth and counted to ten. "For your information, Brody Wilson, I am an adult and I was an adult the whole time I was with Roger. Yes, in hindsight, I may have made some unfortunate choices, but I wasn't some naive waif ripe for the picking. Yes, I fell for his charm, but should I let that turn me bitter? What kind of example would I be teaching Elliott?"

He whirled around toward her. "I meant—"

"I know what you meant, and it's insulting." She tried to swallow a lump in her throat, but it wouldn't go away. Brody might be right about Roger taking advantage, but she didn't go into anything blindfolded. Sure, maybe she should have suspected something, seen through Roger's veneer, but hindsight was twenty-twenty, so she'd forgiven herself. Another choice. To have Brody think she was some child angered her. She blamed her bedraggled appearance in the ER for his opinion. She never should've told anyone about Brody being Elliott's uncle until she'd recovered and could present herself from a more powerful and composed position. Instead she'd been wearing borrowed clothes and looking like someone who needed rescuing. "I can't regret something that gave me Elliott."

"But Roger should...he should've..." He shoved his hand in his hair.

"Yes, he should have," she agreed. "But there are never guarantees. Guarantees come with car batteries, not relationships. Not everyone gets a happy ending handed to them, so I've decided I need to make my own...for myself and for Elliott."

Tough talk, and yet it still hurt to have her baby's father reject him. She and Roger had already gone their separate ways when she learned she was pregnant. When she'd gone to him with the news, she had thought they could come to a cordial agreement, perhaps with visitation rights. But Roger had totally rejected the idea of fatherhood. He went so far as to suggest "dealing with the problem," which she had no intention of doing.

Considering her background, her optimism was silly, childish even, but as she'd said, it was a choice, one she made every day to honor someone who may have been in her life for a brief time, but who'd comforted her when she needed it: the one foster mother who'd come to a school recital. She wanted for Elliott what Aunt Betty had wanted for her, to see and appreciate the wonders of life. If that made her seem naive, then so be it.

Blinking to clear her vision, she stomped toward the office, but Brody's hand on her shoulder stopped her.

He turned her to face him, his blue eyes stormy as he scanned her face. Throwing the toothpick onto the floor, he said, "I'm an ass."

And just like that, her anger melted away. He continued to study her as if he'd expected something else from her. "What? You were expecting an argument?"

"You could put up a fight." He held up his thumb and forefinger a short distance apart and gave her a devilish grin. "A small one?"

She rolled her lips in to keep a smile from springing out. Sure, her anger had evaporated, but she wasn't giving him carte blanche to trample over her feelings. "If I thought you deserved one, I would."

"Ouch." Their gazes met and held. He ran a finger down her cheek. "I'm sorry… Roger…he… I…"

"You're not responsible for his actions. Why would you feel as though you were? You've been nothing but helpful and welcoming." His light touch made it difficult to keep track of their conversation.

"Our family…the dynamics are…" He sighed and studied a spot over her shoulder. "Complicated."

She could understand that he might have felt conflicted over his father having another child. "Because you and Roger are half brothers? Your father wasn't the first man to have an extramarital affair."

He stepped back and tugged on his ear. "I wish it were that simple. How much did Roger tell you?"

"Not much…he said he had a half brother, but that you isolated yourself from the family." Roger had made it sound as if Brody felt superior to his brother, but now she was beginning to realize, as she went over past conversations, that Roger's attitude could've stemmed from jealousy.

"Did he tell you the circumstances?" A muscle ticked in his jaw.

"He told me his father wasn't married to his mother." She wanted to cup his jaw in her hand, caress it until his stormy eyes cleared and he showed her the devilish grin she was fast coming to enjoy.

"That's true, but it's a bit more unsavory than that." He stood as stiff as the handle of the pitchfork.

"Oh?" What could make him so defensive? He and his brother were close in age, so Brody would've been a child at the time Roger was born. How could he be blamed for anything?

"Roger's mother was our family maid." His Adam's apple bobbed when he swallowed.

"Oh." Good old Roger had left out that part. He'd always said Brody had made him feel inferior, as if it had been on purpose, but now she suspected it was Roger's own insecurity reflected on Brody. No wonder Roger had been jealous of Brody as the legitimate son. Mary knew a lot about feeling like the outsider, whether it was an intentional slight or her own feelings projecting back.

He let out a long, low sigh. "Yeah, live-in maid."

"It broke up your family?" No wonder he was so cynical.

"That's the thing. No. But it did give my mother ammunition…as if she didn't have enough already. She was the one who came into the marriage with all the money and therefore all the power. And believe me, she knew how to wield that power."

"What happened to Roger and his mother?"

"They lived in the pool house on the estate." His expression told her he found it hard to believe, too.

"Oh, wow…that sounds…"

He quirked an eyebrow. "Complicated?"

Among other things. "Yeah, and I take it you're telling me you don't do…that."

He gave a quick shake of his head. "Not anymore."

She dipped her head in a quick nod of acknowledgment. "Good to know."

And she needed to remember that. Elliott was Roger's son, and that would make anything between her and Brody complicated. This whole bizarre situation must be a reminder of his childhood in a strange way. At least she knew up front that anything with Brody wouldn't lead to forever.

Aren't you jumping the gun a bit? Coming to the hospital and offering her and Elliott a place to stay meant Brody was a decent person, not that he was interested in her in any way that might lead to anything physical between them.

"So, you'll accept my apology for what I said? I may not be responsible for Roger's actions, but I'm still bothered by them. Ashamed that he didn't do right by you and Elliott."

"Apology accepted. Frankly, I'm not proud of getting involved with him. Normally I'm a better judge of people. Considering my background, I've had to learn to read people and situations."

"Background?" He cocked his head.

She might as well get this out of the way up front. It still surprised her how some people's attitudes changed once they knew about her past—a past she'd had no control over—and she wanted to know up front if Brody was one of those. As a child she hadn't understood it, but now she suspected people blamed the victim. Brody seemed to have his head on straight, but then, she'd been wrong about people before. She drew in a deep breath. "I grew up in foster care. My mother died when I was six. She was a single mother and there were no known relatives, so I went into the system."

"I'm sorry." He took a step toward her, his eyebrows drawn together. "That's why you were so insistent on Elliott having family. You must've been frantic after the accident."

"You could say that." She touched the gash over her eye. "There was so much blood, I panicked and made sure everyone knew that Elliott was your nephew. In case…well, just in case. Considering Roger had no interest in him."

Brody reached out and pulled her in for a chaste hug. "Don't worry. I may have acted like an insensitive jerk, but if anything ever did happen—which I doubt—I'd be there for Elliott."

"Really?" She put her arms around him. He smelled of hay, horses and fresh air, and she struggled with the urge to rest against his solidness, if even for a moment.

There were so many reasons she should pull away. He didn't do complicated, and their getting involved was that with a capital *C*. She was a single mother who needed to think of her son. Starting something with Brody knowing he didn't do complicated would be stupid. She could be damaging the one thing she'd come for...establishing a familial relationship for her son.

Instead of pulling away, she tightened her arms around him. He responded by fitting her body to his. He used his thumb under her chin to lift her face to his. The look in his eyes mirrored her anticipation, and her heart crashed against her ribs.

"I've needed to know what you would taste like since you first smiled at me," he whispered and fastened his mouth to hers.

His lips were firm but gentle, coaxing a response from her, and she parted her lips, letting his tongue slide against hers. She couldn't control the small sigh that escaped at the intimate contact. More, she wanted more, and leaned closer, aligning her body with his as his arms tightened around her. She was—

The calf butted its head against them and started to bawl, its mournful cries mingled with their heavy breathing. Brody laughed, his breath warming her cheek, and she joined in, her gaze meeting his in a shared moment. Then he dropped his arms and stepped back.

"I'm sorry. I shouldn't have..." His brow furrowed.

"No, it's okay." Strong words, even though she was feeling anything but, her knees weak, her hand trembling as she reached out to bury her fingers in the calf's wiry coat. She cleared her throat, hoping to give her voice strength she didn't feel. "Is she okay?"

"I'm sure she's fine for now," he said as he led the calf

back to the stall and shut the door once he'd gotten her settled. "Probably lonesome and missing Mom."

Mary could relate. She had still had a recurring nightmare of being lost in a maze of corridors and doors leading nowhere. No need for an expert to interpret the meaning.

She went to the calf. "Don't you worry, Eleanor, Brody has another cow to keep you company."

Brody's lips twitched. "Eleanor?"

"I like it," she told him and lifted her chin. "What happens to her now?"

He grinned and touched her cheek with the tip of his finger then stepped back. "Once I know she's healthy enough, I'll put her together with Gertie. Cows are social animals, and they can both benefit from the company."

"Speaking of social…where are the other animals? They don't stay in the barn?"

"During the day the alpacas are in a pen out back and the horses in the fenced-in corral. At night, the barn keeps them safe from predators."

She admired how he looked after these abandoned animals. Her search for him had nothing to do with those bottomless blue eyes fringed with dark lashes or his sexy smile. He'd said he had wondered about her since the first time she smiled at him. Had she smiled at him at the funeral? Had he thought about her as she'd thought about him after that brief first meeting? She started to lift her hand to her still tingling lips, but dropped it. "Wait. Did you say 'horses'? Plural?"

"Yeah. Four." He stabbed the tines of the pitchfork into a bale of hay.

She couldn't decide which was sexier, those muscles straining against his cotton T-shirt or the fact he was helping an abandoned calf get a second chance. "I thought you only had one named Patton."

"Only one is mine. The other three I board for people who have second homes on the lake." He replaced the first-aid kit on the shelf and dumped the used milk bottles into a utility sink located at one end of the workbench.

"Do you use Patton for your farmwork?"

"No, he's not a working horse. He's here to enjoy his retirement."

There had to be a story behind him having the horse. She'd bet there was one behind every one of his animals. Just like this calf. "How did you end up with a retired horse?"

"The owner couldn't take care of it anymore."

"And he brought it here?" How was she supposed to feel about this? Did this make her and Elliott just two more strays Brody was taking in? If so, then she needed to remember that before harboring any more romantic notions. She raised her hand to her lips. *Except he kissed as if he meant it, as if he found her desirable, as if she was more than Elliott's mother.*

"The owner asked if I could take it." He ran water into the sink.

"You run an animal sanctuary?" No wonder he'd been so evasive about what kind of farm he had. Brody wasn't using the animals but taking care of them, giving them shelter and feeding them. Just like her, once again a lost misfit.

"The place has some animals, but that doesn't make it a sanctuary. So what if I take care of them? Can't let 'em starve, now can I?" He banged the bottles against the sides of the metal sink as he washed them.

Okay, then. We'll assume that question was rhetorical.

She considered what he was doing quite noble. Wouldn't it be wonderful to bring Elliott up on a place like this with someone like— *Whoa, slow down, Mary.* She was already weaving fairy tales and needed to stop. Even if she chose to live in Loon Lake, she would not be living on Brody's farm. She wanted him and Elliott to form a bond but she didn't have to live with Brody for that to happen.

"Can I help with anything else?" She wanted to show she appreciated him offering them a place to stay. And doing something physical would help get rid of some of the tension that kiss had created within her.

He wiped his face on his sleeve. "That's not necessary. You still need to be careful of your injuries."

"I know I'll just get in the way, but I'd love to help... if...if you'd show me what to do." Being a part of life on the farm appealed to her, even though she knew her stay here was temporary. Never one to let opportunities pass, she'd enjoy it while she could. And maybe she'd learn some things that would help if her dream of opening a camp for foster kids ever to fruition came.

"I doubt if the doctor would approve that."

"I bumped my head, but my limbs are still intact." She held up her hands.

"All right, but promise you'll stop at the first sign of—"

"Any of those things on the list from the ER?" She grinned when he grunted an acknowledgment. "I will. I promise."

"You could help me inventory."

"Inventory? As in counting things? Don't you have something...something more farmer-like?"

"Farmer-like?" He grinned. "Isn't counting what you're good at?"

It was true; she enjoyed working with numbers because they never let you down. Numbers didn't care about your background. Numbers just *were*. "I suppose so."

A cry from the office interrupted her, and she rushed to get Elliott. She didn't want to give Brody any reason—well, any *more* reason—to regret his decision. Elliott quieted when he spotted her and began kicking his legs, a sign he was happy.

"Wait until you see what Uncle Brody has," she told him as she undid the safety straps and pulled him out of the seat. "Let's go ask Uncle Brody if he thinks it's okay for you to pet Eleanor."

Brody was washing the bottles they'd used for the calf. When Elliott spotted him, he threw out his arms and began babbling.

"I think he wants you to hold him. If that's okay with you."

"Sure." Brody put the bottles on a shelf and wiped his hands, then reached out and took Elliott. After getting him settled against his side, he said, "You want me to show you around, big guy? Your mom tells me you like cows."

As if on cue, the calf stuck her head over the half door of the stall. Elliott's eyes widened, and he squealed. Brody winced and rubbed an ear with his free hand. "Whoa, a little notice next time, big guy."

"Sorry about that. He just learned he could make that sound." Mary laughed. "The first time he did it, he stopped and looked around like he was trying to see where it came from. He was insufferable the first couple days after he realized he could make all that noise."

Elliott reached out, and Brody leaned closer to the calf. Elliott patted his hand against the calf's head and looked to Brody, letting out another—less shrill—squeal. Elliott wrapped his chubby fingers around the calf's ear and tugged. Brody pried Elliott's fist open and took a step back. "I'm sure she appreciates the sentiment, big guy, but maybe with a little less ear tugging. I'm not sure of her disposition yet."

Another string of baby gibberish had Brody chuckling. "Yeah, it's a smaller version of the ones your mom tells me you saw grazing in the fields."

Mary rubbed her knuckles across the calf's head. "Maybe once Elliott and I have our own place, we can get a dog."

Brody's eyes sparkled with mischief. "And what? Tell him it's a miniature cow?"

"Very funny." She made a face at Brody, but in truth she was enjoying spending time together. Almost as if—Nope, she wouldn't give life to *those* thoughts. Brody was getting to know his nephew—that's all. *Are you forgetting that kiss?* Yes, yes, she was.

"I don't think you'll be fooled by a dog, will ya, big guy?" Brody demonstrated for Elliott how to pat the calf. Elliott looked at Brody and babbled something before leaning toward the calf and bringing his hand up and down in a similar motion. "That's it."

"Tell Mom you'd rather have a calf and a built-in milk supply," Brody said in a stage whisper next to Elliott's ear.

"Oh, brother, even I know cows have to have baby cows in order to produce milk." She laughed. "Nice try, but I think we'll start small. Speaking of which, I'm surprised you don't have any dogs around here."

"I'm sure there's a farmer out there giving some stray mutt directions to this place right now."

Mary laughed, and Elliott did, too.

"You think that's funny?" Brody tickled Elliott's belly, sending him into ecstatic giggles. "I'll be sure to send every stray mutt in the county to you and your mom."

"Uh-oh, I guess pet friendly better be at the top of the list when I go apartment hunting."

"Apartment hunting?" He cocked an eyebrow.

Oops, she hadn't meant to throw that out there yet. Sure, she'd been *thinking* about settling in Loon Lake on a permanent basis if she could find work, but she hadn't said anything. And Brody was many things, but a mind reader wasn't one of them.

"You're homeless?" Brody's question broke the silence.

"What? Oh, no, no, no." She rushed to reassure him. Nothing like appearing even more pathetic. She wished she could go back to day one on her "let's go find Brody" project.

Brody moved away from the calf, and when Elliott started to bring his hand to his face, Brody captured it. "I think we'd better clean that hand before you go sucking on it. Maybe Mom can open that box of wipes," he said and motioned with his chin.

Mary wiped Elliott's hands. He brought one to his face and babbled at it before making a fist, which he tried to fit into his mouth.

"I put a teething toy in the freezer this morning. If you want, I can take him back in the house."

"I'll come with you, and you can explain about apartment hunting."

"Fine." They started toward the house while she told him about the insurance company she'd been working for and how it had been swallowed up by an even larger one and she'd lost her job. The lease on her apartment in Hartford was also expiring, so she'd decided to put her belongings in storage and come to Loon Lake to let Elliott connect with his uncle while she waited for responses to her résumé. "I figured we might have to move anyway, depending on job offers I get. I was hoping I might be able to find a rental on a monthly basis, either here in town or close by."

"That makes sense, except the part about finding a rental in Loon Lake." He frowned. "There's one small apartment building, and most of the lake cottages are already rented for the summer season. I doubt you'll find much."

"That's okay. I researched the nearest larger cities or across the river in New Hampshire so I'd have a contingency plan."

"That's not what I meant." He shook his head. "I meant you and Elliott can stay here."

"Oh, we couldn't do that." It had been one day, and she already had way too many ideas about Brody in her head.

"Why not?"

"I hate imposing on you. Elliott and I can move to a motel or find someplace to rent while I look for a job." Elliott started to fuss, and she reached out to him.

Brody handed the baby back to her and held the kitchen door open. "That isn't necessary. I have plenty of room here."

"I didn't come here to sponge off you."

In the kitchen, she got Elliott's teething ring and went into the living room. She grabbed a baby blanket and dropped it on the floor.

Brody followed them into the other room. "I know that. Right now, you're like a visiting relative. I wouldn't make you stay in a motel when I have all this room."

"I thought you didn't associate with your relatives?"

"Are you always this contrary?" He lowered his chin and contemplated her.

She gave him a fake grin. "Just living up to my name."

"Maybe I should plant you a garden. What do you think, big guy? Should we plant a garden for your mommy?"

Elliott held out his teething toy as if offering it to Brody.

Brody clicked his tongue. "As tempting as that is, I'll pass, bud."

She tried to arrange the blanket with her free hand while balancing Elliott.

"Here, let me do that." Brody took the blanket and spread it out.

With Elliott settled and rolling around on the blanket, Brody returned to his office in the barn, saying he had paperwork.

Did he need to work or was he glad to get away from them? Sure, he seemed to be bonding with Elliott, which was what she wanted, but having two practical strangers moving in with him must be unsettling. It would be for anyone, and more so for a man used to living alone and, if the townspeople were to be believed, embracing his isolation.

She couldn't forget how Elliott's biological father being Brody's estranged half brother complicated everything. And Brody Wilson clearly didn't do complicated.

Chapter Five

In his office Brody tried to concentrate on catching up on posts in the restoration forum he belonged to and answering emails from persons seeking his expertise, but thoughts of Mary and Elliott kept rolling around in his head.

What had prompted his offer of a place to stay while she searched for employment? Because he wanted to get to know his nephew better? Or because he'd enjoyed that kiss? He'd done his best to push it out of his mind, along with the image of how she'd looked the night before with her sleep tousled hair.

Was it Mary herself that he wanted to get to know better, and not just because she was Elliott's mother?

Elliott's mother. That right there was the problem. Roger was Elliott's father, even if he didn't want anything to do with his son. And in Brody's experience, complications led to headaches and, yes, heartache.

Remembering Mary's talk about summer camps, he

clicked on a search. He shouldn't be encouraging her outlandish idea. If he wasn't careful, she'd be wanting to turn *his* farm into one. No, he drew the line at that. Taking in animals that needed a place to heal was one thing, but kids? The animals didn't demand anything beyond food, shelter and the occasional visit from the local vet. His relationship with them was simple, undemanding. He knew nothing about helping disadvantaged or at-risk kids.

Wait—that wasn't the complete truth. What about Kevin and Danny? He'd spent some time with them, and he knew the teens could've taken a wrong turn if not for Riley and Meg, along with others in town, stepping up when the boys' biological families had failed. Kevin was graduating from high school next month and would be attending the local community college, and Danny was getting his GED and planning to join the military.

He rose and went to the window, his hands thrust into his back pockets. *I would have given anything to spend time at a place like this.* Mary's words bounced around in his head. Opening his sanctuary—God, now she had him calling this place an animal sanctuary. Opening it to others wouldn't change Mary's childhood.

But it might change someone else's life. Damn. His inner voice was nothing but trouble.

Once again his thoughts strayed to Kevin and Danny. Would they be in the same place if someone hadn't cared enough to give them guidance?

Would you give them the same kind of guidance you gave Roger?

Because that had ended so well, with Roger rejecting responsibility for his actions, denying his own son. He shouldn't be surprised. Some things never changed, and Roger had proved that over and over.

He prowled around the small office, trying to get a

grip on his thoughts. Bringing Mary and Elliott to the farm had been the decent thing to do, but he needed them to leave before...

Before what? Before he didn't want them to leave? He didn't do complicated. Sure, he'd be an uncle to Elliott, but nothing more. A beautiful, alluring woman like Mary would find someone to settle down and share her life with, and he'd be relegated to the sidelines.

And that was okay with him, because if his parents were anything to go by, happily-ever-after was fraught with toxic behavior. But that kiss...

That kiss made him wonder if it would be worth taking a chance but that was crazy. And yet, the thought of Mary sitting across from someone else at mealtimes, Mary sharing that certain little smile she got when something amused her or Mary throwing her arms around some other man when he pleased her bothered him. Way more than it should.

Disgusted with his thoughts, he stalked back to the house, where Mary was spooning cereal into Elliott's mouth. The baby bounced in his high chair and began jabbering when he spotted Brody. Elliott's reaction lifted Brody's mood, and he grinned back. He didn't know about other babies, but Elliott was always so happy—his enthusiasm for life was infectious.

"Hey there, big guy." He ruffled Elliott's curls. "Eating again?"

"Tell Uncle Brody you're a growing boy," Mary said as she spooned more cereal into the baby's mouth. "Do you think we could go into town sometime soon? I'll be needing more diapers and baby food."

"Sure, we can go this afternoon." Brody got a can of soda out of the refrigerator.

"Thanks. I'll get ready as soon as he's finished eating." She turned back to feeding the baby.

"I can finish if you want to get ready." He took a sip and set the can on the counter. Truth was, he enjoyed spending time with his nephew.

After Mary went upstairs, he continued to feed Elliott and kept up a conversation, telling him about the animals on the farm. Maybe if he started now he could instill a sense of responsibility in Elliott so he wouldn't turn out like Roger.

Elliott chattered back until he yawned and rubbed his fist back and forth across his face, smearing cereal everywhere—even in his nose.

"A couple more bites?" Brody leaned closer, waving the spoon back and forth, hoping to entice the baby.

"Achoo!" Elliott's sudden sneeze sprayed baby cereal everywhere. Brody jumped back, but not before he was covered in the gooey mess.

"Thanks a lot, big guy." He grabbed a towel and began trying to wipe off himself and the baby.

Elliott poked out a trembling lower lip, and Brody's annoyance vanished. "Hey, hey, it's okay, bud. Let's get you cleaned up. Your mom will think I'm an amateur if she sees you like this."

"Like what?" Mary asked from the kitchen doorway.

Brody glanced up and totally forgot about the mess as awareness and appreciation flowed through him. Mary had on a blue sweater that complemented her dark eyes, olive skin and lustrous curls. Even the healing gash over her eye didn't detract from her beauty. Oh, man, he needed to stop staring.

"Oh, dear, look at the two of you." She pressed her lips together as if to suppress a laugh. At the sink, she rinsed out a washcloth and turned back to the pair of them, contemplating them as if she couldn't decide whom to wash first.

Brody reached for the wet cloth. "Here, let me. No sense in all three of us being covered in cereal."

"Sorry about that," Mary said, but Brody arched an eyebrow to let her know he wasn't buying it and she grinned.

He took the wet cloth from her, his fingers brushing hers and jolting him with that spark of awareness—awareness that Mary was more than Elliott's mother.

Turning from temptation, he concentrated on getting his nephew cleaned up. Not easy with a moving target, but he wiped Elliott's face and pulled him from the high chair.

Mary reached for her son, but Brody kept him out of reach. "Let me make sure I got it all."

"That's right. This sweater belongs to Meg Cooper." She smoothed the long sweater over her hips.

"I meant you look nice. Not that you wouldn't look nice in something else." *Or in nothing at all.* He sighed. At least no one could accuse him of being a smooth talker.

"It's a Hepburn sweater, and they're popular and classic for a reason."

"Would you please tell your mom I'm trying to tell her how pretty she is? Maybe she'll believe you," he said to Elliott in an exaggerated tone, and the baby responded by giggling.

Brody glanced at her. "See? He agrees with me."

"Thank you...both," Mary said, her cheeks pink. "He looks clean. I'll take him if you want to wipe off, too."

Brody glanced at his shirt, which was now liberally sprinkled with baby food. "Yeah, let me get a clean one."

After changing, Brody went back downstairs and followed the sound of Mary's voice to find her on the porch swing with Elliott on her lap, as they watched the horses grazing in the distance.

Mary stood and settled the baby on her hip. "Are the horses friendly?"

"Yes. Do you ride?" An image of her astride a horse, laughing, her hair trailing out behind her, popped into his head before she answered.

"No, but I'm sure I could learn."

"I'm sure you could." Oh, yeah, he definitely wanted to teach her. "For starters, I'll introduce you to them when we get back. I want to get to the drugstore before it closes."

Mary glanced at her watch. "But…"

"They close early on Wednesdays so the pharmacist can take his granddaughter fishing," he explained.

"For real?" Mary gave him a skeptical look.

"Honest to God." He'd gotten used to the pace of life in Loon Lake and forgot it sometimes came as a shock to others. "Small-town living."

"I think we're going to enjoy it here." She gave Elliott a hug. "What do you think?"

Elliott tried to stick his fish-shaped blue teething toy into her mouth. She avoided the drool-covered offering. "Your prescription. I hope it's nothing serious."

"It's not for me. One of the horses is on an inflammatory drug regimen, the vet calls it in and the pharmacy compounds it. Makes it easier." He wiggled his eyebrows. "Believe me, you don't want to give a horse pills."

"I'm sure there's a wonderful punch line out there somewhere, but I got nothing." She made a tsking sound. "Sorry."

He tickled Elliott, who giggled. "Should we let her off this time? Whaddaya think, big guy?"

"You guys are a tough crowd." Mary's lips twitched.

Brody zeroed in on that mouth. If he leaned a little closer, he could—*thwack*. A teething toy collided with his lips. Served him right for having those thoughts about the little guy's mom. He moved out of range of those tempting lips and the fish-shaped toy. "After the drugstore, we'll go to see Tavie. I'm sure she's chomping at the bit to meet you."

"Tavie is Ogle's wife, right? The one who arranged for all the baby things?" she asked as she reached down to get her purse and the diaper bag from the swing.

"Yeah."

"Good. I'd like to thank her for her generosity."

While Brody waited for his prescription, Glenda, the pharmacy tech, kept glancing at the three of them and smiling. He could just imagine the gossip flowing as soon as they left. He'd told Mary when they first walked into the store she could shop around, but she seemed content to stand next to him while he waited. To be honest, he didn't mind the idea of gossip as much as he might have three years ago. Or even three days ago.

A pattering of footsteps had Elliott straining to look over Mary's shoulder. The baby kicked his legs and squealed. Brody turned as Riley and Meg Cooper's six-year-old dynamo, Fiona, barreled down the aisle toward them. Her mass of red curls bounced like marionettes as she skidded to a stop in front of them, her sneakers squeaking on the polished floor.

"Mr. Brody, hi." Fiona gave him a gap-toothed smile, her lower incisors missing.

"Well, if it isn't Miss Fiona." Brody leaned over and gave her a high five, which she returned, setting off giggles, her bony shoulders rising and falling. "Mary, this is Fiona, Deputy Cooper's daughter."

"Glad to meet you, Fiona," Mary said.

Fiona pointed at Elliott. "We're gettin' a baby. Right now he's in Mommy's tummy. Mommy says we're gonna name him James Riley. Daddy let me pick out my doggy's name, but Mommy says *she* gets to name the baby. Daddy says it's 'cuz I picked Mangy." Fiona pushed her pink glasses higher on her nose and studied Elliott. "What's his name?"

Mary's amused smile lit up her face, making Brody's breath hitch in his chest. He could look at her all day and not get bored.

"His name is Elliott." Mary squatted and balanced the baby on her knee to give Fiona a better look. "Elliott, can you say hi to Fiona?"

"Hey." Fiona leaned closer, resting her hands on her knees. "Elliott is the name of the boy in *E.T.*"

Mary caught Elliott's chubby hand in hers when he reached out, making a grab for Fiona's hair or her wire-rimmed pink glasses, both enticing targets for the curious baby. "Do you like that movie?"

"Uh-huh, Daddy watched it with me. And he didn't even complain when I wanted to watch again. Mommy said—" Fiona waved a finger back and forth "—Daddy has had to watch that dang movie a *mill-ee-yawn* times, young lady."

Elliott kicked his legs and tried to catch Fiona's finger. Laughing, Mary said, "Sounds like you have a very patient daddy."

"I guess." Fiona straightened and studied Mary. "Are you that lady Mommy says is living with Mr. Brody on his *aminal* farm?"

Brody tugged one of Fiona's pigtails. "Her name is Mary. She and Elliott are visiting me."

"Daddy visited us, then me and Mommy married him.

And now I'm Fiona Cooper. Mr. Brody?" Fiona gazed up at him expectantly. "Are you gonna marry Elliott's mommy and change his name?"

"No, it's not like that." Brody ran a finger under his shirt collar and avoided eye contact with Mary. "I mean… this is different. Your daddy was always your daddy, Fiona. Even before he and your mommy got married. But Elliott…well, Elliott's my nephew and he's visiting."

She canted her head and looked up at him. "So you're *not* gonna marry Miss Mary and be Elliott's daddy?"

"Absolutely not. I mean Elliott isn't… I'm not… Mary doesn't…" *Stuff a sock in it, Wilson.* He glanced around. Where the heck was Meg? And why wasn't she supervising her chatterbox of a daughter?

Fiona's gray eyes were large behind the lenses of her glasses as she shifted her gaze from him to Mary. "But—"

"Fiona Bridget Cooper!" Meg hurried up the aisle and placed her hands on her daughter's slender shoulders. "What did I tell you about wandering off?"

"Not to do it?" Fiona glanced up at Meg. "But, Mommy—"

"But, Fiona," Meg mimicked and stuck out her hand. "Hi, I'm Meg Cooper. You've already met my husband, Riley, and…" She put her arm around Fiona's shoulders. "My daughter."

"Mommy." Fiona tugged on Meg's maternity top and pointed to Elliott. "His name is Elliott. I told them we're getting a baby boy soon."

"Yeah, not soon enough." Meg laughed and rubbed her protruding belly. "I see all the things I've heard about what an adorable baby he is are true."

"Thank you. And I can't thank you enough for the loan of the clothes," Mary said as Meg gushed over Elliott.

Meg waved a hand in a dismissive gesture. "Glad to help, and I think that sweater looks better on you than me."

Fiona tugged on Meg's shirt again. "Mommy, Mr. Brody says he's not going to marry Miss Mary and be Elliott's daddy."

"That's not any of our business, sweetie." Meg blushed and shot them an apologetic glance. "Sorry we can't stay and chat, but we're meeting Riley for his lunch break, and we're running late."

Brody glanced at Mary as Meg marched her daughter away. What the heck was she thinking? He winced at his reaction to Fiona's marriage question.

"Well, that was awkward. I guess I should be thankful no one can understand what Elliott is saying." Mary laughed, watching Meg and Fiona walk up the aisle.

"Brody?" The pharmacist cleared his throat. "Any questions?"

"I'm good. Thanks, Rob." Brody turned and took the white bag but couldn't fight the maudlin thoughts assaulting him. They couldn't be because he was envious of Riley's family situation. Because he wasn't. Nope. Not one little bit.

Mary followed Brody to the truck, a dozen thoughts and emotions vying for attention. She hadn't come here for any sort of personal relationship with Brody other than the one between him and Elliott. He'd taken a physical step away from her when Fiona had asked if he was going to marry her. She wasn't sure if his action had been conscious or not. Oh my goodness, one kiss from him and she was dithering like a schoolgirl. She laughed at her foolishness.

Brody glanced at her. "What?"

"Meg must have her hands full with Fiona. How long have they lived in Loon Lake?" Mary asked as Brody pulled up to the traffic light. She figured Meg Cooper might be a good source of local information. "She sounds like she's from Boston."

"You're right. She spent summers and school vacations here and then moved permanently into her family's cottage by the lake about four or five years ago."

"Did she meet her husband here?"

"They'd known one another since childhood. He spent summers here for a while, too. Riley is friends with Meg's brother, Liam," Brody said.

"But they married recently?" At least that's what she'd gathered from Fiona. She had a feeling there was a story in there somewhere.

Brody nodded. "A little over a year ago."

"I should've gotten her phone number. She might be able to point me in the direction of a few things." And Mary hoped Meg might know of some places for rent. She hadn't missed the speculative glances the pharmacy tech had given them, even before the little girl had shown up with her awkward questions. No wonder Brody was freaked out by Fiona's bluntness. She was, too, but his reaction gave her a clear view of reality. Which was fine. She'd come here to give Elliott a link to family, that's all. So where was this disappointment coming from?

"I can give you Meg's number. I'm sure she won't mind." He frowned. "But you know I'll be happy to help you with whatever you might need."

"Know a good pediatrician? Or gynecologist?" She grinned.

He chuckled. "Okay, you got me there."

Before Mary could find a way to talk about their situation, they pulled into the gravel lot in front of the general store.

Loon Lake General Store looked like it belonged on the set of a television show featuring a small-town sheriff and his bumbling deputy. Two ancient gas pumps stood in front of the two-story barn-red wooden building. The entrance was an open porch with hand-painted black-on-white signs, hung between the posts that advertised Vermont cheese, maple syrup and video rentals. On one side of the porch, there was a black deacon's bench, and on the other a freezer with bagged ice for sale.

The store fit with her image of the town and its residents. She unbuckled her seat belt and winced when her right shoulder protested. The bruising from the safety strap was easing but still reminded her she'd been in a crash.

Brody glanced at her. "Wait and let me help you get out."

"I'm fine, it's just a little stiffness," she said and waved him off, but he rushed around and helped her anyway.

Brody unlatched the infant carrier from the back seat. When she reached to take it, he said, "I've got him. You need to take it easy, doctor's orders."

She rolled her eyes but fell into step as they walked across the parking lot, their feet crunching on the gravel, their arms bumping. Even that impersonal contact sent shivers of awareness through her, but Brody's "absolutely not" answer to Fiona's blunt question tempered her feelings. This was all about Elliott. As a baby, he had no control over who was or wasn't in his life. But she vowed not to be an easy target for any man, even one with eyes fringed with thick, dark lashes designed to make women swoon. How had she not seen Roger for who he was long before Elliott? Nope, she wasn't getting into the what-if trap. She loved their son enough for the both of them. Brody was nothing like Roger, she could see that blind-folded, but his reaction to Fiona's question told her all she needed. She'd let him get to know Elliott, but she would never throw herself at him.

An old-fashioned bell jingled when Brody opened the door. He stepped aside, holding the door so she could enter ahead of him. Talk about stepping back in time. The in-terior of the store was an explosion of color. Open shelv-ing displayed boxes, cans and jars of all shapes and sizes. Wooden barrels full of bulk dry goods stood in front of a glass display case with deli meats and cheeses.

But what held Mary's attention was a display of glass wind chimes and sun catchers. The colors and workman-ship reminded her of pictures she'd seen of Chihuly glass sculptures, although on a much smaller scale.

"It's high time you brought them to meet me, Brody Wilson." A seventysomething woman with teased hair reminiscent of earlier times greeted them from behind a long wooden counter located at a right angle to the en-trance. "Everyone in town has met them but me."

"That's hardly true," Brody shot back.

The older woman speared him with a glare. "You in-troduced her to Bill Pratt over at Hilltop. How do you explain that?"

Mary's instinct was to defend him, but the woman winked at her before turning back to confront Brody.

"Bill hasn't given me half the grief you have," he mut-tered.

"Ha! That's not what I heard." The woman's penciled eyebrows rose. "If the story about him bringing you a calf to bottle-feed is true."

"Oh, it's true." His tone was resigned.

"That granddaughter has him wrapped around her

finger. So…" The woman hitched her chin at Brody. "Introduce me already."

Brody rolled his eyes. "Mary Carter, I'd like you to meet Tavie Whatley."

"It's a pleasure." Mary stepped forward and shook hands.

"Nice to *finally* meet you, Mary." Tavie squeezed Mary's hand before letting go. "Now, Brody Wilson, you set that baby up here so I can see him, proper like. I've heard from everyone how adorable he is."

Mary gave Brody a puzzled glance. "Why is everyone talking about Elliott?"

"Don't worry, you'll get used to how quick news travels around here." Brody set Elliott's infant seat on top of the counter. "And they love it when they have someone or something new to talk about."

Tavie leaned over Elliott and cooed. "Isn't he just a sweetheart?"

Elliott gave Tavie a wide, gummy grin, kicking his legs and making Tavie laugh in delight. Mary lifted him out of his seat and rested him on her hip after pulling the teething ring out of her purse.

"I can see why the nurses at the ER were so taken with him." Tavie reached over and danced her crooked fingers up and down his chest, grinning at the peals of baby giggles.

"Thank you." A sense of belonging and connection filled Mary. Despite the inauspicious beginning, coming to Loon Lake had been the right decision. The care between Brody and Tavie was evident, even in their good-natured sparring; this type of camaraderie had been what Mary had longed for her entire life. She was still very much a stranger, an outsider, but she hoped with time she and Elliott might belong, too. "I've been wanting to thank you for your generosity with all the baby things."

Tavie waved her hand in the air as if to dismiss the act of kindness. "You're welcome, dear, but all I did was make the arrangements."

"Yeah, Tavie is Loon Lake's benevolent dictator," Brody teased.

"What can I say?" Tavie sniffed and touched her hair in a smug gesture. "Responsibility walks hand in hand with capacity and power."

Brody's eyes widened. "Really."

"Yes really, Mr. Smartypants." Tavie sniffed and winked at Mary. "It was on my daily calendar of quotes."

"And I'll bet you've been waiting for me to come in here so you could use it." Brody's throaty snicker released a swarm of flutters in Mary's stomach.

Tavie clucked her tongue and reached under the counter. Straightening, she tossed a box of toothpicks at Brody, which he caught one-handed and pocketed with another deep chuckle that sent a tingle along Mary's spine.

"I think we got you outfitted with baby furniture, but if you need anything else, just let us know," Tavie told her.

Heat rose in Mary's cheeks. She was grateful for the generosity of the town's residents, but something inside her balked at being a charity case. Did everyone assume she needed a handout? Some first impression she must've made. She wanted people to like her, not feel sorry for her. "I appreciate your generosity, but I can buy whatever my son needs."

Tavie shook her head, her halo of teased hair moving with her. "It's not charity, sweetie, it's neighbors helping neighbors."

"But I'm a stranger here," Mary protested.

"Yes, but you're with Brody now, and he's one of us.

Whether he likes to admit it or not." Tavie tapped fingers on the counter like a judge using a gavel to pass judgment. "And Brody can haul the stuff back here once you get settled with your own things. See? Problem solved."

The bell above the door tinged, and Ogle Whatley stepped inside the store. He nodded. "Brody. Mary."

Tavie looked up from entertaining Elliott. "Ogle picked up your car this morning."

"Any idea of the extent of the damages?" Brody asked before Mary could say anything.

Ogle rubbed his shiny scalp. "I'll need to look it over a bit more, but most of the damage appears to be cosmetic. 'Course, the insurance people will have the final say."

"Thank you," Mary said, still trying to process the kindness of these people. Of course, some of it was due to Brody, but it was still amazing and unlike anything she'd experienced before. "I will be sure to get the insurance claim started today. Oh, and my suitcases and items are still in the trunk. I don't suppose—"

"Ogle, see what you can—" Tavie began.

"Already on it, dear." Ogle saluted his wife and motioned for Brody to follow him.

"Let me go see what I can do." Brody touched Mary's arm. "If there's anything you need while we're here, Tavie can put it on my tab."

"I can pay my own way," Mary said. Living in a small town, even one as friendly and helpful as Loon Lake, would take some getting used to. She couldn't pop down to the bodega on the corner if she ran out of diapers or baby food, but having other people who would know and love Elliott would be worth any inherent inconveniences.

After the men left, Tavie held out her hands. "May I hold him while you pick up whatever supplies you need? It's been a long time since I had a young'un to fuss over.

My youngest grandbaby is off flyin' helicopters over there in Afghanistan."

"Sure. He's not shy around strangers. At least not yet." Mary handed him over. "You must be proud of your grandchild."

"We are proud of him. 'Course, he'd make me a lot happier if he was home and safe," Tavie told her. "It's not like we don't have helicopters around here. They used one a ways back to pluck some hiker who got turned around over there in New Hampshire on Mount Washington."

"I hope your grandson comes back safe and sound," Mary said. "And soon."

While Tavie entertained Elliott, Mary went over to the display of wind chimes and bird feeders she'd noticed when they'd first entered the store. The blown-glass shaped to look like jellyfish caught her eye. She loved the whimsical hand-painted seahorses and tropical fish in between the tentacles of the jellyfish.

"Aren't they beautiful?" Tavie, with Elliott perched on her hip, came to stand next to Mary.

Mary nodded with enthusiasm. "I love listening to them. And these are fun just to look at. They remind me of miniature Chihuly glass sculptures."

"I don't know what Chihulys are, but a few of these would sure look pretty on that front porch of yours." Tavie bounced Elliott on her hip. "As long as you placed them in a protected spot."

"Oh, I'm just staying on the farm temporarily." Good heavens, did people think she'd moved in with Brody?

"You and this little guy here will be good for Brody, bring him out of his shell."

"But I'm just—"

"*Yeah*, I 'spect that now you're here, Brody will be more visible in the community. I'm sure the three of

you will be joining us for the Independence Day picnic
on the green."

"The picnic sounds like a highlight for the community," Mary said, trying to be noncommittal. How had
a discussion of wind chimes deteriorated into this? And
why did Brody not want to involve himself in the community? Strange, because everyone seemed to like him.

"Yup, even Des Gallagher—he's the one who makes
these…what did you call them? Chihulys? Anyway, he'll
be there with a booth in the craft fair. Like Brody, he's
a veteran, doesn't say much. Lets his artwork speak for
him, I reckon."

Before Mary could form any sort of comment, Elliott tried to grab a bird feeder made of delicate china
teacups. The cups held seeds and the saucers formed a
perch for the birds.

Tavie took a step back. "As gorgeous as they are, I
don't think your mama wants to buy all of Des's cre-
ations. Let's go find something more age appropriate."

Mary enjoyed listening to Tavie and Elliott as she
strolled around the store and picked up the supplies she'd
need, her footsteps echoing on the raw wooden floors.
She paused in front of a display crammed full of glass
jars stocked with all sorts of sweets. She'd never seen
anything like it except in pictures or movies. It was easy
to imagine an older Elliott asking for a treat. *Whoa, slow
down. Don't get ahead of yourself.* She couldn't put all
her hopes and dreams into staying in Loon Lake. Experience had taught her the evanescent nature of people and
places in her life. She touched her fingertips to her lips as
she recalled Brody's kiss. Had it meant anything to him,
or had it been to satisfy his curiosity? He'd admitted that
he'd wondered what kissing her would be like, so maybe

that was what had prompted it. She needed to be wary of projecting her feelings onto his actions.

"There you are. Finding all you need?"

Brody's deep baritone from behind caused her to twirl around and the items she'd been juggling in her arms slipped, spilling to the floor.

"Hey, you okay?" Brody frowned and touched her arm. She nodded, and he squatted to gather her things. "You're sure you're okay? You seem a bit jumpy."

Are you gonna marry Elliott's mommy and change his name?

Now you're here, Brody will be more visible in the community.

Would he feel pressured by her staying on his farm? Heck, she was feeling it, so he must be. "I don't want Elliott and me being here to make any trouble for you."

"Trouble? What do you mean?" A deep frown creased his brow.

Yeah, what did she mean? She shrugged and searched for words to explain. "From what Tavie said, it feels like the town is…is reading into my staying with you and… and I don't know if there's someone you don't want getting the wrong idea…about us, I mean. Fiona is the one who asked the question, but others are looking at us and wondering."

"C'mon, Mary, you're not going to let something a six-year-old says affect you. As for the town, jumping to conclusions is part of what they do. Don't worry about it." He took the mangled box of baby cereal and set it on the floor. His hand captured hers, his intense gaze steady on her. "I'm glad you're here, and I'm enjoying getting to know Elliott. We'll just take things as they come and—"

"Land sakes, what're you two doing down there, actin' like a couple of gorbies in mating season?" Tavie stood at the end of the aisle with Elliott snuggled against her shoulder.

"I'm just helping Mary pick up the things she dropped." Brody scooped up the rest of the items and rose, pulling her up with him. When she reached for her things, he said, "I got 'em."

He started to follow Tavie, but Mary stopped him with a hand on his arm. "What are gorbies?"

"Gray jays…birds. Don't worry, you'll pick up the lingo after you've been here for a while." He laughed and shifted the things in his arms.

"Must be nice to belong somewhere," she said on a quiet sigh. Brody acted as if he belonged, but his speech didn't have the same characteristics of the people she'd met. "Did you spend any time here growing up?"

"Nah, but they don't hold it against me."

So these people had welcomed him. Her whole life she'd been searching for the place she belonged. She'd like to think that place might be here in Loon Lake. "How long have you lived here?"

"Since I got out of the army…about three years," he said.

"How did you pick Loon Lake?" She found she wanted to know all she could about him…and not just for Elliott's sake.

"A helicopter pilot I met in Afghanistan spoke about the town, so I decided to check it out."

She couldn't help grinning. What were the chances? "Tavie's grandson?"

"Now that you mention it, I believe he was." Brody laughed, the corners of his eyes crinkling and setting off flutters in her stomach. "See? You're already becoming a part of the community."

"Well, Tavie did mention that her grandson flew helicopters," she confessed, but his words affected her. More than they should have. Maybe she'd found a place to fit in, a place to belong to, a place to raise Elliott. A place to call home.

Tavie handed Elliott to Brody so she could ring up Mary's purchases. Once in Brody's arms, Elliott kept up a string of baby gibberish, and Brody nodded and smiled as if he understood what Elliott was telling him. Watching them, Mary had to blink to clear her vision so she could see the number pad to key in her PIN as she paid.

Finished bagging the items, Tavie leaned over the counter and gave Elliott's cheeks a gentle squeeze between her thumbs and forefingers. "Such a sweetie. Be sure to bring him back soon. And if you need anything, Mary, just give me a holler."

Brody looped his free arm under the infant seat handle and picked it up. "Tell Ogle we'll be in touch about Mary's car."

Tavie pulled out a small box from under the counter and set it in the empty infant seat. "Don't forget these."

Mary started to reach for the box, but Brody shook his head. "I got it."

Tavie grinned and winked. "Great meeting you, Mary. If I don't see you through the week, I'll see you through the window."

Mary laughed as they made their way to Brody's truck. "She's quite the character."

"Hmm, she is."

At the pickup, Brody handed Elliott back to Mary and strapped the safety seat back into place. Before stepping aside, he laid his small box on the floor.

She looked from the package to him, and he shrugged.

"Tavie's been after me to buy some of Des's things. She calls it 'supporting the local artisans.'"

Mary's breath caught in her chest. Had Tavie told him how much she'd admired the wind chimes? *Don't be silly. It's like he said. He was supporting local craftsmen.* But she couldn't help smiling to herself as she climbed into the truck.

Chapter Six

As per usual, Brody had excused himself after supper, saying he had to check on the animals and do some work in the barn. She would've liked to have accompanied him, but she hated to interrupt Elliott's bedtime routine. *Yeah, and what about the fact Brody never invites you?* She'd broached the subject one night, and the panicked expression on Brody's face had told her all she needed to know. So she'd spent her evenings for the past week stargazing from the porch and was often asleep when Brody came back into the house.

The tinkle of wind chimes greeted her as she let the screen door swing shut. Brody had hung the glass ones just inside the door so opening and closing made them chime but still protected them. She set the mug and baby monitor receiver on the floor next to the swing and used the light spilling out through the windows to admire the workmanship in the sun catchers. Brody had hung three jellyfish between the porch columns. They reflected the sun but had no moving parts to break. When she mentioned she liked the sound of wind chimes, he'd hung nonbreakable ones, too. He might disappear from the house every night, but he seemed to know she enjoyed sitting on the porch in the evenings, because he'd also put up a hummingbird feeder and cushions on the swing.

His thoughtfulness brought tears to her eyes, but it also stung to think she'd soon be leaving the farm for a place of her own. And she needed to get serious about looking for a place instead of falling into the cadence of life here.

The screen door's hinges squeaked. "Stargazing?" Brody strolled onto the porch, the door slapping shut behind him.

"Still a little early for that." She set her empty mug on the floor. "For now, I'm admiring the jellyfish."

He touched a finger to one. "Des is a decent guy."

She pushed her foot, setting the swing in motion, its gentle sway comforting. She couldn't be sure if her admiration of the glass ornaments had prompted him to buy them since Brody seemed determined to downplay his generous nature, but it warmed her to think so. "They're beautiful. I guess I will make outdoor space or a small balcony a priority."

He pointed to the empty spot next to her on the swing. "May I?"

"Of course."

Brody eased onto the swing, his weight setting it off into a crazy rhythm, but he used his foot to return it to its gentle motion. He'd been hiding out in the barn in the evenings after Elliott went to sleep because it was getting harder and harder to keep from touching Mary. And he wasn't sure what he thought about that.

"How is Eleanor?" Mary asked. "She seemed happy

to see Elliott and me when we checked on her before supper."

"You think so?" He chuckled at her insistence on treating the calf as if it were a dog, but her attitude spoke to something deep within him. Not that he was about to explore those feelings. Or any other feelings, for that matter. Instead, he'd concentrate on whether to get Mary and Elliott a dog. The Coopers' mutt was cute, even if it had the unfortunate name of Mangy. He should ask Riley where he'd gotten the dog.

She worried her lower lip. "Maybe I should have checked on her again in case she was lonesome."

"She's fine, bedded down for the night. We can put her in the pasture with Gertie tomorrow, if that will ease your mind." He'd let the old cow near the calf's stall a few times so she'd get used to her. He knew they could be fearful in new situations, so he'd take it slow.

"Yes, thank you." She turned toward him, her face split with a smile, her eyes sparkling.

He swallowed, trying to think of something to break the tension swirling around them. "So…you, ah, you like stargazing?"

"It's nice without all the light pollution from the city…" Her voice trailed off.

"It is." He leaned closer, and his heart rate increased. Where did this desire to know her thoughts come from? "Is there a reason you enjoy it so much?"

"As…as a kid, I had a silly dream of going into space." She breathed out a quiet laugh. "With Nathan Fillion and the crew of the *Serenity*."

"Ah, a *Firefly* fan." He rested his arm across the back of the swing. Jeez, could he get any more obvious? He hadn't been this awkward or juvenile in years.

"Uh-huh," she said and seemed to relax. "What about you? What were your dreams as a kid?"

Her hair brushed against the skin on his bare forearm, making it hard to concentrate on their conversation, but if he didn't at least try to make small talk, she might leave. "I wanted to be Bond. James Bond. I guess I'd be more Jason Bourne, since I'm not British."

"Well, I think you're even cuter than Matt Damon." She glanced at him with that infectious smile.

"Taller, maybe." He laughed, but his chest expanded at the compliment. Why had he been avoiding spending the evenings out here with her? At the moment he couldn't think of even one reason.

She shook her head. "Matt Damon isn't short."

"Not to you maybe…you're, what? Five three or four."

"Three and a half, if I stand ramrod straight. You're what, six two?"

He grinned into the darkness. "Yeah, something like that."

She moved her head to peer at him through the dim light. "What? Tell me."

"Six one and a half…if I stand ramrod straight," he mimicked.

She playfully bumped his shoulder.

Her touch sent a shiver racing through him, leaving him wanting more. When was the last time a simple, playful gesture had meant so much? "So, have you caught a glimpse of the *Serenity* yet in your nightly observations?"

"Very funny. I don't think I've ever been this far away from the city's light pollution. The sky…it's…it's amazing out here."

"Yeah, I looked up a lot when I first moved here." He studied the graceful curve of her neck as she studied the night sky. There was a spot where her neck and shoulder met that was begging to be kissed and caressed. He suppressed a groan.

"And now?" she asked with that breathless, husky quality to her voice.

Aw, man, she was killing him. He shifted and had to steady the swing again with his foot. "Now it's just there. But thank you for reminding me to stop and take a look."

"The more I see and experience, the more convinced I am that Loon Lake is the place I want to raise Elliott."

"You do know that once he's grown, he'll run off to the city to look for excitement," he teased.

A soft curve touched her lips as she glanced at him. "Yeah, but at least I will have given him a good start in life. He'll always have this place to come to if he needs it."

"He'll always be welcome here." *And you, too.* For someone who'd come here seeking isolation, he'd sure changed his tune. Temporarily, he reminded himself. He needed to remember Elliott was his nephew, thereby complicating matters. And what exactly was his objection to complicated?

"Sorry. By here, I meant Loon Lake. Don't worry, we're…uh…we're not permanent houseguests." She glanced at her hands in her lap.

"I wasn't worried," he assured her in a quiet tone and touched her shoulder.

"Meg Cooper said I might be able to rent the house next to theirs for a short time. She said she'd approach the owners and see."

"There's no rush." The speed and ease with which Mary and Elliott had fit into his life surprised him.

"Thanks, but it can't be easy for a confirmed bachelor

to be bombarded with everything that goes along with housing a mother and baby."

Brody used his foot to set the swing moving again. Mary talking about moving out didn't bring the relief it should have—the relief it would have a week ago. The fact that he wasn't happy to hear her talking about getting her own place made him uneasy. He didn't do long-term relationships. He'd experienced the fallout when they turned bitter and wasn't wishing that on anyone. Mary moving on would be a good thing, a smart thing. For both of them. And yet the thought of her leaving left him feeling...what? Like something would be missing from his life. No, that was crazy. She and the baby had been here less than two weeks. And yet, he'd fallen in love with the little guy. If he wasn't careful, he might feel the same about Elliott's mother.

"Was the army a dream of yours?"

It took a moment for Mary's question to register. He pulled his thoughts together. "After the attacks on September 11, my thoughts turned to the military."

She touched his chest. "You would have been young."

"Seventeen and impressionable, I guess." He blew out his breath, trying to stay on topic when all he wanted to do was pull Mary into his arms and...and what? Ride off into the sunset? Safer to stay on topic. "I was eager to make a difference."

"How long were you in?" She dropped her hand into her lap.

He wanted that hand on his lap. "Fourteen years."

"That's well over halfway to a career and retirement. Why did you leave?"

He inhaled—was he going to do this?—held it for a few beats and exhaled. "I suffered a central retinal vein occlusion—a CRVO. It's a blockage of the major vein in your eye. Like a stroke. It affects your vision in that eye. The sight in my left eye was—is—compromised."

He'd left out the details. There was a lot he couldn't share, some because it was still classified military intel and some because he wasn't ready. Even with Mary.

She placed her hand on his arm. "Were they able to do anything about it?"

Her hand on his arm was comforting. But he didn't need comforting about his past. The past was just that. Past. "They can treat it, but the loss is permanent. I will always have blurry vision in that eye, but eventually my right eye became dominant. The whole thing affects your depth perception, but your brain learns to compensate for that, too."

"And that meant you had to leave the army?"

"They wanted to stick me behind a desk. I didn't join the army for that. I was Delta Force, not a clerk, so I bailed when my time was up." He used the hand on the back of the seat to toy with her hair, enjoying the silky strands running through his fingers.

"I'm sorry."

"Don't apologize." His fingers traced the curve of her ear. "It's not your fault."

"Knee-jerk reaction." She leaned closer, almost snuggled into his body. "I hate that you had to give up your career."

He opened his mouth to tell her he was resigned to losing his army career. "I'm… I'm going to kiss you."

He brought his mouth closer to hers, giving her time to say no or push him away, praying she would do neither. She blinked and parted her lips as if in anticipation. He lowered his mouth to hers.

Her lips were soft and warm under his, and her scent

swirled around him, sending his blood racing through his veins to gather—

A cry came over the baby monitor, and they jumped apart like guilty teens caught necking on the porch by an overprotective dad.

He stared at her, his breath coming in short gasps along with hers. Another cry over the monitor broke the spell. "I have to confess… I enjoyed that."

She swallowed, her muscles working in her slender throat. "Me, too."

He caressed her cheek with his fingertips, savoring the soft, warm skin.

Elliott cried again, and Mary winced. "I should check on him."

Brody rested his arms on his thighs as the door shut behind Mary. He should be grateful for the interruption. So why wasn't he?

Mary changed Elliott's diaper and rubbed his back before laying him down. He yawned and drifted back to sleep. Satisfied he was okay and a dream or noise had disturbed him, she went into her room and got ready for bed.

She couldn't stop thinking about the kiss and what might have happened if Elliott hadn't interrupted them. Torn between relief and frustration, she stared at her reflection in the mirror as she brushed her teeth. Would getting physical with Brody be a mistake or the best thing that had happened to her? He'd already told her he didn't do complicated relationships. And yet watching him with Elliott and with the animals, she knew he possessed a deep capacity for caring. He might deny it, but Brody Wilson cared with all his heart.

Before getting into bed, she opened the bedroom window, enjoying the sound of the wind chimes tinkling in the evening breeze. He'd shrugged off his purchases, but it had melted Mary's heart to think he might have bought them for her enjoyment.

She turned off the bedside lamp and tugged the covers over her, and exhaustion soon pulled her under.

Bright sunshine streamed through the windows when she awoke. What time was it? Was Elliott still sleeping? She rushed into his room, but his portable crib was empty. Not bothering to dress, she threw her bathrobe on and tied the belt and followed the murmur of voices down the stairs and to the kitchen. She hesitated in the doorway, her hand curled around the door frame.

Brody sat in a chair pulled away from the kitchen table with Elliott in his arms. The baby drank from a bottle as he gazed up at his uncle, who looked relaxed and natural. If she'd had any misgivings about coming to find Brody, they melted away. At least this time she'd made a wise choice. Now she needed to be careful not to ruin it by falling in love.

Brody glanced up. "Good morning."

His smile had her pulse in overdrive. "Did he wake you?"

"No, I was up and heard him chattering to himself and went to check on him."

She stepped farther into the kitchen, the wood floor cool on her bare feet. "You should've woken me."

"I figured I'd let you sleep. I know he's kept you up the past few nights."

"Thanks. He's teething. But I—" She broke off to stifle a yawn. "I'm sorry if he's kept you awake, too."

"He hasn't."

"But he must've if you knew he's been keeping me up," she couldn't help pointing out.

"I've been awake, but it hasn't had anything to do with Elliott."

"Oh?" She glanced at him, but he didn't elaborate. As much as she wanted to know what demons kept him awake at night, she didn't have the right to ask. *Listen to yourself.* He was Elliott's uncle, and she was a houseguest. Period. A couple of kisses didn't equal a relationship. He'd offered her a place to stay until she got on her feet in Loon Lake.

"Do you know of any places in town that are hiring?" she asked.

"Hiring?" His brows pulled together, and he frowned.

"I need a job. Getting employment is important so I'll know what rent I can afford. I don't want to dip into my savings if I can avoid it. At some point I'd like to be able to buy us a home of our own. Someplace permanent." A forever home. Something she'd never had but had longed for with all her might. Maybe an old farmhouse that she could restore as time, talent and resources permitted.

"You don't have to rush out and take the first job that comes along. Take your time finding the right one."

"I don't want to overstay my welcome."

"You haven't." Brody grinned at Elliott, who reached up and grabbed his nose. "You and this little guy can stay as long as you need. Right, little dude?"

Elliott kicked his legs and squealed. *"Doooo."*

Her lungs expanded, and she exhaled on a laugh. "Did he just say 'dude'?"

Brody chuckled. "I think he did. Something wrong with 'dude'?"

"Nothing. It's just not the first word I expected my son to learn." Elliott was making sounds, nothing more, but she took the opportunity to learn more about Brody. He wasn't the most forthcoming guy she'd known. "Where did you get that, anyway? You don't look like a surfer."

"I'm not, but I knew someone who…was." Brody's blue eyes clouded over.

"A friend?"

"We were in the army together. Sean was the stereotypical West Coast surfer, although I suspect a lot of that was put on. But it worked. Had women flocking to him." His smile was tinged with sadness, the kind of bittersweet smile people got when they remembered the good times with someone they'd lost.

"Wha—" She stopped to clear her throat. "What happened to him?"

"He received what doctors label traumatic brain injury while rescuing a fellow soldier." Brody's voice was flat as if reciting facts, as if pushing the associated feelings away.

She yearned to comfort him, but words escaped her. Every platitude that came to mind had a hollow ring to it. And she feared physical comforting would lead to places they might regret.

Elliott scrunched up his face and grunted. Brody lifted him higher. "Uh-oh. I think it's time for Mommy to take over."

The moment had passed and, although she wished she'd been able to find the right words, she let it go and concentrated on the immediate. "Funny how that works."

"I could always switch with you if you'd rather muck out the stalls." He lifted his eyebrows as if trying to entice her.

"Hmm…" She pretended to think it over. "I guess I'll stick with my son." She reached for Elliott.

"Sorry, gotta go to Mommy." Before letting go of his nephew, Brody cupped his hand over Elliott's curls. "But I was rooting for you, big guy."

Mary took Elliott and wrinkled her nose when she got

a whiff. No wonder Brody was so eager to escape to the barn. Brody went into the mudroom.

"Before you go to deal with your...uh, stuff, have you heard anything from Ogle about my car?" she asked before he left.

"He said he's waiting for the parts he ordered." He stood in the doorway, pulling his boots on. "Why? Do you need a lift somewhere?"

"I need a haircut, and Meg recommended a place in town, Colleen's Cut and Caboodle."

He laughed. "Catchy. Does this afternoon work?"

"Ha. I can see you haven't gone to many hair salons."

He frowned in confusion. "Is that a no?"

"It means I'll have to call the place and see if they have any openings available." She shrugged. "Maybe we'll get lucky."

A strange look crossed his face, but he lifted one shoulder in a careless shrug. "Okay, just let me know."

After dealing with Elliott's diaper and giving him a bath, Mary sat him on a blanket in the living room and called Meg's hairdresser. As luck would have it, there had been a last-minute cancellation.

That afternoon on the drive into town, Brody said he needed to pick up a few things from the feed store, so he dropped her off and told her to text him when she was done.

"Are you sure you don't mind taking Elliott with you?" she asked as Brody pulled up in front of the salon.

"Go," he said and waved his hand. He glanced in the rearview mirror. "Us guys will be fine, won't we, dude?"

Elliott waved his stuffed bear up and down. *"Dooooo."*

"See?" Brody chuckled as Mary got out of the truck, and the sexy sound followed her into the hair salon.

"Welcome to Colleen's," a teenage girl with bright purple hair greeted her.

Mary returned the girl's smile but took a quick survey of the salon before stepping up to the counter.

The girl fluffed out her purple locks. "Before you ask, we ran out of purple dye yesterday."

Mary snapped her fingers. "Just my luck. I have an appointment. Mary Carter."

"Oh, you're the woman with the baby who's staying with Brody Wilson," the girl said with a cheerful grin.

"Ashley." An older woman with plain blond hair approached the counter and shook her head at the teen.

Ashley just shrugged. "It's not like it's a secret. Kevin told me he and Danny brought some baby stuff out to the farm."

"It's okay. I'm learning how fast news travels around here." Mary smiled at the two women.

"Living in Loon Lake is like playing six degrees of Kevin Bacon." The older woman shook Mary's hand. "I'm Loretta—we spoke on the phone."

Mary followed Loretta past several other customers, who smiled and said hello. The woman kept up a steady stream of friendly conversation as she trimmed Mary's hair. After she'd finished, she insisted Mary show her pictures of Elliott. Mary dug out her phone, and soon other customers came over and oohed and aahed over him.

"Be sure to bring him in here so we can say hi," Loretta said.

"And we won't complain if you bring that fine-looking Brody Wilson in, too," another woman commented.

"Ladies, please," Loretta said but couldn't hide her grin.

"We may be old, but we're not dead or blind," a woman said to a round of "hear, hear."

"Pay no mind to them." Loretta guided Mary to the front of the salon.

"It's okay," Mary told her. Heck, she wasn't blind either.

"Should I put you down for a trim in about six weeks?" Ashley asked as Mary paid. "You can always change it if something comes up."

Mary glanced around the small salon, smiling at the women who were there. When they smiled back, she nodded. "Yes, I'd like that."

Brody texted Mary while the kid from the feed store loaded supplies into the bed of the truck. The café was located two storefronts away from the hairdresser, so he told her he and Elliott would wait for her there. He had no idea how long it took for women to get their hair cut. In his opinion, Mary's hair looked fine, but he'd kept that to himself.

Brody set Elliott's infant seat on the table in a booth by the windows and marveled at how the baby's smile and dark eyes attracted everyone's attention.

"You're a male version of your mom," he whispered to his nephew.

The door to the café opened, and Mary stepped in. Brody's heart beat against his chest, and he had to swallow several times to keep from drooling.

Elliott kicked his legs and began babbling when he spotted his mother.

"Hello to you, too, sweetie." Mary squished his chin.

"I thought you were getting your hair cut?" Brody asked as she slipped into the bench seat across the booth from him.

Trudi, the waitress who'd led Mary over to the booth, gasped and bopped Brody on the head with her order pad. "Brody Wilson, what is wrong with you?"

"Hey." Brody brought his arm up in a defensive gesture.

"You do not say something like that to a woman just back from the beauty salon," Trudi sputtered.

Elliott drew their attention when he burst into infectious baby giggles.

Brody turned to Elliott. "You think that's funny, do you?"

The baby laughed harder, and Brody put his hand around Elliott's stomach and tickled him. "Don't encourage her, dude. We guys have to stick together."

Mary ran her fingers through her hair. "Maybe I should have gotten purple like Ashley."

"Is that what color it is this week?" the waitress asked.

Mary nodded. "I'm not sure purple would work with my natural hair color, though."

Trudi tilted her head as if studying Mary's hair. "Yeah, I'm not sure that—"

"You two can't be serious," Brody interrupted. "I love Mary's hair. It looks great just the way it is."

"Now, that's the right answer," Trudi said and winked at Mary. Lifting her chin, the waitress leaned toward Elliott. "Let that be a lesson to you, young man."

His response was to blow spit bubbles and giggle.

"What can I get you two to eat?" Trudi's pencil hovered above the order pad.

Brody motioned toward her pad with his head. "I see that thing is good for something other than hitting me?"

"Don't tempt me," Trudi shot back. "The special today is fresh lobster roll."

Heck, he'd let Trudi whack him all she wanted if it meant putting that grin on Mary's face. "Do you like lobster?"

"I love it, but—"

"We'll take two," Brody said and tucked the menus back into their place between the napkin holder and the salt and pepper shakers.

"Curly fries?" Trudi stuffed the order book into her apron pocket.

Brody raised his eyebrows at Mary, and she nodded.

"Good choice." The waitress hitched her chin at Brody's empty white ceramic mug. "More coffee?"

He raised his hands. "No, I've had enough. Just a water refill to go with lunch. Mary?"

"Water's good for me."

The waitress trotted off, and Mary turned her attention to Elliott. "Have you been behaving yourself for Uncle Brody?"

"Your son is quite the little flirt. He's been entertaining the ladies." He grinned and canted his head toward Elliott. "If I'd known babies were such chick magnets, I might have gotten one a long time ago."

Mary rolled her eyes. "I doubt you need any help in that department."

"He wouldn't if he didn't keep to himself out on that farm of his." Trudi appeared and set a red plastic tumbler in front of Mary and used a pitcher of ice water to fill it and refill Brody's. "He'd like nothing better than for all of us to think he's an ogre like that…you know, that green guy in my grandkids' movies."

An impish grin stole across Mary's mouth. "Shrek?"

"That's the one." The waitress placed a hand on her hip and lifted the pitcher. "Your lobster rolls should be out soon."

"So, Shrek?" Mary pulled the wrapper from her straw and crumpled it between her thumb and fingers.

"They're not happy unless they're gossiping about someone," he grumbled, but his attention was on those lips. Kissing her had been a blunder, because now he knew how they tasted. And those tastes weren't enough. Nowhere near enough.

"That's not fair." She stuck the straw in her glass. "They all seem very nice."

"Yeah, right," he said as he touched his head, but he ended up grinning like a fool. Being around Mary and Elliott had that effect on him.

She smoothed a blanket over Elliott as his eyes grew heavy and he began to doze off. "Did you get all you needed at the feed store?"

He nodded and sipped his water. "I also made an appointment with a farrier to come to the farm to take care of Patton and the other horses' feet."

"Patton is your horse, right? Is there something wrong?" She placed her elbows on the table and leaned closer.

"Yes, Patton is mine and this is just routine. Their hooves need trimming about every six to eight weeks." Her concern for the animals touched him like a hand around his heart.

Mary flipped her hair over her shoulder. "Just like my hair."

"I'll be sure to compliment them on their trimmed feet," Brody said and they both laughed.

Elliott startled and opened his eyes but brought his thumb to his mouth and dozed off again.

Mary and Brody talked about the horses until the waitress came back with their lobster rolls.

Trudi set their plates on the table. "Will we see the three of you at the Independence Day picnic? It will be a good way for you to introduce Mary around."

"I don't—"

"I'd love—"

"Oo-*kaay*, I think that's my cue to leave." The waitress's gaze bounced between them, and she winked and scurried away.

Brody cleared his throat. "Look, if you—"

Mary shook her head. "Ogle said my car would be ready by then, so there's no need for you to worry about it if you prefer not to come."

Brody frowned. "It's over a month away, so we don't have to decide today."

He didn't have a burning desire to attend the annual town picnic, but having Mary say she didn't need him to accompany her bothered him. The fact it bothered him was even more disturbing.

Chapter Seven

"There's a baseball game on tonight." Brody winced at the lame attempt at small talk. How many times had he squashed the urge to tell her what he'd planned for tonight? It wouldn't be a surprise if he told her.

"Oh?" She gave him a curious look as she loaded the dishwasher.

He handed her the rest of the dirty dishes from supper. "Yeah, I thought I'd watch it."

"Okay."

She was looking at him as if he'd lost his mind, and he couldn't blame her.

Before he embarrassed himself further, he went into the living room and put on the game. But he would've been hard-pressed to tell anyone the score, because he kept glancing at his watch, not wanting to lose track of the time.

It had been three days since Mary's trip to the hair salon, and each night he'd forced himself to remain in the house after supper as a test to his willpower. He would acknowledge his physical attraction to Mary, but he refused to let it rule his actions. But tonight was different.

When Mary picked Elliott up off the blanket on the floor to put him to bed, Brody followed. After they'd gotten Elliott tucked in, Brody touched Mary's arm as they walked out of the room. "There's something I want to show you. I should've explained, but I didn't want to spoil it."

"What? What is it?"

He checked his watch. "We have a few minutes."

"Oh?"

"Follow me," he said and went to the stairs.

She followed a step behind. "I don't understand."

"You'll see." He led her to the front door, hoping his surprise didn't fall flat. How many times had he wanted to blurt out his plan?

"Where are we going?"

"Outside." It was too late to turn back now, so he'd have to power through this and hope she wouldn't laugh.

"I know that. But why?"

Before his better judgment kicked in, he took her hand in his. "Something I want you to see."

"But it's pitch-black out there. How am I supposed to see anything?"

Brody squeezed her hand and led her through the door.

"What if—"

He held up the baby monitor. "We'll be in sight of the house at all times. I promise."

He brought her to the front yard, away from the trees, and checked the illuminated dial on his watch again.

He stood close and let go of her hand so he could wrap his arm around her shoulder.

"Be watching up there," he said and pointed skyward.

They stood gazing up for several minutes, her scent filling his head.

"Ooh, there's Cassiopeia and Cepheus." She turned. "Did I tell you I spotted them the other night? Is that why—"

"No, this is better." *Please let it be so.*

She drew in a breath as if affronted but spoiled it with a grin. "Better than Cassiopeia and Cepheus? Is that possible?"

"Brat." He flicked her nose, then pointed toward the sky. The urge to kiss her was strong, but if he did he wouldn't stop and they'd miss it. "Keep watching."

Her head followed his pointing finger. "What am I looking for?"

"You'll see it in a minute." He grinned at her growing impatience.

"I don't understand," she said, her tone doubtful.

"You told me how you used to look at the night sky and wonder about all the things up there." He squeezed her shoulder, drawing her closer.

"It was silly…childish…." She shuffled her feet and glanced down.

"No, it wasn't. I named my alpacas Lost and Found. I would be the last one to tease." He hugged her closer and placed a kiss on her temple, not wanting her to feel foolish for divulging a girlhood dream.

"Keep your eye on the sky." He directed her head in a northeasterly direction.

She stood up straighter as if snapping to attention, telling him she was looking in the right place. Good, because he couldn't turn away to check, hated to even blink, not wanting to miss even a second of her fascination.

"I see a light…but that's not an airplane…what is it?" Her tone was tinged with wonder.

"It's the International Space Station," he told her. She turned to look at him, but he guided her head back to the sky.

"For real?" She sucked in a breath.

"For real." The tension coiling inside him escaped as a laugh. Her delight raised the hairs on his arm. He'd been worried she would scoff.

He couldn't take his eyes off her, but he knew where the space station was because she tracked its progress across the sky until it disappeared into the horizon. "There are astronauts in it right now," she whispered as if talking to herself.

"Yup." He tightened his arm around her. "Not the *Serenity* crew, but astronauts nonetheless."

She turned and cupped his cheek with her palm. "I don't know how to thank you."

There were a few ways—*No, don't spoil this moment for her*—but he did lean into her palm. "I didn't do much except look up the trajectory on the internet and figure out where it was going to be and when."

"It's…it's…" A smile slowly spread across her face. "Thank you. Really… I don't know what to say."

"You're welcome." He shrugged, but every hair on his scalp stood at attention at the expression on her face. "It's not a big deal. It's not like it cost me anything."

"Cost doesn't matter. It was very thoughtful. No one has ever taken the time to set up something like this." Her smile was eager, her face infused with delight.

He laughed, feeling lighter than he had in the past three years. "I didn't arrange for the space station to fly over this little patch of Vermont. It's just up there if you know where to look and when."

"But you remembered something I'd said and went to

the trouble of looking it up and showing it to me." Her voice was soft, husky, tinged with wonder.

"I confess I've come out here before to see it." He brushed the hair off her face. "But this has been the most enjoyable time."

"Ouch." She slapped at her leg.

"Mosquitoes?" His disappointment outweighed the situation.

"I don't know, but it bites, whatever it is." She brushed her leg.

He dropped his arm. "We'd better go back inside."

"Next time we'll have to remember the bug spray," she said as they headed for the house.

The way she said "next time" filled him with warmth. He reached for her hand, laced his fingers through hers and squeezed. No matter what happened in the future, he'd remember this night, this incredible feeling.

The next morning, Mary ended her phone call and fought the urge to squeal the way Elliott did when something pleased or surprised him. Grown women didn't squeal…at least not out loud, but she was still floating from last night. Just thinking about Brody's thoughtful gesture made her giddy. No matter what the future held, nothing would tarnish her memory of the previous evening.

She scooped Elliott up from his high chair and wiped his chin. "Let's go find Uncle Brody and tell him about Mommy's phone call."

It didn't escape her notice that her first reaction to good news was to find Brody. He'd left a note on the table saying he'd grabbed some breakfast and would be in the barn if she needed anything. She recalled him saying today was the day the farrier was coming.

In the barn she found him brushing one of the horses.

"Did they get their new shoes already?" she asked as she entered. She went to stand closer to him, and Elliott began babbling to the horse, who twitched its ears.

Brody stopped his brushing motions. "Not yet. What's up?"

"What makes you think something is up?" She had trouble containing her excitement.

"You're doing that thing." He motioned toward her with the brush.

"Thing? What thing?" She glanced down at herself. What was he talking about?

He went back to brushing the horse but glanced over at her, his lips twitching. "Balancing on your toes."

"I do?" Heat rose in her face. Why had he noticed such a thing?

"Uh-huh." He stopped brushing and crossed his arms over his chest and studied her. "When you're excited or happy about something. Tell me your news."

She couldn't hold back any longer. "I have a job."

"You do?" His head jerked back, surprise stamped on his features.

Another expression crossed his face, but it disappeared so fast she couldn't place the emotion. She tempered her excitement. "It's just part-time, but it's a start. And it could lead to full-time at some point."

He watched her, amused. "Congratulations, but tell me, how the heck did you get a job without leaving the house? Correct me if I'm wrong, but weren't you here all morning?"

"Thanks!" She laughed, a giddy sensation washing over her—not from her news but from the glint in his blue eyes. She hugged Elliott closer. "You were right about news traveling fast in Loon Lake. Someone mentioned to

Mr. Burke that I was looking for some accounting work, and he called me."

"Burke?"

"Randall Burke is a CPA. He works from a small office at his home and is looking to cut back in preparation for retirement. Someone told him I'm a CPA, and he called."

He nodded. "And I'll bet that someone was Tavie."

"Probably, but I don't mind." She kissed Elliott.

He set the brush down and patted the horse. "How about a celebratory dinner?"

"Sure. What would you like me to cook?"

He laughed. "I meant I'm taking you out. We'll go to Angelo's."

Angelo's? What was he suggesting? She might not have been in Loon Lake very long, but even she knew that was where couples went for dates. "That's not necessary."

"I think it is, and I'm not taking no for an answer."

"Well…okay. Thank you." Going to supper wouldn't be like a date or anything—they'd have Elliott with them. So it would just be a family—oops, not that, either, at least not in conventional terms.

"We'll ask Meg if she'd be willing to watch Elliott so you can enjoy yourself without having your meal disrupted. I know Riley is on nights this week. I'm sure she and Fiona would love the company."

It's a celebratory dinner…nothing more. Maybe he didn't want to have to worry about Elliott disrupting *his* dinner.

"Is there a problem with leaving Elliott with Meg?"

"What? Oh, no, that would be fine as long as she doesn't mind. I'll give her a call." She bounced Elliott on her hip. "Would you like to see Fiona?"

Elliott's answer was to squeal, even if he had no idea what all the excitement was about.

"I guess that's a yes," Brody observed.

"I'll go call her."

"Great. Let me know and I'll make reservations."

Mary called, and Meg was eager to watch Elliott and said Fiona would be ecstatic. Despite her earlier caution, Mary was excited, too.

That evening Mary dressed with care. She'd packed a plain black dress in anticipation of job interviews. Although this wasn't an audition for anything, her fanciest jewelry helped it fit the occasion. The way Brody's eyes widened and his smile when she came downstairs told her she'd made a good choice.

At the restaurant, the hostess greeted them. "Our new outdoor deck overlooking the lake is open, if you're interested."

"Mary?" Brody glanced at her.

"That sounds lovely." *And romantic.* It was getting harder to remember this evening wasn't a date.

A pergola strung with thousands of twinkling lights covered a flagstone patio scattered with tables and small trees, tiny lights wound around their trunks and branches. Each table held flickering candles in glass lanterns.

"It's like a fairy tale," Mary said as she tried to take it all in.

"I'm glad you like it." Brody rested his hand on the small of her back as they wound their way through the tables to one overlooking the lake.

"This is gorgeous." Mary felt as though her head was on a swivel as she tried to take it all in. "Have you ever been here before?"

He nodded. "Once, but this area is all new."

She couldn't help wondering whom he'd come with,

because this wasn't the type of restaurant a couple of friends would choose for a night out. No, Angelo's was a romantic setting better suited to couples. *But you're not a couple*, her inner voice reminded. "It's lovely. I'm glad the weather is pleasant enough to be out here."

He made a sound of agreement and picked up his menu, so she opened hers. The waiter returned with water and warm bread.

After the waiter left, Brody directed her attention to a spot on the other side of the dark water. "I'm not sure if you can see much in the dark, but the Coopers live across the lake beyond that stand of trees."

She glanced across the water. "Huh, I didn't realize Meg and Riley lived so close to the water."

"Yeah, the homes on that side are hemmed in with trees, but they have a path down to the lake. It had gotten overgrown, but a few of us cleared the way, widened it and put in pavers as a wedding present."

"What a great gift." She took a slice of bread and dipped it in the olive oil and herbs.

"I was just muscle."

"I'm sure they were pleased."

"That reminds me." He set his bread on the small plate and pulled a clumsily wrapped package from the inside of his jacket. "To celebrate your new job."

"I thought that's what this was for." She waved her hand around the patio.

He shrugged. "It's a small gesture."

"Good, because it's a small job…for now."

Goodness, she hoped he didn't notice how much her fingers trembled as she unwrapped it. She hadn't received many presents in her life, and while she appreciated him going out of his way to celebrate her job, she didn't want him to know how much this meant. She didn't want pity from Brody. No, she wanted so much more. And that scared her.

"Well?" He motioned his head toward the half-opened present.

"Oh, sorry." She tore the rest of the paper and opened the box. Inside, nestled in balled-up newspapers, was a kid's magic wand, the kind she might find at a dollar store. She held it up.

"To make all your dreams come true," he said gruffly.

His flushed face told her he found his little bit of sentiment embarrassing. That warmed her heart as much as the gift itself.

She tapped him on the shoulder. "Look. It works."

If she hadn't been watching so closely, she might've missed the flash of panic in his eyes before he blinked and it disappeared. Yeah, he wasn't ready for forever. Was she chasing an unattainable dream? One as outlandish as imagining herself aboard the International Space Station last night? *Quit being silly and enjoy the evening without any worries about tomorrow.*

The waiter returned. "Are we celebrating something this evening?" he asked and motioned to the package.

"My new job." *One that will allow me to stay in Loon Lake permanently.*

"Congratulations," he replied and took their orders.

While they waited for the meal, Brody asked her about her previous job.

After describing her job at the insurance company, she gazed at him across the table. "What about you? What sort of things did you do in the army?"

"The parts that aren't classified are rather boring, I'm afraid. Heck, some of those are, too."

"Are you saying it's above my pay grade?" She was enjoying this moment of closeness.

He furrowed his brow, but the flickering candlelight caught the twinkle in his eyes. "Are you making fun of me?"

"Absolutely not," she said in as serious a voice as she could muster. "I'm the one who imagined herself aboard the *Serenity*, remember?"

"I would never make fun of that." His manner turned serious, and he reached out to touch her hand resting on the table. "I understand about wanting to escape the realities of a childhood we had no control over."

"Is that what I was doing…looking for a way to escape?" Adults in her life had scoffed at her flights of fancy, so she'd learned to internalize her daydreams.

He leaned back against his chair. "That's what I was doing when I imagined myself as James Bond."

"I hadn't thought about it like that." She flinched at her breathless tone.

The waiter returned with their meals, and they ate in companionable silence for several minutes.

A splash brought her attention to the lake, but it was difficult to see anything in the water's inky darkness.

"It's a loon," he said and took a sip of water.

She nodded. "Ah, yes, Loon Lake.'"

They talked about the town as they ate. When the waiter appeared with the bill Mary reached out, but Brody waved her off. "I invited you. I pay."

"Thank you." Mary gathered her purse.

"How about a walk by the lake before we go?" Brody pointed to a short flight of steps leading down to the lake. "There's a boardwalk, so it should be an easy stroll."

Her heart turned over at the prospect of walking along the lake in the moonlight with him. *Not a real date*, she repeated to herself. "I'd like that."

He reached for her hand, and she slipped hers into

his. A shiver of excitement raced through her at the calluses on his palm.

He was so quiet and still beside her, she couldn't help but wonder what he was thinking. Was this a simple dinner between friends to celebrate her job? Or was it a romantic date?

"I—"

"I—"

"Ladies first." He dipped his head.

"I wanted to thank you again for tonight." *Coward.*

"My pleasure." He squeezed her hand. "It's getting late. I suppose we should go relieve Meg."

"Yes, I think so," she agreed, but she had a feeling that wasn't what he'd planned to say. She swallowed her disappointment. It would be a shame to let something so petty ruin her wonderful evening.

Meg answered the door, and a curly-haired dog pushed his nose through the opening.

Meg grabbed its collar and opened the door wider. "Hey, guys, c'mon in. Mangy, sit."

The dog whined but sat. Mary crouched to pet the friendly dog as soon as Meg closed the door. "I'll bet Elliott loved you."

"He got a kick out of him," Meg agreed.

Brody rubbed the dog's ears. "He seems very well behaved."

"For the most part," Meg said and led them into the small living room scattered with toys.

Brody turned to Mary and cocked an eyebrow. "Maybe Meg could give you lessons for Eleanor."

Mary pulled a face at him but ruined it with a grin. "Very funny."

"Oh, you have a dog?" Meg frowned when Mary shook her head. "Then who's Eleanor?"

"Mary's calf," Brody said in a serious tone, but Mary caught the twitch of his lips.

Meg's eyes widened. "You have a calf?"

"One of the farmers brought her to the farm when the mother rejected her," Mary explained.

Brody was nodding, his blue eyes sparkling with humor. "Uh-huh. And Mary treats it like a dog—the calf follows her around, plays fetch and—"

Mary smacked his shoulder. "Cut that out. She's going to believe you."

Meg laughed, and when her gaze bounced between the two of them, Mary caught the other woman's speculative expression.

Mary attempted to divert Meg's attention. She didn't need gossip about them flying around town. Not that Meg Cooper would be spreading gossip, but Mary wanted to be proactive. "I hope Elliott wasn't any trouble."

"No trouble at all. He's so sweet, but I think he's getting a tooth."

Mary frowned. "Oh, no, I hope he wasn't fussy."

"Nah, Fiona and the dog kept him entertained until all three fell asleep." Meg waved off Mary's concerns. "Now tell me about Angelo's."

"It was amazing. We sat out on the patio area."

"Ooh, how was it?" Meg glanced at Brody before turning her attention back to Mary. "I've heard it's very romantic."

"It has tons of twinkling lights and views of the lake." Mary tried to sound as casual as possible, but warmth flooded her cheeks. Luckily Brody's attention was on the tug-of-war with the dog.

Meg sighed. "Riley and I still haven't gotten there, but we've seen the lights from across the lake."

"Any time you want to go, let me know," Mary said. "I'd love to return the favor and watch Fiona."

"I may take you up on that if we can plan before this one comes along." Meg rubbed her stomach. "It would even be worth the heartburn."

"Oh, no, are you having problems with that?"

Meg nodded. "Some. Did you?"

"Some," Mary said, and they both laughed.

Meg rubbed her stomach. "And what about—"

"Ladies, I love a good pregnancy discussion as much as the next guy, but I think I'm going to suggest it's time for Mary and me to leave." Brody relinquished the dog toy and stood.

Meg turned to him. "I never realized you were such a coward, Brody Wilson."

"I think he could tell where this was headed," Mary suggested.

Brody chuckled. "No place I want to be, that's for sure."

They went down a short hall to a bedroom lit by a low-wattage light next to a crib. The room was in the process of being decorated as a baby boy's nursery, with a mountain mural on one wall and a penciled outline of a moose on another.

"As you can see, we're not finished yet," Meg said.

"It's lovely. I'll have to pick your brain for ideas when Elliott and I get our own place." Now that she had a job, her days on the farm were drawing to a close. *No, don't spoil tonight.*

"Next time you should plan on leaving Elliott all night," Meg suggested as Brody picked up the sleeping baby.

"Well, I…" Mary had no idea how to respond.

"Thanks, Meg, we will," Brody said as Elliott snuggled against his shoulder.

Chapter Eight

The next morning Mary awoke to voices outside her window, which overlooked the front yard. She crossed to it, but the porch roof blocked her view of the steps. She threw some clothes on and checked on Elliott. He'd awoken last night after they'd arrived home and had been fussy off and on during the night. She'd massaged his gums and let him suck on a cool, wet washcloth, and since both gave him a measure of relief, she knew her teething assessment was correct.

She grabbed the baby monitor receiver and went downstairs. Last night was even more reason they needed to find their own place. She couldn't keep disrupting Brody's nights with a fussy baby.

The open front door showed Brody talking with Ogle and a teen on the porch.

Ogle looked up when she approached the doorway and lifted his baseball cap. "Mornin', Mary."

"Good morning, Ogle and…" She glanced over at the teenager and smiled. "Kevin, right?"

"Mornin', Miss Mary." The kid nodded and shuffled his feet.

She stepped onto the porch, and sure enough, her car was on the other side of Brody's truck and looking like it had before the accident. This was a good thing, she told herself. So why wasn't she happier?

Ogle swatted a fly away with his cap. "The body shop called this morning, so Kevin and I went over and picked her up. We drove it around a bit to be sure everything was workin' proper like."

"I can't thank you enough for all the help." Mary gave Ogle a hug and turned to Kevin, remembering Brody had told her how the motherless teen had been neglected by his alcoholic father. "You, too, Kevin," she said and grabbed the teen into a quick embrace.

After she dropped her arms, Kevin stepped back and shoved his hands in his front pockets, hunching his shoulders and ducking his head, but he couldn't hide the ear-to-ear grin or the red cheeks. Mary understood how simple gestures could mean a lot to a kid who at one time had been made to feel expendable or inconsequential.

Ogle clapped Kevin on the back. "We'd better head back. Tavie said she had some things she wanted you to do today."

Kevin nodded and loped to Ogle's truck, but before getting in, he turned back. "Uh, the Coopers are having a cookout to celebrate my graduation and they…uh, said I could invite anyone I wanted… I know you two don't know me, but…well…"

"We'd…" Mary began and glanced at Brody, who gave her a slight nod. "We'd love to come. I'll be seeing Meg Cooper later, and I'll get all the details."

After Kevin and Ogle had left, Mary turned to Brody. "I hope you don't mind my accepting for both of us."

Brody closed his eyes for a moment. "I can't fight both of you."

"Both?" She had no idea what he meant. Surely he wasn't talking about Elliott.

"You and the town." He stepped off the porch. "If I stand around here much longer, I might be tempted to do something I shouldn't, so I'm going to check the horses' feed."

She wiped her palms on her jeans. "Will you come back for breakfast? I was thinking I'd use that leftover bread for french toast."

He hesitated for a moment then nodded. "I'd like that."

"Give me half an hour?" She needed to at least brush her hair before fixing breakfast.

"Sounds good." He turned and headed across the yard, moving with a lithe stride.

A touch of makeup wouldn't hurt, either.

In the barn, Brody worked filling the horses' buckets with oats, but thoughts of Mary and what might've happened last night if Elliott had gone straight to sleep when they got home kept intruding. Sure, they shared sexual chemistry, but he liked her, he enjoyed talking to her or just being with her as much as he enjoyed looking at her; that knowledge made her even more dangerous to his equilibrium.

She'd said half an hour, so he checked his watch, feeling like a schoolboy waiting to get a glimpse of his current crush. After what felt like the longest half hour of his life, he headed into the house.

As usual since Mary's arrival on the farm, his kitchen seemed to reach out and touch him—the warmth, the smells and Mary's cheerful voice as she kept up a stream of chatter with Elliott. He paused in the mudroom. *That baby in there is your nephew.* Nothing would change that fact.

Do you want to get mixed up in those family dynamics again?

"It's just breakfast," he muttered under his breath.

"Oh, good, you're here." Mary began putting things on the table.

He washed his hands at the sink and leaned against the counter as he dried them, admiring her backside while she set their food on the table. *Just breakfast, huh?*

Brody patted Elliott's head before sitting down next to the high chair. "Hey there, big guy, are you in a better mood this morning?"

Elliott banged the wooden spoon he had clutched in his hand on the tray of the high chair and let out a string of baby babble.

Mary passed the plate of french toast. "I'm sorry if we kept you awake last night."

"No problem." He didn't tell her that thinking about how lovely she looked in the flickering candlelight at the restaurant would've kept him awake anyway.

While they ate, Mary told him how she'd offered to help Meg with the preparations for Kevin's party.

"Now that I've got my car, I'll go into town and pick up some baking supplies," she said as she poured maple syrup on her breakfast.

"Do you want me to go with you?" He dipped his piece of bread into the amber syrup on his plate.

She cut her french toast into bite-size pieces. "No, that's fine. I don't want to intrude on your time. Besides, I have to start learning my way around town."

Disappointment curled in his belly, but he didn't argue

with her. She was a visitor, not a hostage. And he wasn't going to follow her around like some lovesick puppy dog—even if he wanted to be everywhere she was.

"Meg suggested going to the Pic-N-Save, but will Tavie get mad at us for shopping somewhere other than her store? She's been so generous to me." She stuck the last pieces into her mouth.

"Don't worry. They coexist peacefully." Brody speared the last piece of french toast from the platter in the middle of the table and dangled it from his fork. "Share?"

She held up a hand. "I'm done."

He dropped the piece onto his plate and reached for the syrup.

"I'll check out the Pic-N-Save this morning." She picked up her empty plate and brought it to the counter. "I'll get Elliott ready as soon as I clean up the kitchen, and we'll get out of your hair for a while."

"Why don't you leave him here with me?" Had he lost his mind?

"You don't mind?" She opened the dishwasher.

"We'll be fine." He leaned close to the baby. "Won't we?"

"Dooo," Elliott declared and then whacked Brody on the nose with the spoon.

"Elliott," Mary cried.

She stepped toward the high chair the same time as Brody started to move. She tripped over his foot and lost her balance, then Brody grabbed her and she landed on his lap with a startled "oomph."

Brody's arms tightened around her and held her for a moment, savoring her weight on his lap—that luscious backside he'd been admiring pressed against him was intense pleasure, intense torture.

Before either could move or speak, Elliott squealed

in delight, as if they'd arranged the entire thing for his benefit.

"Sorry." Mary scooted off his lap.

"My fault. Me and my big feet," he said, but he wasn't sorry even though he had to remain seated for an extra few minutes so as not to bring attention to his current condition.

After Mary left, Brody put Elliott on the floor to let him practice rolling over and crawling. He'd been reading child development articles on the internet and knew learning to crawl was an essential milestone. Elliott rolled onto his stomach, and Brody set a series of baby toys on the blanket but out of reach.

Tires crunching on the gravel in the driveway had Brody going to the front door. It was too early for Mary to return.

But it was her, and she was pulling a box out of the back seat. She approached the house carrying the cardboard carton.

He scooped Elliott off the floor and went to the door.

"What have you got there?" The way she'd been carrying the box out in front of her aroused his suspicions. He reached down and grabbed Elliott's bouncy seat from beside the door. On the porch, he set it down and strapped the baby in.

She stuck her chin out, a habit he noticed when she was going to dig her heels in over something. Great, yeah, he was right to be suspicious.

"I was on my way into town when I saw some boys gathered around something and poking it with a stick, so I stopped to see what they were doing." She set the box beside her on the sidewalk leading to the porch and pushed her loose hair out of her face. "Their behavior disturbed me."

He cocked an eyebrow. "Was this an example of responsibility walking hand in hand with capacity and power?"

"I was putting it into practice." She nodded, her dark eyes sparkling.

A laugh broke from his chest. "And what capacity and power were you in possession of?"

"I was older and bigger...well, older, anyway." She quirked a smile at him.

Did that box just move? "What do you have?"

She cleared her throat. "A crow."

"A what?" He scowled.

"I think it's been injured." She undid the flaps on the box. "Even after I chased the boys off, it didn't fly away."

He blew his breath out and stepped off the porch. "Maybe an injured wing."

"I figured you'd know what to do."

Stop looking at me as if I can solve every poor creature's problems. But he was starting to like the way she looked at him. "Me? Why would you assume I know what to do? Whatever gave you the idea that—"

"Because you knew what to do with the calf." She enunciated as if explaining something to a child.

She was killing him with the way she looked to him as if he had answers. There was a time when he assumed he did have them, but that was all in the past. Just like his family, his military career, his Delta team. Aw, hell, she was still looking at him, looking *to* him. "This is a crow, Mary, not a calf."

"I know that," she sputtered, her dark eyes snapping sparks at him. "What else was I supposed to do? Huh? I couldn't just leave it there, even after I chased the boys off. Without the ability to fly, it's helpless. I felt sorry for it."

How was it possible he found her even more appealing when her gaze was shooting daggers at him? He shifted, trying to ease the sudden tightness in his jeans.

She drew her lower lip between her teeth, glancing around as if she'd see an answer somewhere. Then she squared her shoulders and drew up taller. "Okay. Where would you go to find out what to do? There must be a local…" She shrugged. "I don't know. Some sort of agency. A forest ranger or a wildlife and fisheries agent… someone somewhere so I could find out what to do."

She must've taken his silence as unwillingness to help. Hell, he'd been too busy thinking X-rated thoughts to form a coherent answer. And the thing was, he couldn't fault her for expecting him to help, considering the menagerie he had accumulated in the three years he'd been here. And he admired that she'd cared enough to stop. "You'd go to all that trouble?"

"I would."

He blew out a breath and bowed to the inevitable. "Let's get it settled in the barn for now and I'll—"

"You're going to help?"

Good Lord, she bounced on her toes and he was putty in her hands. "What the heck, I've got a bottle-fed calf, some maladjusted alpacas and crazy chickens, so a crow that can't fly should fit right in."

"Thank you," she said, but her smug smile told him she'd known he'd end up helping.

No wonder the female population of Loon Lake thought he was a pushover. Because he damn well was. But he liked that Mary had turned to him. He grunted and pointed to the barn. "Bring it in there."

"Thank you." Mary said as she picked the box back up again.

"Yeah, you already said that," he muttered and retrieved Elliott and his bouncy seat from the porch. "I hope you're taking notes, big guy. Maybe you can avoid my mistakes."

"I heard that," she said over her shoulder.

"I'm sure you did."

"I told you I knew someone who could help," she told the box.

"Like with the calf, I will do my best, but—"

"I know it's up to Mother Nature." She set the box down.

He put Elliott in the office, sequestered away from the crow to avoid any harmful germs the bird carried. "Tell me what happened."

Her look grew fierce. "They had a stick and I grabbed it out of one of the tormentors' hands and threatened to hit him with it."

Good Lord, she could've been hurt. "How old were these boys?"

She puffed out her cheeks and blew out the trapped air. "They looked around twelve or thirteen, maybe."

Calm down, they were just kids. "How many were there?"

"Four, but don't worry, I learned how to take care of myself. Not all of the foster homes I was placed in were…"

His head shot up, and he drew in a sharp breath. "Were what?"

She shrugged as if unaware of his distress. "Safe or even friendly. Anyway, after giving those boys a piece of my mind, I used my sweatshirt to cover it and get it into the car."

The nonchalant way she described some of her treatment as a child in foster care sliced him open like a Ka-Bar knife. It hurt to know he was helpless to do anything about it. No wonder she wanted to help.

"Is that okay?"

"What? I'm sorry, is what okay?" He'd missed her question, too busy planning mayhem on anyone who'd been mean to her, including his own brother.

"If I set the box down here?" She motioned with her head at the workbench.

"Sure. We'll need a place to keep it contained, since it's not like I have birdcages lying around." He was doing his best to resist the urge to take her into his arms, comfort her. Lord knew if he did, he'd end up doing things they might both regret. Or not.

"What? No birdcages?" She set the box down and wiped her hands on her shirt. "Tsk, tsk. A gross lack of foresight on your part."

"For which I humbly apologize." He bowed his head.

"As well you should." She scowled but soon dissolved into a giggle.

"I'm going to go in the house and get an old sock." *And wrangle my libido into submission.*

"A sock? For what?"

"To keep its wing immobilized while it heals."

"See? I knew you'd know what to do." She went to the sink and began washing her hands.

Did she have any clue how she was tying him in knots? Shaking his head, he headed to the house.

When he got back to the barn, Mary was talking to the crow in low, soothing tones. His gut tightened at the husky quality to her voice when she spoke like that.

"This should work." He held up a sock with the foot

cut off, leaving the ribbed portion intact. "It will act like a cast."

"Cool."

"Now we have to…" He made the mistake of looking at her and lost himself in her smile.

"Have to what?"

"Huh?" He mentally shook himself. *Stay on task, soldier.* "We'll have to get it around the bird."

"How do we do that?"

"Very carefully," he managed with a straight face.

She rolled her eyes. "I walked right into that one."

"Rule number one when you live on a farm with animals." He touched the tip of her nose with his finger. "Watch. Your. Step."

Brody located two pairs of heavy-duty gloves on his workbench, grateful he hadn't gotten around to tossing the old, tattered ones. He gave Mary the better of the two. "Let's see if we can do this without getting pecked."

"Crows are pretty smart. Maybe he or she will understand that we're trying to help."

"We'll keep its head covered. It keeps wild animals calm." Brody put a scrap of cloth over the bird's head. "Here. Can you hold that in place while I slip the sock around the body?"

The crow squawked and tried to peck him, but the gloves did their job and he got the makeshift cast on.

He poked around until he located a bale of hardware cloth and brought it to a stack of lumber. "It will need someplace safe to stay while it heals."

"You might need this." She lugged a toolbox over. "Tell me how to help without trying to argue with me."

He laughed and brushed a curl off her cheek. Resisting the urge to touch was a losing battle. "I'll need you to hold up the sides until I can get them nailed in place."

"What were you going to use the wood and all this wire for?"

"Fencing." He gathered the supplies and set them down in the middle of the barn so he'd have space to work.

"What were you going to fence in?"

"The fence was to keep something out." He began laying out the boards in a square pattern. "If I plant a garden, I need to keep the poachers out."

"Poachers?"

"Rabbits, mice, raccoons and other assorted varmints." He scrounged up his best glower. "And don't go giving me grief about bunny rabbits needing to eat."

She pouted. "Well, they do."

Man, she made pouting desirable. "Uh-huh. Hand me that hammer, please."

She handed it to him. "What kind of things would you plant in your garden?"

"The usual…tomatoes, cucumbers, peppers, squash… maybe some watermelon." He hammered the nails.

"It would be fun to watch them grow." Her tone was wistful.

"If you like standing around and watching things grow." Yeah, and he'd be the first in line to watch her.

She punched him on the shoulder. "Quit making fun."

"But you're such an easy target." He couldn't hide his grin.

She stuck out her tongue. "Brat."

"Can't wait for Elliott to start copying you." He pounded in another nail.

She clamped her mouth shut and glanced toward the office as if she expected Elliott to be watching.

He chuckled. "Could you hold this in place for me?"

As they worked, Mary told him about a magazine article she had read recently while in the pediatrician's waiting room about crows and their intelligence, going on and on and citing examples of their abilities. If not for enjoying the sound of her voice, his eyes might have glazed over.

Still, he couldn't help pulling her leg. "How long have you been waiting to use that trivia?"

She frowned. "It's not trivia. It's scientific fact."

"Well, this crow was smart enough to get injured while you were around."

"All I did was save him from walking here. I'm sure he would have found you sooner or later."

"You think so?" He raised an eyebrow in amusement. Damn, he needed to pay attention to the job at hand or he'd be nailing his fingers.

"I know so." She nodded once.

He used a pneumatic staple gun to fasten the hardware cloth to the frame and screwed in the hinges for the door. Poking through his toolbox, he found a hook-and-eye set to use as a door latch.

He stood back to admire his handiwork. "I think that should work until it recovers."

"Serenity."

He turned to look at her. "Beg pardon?"

"That's what I've decided to name the crow. I don't know whether it's male or female, but Serenity is gender neutral."

He scratched the back of his neck. "Serenity, huh?"

"Unless you have a better idea?"

"Not a one." Oh, he had lots of ideas, but none that included a crow. Or clothes.

She got the box with the crow and he put it inside the cage, leaving the top open so the crow could hop out when it wanted. He shimmied back out of the cage and secured the hook.

She sighed. "I hate locking it up."

"It's more for protection."

"I know, but whenever people say it's for your own good…"

Brody ran a hand through his hair. When he decided to buy the farm, he'd had visions of becoming a hermit; back then quiet and solitude had been his friends. But the residents of Loon Lake, while giving him his space, had somehow woven a spell and claimed him as one of their own. Now he was sharing his home with a baby and discussing a wild crow with a beautiful woman.

When he first brought them here, he'd been looking for reasons they needed to leave. Now he was looking for reasons to keep them here. And that was dangerous.

She studied the bird. "I need to look up what to feed it."

"Peanuts in the shell, fresh fruit, mealworms and *mmmhhff*—"

She threw her arms around him. "Thank you."

The sweet, flowery scent of her hair surrounded him. Oh, man, he was in trouble.

He stood motionless, fighting the urge to throw his arms around her, because if he did, they'd end up on the floor of the barn in a tangle of— *Stop! She's here because you're her son's uncle.* And that was a fact no amount of time, space or wishing would ever change.

She must've realized how stiffly he was holding himself, because she dropped her arms and would have backed away if he hadn't caught her hand. He couldn't let her go thinking he was rejecting her. He swallowed hard. What could he say? "Mary, I…"

She tugged her hand free. "It's okay. I get it. Complicated."

She'd collected Elliott and disappeared before he could form a coherent thought, let alone a verbal answer.

Chapter Nine

Distance. She needed distance. Mary marched across the yard, into the house and up the stairs. She left Elliott, asleep in his seat, in his room and went into hers. She balled her hands into fists. What was wrong with her? Elliott was six months old, so her rioting hormones had settled back to normal. Never in her life had she thrown herself at a man. Even with Roger, he'd done the pursuing. No one in her life had ever pursued her with such determination as Roger had, and she'd let ego cloud her judgment. Had she somehow done that again?

In the bathroom she washed her face and began brushing her hair. Once Elliott woke, she'd go into town and check out some of the businesses on Main Street. She'd noticed a bookstore and a needlework shop, both customers of Randall Burke's. She could introduce herself and let them know Randall would be doing less and less.

"Mary?"

She twirled toward Brody's voice, the brush slipping out of her hand and clattering onto the tile floor.

"Sorry, I didn't mean to startle you." He held up his hands, palms out.

"No problem. I didn't hear you come up the stairs." She stooped to pick up the brush and used those few seconds to compose herself.

"I…" He tugged on his ear. "I want to apologize for my behavior."

"What do you mean?" She wasn't making the mistake of assuming or taking anything for granted. She needed to know where she stood with Brody.

"I gave you the impression that I didn't want your kisses. Nothing could be further from the truth." He ran his hand through his hair. From the state of it, it appeared he'd been doing that quite a bit.

"I shouldn't have thrown myself at you." She set the brush down. "It was…inappropriate."

Good Lord. She sounded like some hapless heroine from one of her Regency romances.

"Inappropriate?" His eyebrows shot up to disappear under his disheveled hair.

"Impulsive?" And how was this better?

"I'd say inevitable." He stepped closer and reached out, hooking his hand around her waist. "Please? Let me apologize for giving you the wrong idea."

"Well… I…" She pulled back enough to look at his face but not enough to slip from his embrace. "I gotta be honest and say you're confusing me with your mixed signals."

"I know." He pulled her closer and rested his forehead against hers. "I didn't want you to think I was taking advantage of our situation. I needed to be sure you weren't just expressing gratitude for my help with the crow."

"That wasn't gratitude. Believe me, I know the difference," she assured him and ran her hands across his back, enjoying the way his muscles flexed under her fingers.

He exhaled, his breath warming her face, warming her heart. "Mary, I... I've wanted you from the first moment I saw you."

"You have?" Her heart pounded as their breath commingled.

"You don't look convinced." His arms tightened around her.

"Well—"

He eased her closer, fitting her against him, her softness to his hardness. And oh, boy, his muscles weren't the only things hard on him. She wiggled closer.

"Mmm." His lips fastened on hers. He lifted his head, his blue eyes dark with desire. "What say you now?"

"Huh?" She was lost in a haze of desire.

"Are you convinced I want you every bit as much as you want me?"

She ran her tongue over her teeth, then her lips, feeling powerful when his pupils dilated. "Maybe I could use a little more convincing."

He lowered his head. "I'll see what I can do."

He deepened the kiss as she lifted her arms from his waist to loop around his neck, urging him closer.

He lifted his head, his blue eyes intent. "If...if this isn't what you want—"

She silenced him with her fingers over his lips. "I'm an adult and I understand ramifications... I also know what I want."

"Thank God," he muttered and scooped her up. "Your bed or mine?"

"Wait. Do you have condoms?"

"Mine it is."

In his room, he laid her on the bed and shucked off his boots before joining her. He brought his mouth down on hers and she opened immediately for him, her tongue meeting his. Without lifting his mouth from hers, he began unbuttoning her blouse. After getting the first few buttons undone, he reached under the fabric to cup her breast. He pinched the nipple through the fabric.

He lifted his mouth from hers to trail kisses along the skin he'd exposed.

She buried her hands in his thick hair and tugged him closer as he kissed his way to her breasts. He ran his tongue over the lace covered valley.

"This is convenient." He grinned and flicked open the front clasp of her bra.

He captured a nipple with his mouth, but, as much as she hated to, she pulled him away. "Careful. You might get more than you bargained for."

"I don't under—oh." He grinned. "I guess those belong to the little guy for now."

"I'm weaning, so most of his feedings are bottle, but I don't want to send the wrong message to my body."

"Gotcha."

Abandoning her breasts, he undid the remaining buttons and pulled the fabric apart. He slowly worked his way down to her navel and circled it with his tongue.

Abruptly he sat up and pulled his shirt over his head. He grabbed a condom from the nightstand, set it on the bed and eased back down next to her. She ran her hands over his bare chest, admiring the muscle definition and the sprinkling of dark, curly hair. "This farming business agrees with you."

He chuckled, that delicious low sound that made all her hormones stand up and salute.

"I keep up with my military routine between all that

farming." He flexed his abs and grinned, obviously pleased with her admiration.

He laid back and pulled her with him so she landed partially on top. She kissed his chest and licked his flat nipples until he sucked in a breath and rolled over, reversing their positions.

He unsnapped her jeans. "Let's get you out of these so I can see you."

She quickly shimmied out of the jeans and tossed them aside.

He started to pull her panties off and stopped, sucking in a sharp breath. "Mary?"

The tattoo. How could she have forgotten about it? Maybe because this was the first time anyone other than the artist had seen it. And she hadn't realized that letting someone see the tattoo would feel like exposing herself.

She started to pull away. "You don't like it?"

He tugged her closer. "I do… I do…it's just…it's a surprise. I wouldn't have imagined."

His tone had held a note of wonder, along with… amusement? Was he laughing at her?

"Maybe it's like you said. A surprise." She lifted one shoulder. "I got it after Elliott was born."

"What is that symbol?" He pulled her lace panties off and continued to explore.

"It's Japanese for 'dream.'" A delicous shiver raced through her at the touch from his callused fingers.

Something flickered in his deep blue eyes. "Thank you."

"For getting a tattoo?" How was she supposed to follow this conversation when he was doing all these distracting things to her?

"For allowing me to be the first to see it."

"My pleasure," she said, but it came out more like a groan.

"No, but let's hope this is," he growled and lowered his head.

He teased her with his tongue until she was crazed with need. When he finally stroked the spot that had been begging for attention, she buried her hands in his hair. She bit off the cry when the wave of pleasure hit her.

"That was…" she trailed off, savoring the moment. For once, she was more than any of the labels others had foisted on her—foster child, accountant, single mother.

He looked up and grinned smugly. "I'm glad."

She frowned. "But you still have your pants on. Aren't you…?"

"Oh, I most certainly am," he said and shucked his pants off along with a pair of gray boxer briefs. "And you are, too."

"Again?" She shook her head. "No, I've never…"

"Then I need to rectify that." He dipped his head and captured her mouth.

He kissed, stroked and explored her body, making her feel not just feminine but desired and special. When he had worked her into another frenzy, he ripped open the foil packet. Nudging her entrance, he moved slowly as her body adjusted to him. Another gesture that made her feel treasured. He set a rhythm that had her climbing toward another release. Was that even possible? He put his hand between their bodies and found that sensitive bud. Not just possible…inevitable.

"Yes, please." She writhed and twisted on the mattress, the sheets clutched in her fists.

One last powerful thrust and they simultaneously fell over the edge.

They lay entwined as their breathing slowed, his fingers making lazy trails across her bare skin.

"You're very talented," she whispered.

His expelled breath blew wisps of hair across her forehead. "And you're a dreamer disguised as an accountant."

"Number crunchers can have dreams, too."

"Tell me your dreams, Mary," he coaxed and tightened his arm around her.

"Why?" She brushed her hand across his chest, enjoying the way the crisp hair felt against her palm. "Are you going to wave my magic wand and make them come true?"

His blue eyes darkened and her pulse picked up at his sudden intensity. "I would if I could."

She walked her fingers up and down his chest. "You do have a wand…not sure how magical it is…"

"Challenge accepted." His voice rumbled in his chest. "I will have to demonstrate again how magical my wand is."

Again? She giggled, feeling carefree and just a bit reckless.

A frantic cry came from the other room.

"I give him kudos for impeccable timing." Brody sighed and kissed her forehead. "Do you want me to get him?"

She shook her head and reluctantly swung her legs off the bed. "No, but thanks."

With a furtive glance at him sprawled on the bed, she picked up her clothes and quickly dressed. She was going to need time to look at their situation logically and seeing Brody with Elliott would cloud the issue. Sex, even mind-blowing sex, wouldn't magically change Brody's opinion of long-term relationships any more than her dollar-store wand would. But time might help, just as time would heal the crow's wing.

Brody had escaped the house and sat in his office in the barn. He balled his hand into a fist when he caught sight of his reflection in the blank computer screen. What had he done? Relaxing his hand, he tunneled his fingers in his hair and tried to think logically. They were both adults who'd acted on a mutual desire.

Yeah, was that how your father justified himself?

He jumped out of the chair, and it rolled away. With a muttered curse, he moved it out of the way as he paced. He wasn't his father, with a wife and son who might get hurt by his actions. And Mary wasn't an employee. She was educated and not dependent on him for an income. As a matter of fact, she had a job with potential and—

He snapped his fingers as an idea formed in his head, and he rummaged through his desk drawers until he found a tape measure. Grabbing a pencil and notepad off the desk, he left the barn and went to the bunkhouse.

A week later, Brody hurried through his morning routine in the barn. He and Mary had settled into a comfortable pattern of spending time together during the day and making love at night. Simply thinking about Mary had his body reacting.

After finishing up in the barn, he let himself into the kitchen. Mary looked up from the baby cereal she was mixing. As usual her smile stopped him in his tracks.

Elliott also looked up and squealed. Brody chuckled, getting a charge out of the baby's reaction. A month ago it would have sent him running for the hills, but the baby's happiness and delight at everything was hard to resist. Elliott had inherited Mary's enthusiasm, drawing people to him.

"Hey there, big guy, your mom tells me you have a tooth." Brody hunkered down in front of the high chair. "Wanna show it to Uncle Brody?"

Elliott shook his head. Something he'd started doing, no matter what anyone asked him.

Brody reached under the food tray and tickled his foot, sending him into spasms of irresistible baby giggles. "Aha, I see it."

Mary laughed and brought the cereal bowl to the table. "You were up early."

"I had some things to do." He tried to sound casual, but his heartbeat had kicked up, so he went to the sink and washed his hands.

She began feeding Elliott. "What's going on?"

"What do you mean?" He took his time drying his hands.

"There's something else going on. You get a little sparkle in your eyes when you're pleased about something."

He did? So much for keeping his "spy skills" after leaving Delta Force. Or was she that attuned to him? And if so, how did he feel about that? The idea that she might be able to read him was unsettling.

"Well?" She glanced up. "Are you going to tell me or keep it a secret?"

"I may have something I want to show you." He hung the towel back on the rack.

"What is it?" She paused with the spoon partway to Elliott's mouth, and the baby scowled at Brody, as if knowing he was the cause of his mother's inattention.

Brody hitched his chin toward Elliott. "Your son is waiting for that spoonful."

"And you're avoiding answering my question," she said but spooned the cereal into Elliott's open mouth.

Brody pulled out a chair with his foot and sat. "I'll show you after he's finished with breakfast. He needs his strength to push those teeth out, huh, big guy?"

Elliott shook his head, and they both laughed.

Mary scraped the bowl and spooned up the last of

the cereal. "Let me wash his face and give him a bottle. Where is this thing you need to show me?"

"Outside."

She wiped Elliott's face and hands before handing him a bottle. "The sun is shining, so it can't be another space station."

"There is no other space station," he teased.

She clicked her tongue. "You know what I mean."

He stood and tapped his fingers on her shoulder. "Hurry."

She slid out the tray and pulled Elliott out of the seat.

"Here, give him to me." Brody reached out and took Elliott, settling him on his hip. Then he reached for Mary's hand with his free one and led her outside.

"Where are we going?"

"I want to show you what I've been doing in the old bunkhouse."

"You said you were just cleaning it out and using that as an excuse to give Kevin and Danny some odd jobs," she said as they walked the short distance to the building.

"True. But that's not all." He stopped by the door and dropped her hand while he fished a key out of his pocket.

"A key?" She seemed startled. "But you don't even lock your house. Why are you locking this place?"

"I didn't want you to stumble in here and spoil the surprise." He opened the door with a flourish then stepped aside so she could go in first.

Mary blinked as she glanced around. She frowned as she took in the home office he had made.

"I know it's a ways out of town, but you'll be able to meet with clients if you want." He pointed to a desk and computer station he'd set up. "And there's a bathroom down the hall. I cleaned it up some but thought you might like to decorate it."

She turned to him, her eyes wide. "You did all this for me? I don't know what to say... Tha-thank you."

What the...? Sure, she was saying all the right things, but she wasn't excited...not the kind of joy she'd displayed when he agreed to take the calf or when he helped her with the crow. He'd known her long enough to know when something pleased her.

His chest squeezed, threatening to cut off his air supply. She wasn't bouncing.

He glanced again at her feet planted firmly on floor. Why did he bother trying to please other people? He hadn't ever been able to do anything to please his parents, so what made him think he could please Mary?

"And that's not all." Maybe this would be what she wanted. He tugged her hand and pulled her toward the farthest end of the building, where there was a kitchen. He hadn't planned on this part, at least not yet, but maybe this would please her. "This part could be turned into living space. It'll be a while before it's finished, but I thought you might like your privacy."

"Privacy?"

He nodded and glanced around. "I can turn this into an apartment for you and Elliott...if...if that's what you wanted."

"Oh." She licked her lips.

Maybe she wasn't seeing the potential. "I know it doesn't look like much now, but it's still a work in progress."

"It's...it's..." Mary bit her bottom lip. "You didn't have to go to so much trouble. I... I could've found some place in town."

"I know it's not as convenient as an office in town, but rent might eat up your profits."

"I see," she said.

He tried to swallow past the lump in his throat and

couldn't. What had made him think she'd be happy staying on the farm? Staying with him?

After putting Elliott down for his morning nap, Mary wandered through the empty farmhouse, her footsteps seeming to echo on the hardwood floors. As much as she loved the place, it felt barren without Brody. He'd ridden off on Patton several hours ago. Exercise or avoidance?

You knew this was fleeting. It's your own fault for falling in love with the farm. And with its owner.

She couldn't deny it any longer. She'd fallen in love with Brody, a man who said he didn't do long term, a man who didn't do complicated. Elliott's biological father was Brody's estranged half brother, a fact that could never, ever change, no matter how much she or he might wish.

Had Brody decided to put her in the bunkhouse before or after they'd made love? She'd thought the desire had been mutual, but maybe she'd been fooling herself. *Like you did with Roger?* No, she argued with herself, this was different. She understood now—after it was too late—that she hadn't taken the time to get to know the real Roger.

Brody proved in so many ways he was capable of deep compassion, and yet he locked himself and his heart away here on the farm. He cared for the animals, expecting nothing in return. He'd come to the hospital and opened his home to her and Elliott. And he'd bonded with Elliott. Brody wasn't dispassionate. She'd bet he cared too much and that frightened him.

Could she show him, prove to him that loving someone was worth the risk?

"Brody?"

Brody grunted as he draped the saddle onto the sawhorse and turned to face Mary. She lingered inside the door to the barn, uncertainty apparent in the way she stood, the way she worried her lower lip. He'd ridden Patton, trying to let his anger and frustration run its course. "Yes?"

"Could we talk for a minute?" She rubbed the fingers of one hand over the back of the other.

"Right now? I've got a lot of things to take care of." Like putting off hearing how she wasn't happy here, how she wanted to leave.

She swallowed, her neck muscles working. "Elliott's down for his nap, so it's a good time for me."

Might as well get this over with. Putting off the inevitable never accomplished anything. He strolled into his office and pointed to the chair next to his desk. "Sure. I suppose my stuff can wait."

God, he sounded like a petulant child.

Mary followed him into the office but didn't sit. She paced back and forth instead. "If you needed us to leave, all you had to do was ask. I am through staying places I'm not wanted."

"I—wait, what? Leave?" Where was this coming from? He wanted the opposite. That's what this whole futile exercise had been about—getting her to stay on the farm. "I didn't do it because I want you to leave."

She stopped pacing and faced him. "Then why? Why do you want to put us out in the bunkhouse?"

He ran a hand across his mouth and sighed. How was he supposed to explain it without sounding like an arrogant ass? "I…oh, hell, I may as well come out and just say it. I don't want you to feel obligated."

"Obligated?"

"I…" He tunneled his fingers through his hair. "Obligated because I was letting you live here."

"But aren't I paying my share? I've helped out with groceries and working with the animals. Did you want me to chip in more money? I can... I've gotten a lot of work from Randall. More than I expected."

"You're paying more than your share." Talk about making a mess.

She frowned and shook her head as if trying to make sense of what he was saying. "Then what?"

"I didn't want you to think I was expecting sex in return for...for anything." *I want you to come to me free of obligation.*

She blew out her breath. "You must have a low opinion of me if you think I'd sell myself for a couple of lobster rolls at the café. I am worth a heck of a lot more than that."

"No, Mary, wait!" He reached for her before she could get away. With his hands resting on her shoulders, he turned her to face him. "This is coming out all wrong. This was all me. I wanted to be sure you felt on equal footing with me. I didn't want you to regret it later or for you to think I assumed anything because I had all the power."

"What makes you think you have all the power?" She looked at him as if he'd sprouted horns. "I can leave anytime I want. I have enough money to support myself, and I have new friends here who are willing to help. Meg told me the cottage next to theirs is available if I needed a place. Her brother is going to be renting it while he's helping Riley with the addition to their home, but he isn't going to be able to come yet."

His heart pounded in his chest. Had she been looking for a place to rent? "Were you thinking about leaving?"

"Only because I thought you wanted us to leave."

"I don't want you to leave. I've enjoyed having you here and getting to know Elliott." There. He said it. *Yeah, but you left out the part about falling head over heels.* He was still shying away from giving his feelings a name.

"Okay…" Mary said. "That's what you don't want… what is it that you *do* want?"

"What about some simple fun?"

Something flickered across her face and disappeared before she tilted her head back and eyed him. "Fun? What does that mean?"

Pulling her closer, he lowered his head and kissed her. Her mouth was soft, pliable under his, and he nibbled at her fuller bottom lip. Finally lifting his head, he said, "Does that answer your question?"

At first she looked a little shell-shocked, but a smile soon spread across her face, lighting her eyes. "Elliott usually sleeps for at least an hour or two during his afternoon nap."

Her breathless tone wreaked havoc with his senses, swamping him with need. Without another word, he scooped her up and carried her into the house, not stopping until he reached the top of the stairs. He hesitated for a moment. Glancing down at her, he grinned. "There's a new box of condoms in my room."

Chapter Ten

"So I've been doing it wrong all this time?" Mary asked from the doorway of her office. The two weeks since he'd shown her his surprise had flown by and today Brody was using a laser level to mark a spot on the wall behind her desk. Her plan had been to pick a spot, hammer in a nail and hang the framed photograph of a sunset on Loon Lake. She'd fallen in love with the rich colors, and once the local photographer had explained the process of creating high-dynamic-range digital photographs to her, she knew she had to have the picture.

Brody made a chalk mark on the wall before turning. "What was your plan? To eyeball it and hammer in a nail?"

"Something like that." Which was sad, because then she wouldn't have had the pleasure of seeing him with his tool belt.

He tsked his tongue and turned back to hammer the hanger in place.

Despite her initial reluctance, Mary liked her office and, considering how many times a day Brody popped in, she no longer believed he'd been trying to get away from her. Aside from Elliott, Brody was by far her most frequent visitor, but she'd also had a few prospective clients drop in. Her boss, prodded by his wife, had retired earlier than expected and she'd taken over the accounting business. Although she wondered how much of her foot traffic was urgent need of her services or curiosity over Brody and his farm.

The days were turning warmer, and Brody had installed a screen door so she could enjoy the gentle breeze and the wind chimes he'd purchased. Somehow a week had morphed into a month, and she had to keep reminding herself that this wasn't her life but a temporary arrangement. She and Brody had agreed to explore their chemistry with a no-strings-attached policy. She wouldn't have minded strings, but Brody wasn't ready and maybe never would be. That was something she would have to accept when the time came. And that time would come, because she couldn't carry on this way forever. It wouldn't be fair to Elliott to let him get accustomed to having Brody in his daily life and then snatch it away. And she needed to think of herself, as well. She wanted someone who could make a lasting commitment.

"Mary?"

She mentally shook herself. "Sorry."

He held up the framed photograph. "Do you want the honor?"

"That wouldn't be fair, since you did all the work."

He motioned with his head. "C'mere and we'll do it together."

It was as if her heart had outgrown her chest. She

wanted nothing more than to do things together with him. "Deal."

After hanging the picture, they stepped back to admire it.

"We do good work." He bumped her shoulder with his. "I'm going to remove the sock from the crow today. Want to help?"

Before she could respond, Elliott, who'd been sleeping in the playpen, woke up. She picked him up and cuddled him. "I guess this will be the big test to see if the wing has healed."

"We'll see," Brody said and patted Elliott's back as he snuggled against Mary's shoulder. "I built an enclosure on the side of the barn."

"What was wrong with the cage?"

"It will need—"

"Serenity."

He huffed out his breath. "*Serenity* will need a week to see if the wing is healed and to regain strength."

She grinned, because the twinkle in his blue eyes told her his annoyance was all pretense. "You built another enclosure?"

"This one's more like a lean-to on the side of the barn."

He lifted a shoulder and let it drop as if his actions were no big deal. Except to her they were and one of the reasons she was falling more in love with him each day. By staying she was opening herself to heartache, but if she didn't stay and try to get him to see this could work, that they could work, she'd regret it for the rest of her life.

"Mary?"

"I'm sorry, what?" She needed to concentrate on reality, enjoy the present instead of fantasizing about a future that might never come to pass.

"Did you want to see the enclosure?"

* * *

For the next week they watched Serenity regain its strength and ability to fly. She would soon have to find that within herself. She and Elliott couldn't stay in this suspended animation forever.

Last night they'd attended the party given by the Coopers for Kevin's high school graduation. Their arrival together didn't go unnoticed, and people had started treating them as if they *were* a family.

Brody came into the kitchen as she finished giving Elliott his breakfast.

"I think we should release the crow—er, Serenity—this morning," he said as he poured himself a coffee. "I would say the wing is healed."

"Then it's time." Mary sighed. "Let me get his diaper changed first."

After she'd gotten Elliott cleaned up, they walked across the yard to the enclosure Brody had made. He'd dismissed the structure he'd put together as a mere lean-to, but it was so much more than that. The care that had gone into building it was evident, like the care that went into everything on this farm.

She had to clear her throat before she could speak. "What do we do?"

"Open the door and leave it open. It might get skittish and not want to fly out if we're standing around, so we'll go inside the office. We can watch from the window in the door."

The crow was still a wild creature, despite becoming accustomed to human care, so that made sense. She nodded and sniffed.

"Hey." He touched her shoulder. "What's wrong?"

She gave a quiet little laugh. "I can't decide if I'm happy or sad."

He squeezed her shoulder. "It's okay to be both."

"We may never see it again." She should be rejoicing at saving a wild creature and releasing it to its natural habitat, but she was feeling selfish and couldn't shake her melancholy. *Backbones, not wishbones.*

"Would you prefer keeping it locked up?"

Her head jerked up at his words. "What? No, of course not. Not if it can fly."

"Would you have preferred leaving it to its fate with those boys?" he asked with a significant lifting of his brow.

She let out a laugh. "I know what you're doing."

He ducked his head to look her in the eyes. "Is it working?"

"Absolutely not." She grinned and pushed his shoulder. "Now go open the door. I'll be inside."

In the office area, she put Elliott in his bouncy seat. Brody stepped in and shut the door. She joined him at the window, and they watched as the crow hopped out of the cage, glanced around and took off, flapping its wings and then gliding away until it was out of sight.

She couldn't prevent another sniff as she turned away from the window. "Do you have any tissues in here?"

"Don't cry," he said, a twinge of annoyance lacing his tone, but he eased her against him. "You did a good thing."

"*We* did a good thing," she corrected him. "And I'm not crying. I happen to have sweaty eyes."

"Ah, I see." He touched her cheek and motioned toward the desk with his head before stepping back. "Check the top drawer for tissues."

She pulled out the top drawer, and Brody's smiling face stared up at her from a creased and dog-eared snapshot. Standing next to Brody were three other smiling men, their arms thrown around one another's shoulders, mugging for the camera. They all wore tan T-shirts and desert-camo pants.

She picked up the picture and sank into his office chair. How young and carefree he looked. He'd told her about why he'd left the army, but not about what that decision had done to him. But he must've hung on to that picture for a reason. Brody didn't strike her as a sentimental guy. His home wasn't full of those tchotchkes people kept as reminders of people or places they loved, nor had she seen any pictures anywhere.

He'd said he'd come to the farm after getting out of the army. Had he needed the peace and solitude of this place?

"Mary?" He glanced at her over his shoulder. "Did you find any?"

"Uh, I found this." She held up the picture, tissues and tears forgotten. "Who are these guys?"

"My Delta Force team." He took a few steps toward her and reached for the photo.

She handed him the picture. "You looked like great friends. Was this picture taken in Afghanistan?"

"No." He stared at the photo, deep creases marring the skin between his eyebrows. "The exact location is classified, but let's just say it was somewhere on the African continent."

"Oh, so you didn't just go to Afghanistan?" She'd assumed his military service had all been there.

"Delta Force gets sent all over the world."

"Are those guys still in the army?" She wanted to know all she could about this man. *Do you think knowing more will help convince him to ignore your situation?*

"I didn't stay in touch." He shrugged as if it was of no importance, but she had spotted the longing in his eyes as he stared at the photo, as if he missed them.

He set the photo back on the desk and she picked it up, glancing at the back, but it was blank. "What're their names?"

He paused for a moment before using his index finger to rest under each face. "Landry Collins, Jeff Bowen and Sean Kennedy."

"The surfer dude?"

He nodded and she glanced at the photo again. It was as if the camera had caught not just their likenesses but their closeness, as well. Brody's eyes were filled with sorrow when he looked at the picture. "What happened?"

"A central retinal vein occlusion happened."

Her stomach churned. She hated feeling so ineffectual. "But the eye thing wasn't your fault. You couldn't help it."

He clicked his tongue. "Fault or not, I let them down."

Damn, the man was stubborn. "You make it sound like it was my fault for being in foster care."

His head jerked back. "What? No. That makes no sense. You had no control over what happened to you."

"Exactly. It stinks, but it's not your fault. Had that happened to one of them, would you have just walked away? Left him to his fate?"

"No way. We didn't leave anyone behind."

"I guess they felt that way about you, huh?"

He expelled his breath. "I see what you're doing."

"Is it working?"

He chuckled, but before he said or did anything, tires crunched on the gravel in the driveway.

Disappointed, she checked her watch. "That must be my new client. I better get into my office."

She reached for Elliott, but Brody put his hand on her arm. "Leave him here. He's fine. I'll keep my good eye on him."

Her jaw dropped. What was she supposed to say to

that? And before she could stop herself, she grinned and it morphed into a laugh.

"I love it when you laugh," he said and leaned over until his lips pressed against hers. A car door slammed.

"You'd better go," he whispered.

Brody stared at the door she'd walked through. When was the last time he'd been able to joke about what had happened with his eyesight? Had he ever? For some reason, talking to Mary was easy and helped to put things in perspective.

He picked up the old picture and rubbed his fingertip across the familiar faces. Was Mary right? Should he have kept in touch? After their last mission went sideways because of his condition, he'd shut himself off. But he wouldn't have blamed any of them if the situation had been reversed. So why was he blaming himself?

Needing to do something physical, he checked to be sure the straps on Elliott's little seat were secure. Satisfied, he picked up Elliott and the seat and walked around to the front of the house. When he'd first moved in, he'd removed most of the overgrown bushes around the front porch. They'd been in such bad shape, he'd decided starting with new growth seemed easiest. He hadn't gotten around to replacing the ones he'd removed. The last time they'd been to the Coopers', Mary had admired their rhododendrons and he figured those were as good as any other bushes. His choice had nothing to do with the fact Mary had said how much she liked them.

Brody set Elliott and his seat on the porch, and a small pile of trinkets on the top step caught his eye. "What the…?"

He hunkered down and poked at the bottle cap, a piece of discarded foil from a cigarette pack and a… He picked up the piece to examine it and realized it was a Lego brick. Rising, he glanced around, but the deserted yard held no answers. The pile was too neat to be anything but on purpose, as if a child had laid treasures out for someone to admire. Brody scratched his head and glanced over at Elliott. He could imagine Elliott doing something like that, but not for another couple of years.

He pulled out his tape measure and pad and pencil. Much like he'd done with the bunkhouse and Mary's office, he sketched plans for rhododendron bushes along the front porch.

A car drove past. Mary's new client, he thought, and nodded his head to acknowledge the driver's raised hand.

Soon after the car disappeared down the driveway, Mary came to the front door. "There you are. What are you doing out here?"

He slipped the pad into his back pocket and pointed to the pile of trinkets. "Wondering what this is."

She stepped onto the porch and peered down at the items. "It couldn't have been blown there. The pile is too neat…unless you…"

"Nope. Found it like this."

"That is strange." She shook her head. "Do you think it could be Serenity?"

"Has enough time passed to gather this stuff?"

She shrugged. "Maybe the other crows helped."

He quirked an eyebrow at her. "More of your crow trivia?"

"Don't laugh. I—"

Elliott woke up with a startled cry.

"Oh, sweetie, did you have a bad dream?" Mary reached down and unfastened him. "How 'bout we sit on the swing for a few minutes."

With Elliott perched on her hip, she started for the

swing, but he reached out and tried to grab the sun catchers. When she skirted past the tantalizing hangings, he kicked his legs and began to cry in earnest.

She kissed his cheek. "Sorry, sweetie, those are pretty to look at, but we can't touch."

She sat with him on the swing, but he continued to fuss, pointing to the delicate glass.

Brody stepped over and reached out. "Here, let me."

He lifted Elliott into the air and made airplane noises until the tears dried up and the baby was giggling.

"Would you like to go to the lake this afternoon? We can play hooky." He lifted Elliott above his head. "Would you like that, big guy?"

"Hooky? I didn't even do that as a kid."

He sat next to her on the swing with Elliott on his lap. He bumped shoulders with her. "Bet you were one of those girls who followed all the rules."

She laughed. "Pretty much. I kept my head down and tried to blend into the background."

He reached over and captured a lock of wavy dark hair between his fingers, marveling at how soft it was. "I find it hard to believe you blended into the background."

"Yeah, well, I did."

She stared straight ahead, but he'd bet she wasn't seeing anything. Her eyes were clouded, and he wanted to wipe out her bad memories. He brushed the backs of his fingers across her silky cheek.

She blinked and turned her head. "I didn't want anyone to notice me."

"Why?" How could someone so vibrant go unnoticed?

"Because then they might remember I was 'that foster kid.'" Her smile was sad as she continued, "I preferred going unnoticed to that, especially in high school."

What? No way was he buying that. "Guys had to have noticed you."

"There was one boy I liked. He was quiet and seemed nice. He used to tell me about a video game he was designing." Her tone had taken on a wistfulness. Then she grimaced and braced her shoulders. "The other kids in the foster home called attention to us, and I was forbidden to go out with him. One of their other foster girls had gotten pregnant, and they said it wouldn't happen again on their watch." She spread her arms and smiled wryly. "It didn't happen then, but it did happen."

He didn't say anything but in a perverse way, he was glad it had happened. If not for Elliott, they might not have found one another. He wouldn't have had the pleasure of getting to know Mary Carter.

Their current arrangement wouldn't last forever. Loon Lake was a small town, but there were single men, one of whom might want something more than he did. She and Elliott deserved a forever family, considering her background. He could understand—and accept—her wanting more than he could give. But not today.

Chapter Eleven

Brody glanced at his watch as he checked the horse stalls for fresh water and oats before going to the pen he'd constructed for Lost and Found and giving them some chopped carrots as a special treat. Elliott always got a kick out of watching the alpacas eating their vegetable treats, but Mary had taken him with her into town that morning. She had volunteered to help with the luncheon at the church. Brody had offered to watch Elliott, but she'd said it wasn't necessary because the church had a nursery available. And he wasn't disappointed by that. Not one bit.

Going about his chores was a lot faster without Mary and Elliott here to distract him. He'd come to the farm looking for isolation and had taken on the abandoned animals because he couldn't turn his back. Now, taking care of them was the price he paid for his solitary lifestyle.

But Mary had jumped in with both feet, taking care of the animals with enthusiasm. He glanced at his watch again. What had delayed her? He shoved a toothpick into his mouth. Concern for her safety was the reason for his thoughts. It wasn't as if he missed her or anything like that. He enjoyed living alone and he—

Her car interrupted his thoughts, and he went toward the front of the house, all the while telling himself he wasn't rushing out to see her.

And when did you start lying to yourself?

She was bending over, getting Elliott out of the back seat when Brody came around the corner of the house. He swallowed hard at the sight of her backside extending from the open door.

When did you start letting your libido run the show?

She scooted back out and turned toward him. "Oh, hey. Sorry we were gone so long. We made a little detour on the way hom—on the way back."

"Uh-oh, dare I ask?" He pulled an exaggerated face, sending Elliott into gleeful giggles.

"Relax. No wild creatures today, but I did pick up some suet cakes to hang in the tree for Serenity." She used her key fob to unlatch the trunk. "And some vegetable plants for me…you said this morning before I left that it was okay to plant some."

He recalled her saying something about vegetable plants, but he'd been too busy thinking about that tattoo and running his tongue across it. Damn, what was wrong with him? The relationship rules were his, and yet he'd done nothing but break them since seeing her dressed like a lumberjack in that ER. If he wasn't careful, he'd be in the middle of family drama if Roger came looking for Mary or Elliott. Had history taught him nothing? "I haven't fenced the area off yet."

"I've got that covered." She grinned and pulled out a piece of decorative white plastic fencing.

Her guileless expression gutted him, and guilt for allowing their relationship to turn physical rushed in. The emotion rankled him. Mary wasn't naive. She, of all people, knew the ramifications, the consequences. He had no reason to feel guilty. "I hate to break it to you, but that fence won't keep anything out."

She grinned. "I'm sure it will be fine."

He blew out his breath in frustration. "You've been warned, don't blame me if—no, when—this doesn't turn out the way you expected."

"I've told you before, I'm an adult and not into blaming others for my mistakes. I know what I'm getting into." She adjusted Elliott so he rested higher on her hip. "I've known from the beginning. Now if you'll excuse me, my son needs his diaper changed and a nap."

Torn between wanting to run in and apologize for his behavior and keeping a handle on the situation, he got everything out of the trunk and piled it near the porch. By the time he'd finished, so had his anger.

Before dawn, Brody slipped out of bed and picked his pants off the floor. With the jeans still in his hand, he watched Mary sleep. If he woke her, they could repeat last night's activities. The makeup sex had been worth swallowing his pride and apologizing.

Despite his warnings, she'd gone ahead and planted her garden and put up the decorative fence by the time he'd come back to the house for supper. Later today he'd be sure to build her a fence designed to keep her vegetables safe from pests. Of course it would never be one hundred percent safe, because some creatures could burrow under the fence and into...into his heart.

He tried to discount that last thought but she had burrowed into his heart. He yanked his pants on, grabbed his shirt and socks, and left the room. Why did he feel as though he were sneaking away?

After making coffee, he stepped onto the porch to enjoy the sunrise. Glancing over at Mary's little vegetable patch, he choked on the sip he'd just taken. He slammed the cup onto the porch rail and hurried down the steps. Something had gotten into the garden and ruined it.

He muttered a string of curses as he surveyed the damage. This was one time he'd give anything to have been wrong. Her dark eyes had sparkled with joy as she'd surveyed her small vegetable patch—even his pessimism hadn't dimmed her enthusiasm. She'd worn that special smile he'd come to enjoy.

Hell, this was reality, and she needed to deal with it. But hadn't she been doing that her entire life? He turned on his heel and marched back to the house, grabbing his coffee mug and gulping down the contents on the way in.

He scribbled a note and propped the paper against the salt and pepper shakers on the kitchen table. He grabbed his keys and went out to his truck.

"A fool's errand," he muttered as he yanked open the driver's side door. And he was that fool.

Mary sat on the top step and drew her knees up against her chest as she surveyed her ruined garden…again. This time from a distance, as if that would make it hurt any less.

She swallowed back useless tears, closed her eyes and rested her cheek on her knees. Brody had warned her, but she'd gone ahead and planted the garden. He'd warned, but she'd gone ahead and fallen in love with him. Not just him, but with the farm, the town, the animals…even the stupid crow, who had flown off without a backward glance.

And you're going to just give up? Sit around and feel sorry for yourself?

She sat up straight and braced her shoulders. If last night was any indication, Brody's ardor hadn't dimmed. If she didn't at least try to make him see how good a future together could be, she'd regret not trying. After mentally promising not to embarrass herself by clinging if Brody lost interest, she stood up and dusted off her pants. Elliott would be waking and wanting breakfast so she went back inside.

A short time later she heard Brody's truck return, but he hadn't come in the house, and she resisted the urge to rush outside. The "I told you so" over the garden was inevitable. And heck, she couldn't blame him. So instead, she stayed in the house and made a plate of pancakes and left them in the oven to stay warm.

"Let's get you cleaned up, sweetie," she told Elliott and rinsed out a face cloth.

"Mary?" The front screen door opened with its usual squeak.

"In the kitchen," she called.

"Could you come here? I don't want to track dirt through the house."

"Let's go see what he wants." Probably to show her the ruins of her garden. She picked up Elliott and went through the living room to the front door.

Brody stood in the doorway, holding the screen open. "Your secret admirer has struck again."

"My what?"

He put his arm around her shoulder and pointed to the top step. Sure enough, a small pile of goodies rested there.

"How do you know they're for me? Maybe they're meant for you," she teased.

He hunkered down and picked up an item, holding it on his flat palm so she could see. "There's an earring in there today. I think it's for you."

She tilted her head and studied him. "Hmm... I don't know...you might look like quite the rake with an earring."

"A what?" He scowled. "I have no idea what that is."

"Sorry. I've been reading a lot of Regency romances." She laughed, and Elliott soon joined in.

"And don't you try to tell me you know what she's talking about, big guy." Brody tossed the earring onto the sidewalk and tickled Elliott's stomach, making him giggle even more. "Tell me what you're—"

A furious cawing interrupted him, and a crow glided to the ground near their feet. The bird picked up the earring and dropped it back on the pile before flapping its wings and returning to its perch in the tree.

Brody guffawed. "Looks like we were right about your admirer."

She nodded, her throat too clogged to speak. Elliott was straining every which way, trying to see where the crow had gone. She hugged him closer, reveling in the fact she'd made a difference in someone's life, even if that someone was a wild bird. Aunt Betty would have been proud. Maybe someday she'd be able to do it on a grander scale with a summer camp for—

"...still need to get a fence around it," Brody was saying.

"I'm sorry, what?" She blinked, trying to clear her thoughts.

"I said I need to put up a fence around your garden."

Her shoulders sank. "But it's destroyed."

He quirked an eyebrow. "Is it?"

She walked to where the porch wrapped around the side of the house and glanced over to the spot that had once contained her small vegetable patch. Wood and hardware cloth similar to what they'd used for the crow's cage were piled next to neat rows of plants. Wait...*plants*? But all hers had been eaten or mangled.

"You...you..." she sputtered, trying to take it all in. "Is this what you were doing? Your note just said you needed to run an errand."

"I saw the garden when I came out this morning."

"And you went out and got replacement plants?" Instead of telling her, "I told you so," he'd done this.

He cleared his throat. "Like I said before, I had planned on planting a few things and—are you crying?"

"No. I just...just..." She sniffed. Her reaction was silly. This was a garden, after all, but it represented so much more.

"Have sweaty eyeballs again?"

She burst out laughing, and Elliott joined in.

Two weeks had passed since he'd helped Mary with her garden, and life on the farm had settled into a comfortable pattern. Was that the reason he'd agreed to come to the annual Independence Day picnic? Brody gripped the cardboard tray holding popcorn and drinks tighter as he wove his way through the crowd, nodding in acknowledgment to the people who greeted him. It looked as if most of the residents of Loon Lake had gathered on the town green to enjoy the weather, the food and the music.

Why had he let her talk him into this?

Talk you into it? Are you delusional?

Delusional was the word for it. Mary had said she was coming, and he'd offered to come along. Not a lot of arm-twisting going on. He caught sight of Mary and Elliott up ahead on the blanket they'd spread out earlier. In a few moments, they would look like all the other families, but she must know he'd accompanied them to the picnic to help her and Elliott assimilate into life at Loon Lake. Happy families didn't exist, even in idyllic settings like this with green grass and a bright white gazebo. As if to punctuate his thoughts, the band began playing a John Philip Sousa march. Yeah, he got it. Small-town America, but he'd bet Kevin and Danny would agree with him about families. No, what he and Mary were doing was having some fun. Definitely not forming a forever family.

Except the things he was feeling weren't uncomplicated. No, they were veering more into forever, soul-deep, past-the-point-of-rescue territory. He could lay out all the logical, rational reasons in his head, but his heart wasn't getting the message.

Mary held on to Elliott's chubby hands, allowing the baby to pull himself up, his legs shaking under the unaccustomed strain of holding his weight. He'd be walking in another three or four months. Brody frowned at the thought. How long before Mary got tired of their arrangement? And why the hell was he thinking in terms of her getting tired of it? He was the one who should be setting limits. And sticking to them.

Elliott bounced up and down while Mary held him upright. The baby's face lit up when he saw Brody. "Daaa. Daaa."

Brody came to a stumbling halt, a tingling in his gut. Thank goodness the drinks had lids. Elliott was making sounds, not forming words. He had to believe that because he had no freaking idea how to be a father...except to not do the things his own had done. He swallowed hard. That was no way to parent.

Mary turned around, but her attention quickly skittered back to Elliott. "That's Uncle Brody, sweetie. Can you say Brody?"

"Da." *Bounce.* "Daa." *Bounce.* "Daaa."

Elliott was babbling sounds, not making conscious decisions. At least that's what the article he'd read on the internet had claimed. Babies made sounds. Nothing to see here, folks. Just practicing new sounds. Brody mentally kicked himself and took the last few steps to reach their spot. He leaned down and placed the tray on the blanket out of reach of active baby feet.

"Hey, Mr. Brody, Elliott is calling you Daddy."

Brody straightened and turned to find Fiona Cooper standing behind him. "Hello there, Miss Fiona."

"Elliott called you Daddy," she repeated, her eyes large and serious behind her glasses.

"Nah, he's just making baby sounds." He rubbed the back of his neck.

She nodded her head. "Yeah, he was. That's the way babies say it, 'cuz they can't talk good."

"Sounds like they're not the only ones," Meg said as she joined them and gave Brody an apologetic smile. She tapped Fiona on the shoulder. "Go help Daddy with our stuff, please."

"But, Mommy."

"But, Fiona." Meg gave her a look.

Fiona heaved an exaggerated sigh but said, "Yes, Mommy," and ran off.

Meg watched her daughter until Fiona was with Riley, then shook her head. "Kids. Sorry about that."

Mary smiled, but Brody couldn't help noticing she'd remained strangely silent. What was she thinking?

He rubbed a hand across his face. He'd rather be behind that damned desk, buried in army paperwork than here, right now. Was it too much to hope for a freak rainstorm to cancel the rest of the day? How about Fiona Cooper developing laryngitis? No? Better believe he'd spend all next week saying "mama" to Elliott until the baby learned some new sounds.

"I'm back." Fiona returned dragging a folded canvas lawn chair. "Here, Mommy. Daddy says the biggest one is for you so you don't get stuck."

"Blabbermouth," Riley muttered as he approached.

Brody smothered a laugh, but Riley motioned to Elliott and poked Brody in the ribs. "Your time is coming."

Brody grinned, but his gut twisted. He couldn't have Elliott calling him Daddy. Could he? Mary never encouraged that. She'd seemed to make it a point to refer to him as Uncle Brody.

But she's not jumping into the conversation, is she?

"Daa...daa," Elliott persisted, enjoying being the center of attention.

Riley laughed. "See? What did I tell you?"

"Nah, man, it's just noise." Brody swallowed. He glanced over to Mary but couldn't catch her attention. He cleared his throat. "Mary? Did you say you wanted to see the craft booths?"

"Sure." She scooped up Elliott and secured him in the umbrella stroller they'd brought. "Meg, did you—"

Meg held up a hand. "I'm good. Riley's going to wait on me hand and foot this afternoon."

"I am?"

Meg raised an eyebrow at her husband. "I might get stuck."

"Ouch." Brody sucked in a loud breath and placed a hand on Riley's shoulder. "Good luck with that."

Riley grunted and brushed his hand away. Brody laughed and grabbed the umbrella stroller, lifting it when Mary struggled to get its wheels clear of the blanket.

"Poor Riley," Brody said as they walked away, wanting to break the silence. What was going on in that beautiful head of hers?

Mary turned her head and glanced back at the Coopers. "I wouldn't say that."

"Huh?" He turned. Riley and Meg were locked in an embrace.

Brody didn't miss Mary's wistful expression at the Coopers' PDA. Beads of sweat broke out on his forehead. Was that what Mary was longing for?

"Meg deserves her happy ending," he said, remembering Meg's struggles as a single mother.

"I'm sure she does." Mary stopped when one of the stroller wheels got stuck in a rut in the grass.

Ouch. Open mouth, insert foot. "I meant—"

"I know what you meant." She backed the stroller out of the rut.

"Here, let me." He reached for the stroller handle.

"I got it." She maneuvered it around the indentation.

He blew out a frustrated breath. Damn, he hadn't meant to hurt her feelings, but he might never get his foot out of his mouth if he continued to botch his explanation. Better to let it drop. "About Meg, I—"

"Mary, I'm so glad you were able to come." A distinguished-looking, gray-haired man dressed in khakis and a red golf shirt approached.

She smiled and shook the man's hand. "Me, too, and I'm so glad the weather held out."

Brody glanced at their clasped hands and shifted his weight from one foot to the other. She turned. "Reverend Cook, I'd like you to meet Brody Wilson."

Reverend? Aw, man, he was in rare form today. Jealous of— Wait, no. He wasn't jealous, because that would mean—

"Brody Wilson, nice to *finally* meet you." The pastor smiled broadly.

His face on fire, Brody shook hands with the other man. "Uh, same here, Reverend."

The other man chuckled. "Putting people on the spot is one of the perks of my job. And sadly, I confess I rather enjoy it."

Brody laughed, despite the embarrassment, and the pastor winked.

"Brody is Elliott's uncle, and he's been kind enough to put up with us while I get my feet on the ground in Loon Lake," Mary said.

She was making sure to clarify for people that he was Uncle Brody and nothing more. That was the truth, and yet it pinched like a new dress shoe. Maybe *she* didn't want anyone seeing them as a family. *Hey, dumbass, he's the church pastor. What did you expect her to say?*

"You're the one with the animal sanctuary out at the old Miller farm," Reverend Cook said.

Brody grimaced. "I'm not sure I'd go so far as to call it a sanctuary."

"Well, whatever it is, I think it's great and a fine example to be setting for little Elliott here." The pastor hunkered down in front of the stroller. "Hello to you, young man. My daughter tells me you're a joy to have in the nursery."

Elliott kicked his legs and giggled as if to agree.

The pastor straightened. "I won't hold you up any longer, but before you go, I'd like to extend an invitation to the three of you for dinner at the parsonage."

Brody shuffled his feet. What was he supposed to say to that?

"It's a thank-you dinner," the pastor said, as if sensing reluctance. "Mary was a big help getting our church secretary up and running with the new accounting software."

Someone called out to the pastor, and he patted Mary on the arm. "At least think it over. Now, duty calls. Something about judging pies. Wouldn't want to miss Clara's delicious strawberry rhubarb."

Brody turned back to Mary. "You've been helping in the church office?"

She began walking again. "The new secretary wasn't familiar with the program they had, and I gave her some basic pointers."

Several people waved and called out as they made their way to booths that were set up to display local crafts for sale.

Brody nodded to them, but he had no idea who they were. "How do you know all these people?"

"I met some of them at the luncheons and others through Randall Burke." She shrugged as if it were no big deal.

"What luncheons?" How did she manage this whole existence without him noticing? And how did he feel about that? Glad. Yeah, he was glad she was fitting in, making a life for herself here. But one that apparently didn't include him. And his determination to stay aloof, not to get involved was now mocking him as he yearned to be a part of the life he imagined her living.

Her brow furrowed, she peered at him. "You're the one who first told me about the luncheons way back when I mentioned my idea for camp. It's a soup kitchen, but everyone agrees there's less stigma with the term *community lunch*."

"Of course." He closed his eyes and pinched the bridge of his nose. He wanted her to be a part of Loon Lake, with or without him. He saw how much she enjoyed being accepted and being a part of this town, especially considering her past. He rejoiced in her fitting in. And she had. She'd been busy building this whole other life without telling him or including him. Without him. Period, full stop.

"I said we're going to try our luck." She had stopped in front of a sign that said Fish Bowl Toss. Hanging stuffed animals lined the sides of the small booth. Glass goldfish bowls were on a table at the back.

She gave him a sheepish grin when he raised an eyebrow. "What? It's for charity."

He clamped his mouth over a laugh and raised his hands, palms out, to indicate he wasn't judging her.

She handed over a few bills and took three squishy balls from the attendant. "Elliott, pick out which prize you want."

After three shots and three misses, she bent down to Elliott in his stroller. "Sorry, sweetie, I guess I was too confident in my abilities."

Brody pulled out his wallet. "Let me try. Like you said, it's for charity."

The attendant handed him the three balls he'd retrieved, and she took Elliott out of the stroller for a better view.

Brody made all three shots and laughed when Mary stuck her tongue out. Damn, she was beautiful and he was in so deep, he might never crawl out.

The attendant pulled down a large stuffed panda and handed it over. "Your dad's a good shot."

"He's not my son, he's my nephew," Brody replied and winced. And again with the foot in the mouth.

But it felt more like a knife to the chest. He wanted to watch Elliott grow up. Wanted to be there not just for those first faltering baby steps but for those tentative steps into adulthood.

What if Mary started a new life away from Loon

Lake? He'd be nothing more to Elliott than a picture stuck to the refrigerator and a disembodied voice on the phone.

Mary did her best to enjoy the rest of the afternoon and evening, but she could see how uncomfortable Brody was with people treating them like a family. Her hopes for convincing Brody that what they shared was more than friendship with benefits were fading. No amount of wishing would take away the fact Elliott was Brody's nephew, not his son.

As much as she enjoyed sitting with Riley and Meg, witnessing the way they gazed at one another or the simple touches between them made Mary's heart ache. She wanted that for herself, and if she wasn't going to find that with Brody, she needed to accept it. And as much as the thought hurt, she might need to look for it elsewhere.

"Something wrong?" she asked as they loaded their things into the truck at the end of the night.

Brody sent her a surprised look. "No. Why?"

"You had a fierce scowl on your face." She knew he might have been uncomfortable today, but she hadn't detected anger.

He put the cooler onto the truck bed. "Sorry. Didn't mean to."

"It's okay. I guess I shouldn't have dragged you here." She glanced around at the other families loading things into their cars. "I guess we don't belong."

"You didn't drag me." He turned to look at her. "And you and Elliott belong here just as much as anyone. You're now a part of this community."

She put the folded blanket on the back seat next to Elliott's car seat. "I meant we need to be careful what sort of picture we present."

"We're friends enjoying a summer picnic and concert." He raised the tailgate. "I'm glad I came."

"You are?" Could she have misinterpreted his behavior today?

"Sure." He slammed the tailgate shut. "You got some new business, right?"

Was that what he'd thought this was about? Was that why he'd come? "Yeah, but—"

"Then it was worth it. Not a wasted outing."

She licked her dry lips, ignoring the heaviness in her chest. "You're right."

"Ready to go?"

"Yes." *No*, her heart screamed.

Chapter Twelve

Was she imagining things? Looking for trouble where none existed? Mary bunched up her pillow but couldn't find a comfortable position.

After the picnic, they'd come home and put Elliott to bed and gone up themselves soon after. She and Brody had made love, but he seemed to be holding back, putting up his defenses. Instead of spooning while they fell asleep, he'd rolled onto his stomach. Had the townspeople seeing them as a family spooked him?

And how much longer could she hold out hope before facing reality? Questions twirled around in her head, making sleep impossible. Sighing heavily, she slipped out of bed. Maybe a glass of water would help.

She checked on Elliott and went to the window to let in some night air, but as soon as she raised the sash she smelled it. *Smoke.*

Rushing back to the bed, she shook Brody. "Wake up." His eyes flickered open. "What?"

"I smell smoke."

He jackknifed into a sitting position. "In the house?"

"No. Outside. I opened a window in Elliott's room. I could smell it, but I couldn't see anything."

He jumped up and began pulling his pants on. "You and Elliott should go outside just in case."

"Okay." She was already on her way to get her son. "Should I call the fire department?"

"Let me check it out first," he called from the hallway.

The back door slammed as she got Elliott out of his crib and wrapped a blanket around him. Carrying Elliott close to her, she ran from room to room upstairs, sniffing and turning lights on before going downstairs and doing the same thing. She grabbed her cell phone off the counter where it was charging.

She clutched a protesting Elliott to her chest and ran out the back door, her gaze going to the bunkhouse— her new office—and the plumes of smoke coming from the open door.

"Brody?" she yelled, and Elliott began crying. "Shh, it's okay, sweetie."

She moved closer but remained a safe distance away, not wanting to expose Elliott to the smoke. She called for Brody again before using her cell phone to contact an emergency dispatcher and explain the situation.

After what felt like an eternity in which she felt helpless, he emerged from the burning building, carrying something in his arms. Coughing, he sank to his knees, dropping her framed photo of Loon Lake and her laptop onto the grass.

She ran over to him. "What the heck are you doing?"

"Getting your—" He broke off in a fit of coughing.

Had he lost his ever-loving mind? "Stop it. The fire department is on their way."

"It'll be too late."

He started toward the building again, and she grabbed for him with her free hand, but he slipped away.

She wanted to scream and cry, but one glance at a confused Elliott told her she needed to remain calm. But dammit, she'd never felt so helpless in her life. A childhood spent at the mercy of strangers didn't compare to this.

The scream of sirens captured her attention, and she ran into the front yard. The first to arrive was a sheriff's department vehicle, and Riley Cooper jumped out and ran to her.

The next hour passed in a blur of fire trucks, police and paramedics. After checking on Brody, Riley came and sat with her and Elliott on the porch steps. He assured her Brody had been given oxygen by the EMTs and shouldn't require anything more unless his symptoms worsened. Riley helped keep Elliott entertained until he got a call to respond to another situation.

"Want me to get Brody to come and sit before I leave?" Riley asked, but she refused and he left.

She was having flashbacks to the day of the car accident and Elliott must be, too. And she wasn't sure she could deal with her overwhelming emotions, plus Brody. The paramedics and all but one fire truck had left when Elliott fell asleep. After putting him back to bed, she went through the kitchen and stepped outside.

Brody spotted her and came over. "I'm sorry about your office. I saved what I could."

She glared at him, grinding her teeth, her pulse racing. She had to take a deep breath before she could speak. "How could you?"

His mouth dropped open. "That's the thanks I get for saving your things?"

"Who told you to do something so stupid?" She pushed his shoulder with each word. He could've been killed. Just the thought stole her breath.

"Stupid?" His eyebrows slammed together.

Her arms flailed around. "To put your life in danger for some stupid stuff."

"Stupid stuff?" His head jerked back. "But you said how much—"

"I don't care. It's just stuff." And it was true. Nothing was worth risking his life over.

"But you were so proud of having your own office."

"You don't get it, do you?" No possessions were more precious than his life.

He threw his hands up. "Obviously not."

"I'm not happy because I have some stuff." She ground her molars.

"Will you quit saying *stuff* like it's nothing?"

"It is nothing. I'm happier than I've ever been because I have a place to belong."

"Not anymore." His voice had risen several decibels.

"I'm not talking about a building. I have Loon Lake and all the people in it." Tears rolled unchecked down her face and dripped onto her shirt. "That's what matters to me…not physical things. Home to me is going into town and having people waving hello or Meg Cooper calling and asking if I wanted to join her for a girls' night out with some friends."

"But I didn't want you to lose your st—" He clamped his mouth shut over the last word. Someone behind him cleared their throat and he turned around.

"Sir?" One of the firemen stood there looking uncomfortable at overhearing their argument. "We've finished mopping up. No more hot spots."

"Thanks."

"If you'd like to follow me, I can show you where the fire started. We believe there was a short in the electrical wiring."

Brody followed the fireman, and blinking back tears, she turned and went into the house.

Brody found Mary in her bedroom, tossing clothing from an open dresser drawer into a beat-up old suitcase on the bed.

"What in the world are you doing?" he demanded from the doorway, his fingers fisted around the doorjamb.

"I can't do this anymore."

What the...? He squeezed his fingers until they were white under the soot still clinging to them. "Define *this*, please."

She stopped moving and glared at him. "I'm not going to fall for someone else who sees me as disposable."

"Disposable? Where did you get an idea like that?" Damn her for lumping him into the same mold as his worthless brother. He was sick and tired of always being the person responsible for having to pick up the pieces. "I was the one saving your stuff. How does that make me see you as disposable?"

"Because you risked your life...risked leaving Elliott and...and me." She choked out the last word and threw her arms wide. "And for what? A bunch of meaningless, replaceable *stuff*."

"But I was doing it for you." He stepped into the room. "Those things were all you had in the world."

"You still don't get it." She stalked toward him.

He stood his ground. "Maybe you need to explain it."

"I love you!" she shouted at him, and when he backed away, she followed him and poked him in the chest. "I love you...heart in my throat, can't imagine my life without you, love you. And you'd rather run into a burning building than stay safe with me. Is that clear enough for you?"

Love? He started to choke, but this time it wasn't from smoke inhalation. No way. They were enjoying themselves. Scratching an itch. What they shared wasn't supposed to go that far. Anything else would be a grave mistake.

She lifted the bag off the bed with a grunt. "I'm not going to put myself through that. And I'm not going to put Elliott through that, either."

She swept past him, and he let her. He stood by like some dumbass while she collected Elliott and stomped down the stairs, baby in one hand, suitcase in the other. He stood motionless at the top of the stairs while she went out the front door and shut it behind her without looking back.

He trudged to the upstairs window and watched as she strapped Elliott into the back seat of her car. Then she threw things into the trunk, climbed into the front seat and slammed the door, the sound reverberating in the still air. He resisted the urge to run down there and tell her he loved her.

He stood in the window long after the car disappeared. He stood leaning against the windowsill until the sun was high in the sky.

You knew this had to end. You're not that guy.

He debated getting in his truck and going after her. But what would that accomplish? Let her cool down and…

And what? Decide she wasn't in love with him? Her words had stunned him, ripped through him. So instead of following her, he took a shower and put on clean clothes. But he could still smell the smoke. As if it had seeped into him.

Not bothering with coffee or breakfast, he walked to the barn. Chores would keep his hands busy even if he couldn't shut off his mind. Where was she? He let the animals out and cleaned their stalls. Would she leave Loon Lake?

A car door slammed. Mary? He dropped his tools and rushed toward the opening of the barn. More doors slammed before he got there.

The sight that awaited him in his driveway was not something he could've predicted. Judging by the number and variety of pickups, half of Loon Lake was on his farm. The truck parked closest to the barn looked familiar, as did the attached trailer. Sure enough, Bill Pratt, the farmer who'd dropped his calf off, approached him.

Bill tipped his cap. "We're here to help."

"Help?" Brody stood with his jaw slack, trying to take it all in.

Ogle Whatley stepped around Bill. "You tell us what you want done and we'll do it."

I want Mary back. What was he thinking? Life was better alone. Uncomplicated. He was fine. Or he would be in a few days.

Ogle clapped Brody on the back and squeezed his shoulder. "We're here to clean up and haul away the ruins and rebuild, if rebuilding is what you want."

"Why would you all do that?"

"Simple," Ogle said. "You're a part of this community, son, and we look after our own. Bill here brought his trailer to haul away the debris."

True to their word, the men got to work loading up the burned debris. Brody went into the barn and got gloves to help.

Brody wasn't sure how much time had passed when

he looked up to see more cars arriving. He left the men and strolled over to the newcomers.

"We're here to be sure everyone gets fed," Tavie called as she got out of a car.

She sniffed as she approached. "*Glory*, Brody Wilson, you smell like smoke. Don't tell me you've been sneakin' down to that new mini-mart for cigarettes."

"Of course I smell like smoke, Tavie." Brody pointed to the burned rubble that used to be Mary's office. "Hel-*lo*."

"You don't want that precious little guy to be breathin' in secondhand smoke," Tavie went on as if he hadn't spoken.

The thought of Mary and Elliott felt like a dull knife to the gut, and Brody waved his hand in a dismissive gesture and stalked off to the horse fencing. He knew he should be working with the others, but he needed to take a moment. Mary and Elliott were gone. Each time that thought entered his head, he felt the loss. How could Mary love him? He was a freakin' hermit who lived with a bunch of unwanted animals. She'd been in town a short time and already knew more people, had more friends than he did.

Ogle strolled over to the fence and rested a foot on the bottom rail. "Tavie. Don't take it wrong."

Brody shrugged. Ogle had been within earshot when Tavie had badgered him.

Ogle rolled a toothpick from one side of his mouth to the other. "It's her way of lovin' people."

Brody raised his brow and glanced askance at the old man.

"When I got back from doin' my time in 'Nam, I was so wrung out I didn't even tell her when I was a-comin' home, but she was there when my plane landed with a big smile and a huge flag. I was wearin' my uniform, and back in those days, people weren't so grateful for your service like they are nowadays. Tavie, she stared down anyone who tried to say somethin' negative."

Brody nodded, picturing Tavie taking on Ogle's detractors. "Sounds like she was pretty supportive."

"On the drive home, she scolded me the whole way for not writing to her enough and for not tellin' her when I was gettin' home."

"How'd she know when to expect you?"

"She didn't. Just showed up every damn day and waited." Ogle touched Brody's shoulder. "She don't know how to love any other way, son."

Brody pulled away. "Maybe I don't want all these people loving me."

"The way I see it, you ain't got much choice." Ogle chewed on his toothpick. "People gonna love you, whether you want it or not."

Brody pushed his chair back and grabbed his mug of coffee, swearing when the hot liquid sloshed onto the table. He'd clean up the spill later. Two days had passed since the fire, and he couldn't stay in his kitchen one moment longer. Truth was, this was where he felt Mary's absence most. He missed watching her bustling around cooking breakfast or sitting there feeding Elliott. He missed their happy chatter. His gut twisted at the thought of all the meals he'd be eating alone from now on. No more sharing the day's activities while they ate supper. No quiet discussions over coffee and a piece of pie.

He pushed open the front door and stepped onto the porch and saw the bottle cap on the top step.

He kicked the token of appreciation off with his foot. "Son of a—"

A furious squawking from high in a tree cut him off.

"Get it through your head, bird. Mary. Is. Gone. Gone…

as in not coming back." He swore. Could he get any lower?
Yelling at a damn bird. His shoulders slumped, and he
dropped onto the steps and sat staring at his feet as if he'd
find the answers in his scuffed and dusty boots.

A crow landed in the dirt a few yards away from the
bottom step. Hopping over, the bird picked up the bottle
cap and strutted back and forth across the cracked sidewalk with the present in its beak.

The bottle cap landed next to his right boot. Brody
looked up and barked out a mirthless laugh. "Haven't
you been listening?"

The crow tilted its head and stared at him.

"What?" Brody scrubbed a hand over his face. "Yeah,
yeah, I get it. I screwed up."

People gonna love you, whether you want it or not.

The crow cawed and flew off, its wings flapping in
the still air.

"Same to you," he called after the animal.

He took a swig of coffee and grimaced at the cold and
bitterness. How had he lost track of so much time? He
swung the mug in an arc, dumping the rest, and turned
to go back in the house. But Riley Cooper's black pickup
rumbled down the drive.

Was Riley bringing Mary and Elliott back? Damn, but
his heart skipped a beat at the thought. What a dumbass.
Why would she come back with Riley? She had her own
car. He should be glad she was gone. He had the place
to himself again. No more tripping over baby stuff, no
more sink full of baby bottles needing to be washed. Why
couldn't she wash them after she used them?

Still, his shoulders slumped when it appeared Riley
was alone.

Riley pulled up in a spew of gravel and dust and cut

the engine. He jumped out of the truck and walked up to the porch. "Hey, man."

Brody squinted at him. "Not you, too."

"Me, too, what?"

"Here to talk some sense into me."

Riley hooted with laughter. "I don't think that's possible, Wilson."

Brody rolled his eyes.

"Actually, I came for another reason." Riley shrugged. "But since you asked for my advice…"

"I didn't ask—"

"You'd be surprised what a good grovel can accomplish," Riley continued as if Brody hadn't spoken. "I didn't think Meg was going to forgive me for all the times I messed up, but I figured I had nothing left to lose and everything to gain."

"How did you get her to forgive your sorry—"

"Hey, do you want my advice or not? Because man, you look like—"

"Okay, okay. Can we do this without the editorial observations?" Brody rubbed a hand over his face. He knew full well what he looked like because he couldn't feel this bad and not have it show.

"Just tell her you love her."

"That's it?" Brody blew his breath out through his nose.

"Women already know we're gonna mess up…it's programmed into our DNA, so no need for lengthy explanations. Just beg for forgiveness."

"And tell her I love her?"

Riley held out his hands, palms up. "That's it."

That sounded too easy and Brody tried to swallow the hope that threatened to bubble up. "Why did you really come? You said you had another reason."

"Mary asked me to come and get some of Elliott's things."

What? She wouldn't even come and get her own stuff? His gut churned. Yeah, no way a simple "I love you. Please forgive me" was gonna solve this. "Why didn't Mary come?"

Riley shrugged, making Brody want to body slam him for answers. "Said something about Elliott not feeling well."

"What?" Brody stiffened, his body on full alert. "What's wrong with him?"

Riley strolled to the back of the pickup to lower the tailgate. "Something about a head cold. Meg thinks it could be from cutting teeth. Said Fiona was the same way."

What if it was something more? "Has she taken him to see a doctor?"

"Nah...says it's not that serious."

"How can she be sure?" Brody hated feeling so helpless. He wanted to hit something. "Has she even called the doctor? Maybe she should—"

Riley chuckled. "Calm down, man. There's one thing I've learned. You gotta trust the mom. Intuition or something. I don't know what kind of sh—stuff you went through in Delta Force, but I'm sure you learned to read situations and when to trust that feeling that told you when things were hinky."

"Hinky? Is that cop talk?"

Riley laughed. "Curbing my language. Kids have special radar for bad words."

Brody grunted as he recalled Elliott saying "daa." He had to admit it had freaked him out at the time, but now that he thought about it, instead of the overwhelming need to bolt, his chest swelled with pride.

"You gonna help me or just stand there and stare at my truck bed?" Riley asked, one eyebrow raised.

Brody said a word he wouldn't want Elliott to hear and motioned Riley into the house.

After Riley had left with Elliott's baby furniture in the back of his truck, Brody started to climb the porch steps but changed directions at the last moment. He couldn't face that empty house yet.

I wouldn't blame you, because I know you'd try your best.

Mary's words came back to haunt him as he cleaned out the stalls. Where did she get off believing in him? He wasn't some damn miracle worker. Hell, he couldn't even help his messed-up family. She had no business looking up to him. He'd tried to help Roger and failed. And that failure led to Mary and Elliott paying the price for his screwup brother.

After cleaning out the stalls, he rolled the wheelbarrow over to the compost heap outside the barn and dumped it.

Too bad he couldn't dump the weight pressing on his chest threatening to choke him.

"I love you…heart-in-my-throat, can't-imagine-my-life-without-you, love you."

She'd used those words to describe how she felt about him, but she may as well have been describing how he felt. Times one thousand.

He sighed. Was Riley right? Could he fix this? Could telling Mary how much he loved her and begging her forgiveness work?

He would do all that and more to get her and Elliott back. They belonged here, on the farm with him. He wasn't above begging he missed them so much, but first he had something else up his sleeve.

Feeling more energized than he had in the days since Mary left, he went into the office in the barn and got to work.

Mary hung up the phone after making an appointment with another new client. She was busy with Randall's old clients and her new ones. Soon she'd be able to pay her rent and other personal expenses from her accounting work and not have to dig into savings.

She'd been lucky enough to rent the home next to the Coopers when their son decided to come four weeks early. The baby was fine, but they decided to postpone the extensive remodeling on their home so Meg's brother canceled the lease.

Things had also worked out well with Elliott. She brought him with her to the office, except on days when she had appointments with clients. Those days she had an abundance of people willing to watch him. Even one of the nurses from the ER, Ellie Harding, had volunteered for babysitting duty.

So why wasn't she happy? She'd always told herself that happiness was a choice. You could either see the bright side and be happy or wallow in regrets. She'd chosen to be happy and grateful for what she had. Elliott was healthy and happy, and as for herself, she could support them and make a comfortable life for them in Loon Lake. Again, why didn't all these things give her satisfaction? Why was she constantly on the verge of tears?

Brody. Her melancholy always came back to Brody and missing him. Shaking her head, she got up and poured herself a cup of coffee. Tying her happiness to someone else was dangerous and stupid. She knew better. She'd gotten over Roger. But those feelings didn't come near the scary soul-deep love she felt for Brody.

Getting over him was going to take a long time, but she couldn't—wouldn't—regret their time together. And because of him, she'd been accepted and become a part of life in Loon Lake. As soon as the wound wasn't as fresh, she'd contact Brody. He loved Elliott and Elliott loved him and she wasn't going to stand in the way of their relationship, even if it meant enduring time spent with Brody until Elliott grew older. She was an adult—she could smile and make small talk, ask innocuous questions about his life, the farm, the animals. The women in his life. *Yeeaahh,* that one might be taking things too far.

Mary was engrossed in preparing taxes for her latest client when the office door opened. She glanced up and smiled, but the automatic gesture froze on her lips.

Brody stood in the doorway, his arms full of folders and what looked like blueprint tubes.

"Hey," he said and grinned sheepishly.

"Hey," she echoed.

Had he lost weight? Were those dark circles under his eyes? Were the lines on his face etched deeper? Her fingers itched to smooth out the grooves and rearrange his disheveled hair. She got up and started toward him but stopped.

"I heard you…uh…" He shifted the folders and cleared his throat. "I heard you were accepting new clients."

"Y-yes." Her heart dropped past her knees. He was here on business?

"Good." He stepped farther into the office and closed the door. "Where's Elliott?"

"At the general store. I stopped on the way in this morning and Tavie insisted on watching him. Claims he attracts customers." She swallowed the questions bubbling up. Did he miss her? How were the animals? Was Serenity still leaving tokens of appreciation?

He nodded, and she saw something in his eyes—something like hope. The kind of hope she'd been fighting from the moment he'd opened the door. "Wh-what do you have there?"

He glanced down at the bundle in his arms as if he'd forgotten. "Architectural designs, incorporation papers, spreadsheets."

He quickly dumped his burden into the nearest chair. His gaze still locked with hers, he stepped around the desk until he was close enough to touch.

Trying to ignore how much she ached for physical contact, even the slightest touch, she cleared her throat. "That's an awful lot of papers for someone who hates paperwork."

"I still hate paperwork but..." He shrugged and stared at her as if drinking her in.

"But what?" She tried to throttle the hope that threatened to bring her to her knees.

"It's not a chore when it's for someone you love." He took a breath. "It's for Camp Life Launch."

Her heart pounded so hard it hurt. Did he say *love*? Was it possible? She needed to be sure before she abandoned her pride. "What's Camp Life Launch?"

"It's a summer camp for foster kids. Someone..." He swallowed. "Someone I love very much told me there might be a need for such things, and since I have this farm..."

He did say love...twice! She squeezed the flesh on her forearm between her thumb and forefinger. *Ouch.* She was awake.

When she didn't respond, his shoulders slumped. Breathing deep, he continued. "Anyway... I need someone with knowledge of accounting to help me with the nonprofit side."

He paused when she still didn't react. "Are you going to speak? Argue? Yell? Throw something?"

"I… I don't know what to say." She shook her head, afraid of jumping to the wrong conclusions. "Did…did you say someone you love?"

"I did, but I wanted to tell you about the camp first because I'm hoping after I tell you what else I came to say, we'll be, uh, otherwise occupied and too busy to discuss business." He cleared his throat and continued. "I've been looking into opening a camp for disadvantaged children at the farm. I contacted the guys from my old army unit and they want to help."

"You contacted the guys from the picture?"

"I did." He stepped closer and took her hands in his. "See, this woman and her son came into my life and she brought with her love and sunshine and stars…made me feel things I didn't think possible, made me see all the things I'd been missing."

Tears sprang to her eyes, and she blinked to clear them. "This woman sounds pretty special."

"She is." He lifted one of her hands and pressed a kiss to her palm. "She's way out of my league. Too good for an ogre like me. But we ogres are a pretty selfish bunch and I'm hoping if I grovel and promise to love and cherish her for the rest of my life, she'll forgive me."

"Grovel?" Hope filled her like helium and she clutched his hands to keep from floating away.

"Some advice I received from Riley, who claims to know these things."

A sudden cloud darkened her bright shiny future. "But what about Roger? I can't make him not Elliott's father."

"I can." He tugged her closer. "I contacted him. Told him I was in love with you, planned to marry you and adopt Elliott."

"You did?"

"He's agreed to sign over all his parental rights so I'll be free to adopt Elliott. I told Roger if he ever wanted to get to know his son, he could, but that it would be on our terms, under our supervision."

He hugged her tightly and kissed her hard, as if he'd thought he'd never do so again.

When he lifted his head, he whispered, "I love you, Mary Carter. It's as simple as that."

"And I love you, Brody Wilson."

"Let's get Elliott—our son—and go home."

Home. She liked the sound of that.

* * * * *

COMING SOON!

We really hope you enjoyed reading this book. If you're looking for more romance, be sure to head to the shops when new books are available on

Thursday 21st February

To see which titles are coming soon, please visit
millsandboon.co.uk/nextmonth

MILLS & BOON

Coming next month

CARRYING THE GREEK TYCOON'S BABY
Jennifer Faye

"I'm pregnant."

Xander stumbled back as though Lea's words had physically slugged him in the chest. The back of his knees hit the edge of the bed. He slumped down onto the mattress. Maybe he'd heard her incorrectly.

"Could you say that again?"

"Xander, I'm pregnant. And you're the father."

That's what he thought she'd said.

But this can't be true. Could it?

Xander knew all too well that it was quite possible. They'd spent that not-so-long-ago weekend in bed...and there was the time on the floor...in the living room—

He halted his rambling memories. He didn't normally let loose like that. In fact, he'd never had a weekend like that one. It was unforgettable. And apparently in more than one way.

The silence dragged on. He should say something. Anything. But what? He'd never been in this position before.

He needed time to think because right now all that was going around in his mind was that he was going to be a father. He wondered if this was what shock felt like.

"I...I need a little time to absorb this," he said. "We'll talk soon."

He wasn't even sure if he said goodbye before disconnecting the call. He had no idea how long he laid there staring into space before an incoming text jarred him back to reality.

I'm going to be a father.

The profound words echoed in his mind.

How could this be? Well, of course he knew how it happened. It was a weekend that he would never forget, much as he had tried. Lea's stunning image was imprinted upon his mind.

Still, he never thought he'd hear that he was going to be a father. A father. His heart was racing and his palms were damp.

His mind slipped back to the time he'd spent on Infinity Island. He never thought that it would change his life. But it had. And now he had to figure out a plan. He was known for thinking on his toes, but this was different. This was a baby. His baby.

And he had to do whatever was best for the child.

But what was that?

Continue reading
CARRYING THE GREEK TYCOON'S BABY
Jennifer Faye

Available next month
www.millsandboon.co.uk

LET'S TALK
Romance

For exclusive extracts, competitions and special offers, find us online:

f facebook.com/millsandboon

🐦 @MillsandBoon

📷 @MillsandBoonUK

Get in touch on 01413 063232

For all the latest titles coming soon, visit
millsandboon.co.uk/nextmonth